Dear R

Do you judge your *Scarlet* books by their covers? Or do you choose your romances by the 'blurb' on the back of the book? Perhaps you pick a particular novel off the shelf because of its title, or maybe because of the author's name? You'll notice that each month we provide a list of forthcoming *Scarlet* books, with short outlines giving you a taste of each new story. Does *that* help you to make your selection? Of course, I hope you are buying all four titles each month, but I'd love to know how *you* make *your* reading decisions.

And by the way, how do you feel about sequels? A number of readers have already written to ask if we are planning to publish new books featuring popular characters from already published *Scarlet* novels. If you'd like to see a spin-off of your top-of-the-pops *Scarlet* romance, why not send me a letter for the author in question and I'll be happy to pass it along.

Till next month,
Best wishes,

Sally Cooper

SALLY COOPER,
Editor-in-Chief – *Scarlet*

About the Author

Jill Sheldon (aka Jill Shalvis) is a multi-published romantic/suspense author. *Summer of Fire* was her first novel for *Scarlet*, and we are delighted to bring you *Time to Trust* (formerly entitled Color Me Loved) her second *Scarlet* book – her third *Scarlet* is scheduled for summer '97. In 1995, Jill was a finalist in the prestigious North West region's Romance Writers of America's 'Lone Star Writing Competition'.

Jill majored in journalism and has written many short stories. She lives in Southern California, USA, with her husband and three young children and is an active member of the Romance Writers of America organization, particularly in her local area.

Other *Scarlet* titles available this month:

LOVERS AND LIARS – Sally Steward
THE PATH TO LOVE – Chrissie Loveday
LOVE BEYOND DESIRE – Jessica Marchant

JILL SHELDON

TIME TO TRUST

SCARLET

Enquiries to:
Robinson Publishing Ltd
7 Kensington Church Court
London W8 4SP

First published in the UK by Scarlet, 1997

A copy of the British Library Cataloguing in
Publication data is available from the British Library

ISBN 1–85487–926–X

Printed and bound in the EC

10 9 8 7 6 5 4 3 2 1

To my real-life house-building hero –
my husband

CHAPTER 1

Cord Harrison shouldn't have felt like smiling since he was wet, dirty and exhausted. But, after the carefully structured world his life had become, he found he loved the physical demands of building his house by hand.

Now, with a flick of his wrist he turned the wrench, extracting an ominous creaking noise from the pipe. It didn't deter him, or spoil his basic good humor, even though from his current position on his stomach under the bathroom sink things didn't look good. No problem. He scooted closer, squinting his eyes to see past the now steady mist escaping the pipe.

He swiped at the water streaming down his face and knew with some irony that no one seeing him like this would believe he was the president of HT Designs, famed architectural firm. But he was forced to quickly push the thought from his mind.

Because nothing changed the fact that his plumbing leaked. Badly.

Flipping over onto his back for better leverage,

Cord yanked at the wrench with all his might. At first nothing happened. Finally it budged, slowly. Then cracked. As did some of his good humor. His sharp, surprised curse echoed throughout the empty, half-rebuilt house.

As icy water rushed over him a shout of rich male laughter rang out. Because he recognized the laugh, he ignored it until he'd managed to turn off the heavy flow of water. Slowly he pulled himself out from under the sink, pulling away his cold, sticky shirt from his soaked skin.

A towel smacked him in the face. 'Tsk, tsk, such language.' The heavily amused voice came from the other half of HT Designs, and his closest friend, Seth Thompson. 'Hard to believe you were raised by nuns.'

A fond smile touched Cord's lips as he thought of Katherine, the nun in question. 'Isn't it?'

'You know, it's funny,' Seth said conversationally, making himself comfortable with his usual ease by hopping up on the newly finished tile countertop. 'That nun thing is what people ask about the most. They want to know if that little tidbit is really true, or if our PR people made it up.'

'What do you tell them?'

Seth's grin came fast. 'Since it's usually a beautiful woman asking, I tell them that of course it's true. And that, much as it pains me, you've got one foot in the door of priesthood. Then, out of pure sympathy, I offer myself as a replacement.'

Cord shook his head and laughed, then pushed

himself up to stand where he dripped all over the floor. 'Did you come all the way out here for anything in particular? Or did you just want to see for yourself what physical labor looks like?'

'Physical labor?' Seth smiled. 'Looks more like you've been swimming to me.' He shrugged. 'But suit yourself, man. Just don't ask me to help.' He shuddered at the thought.

'I wouldn't dream of it,' Cord said dryly. Seth's aversion to anything other than the 'civilized' activity of selling designs was well known. 'If you didn't come to help, then what?'

'Besides laughing at you, you mean? You know, it makes me feel better to see the invincible Cord Harrison have trouble with something as innocuous as a broken pipe. But to answer your question – yeah, I had a reason to come out here. Not that I mind the ridiculously long drive out to the middle of nowhere to give you your messages, but I still can't believe you bought out here. It's so far from the city.'

'For peace and quiet, maybe?' Cord wasn't worried about hurting Seth's feelings. They'd been friends too long for Seth to take offense. He squatted before the broken pipe, silently surveying the problem. 'Damn. I would have sworn the plumbing was under control.'

'In this old place?' Seth laughed. 'Are you kidding? Those pipes were here before the gold rush.'

Cord rolled his shoulders, trying to ease the kinks. 'This "old place," as you call it, is a gem. Did you know it used to be a hunting lodge in the 1930s?'

'Looks like it,' Seth agreed. 'And you've recaptured the original rustic charm of the place, no doubt. But you're pretty close to nowhere out here.'

'That's the idea.'

Seth's easy smile faded as he surveyed his long-time best friend with concern. 'What's up with you lately? You work like a demon during the week, then disappear out here every weekend. You've given up all your friends but me, and even I hardly see you anymore.'

'Miss me?' Cord teased, expecting Seth to smile.

But Seth's eyes remained serious. 'Is everything going okay?'

Cord shrugged. He couldn't explain it, even to himself. All he knew was that he was world-weary, tired. He'd been going for so long and so hard, concentrating only on making money and gaining a success that, once achieved, had meant nothing. And it had scared him, deeply. 'I'm fine. I just want to do this.' He gestured around him. 'I really like doing this.'

'And when you finish?'

And when he finished he could only hope that some of his restlessness would be gone. 'Then I'll be finished.'

Seth's face told him that he hadn't eased his friend's mind in the least. 'Well, in the meantime, it's a hell of a long drive out here to come see you.'

'So why didn't you just call?'

'And miss your face when I tell you that *Architectural Design* wants to do an exclusive article on us?'

4

'On you,' Cord corrected. He hated publicity.

Seth sighed – the noise of a man suffering in the presence of a half-wit. 'Cord, HT Designs owes its reputation to you. You know that.'

At the distress in Seth's voice, Cord looked up. 'That's not true. You're just as important as I.'

Seth's lips came tightly together. 'That's another story.' He visibly lightened. 'I don't understand – you have the business world at your feet, women calling night and day . . .' Seth gave up at the long look Cord shot him.

Cord eyed the box of plumbing parts and pulled out the one he needed. He tossed down the towel and slipped back under the sink. He'd fix this sink if it took him all day. He smiled. That was the beauty of it. It was his house, being rebuilt his way, and he could do whatever he wanted.

'Come on, think of the opportunities this will give us with women. You haven't dated in nearly six months, maybe more.'

'Maybe I'm too old.'

Seth laughed. 'You're thirty-three. In your prime. Come on, Cord.'

'Not interested.'

'You say that now because you let yourself get burned with Christina what's-her-name – '

'Seth,' Cord warned him, emerging from beneath the sink.

The warning wasn't necessary. Seth had gone pale. 'Oh, God, Cord. I'm sorry. I didn't even think. You're still upset over Tayna's death.'

Cord sighed. 'Murder,' he corrected. 'And, yeah, I'm upset – because no one should die that way. But my heart isn't aching, if that's what you meant. We'd only gone out twice.'

'I'm sorry,' Seth said again.

Cord looked at him. 'Look, if you're going to hang around, could you at least grab a hammer or something?'

'I'm an idiot,' Seth mumbled.

'No objections there,' Cord said lightly, pushing himself back under the sink. 'Now, get down here and help or go away.'

'All right, all right. I'm going.' He made it to the door. 'Oh, I almost forgot – you haven't seen Lacey lately, have you?'

Cord paused in his speculation of his screwed-up pipes. 'No. Why?'

Seth shrugged, concern clouding his features. 'She hasn't been around.'

'And you're worried.' Where was the part he needed? 'She's okay.'

'It's been three days since she came by for my left-over lunch.'

'Seth, she's a homeless lady.'

Seth squatted into his view and smiled, though a bit wryly. 'A beautiful, young, down on her luck homeless lady, who won't even look at *me* when *you* come in to the office.'

Cord ignored that, knowing that if truth be told Seth was much more appealing than he. Seth's charm was a smooth, elegant kind of handsome. In the office

6

Seth was kidded mercilessly about his *GQ* blond looks and teasing smile, and the fact that he never had trouble finding companions – they lined up at his door. 'Before we took Lacey under our wing she never stayed put,' he said. Then, because some of Seth's worry was beginning to rub off on him, he added. 'It was only a matter of time before she wandered off again. No matter how much we want to help her, it's her life.'

'You're probably right.'

'Maybe she went to visit that sister of hers she always talks about.'

'Maybe. Well, I'm leaving you in peace to fix a pipe.' Seth again started toward the door, then paused, eyeing the difference between his expensive, tasteful tailored clothes and his friend's faded jeans and T-shirt. 'But why you'd want to when you're rich enough to hire a team of plumbers is beyond me. At least you were smart enough to let me hire a painter for you.'

'That's only because I don't like to paint. I want to do everything else myself.'

'I still think you're crazy.'

With long-achieved patience, Cord tuned Seth out and got to work. Later he was startled when he realized two hours had gone by. The pipe was nearly fixed. All it needed was a little tightening –

At the sound of a truck rattling up the long, unpaved drive, Cord sighed. He'd bought the secluded two hundred acres of forest for a reason, a reason that no one but him seemed to respect.

7

Peace and quiet.

Okay, maybe Tayna's death had made him nervous. That the woman had been bludgeoned to death one night less than an hour after their date definitely played a part in it. Overwhelming guilt did too. He hadn't stayed with her that night, as she'd wanted him to, begged him to. But, as lovely and kind as she'd been, he simply hadn't wanted that kind of relationship with her. And now, because she'd been alone, she was dead.

Guilt and regret hung over him, gripping him tight in their sweaty fists. Seth and Katherine kept assuring him he'd get over both, but he was beginning to think they were wrong.

How did one get over death? Especially a cruel, needless one like Tayna's?

Even knowing he probably couldn't have prevented it, even knowing he could have been killed himself didn't ease the lingering blame.

Far below, he heard the knock on the front door and cursed under his breath.

He didn't have to answer it. Maybe he'd be left alone if he didn't. It was worth a try, he thought as he went back to his pipes and tried to forget.

Emily McKay knocked, then stood back to admire the rustic three-story house. She hadn't seen it in several months, not since she had come by before making her bid for the paint job. The contractor had done a terrific job with the renovation and it was, quite simply, a masterpiece.

8

No one answered her polite knock, despite the fact she could see another truck parked at the side of the house. Maybe they couldn't hear her. She pounded harder on the beautiful solid wood double door, thankful that her contract called for a lot of wood staining rather than actual painting. Coloring the natural wood would be an absolute crime.

After another minute she pushed open the door . . . and promptly fell in love. The interior wasn't finished, not by a long shot. Tools were scattered across the unfinished flooring, the walls were streaked with wet drywall taping and the huge brick fireplace wasn't completed. Despite that, there was such personality, such charm, that Emily just stood soaking it in.

The little foyer was all double-glass, designed to protect from the harsh winters, and led into a huge, beautiful living room with tall, open-beamed ceilings and hardwood floors. French doors added light and opened the room to the panoramic view of the woods and hills beyond. It was breathtaking. The glorious morning sun warmed the large room, and for a moment Emily was lost.

Her overactive imagination could picture the walls lined with tapestries, cozy paintings and personal snapshots, the furniture covered with large cushions and quilts, the floor scattered with throw rugs and the grand fireplace lit with a crackling fire.

What a home this place would be. She called out, but no one answered. There was an interesting smell: fresh drywall, new wood and a foresty, outdoorsy kind of scent that came from the myriad windows opened to the spring mountain breeze.

Then she heard a distant ping that came from upstairs – the sort of noise any one of a number of tools could have made.

Climbing the bare wooden curved staircase, she sought out the worker, hoping it was someone from HT Designs. She'd not yet met anyone, having placed her bid for the job through the mail. A Seth Thompson had notified her by telephone that she'd gotten the job.

She found the worker in the bathroom, or at least part of him. Long jean-clad legs stuck out from under the bathroom sink, and for just a minute she stood rooted, staring. Her eyes travelled upward from booted feet to lean, masculine hips and an incredible stomach, exposed by his untucked shirt.

It wasn't her fault, really, since the rest of him was buried beneath the sink. He was talking to himself. His tools were scattered at her feet, plumbing parts piled in a box near his hip. The plumber, obviously.

'Great,' his deep voice mumbled. 'Just great. It was supposed to fit.' One leg bent as he strained with something beyond her view. 'Get in there you son-of-a – '

'Hello,' she called, then bit back a smile at his muffled caustic curse.

Large hands appeared on the counter, followed by long arms which pulled the rest of him out from beneath the sink. Sitting before her, he leveled an annoyed glare at her. '*Who are you?*'

His sharp eyes bore into her and she became uncomfortably aware of two things. One: she was thankful that he was the plumber, not the contractor, and two: he had the darkest blue eyes she'd ever seen. But there was no way she was going to be intimidated, not even by a very large and very irritated man. 'Who are you?' she countered.

'Look, lady, I'm not up for games today.' He moved to his feet in one fluid, graceful motion. She had to tilt her head *way* back to see those eyes settle unerringly on her. They were deep, unreadable, and Emily got the distinct impression that nothing got by this man. He sighed. 'Fine. We'll do this your way. I'm Cord Harrison. Now, who are you?'

'The painter,' she said, allowing herself a small smile of victory. 'McKay Painting, to be exact. I'm here for a walk-through. I start painting tomorrow.'

To his credit, he didn't express the usual disbelief, nor utter a single deregatory remark about a tiny woman like herself doing a man's job. She didn't know whether to be thankful or wary, but assumed the latter was the best bet.

Cord Harrison bent over and picked up a towel at his feet, moving with a surprising elegance for one so large. It wasn't until he started to dry off his arms and face that she realized how drenched he was. His dark, sable-colored hair glistened and his T-shirt clung to his chest and shoulders, emphasizing that this plumber was indeed in decent shape.

'Do you have a name, Ms McKay Painting?'

11

For some reason she wanted to demand that he stick with Ms McKay, but that would have been ridiculous. The building industry wasn't exactly known for its formality on the job site. 'Emily.'

He looked at her, amusement at her stiff tone floating in those eyes of his. 'Well, come on, then, Emily.' He dropped the towel and moved out through the door, obviously expecting her to follow. 'We'll start at the bottom.'

'Start what?' she asked, wondering where the contractor was.

Cord stopped abruptly on the lovely staircase and looked at her as if she were a complete nit-wit. 'Your walk-through. I want to go over the job with you.' His tone was even enough, though his eyes were impatient, as though he couldn't wait to get back to work. 'It's a large job, one that requires painstaking detail on your part. You wanted to start work tomorrow.'

Too many years in a man's world had taught her well. She knew to stand up for herself immediately, knew to be strong, and knew only too well that she would still get barely half the respect she deserved. 'It's not necessary to walk me through this job,' she told him, lifting her chin. 'I know what has to be done and I can talk to the contractor when he shows.' She wished he would change his wet, sheer shirt so he wouldn't be so damned distracting.

'How do you know that I'm not the contractor?' he asked curiously, his dark eyebrows raised.

Even standing a step below her, he still towered

over her. Defiantly she backed up one step, until their eyes were level. 'Because you're the plumber.'

'Ahh,' he said, more seriously, and she was disappointed to see the sparkle drain from his unusual eyes. 'Because I'm dirty and wet? Is that it?'

'That was my first clue,' Emily admitted. She looked past him, down the stairs, trying to find a way to politely put him back on track.

Cord didn't budge, but he gave her a hard look. 'I must say I'm surprised. I would have thought that as a woman painter you would know better.'

'Know better?'

'Do you always judge people so quickly, Red?'

She flushed at the reference to the deep color of her hair, but refused to rise to the bait. It wasn't her fault he misunderstood. He was right about one thing. As a woman painter she knew how badly people could misjudge. 'I'm not judging you at all, Mr Harrison. I'm just trying to do my job. And my name isn't "Red."'

'I see,' he said quietly, still studying her intently. 'Well, Ms McKay, I think the contractor made a big mistake when he took your bid. What do you think of that?'

Emily was well used to men who thought they were superior, but somehow she hadn't expected it of this man. 'I think that it doesn't matter what you think, Mr Harrison. I have a signed contract.' She could worry later about how awkward it would be to work with a subcontractor who didn't like or respect her. After all, it would hardly be the first time.

She could have sworn she saw a brief flare of admiration before he carefully masked it. 'There *is* something you should know,' he said, turning and starting down the stairs again.

'What?' Her eyes took in the thick baseboards, the open ceiling joists, the wide shelving surrounding each and every window and she thought how much work there was to be done in this room alone.

'I *am* the general contractor.'

He continued through the living room into the foyer without a backward glance, leaving her staring after him in stupefied silence.

The next morning, in her own apartment, Emily finally relaxed. The rest of her walk-through with Cord Harrison the day before had gone without incident, though it had been a little strained on her part. She hated feeling foolish. She reached out with her brush. One more touch of blue and the painting of the lake was complete. Pretty good, she thought, stepping back from the wall for a moment. And at twelve feet across and eight feet high, it was also big. *Very* big.

The smile faded as she added a touch of white to the sky, leaning from high on the ladder. If only she could wow the art world with her murals, she would have it made. Then she could afford to tell Cord Harrison to take his job and . . . She sighed. The fact was she couldn't afford to tell him anything. She desperately needed his job.

Painting murals was Emily's first and only true

love. But since her painting didn't put food on the table, or take care of her younger brother, it was time to quit for now and go inside. Backing down the ladder, she heard the door slide open behind her.

'Hey, Sis,' a laughing male voice said from behind her. 'Don't those colors look nice on you?'

She looked down. Her overalls were a rainbow of dried paint. The cloth tied at her side, specifically put there to wipe her hands on, was spotless. Okay, so she could never be accused of being the most organized person in the world. One had only to look in the back of her truck or her kitchen sink to see that.

She turned from the patio wall with a welcoming smile to Joshua, correctly anticipating the fondness swimming in the pale green eyes that were a perfect match to her own. 'What do you think, Josh?'

He eyed the wall carefully. The colors were muted; the water in the round bay a soft blue, the lush green brush surrounding it complementing the misty sky that was streaked with a flock of seagulls. It was so large and so real, a person could almost feel the breeze drift over the water. 'Emerald Bay.' He turned to her with a twinkle in his eyes. 'Our home turf, huh?' He flicked another thoughtful glance at the painting. 'It's huge, of course. And beautiful. The best you've ever done.'

She let out the pent-up breath she hadn't realized she'd been holding. Though only sixteen, Josh had an excellent eye and his opinion meant everything to her. 'I think so too.'

A good foot taller than she, despite her eleven-year

15

advantage, he easily reached out and ruffled her hair. 'Maybe this will be the one. Then you'll be able to stop painting houses for rich snobs who don't want to do it for themselves – '

'Stop it, Josh.' They'd been through this a thousand times. 'That's what we do. We paint custom homes.' She playfully punched his stomach. 'Besides, I don't mind doing it – especially when you actually show up for work to help me.'

He looked suitably chagrined. For a split second. 'But with this painting you'll be able to get a real painting job. You know, like painting murals on buildings and stuff.'

The gullibility of youth, she thought. Had she ever been that way? No, she hadn't. Her youth had been ripped out from beneath her feet. 'I hope so, Josh. But the odds are against it and we need income. Especially for next year when you start college. Tuition is expensive.'

He sighed and shoved an agitated hand through his hair. 'I don't have to go to college.'

It was the age-old argument. She tossed her long braid back over her shoulder and bent to clean up her mess. 'Yes, you do.'

'It'll be too expensive.'

'We'll work it out.' She capped her paints and sent her painting one last, longing look.

'I don't want to leave you all alone.'

Emily straightened, then played her trump card. 'Mom and Dad would have wanted this, Josh. And I want it for you as well.' Desperately.

16

His eyes met hers for one long, telling moment, then skipped away.

'Come on,' she said, not wanting to argue. 'Let's get breakfast. We have a busy day.'

He made a face. 'I don't want to spend my weekend painting.'

'Weekends are the only time you can give me lots of help,' she chided mildly, stripping off her overalls, leaving her in a tank-top and bike shorts. 'And the house is absolutely gorgeous, even if it isn't finished. You'll see.'

'Who's the hotshot owner this time?' he asked, equal amounts of worry and exasperation mixing in his voice.

Emily bit back her frustration. She knew Joshua thought he had good reason to worry. On the last job she'd taken the owner had assumed the painter came along with the paint job. She had fought off his suggestive remarks and roving hands for two long, maddening months.

Somehow she didn't picture having that particular problem with Cord Harrison. He'd taken one scathing look at her and she had known exactly what he was thinking. Short, plain-looking and very bossy. And she'd be willing to bet her first paycheck that his type was tall, leggy, blonde and very friendly – which was more than okay with her. She didn't want to attract *any* man's attention, especially not someone she worked for.

'HT Designs is the owner,' she answered, with some pride. HT Designs was a small but highly successful architectural design company with a reputation that spread across the entire western United States. That she had gotten the job at all was a testament to her own reputation. And to her low bid, she thought wryly.

Josh followed her off the small patio of their apartment and into the kitchen. He put a hand on her arm. 'I hate it that you have to work so hard. Someday soon you won't, you know. I'll take care of you and you can just do what you want.'

She smiled up into his eyes, her eyes stinging with pride. 'We'll take care of each other, okay?'

He hugged her to him fiercely. 'Okay.'

Swallowing past the sudden lump of emotion, she put some water on the stove to boil. Until her first paycheck came in they'd be eating a lot of hot cereal. It had taken her three weeks to find a job this time, longer than they'd ever had to wait before. The building moratorium on the entire Lake Tahoe region was taking its toll. 'Oatmeal again.'

Josh just shrugged negligently and Emily knew that it meant nothing to him, that somehow, despite their meager existence for the past ten years, she had managed to spoil him.

Well, she would hope for the best. She'd hope that Cord Harrison could respect a female painter, that the crew wouldn't be male chauvinist pigs, that she would be able to make the job pay. But most of all she'd hope that Josh remembered to show up to help her out after he did his schoolwork.

Maybe she'd get a chance after work to paint on

her mural again. And maybe, just maybe, someday soon she wouldn't have to take a job painting houses. Then she could paint what she loved. Murals.

Cord leaned against the tailgate of his truck and shook his head. The fact that Emily McKay was a lovely little thing did nothing for his current lousy mood. *She was his painter.* How the hell he hadn't managed to realize the painter was going to be a *she* from her signature on her bid, he couldn't fathom. Small, perfectly curved and very feminine. He shoved his copy of McKay Painting's contract aside and pulled off his sunglasses. Pinching the bridge of his nose, he closed his eyes and tried to get back some of yesterday's relaxed euphoria.

It was no good.

Normally it wouldn't matter what gender his painter was. He wasn't anti-feminist in any way. He loved women – all shapes and sizes. He loved the way they walked, the way they smiled. He loved their unique intelligence, their easy emotions. He loved their softness, their ability to give and nurture life. He *knew* women – in his business he had met more than his fair share of the fairer sex.

Unfortunately, he'd been burned one too many times trying to find a woman who wanted him for something other than his name, his success, his status. And rather then keep trying, risking heart and soul, he had long ago given up.

It was easier to be alone – only no one wanted to let him be.

Damn it, he needed time off from his world, time off to be by himself. Time in which to gain back some luster. Life. And he was going to allow nothing to get in his way.

Not even a beautiful, aloof painter with long, dark red hair and sea-green eyes that positively spoke to him.

'Mr Harrison?'

The subject of his thoughts startled him. He hadn't even heard her drive up, though how he had missed that noisy old truck she drove was beyond him. Turning, he faced Emily McKay. Her eyes were cool, her mouth curved in a polite half-smile. She flipped her long braid over her shoulder.

'Unless you have a preference, I'll be starting with the outside.' She gestured with a thin, elegant hand toward the front of his house.

He glanced at the extensive amount of wood trim, the fine wood siding that made up most of the house, and then back at the small woman before him. 'That's fine.' What he was more interested in was how the tiny woman standing before him was going to stain and paint his huge house.

He stood, nodding toward her scaffolding and ladders sticking out from the back of her truck. 'Want some help?'

Those amazing eyes chilled by several degrees and her voice was soft, yet strong and determined. 'I can handle it. Besides, my crew will be here later.'

She turned from him and went to the back of her truck, efficiently pulling out the smaller painting gear. He watched her for a minute. When she pulled at the scaffolding nothing happened. She tugged again, to no avail. From the advantage of his height, he could see where it was hitched and he moved to help her.

'I said I'm fine.'

'But it's stuck – '

'I can get it,' she insisted.

'Fine.' He backed up and once again sat on the tailgate of his truck. And watched.

'You're stubborn as hell, you know that?' he asked, not surprised when she ignored him. But when she leaned over in her baggy painter's overalls to reach again for the scaffolding and one of her pockets got caught on her ladder, he stood again. 'Look,' he said gruffly, 'I'd sure like to see you handle this by yourself, but I don't want anyone hurt – not on my job.'

'I'll get it,' she ground out.

'Here.' He released her pocket and accidentally brushed up against the bare skin of her arm. He felt the same as he had the time he'd gotten his black and red wires crossed while wiring the kitchen electrical panel. The shock of her skin knocked him back and left him absolutely senseless.

What brought him back to earth was the grounding realization that she felt nothing, nothing at all.

Her disquieting eyes settled on him as she put her hands firmly on her hips. 'I said I'm fine. Now, why don't you be a good contractor and get back to your coffee and donut break?'

Okay, so she was far from helpless. And she liked to be in charge. But he'd be damned if he was about to explain to the irritating woman that he'd not been on a break – he never took breaks.

'That's cops,' he said amiably.

'What?'

'Cops take coffee and donut breaks. Contractors eat bologna and cheese sandwiches and whistle at women walking by.'

'You're laughing at me.'

'And you're judging me. Again.'

She looked at him. 'You're right. My apologies.'

'Accepted,' he said lightly, wanting to laugh at how she'd practically choked on that apology.

He smiled, albeit a wicked one, picturing that cool poise of hers shattered by the end of the work day, when she'd certainly be paint-splattered and struggling with her equipment. Maybe there was some redemption in this situation after all.

Besides, there was always the fun of trying to goad her into losing her restraint and level-headedness. All redheads had a temper. He wondered just how far beneath her composed exterior it lay.

He also wondered why she hadn't felt that physical jolt when they'd touched. It had been unlike anything he'd ever experienced.

His portable phone rang sharply from where it was hooked to his toolbelt. He reached for it, watching Emily saunter up toward his house with a huge ladder tucked capably under her small, but obviously strong arm. He flicked on the phone.

And then, at the solemn tone of Seth's voice, wished he hadn't. 'What's up, buddy?'

'Cord, she's dead. Lacey's dead.'

Air raced from his lungs, making speech nearly impossible. He sank back against his truck, his knees suddenly rubbery. 'What?' he croaked.

'I'm sorry,' Seth said quietly. 'I should have driven out, but . . . Jesus. I didn't think I could drive right now.'

'What happened?'

'Heroin overdose.' Seth's strained sigh sounded over the wire and Cord knew he was equally stunned.

'Lacey didn't do drugs,' Cord said, holding his forehead, trying to think.

'I know. I told that to the police. But try to make them believe that a homeless person wasn't on something.'

'But – ' Cord stopped. 'God. You think –?'

'She was murdered, Cord.' Seth sounded adamant, frustrated. 'There's no way she'd have touched the stuff.'

Cord knew that to be true. It was one of the things that had drawn both Seth and Cord to help Lacey in the first place. 'You told the police, right?'

Seth's laugh was harsh. 'Yeah, I told them I thought she was murdered. For all the good it did.'

Sweat pooled at the base of Cord's spine as the next thought hit him. Tayna, then Lacey. It was too much – simply too much for one person to take.

CHAPTER 2

Emily was late the next morning. She would have liked to have blamed it on the traffic, but there wasn't any on the narrow mountain road that led to the job. Nor could she blame it on her morning's preparation for work. It wasn't as if she wore a lot of make-up or took the time to curl her hair. And if she regretted, just a little bit, that she wasn't more womanly or beautiful, she wasn't about to admit it.

Her tardiness was due to the late night she'd put in sketching her next mural. She'd worked long into the night, struggling to get rid of her odd discontentment.

For once, it hadn't worked.

And now she'd gotten a late start which would throw her entire day off. There was a lot she'd planned on getting done – she had the entire outside of the house to spray – and the fact that she hadn't been disciplined enough to get out of bed with the alarm was a major annoyance.

Slamming the truck door, she went around to the back and started to pull out a heavy box that stored various brushes and pans.

Strong, work-roughened hands pushed in front of her to grab the box before she did. She raised angry eyes, meeting Cord's smiling ones.

'Good morning,' he said cheerfully, pulling the box into his arms. 'Where do you want this?'

Her eyes narrowed, refusing to acknowledge how nicely the sleek muscles in his arms and shoulders bunched together. 'Tell me, Mr Harrison. Do you help all of your subcontractors carry their things?'

'Cord,' he said, turning away from her and walking towards the house, still carrying the box.

'What?'

He stopped and threw her an indecipherable look over his shoulder. 'My name is Cord.'

'I know that,' she said obtrusively, following him.

Damn it, he hadn't answered her question. But at least he hadn't touched her again, like yesterday. She'd actually felt weak-kneed when his warm hands had brushed up against her arm, and the reminder of that was just as embarrassing one day later. She *never* felt weak-kneed.

She had to practically run to keep up with his long-legged stride. 'Would you *stop*?' she called out. He didn't even slow down.

Right then and there she decided that either Cord Harrison was incredibly slow-witted or she hadn't made herself clear enough yesterday. Just in case it was the latter, she tried again. In her toughest teacher-to-bad-student voice, she called, 'I'm quite able to handle my own gear. And what little I can't handle, I have a crew for. Do you understand?'

25

He stopped, then slowly turned, her box still held tightly in his arms. And for one brief, utterly ridiculous moment, she wondered what it would be like to be cradled like that box, against his chest. Held in those amazingly long, sinewy arms.

'Tell me, Red. Is it just me – or do you hiss and scratch at anyone who is nice to you?'

She slammed her hands into her painter's overall pockets so that he couldn't see how they fisted. What was it about this man that caused her to lose control of her temper? She'd always had a formidable one, yes. But never, ever, had she had such a time controlling it. For years she'd been working as a woman in a testosterone domain, and she had learned well. All men were basically after one thing. She'd dealt with it well too, she always thought. Until now.

But maybe, a tiny voice inside her whispered, just maybe Cord was an exception.

'Is that all you're trying to do? Be nice to me?' she asked tentatively, willing to make peace, to give him the benefit of the doubt.

He looked at her strangely. 'Of course.'

'Out back, then.'

'Excuse me?'

'You can bring the box out the back with the rest of my gear that I left there yesterday.' And then she nearly smiled when he merely nodded and turned away to do her bidding. It wasn't so bad letting him have his way and be manly. Actually, it was quite nice. That box was heavy.

He came back for another, and for the first time she noticed the deep lines of strain around his mouth. 'Is – is everything all right?'

He looked at her, silent. And she flushed. She started to turn away, embarrassed that she'd asked, but he stopped her.

'No,' he said quietly. 'Not really.'

'Not really?' Was she doing something wrong? Had he found fault with her work already?

'A friend of mine died yesterday.'

She heard her own sound of shocked surprise, but felt paralyzed. Why was it that just those words touched off a legion of her own horrifying memories? 'I'm . . .' She sighed, then pulled the box from his arms and let it drop to the ground. 'I'm very sorry, Cord. What happened?'

His eyes fixed on a spot far over her head, Cord licked his lips. 'The police say death was caused by a drug overdose.' He shook his head, his jaw tight, eyes hard.

'But you don't believe that,' Emily added, when he went silent.

'She wouldn't have touched the stuff,' he said flatly.

She. Oh, God, Emily thought. He must be devastated. And she'd done nothing but snip at him. 'Cord, I'm sorry,' she said again, inanely, knowing anything else would sound trite. She'd hated that at her parents' funerals – all the . . . triteness, however well-meaning.

'She was a good friend,' he said quietly. 'Nothing

more. But it still hurts. I lost someone else recently as well. It just seemed to hit me suddenly – two friends dead. There aren't many left.' His gaze dropped to hers, deep and full of sorrow. 'I'm sorry,' he said quietly. 'I didn't mean to lay that on you.'

She understood his pain completely. What she didn't understand was why those deep, intelligent eyes of his touched her so.

He abruptly reached for the box she'd dropped. His smile was sad, but genuine. 'Thanks for listening,' he said. And he disappeared into the back of the house.

She let out a deep breath. It might have been good for him to let out his feelings, but what was good for him seemed dangerous for her. She didn't understand how someone she hardly knew could alternately bring out the worst in her and yet stir up such great compassion.

She'd really have to watch these sudden, crazy mood-swings, she thought. Maybe it was only that she'd been up another late night. Maybe it was just that her brother had failed to show up yesterday to help her. Maybe she begrudged spending time painting a custom home to support her and her brother when she'd rather be working on her own mural.

Maybe it was nothing more than the uncomfortably handsome Cord Harrison.

She spent the entire morning working on the house's exterior, enjoying being outside. The weather was typically perfect, blue skies spattered with cotton-puff clouds. If she looked up, she could catch a glimpse of the lake shimmering through the brilliant green forest below. The sounds of the surrounding woods were better than any music. Wind rustled the trees, birds sang, chipmunks bickered pleasantly.

Reaching for the sander, she flipped it on, the noise almost soothing as she ran it along some especially rough areas of the siding. Sometimes the longing to paint overwhelmed her. Like now. When it was at its strongest, it overrode the sorrow and horror of her parents' death nearly ten years before, it erased the difficulty of raising her brother alone and it eased her loneliness, made her forget how she'd gotten that way – at least momentarily.

Because nothing could ever permanently erase the nightmare of her past.

She worked that way, locked in her past, for hours. The sun had moved across the sky when she flipped off the sander and set it down. Standing back to survey her work, she put her hands on her hips. It was looking good. She fumbled through the many pockets of her overalls, looking for the list of things she had planned on getting done.

She found one piece of watermelon candy and absently put it in her mouth before resuming her search. The list was nowhere to be found and she cursed her inability to organize. How was she supposed to handle a job this big if she couldn't organize herself?

'How about a break, Red?'

Her frustrated retort died as she turned and faced Cord. He stood behind her, two cold bottles of soft drink hanging from his fingertips. The man didn't deserve a shrewish painter, nor, she thought as she studied his tired, tense face, did he – or anyone – deserve to lose someone they cared about. But even a grieving contractor could be a dangerous one. And she had to remember – she didn't know this man.

'Nope, no breaks,' she said, plastering an easy smile on her face.

She pulled her hands from her pockets, wishing she didn't feel so grimy and ruffled next to him. Oh, he had a hard-worked look to him – his faded jeans were dusty, his smudged shirt was shoved up above his elbows and the bright red bandanna tied around his forehead held back sweat-dampened dark hair – but his eyes, the color of an early-morning sky a few minutes before sunrise, sparkled with vitality. And a whole host of other things she couldn't guess at. And he didn't smell like someone who'd been working hard; he smelled clean, slightly damp and very male. All together he was one gorgeous, sexy man. Grieving or not, it annoyed the hell out of her.

'What's wrong with a break?' he asked. He tipped back his head and studied her work. 'You've been working hard for hours now. Your arms must be tired from lifting the sander.'

They felt like leaden weights, but she wasn't about to admit it. 'They're fine.' The general contractors of her past had expected her – as a woman – to work harder and better than the rest. She'd spent quite a few years building her reputation, and she wouldn't blow it now because her arms ached.

'Here.' He offered the drink. 'Take one anyway.'

A brief flash of the last man she worked for came into mind. He hadn't hounded about her working too hard, he'd just hounded her. Period. She'd hoped Cord would be different, had been fooled by his easy manner. Though her throat felt parched as the sandpaper on her sander, she regretfully shook her head at the offered drink, thirstily eyeing the condensation dripping off the glass. 'No. Thanks.' She turned away.

'What's the matter, Emily?'

She wouldn't look at him, wouldn't allow him to see how difficult this sort of situation was for her. 'I told you, I don't take breaks. That's all.'

'But you didn't tell me why not.'

Did the man never give up? She bent and fiddled with the equipment strewn across the ground at her feet. 'Wouldn't want to give the boss-man any excuse to go on the rampage.'

He didn't answer and her curiosity got the better of her. She glanced at him over her shoulder, and, though the bright sun blocked out his expression, she could tell his friendly smile had faded.

'I've heard the boss is a good guy. He wouldn't mind if you rested.'

She felt churlish at the hurt in his voice he couldn't quite mask. 'I'm sorry. You're right. You've been very kind so far.'

'*So far*?' he asked, the humor returning. 'Do you expect me to suddenly change my personality?' Once again his smile disappeared as he looked at her. 'Lord. That's exactly what you expect.'

She busied her hands by changing the paper on her

sander, thankful for the distraction. 'I don't expect anything. I just want to be left alone to do my job.'

'I see.'

'I didn't mean to make this awkward. I just work best if I'm left alone.'

'Was it the last contractor you worked for? Or someone a long time ago?'

She stood, but didn't look at him. 'Excuse me?'

'The jerk.'

'What jerk?'

'The one who taught you to be so wary. The one who made it so you can't even enjoy camaraderie on the job site.'

'Is that what this is?' she asked, feeling a little lost. 'Camaraderie?'

'Yes. What did you think it was?'

She lifted her shoulders. Out of her depth, she thought. 'I don't know.' But she knew exactly. She'd assumed he was either tricking her into taking a break he thought she didn't deserve, or he'd been hitting on her. Both assumptions disturbed her.

'You're a quick judge, Emily,' he said simply. 'Maybe you've had to be. But I'm different. No matter what's happened to you in the past – '

'My past is none of your concern.'

'No, it's not. But your present is. You'll be treated as an equal here, that much is a promise. And if you have any problems, I hope you'll come to me with them.' He paused, waiting for her reaction, but she gave him none. Wasn't sure if she could with those dark, serious eyes on her.

His smile was sad. 'You don't believe me. Maybe you'll give me time to prove it.' He thrust out the drink again. 'Go on, Emily,' he said softly. 'Take it. It's just a drink. A very cold drink because you looked thirsty. The end.'

Gingerly, avoiding his fingers, she took the drink. He watched her and she felt ridiculous. 'Thanks.'

He nodded, his face serious, his eyes not giving a thought away. 'I meant what I said before. You've worked hard today, really hard. And I'm not just saying that because you're a woman. I appreciate hard work, that's all.'

'Thanks.' She felt the flush of pleasure and it embarrassed her. How long had it been since she'd gotten simple praise? Too long, since just a few simple words from this man had her acting like a blushing schoolgirl.

She took a long swig of the drink and nearly moaned in pleasure as the cool liquid slid down her throat. A couple of drops escaped and dribbled down the front of her overalls and beneath her tank top. The chill felt incredible, but the sloppiness of the act further embarrassed her.

He made a sound and she shielded her eyes from the sun, trying to see his expression. He raised his gaze from the wet spot between her breasts.

She resisted the urge to cover the spot that now burned from his gaze. Resisted, too, the urge to remind him that he'd just assured her he was different from the other contractors she'd known.

He licked his lips, the first sign of nerves she'd seen

from him. 'Did you get your paints in yet? I want to look at the colors.'

For a startled minute, Emily thought he meant her own mural, but then quickly realized the impossibility. She frowned, trying to adjust to his quick change from easy friendliness to business. Even his face had hardened slightly, almost as if he greatly regretted his attempt at creating a social atmosphere. Or maybe he simply wanted to prove his point about treating her as an equal. Either one would work for her – especially the no social part. That was how she wanted it. Pure business.

'They'll come in tomorrow.'

He backed up a step. 'Okay.'

She held a hand up to her face, again shading it from the bright sun, wishing she could see him more clearly. If it had been two hundred years earlier, he could have passed for a dangerous highwayman. A dangerous highwayman who looked suddenly eager to escape. That knowledge was strangely deflating. 'I'll bring them to you then.'

One thing was certain, she thought as she watched him walk around the house toward the back. The customary uniform for a contractor – snug jeans, flannel shirt, boots and low-slung toolbelt – all definitely fit the man. All too well.

Seth found Cord under a different sink in his large house this time.

When his partner's Italian leather-clad feet came into view from where he lay under the kitchen

34

plumbing, Cord had to smile. 'You're back. I'm dry this time.'

'So I see.'

Cord sat up and tossed aside his wrench. 'What is it about doing this kind of stuff that is so damn satisfying?'

Seth's smile was quick. 'You must not have played with your Meccano set enough as a kid.'

Well, that was certainly true. But that was what happened when one was raised by nuns. They tended to work more on souls rather than motor skills.

'Missed you at the office today,' Seth said casually, leaning against the sink. He fingered the newly placed tile countertop. 'Sheri's driving me nuts, asking me to sign things, prepare stuff, wanting me call this person and that . . .' He shuddered. 'A guy can't just go to work anymore – his secretary's got to hound him.'

Cord smiled, picturing Sheri doing just that. He'd never had a more faithful secretary, or a more loyal one. 'She's just doing her job.'

'She misses you. She grumbled about it today.'

'Sorry I didn't come in. I wanted to finish the tiles in the bathroom.' And grieve.

'Maybe I've just got the Monday blues,' Seth said slowly, 'but I get the feeling you're going to be making a habit of this.'

Cord stood and looked out through the large kitchen garden window. He could see most of his property from this vantage point and he felt something within him swell with pride. He could have left the work for next weekend, but the truth was he hadn't wanted to. 'We've been working hard for years, Seth.'

'Yeah.' Seth smiled fondly. 'Remember the macaroni and cheese days? During the week that's what we'd have for dinner every night.'

'It was all we could afford.' To this day, Cord couldn't stand the smell.

'It's different now. I guess we can do whatever we want. Come in whenever we want, work whenever we want.'

'It was just one day, Seth,' he said, sensing his friend's troubled thoughts. 'A little time off isn't going to hurt either of us.'

Seth came next to Cord and also looked out the window at the lush, foresty view. 'As long as that's all it is.'

'You think I'm going to stop being an architect?' Cord smiled at that. As much as he enjoyed building, designing was in his blood.

'Could you?' Seth asked, serious. He turned from the window and leaned back, crossing his arms over his chest and studying his friend.

Cord shook his head. 'Not likely. But the office runs smoothly enough without me. You do all the managing anyway.'

'I couldn't afford to buy you out, Cord. I mean, if you wanted to leave the partnership.'

'No?' Cord laughed. 'You're the one driving a brand-new red Ferrari.'

'I mean it.'

They both knew exactly how much their business was worth – it had become a source of constant amazement to the both of them. So how could Seth be short money? 'I have no intentions of leaving, Seth,' he said, concerned. 'But – '

'Don't, Cord.' Seth said quickly. 'I know how you are, and I'm fine, really I am. I just overextended myself with some investments, that's all.' He turned away, but not before Cord saw Seth's embarrassment.

Obviously the subject was closed, for now. 'I'll be in the office tomorrow. I just needed . . . some time.'

Seth nodded. 'I still can't believe it. Lacey gone. It hurts.'

How he knew. No matter that they hadn't known her well, he still felt overwhelmed by shock and sorrow. 'I don't understand why anyone would want to hurt her . . . she was so sweet.' That disturbed him greatly, as did the fate that had made Lacey so vulnerable in the first place.

'It's sick. She never did anything to hurt anyone.' Seth looked at him. 'It's good of you to see to her burial. Sheri told me.'

'I'm also trying to find her sister. It's the least I can do.'

'How?'

'I've called Roster.' He was the local private investigator. 'When he finds her, I'll go tell her.'

'I'll come with you.'

Cord nodded. He and Seth had been together for more years than he could count. Always, no matter what the circumstances, they backed each other. 'I also called the sheriff to see if I could put some pressure on to have the autopsy reports checked.'

'A lot of good that'll do,' Seth said with some disgust. 'A homeless person doesn't rate.'

'She does if she has someone to care – and she does. She has us.'

Emily came into view then, talking to a young man that Cord could only assume was one of her crew. They were dressed alike, in those baggy, all-concealing painter's overalls, and he gave an idle thought as to what had happened to his insides when Emily had dribbled her cold drink down the front of her. That quick surge of arousal had startled him, especially since he'd been in the middle of trying to reassure her that he wasn't going to bother her.

She moved out of his view and he wondered if she always wore overalls, and what kind of a figure she'd hidden beneath them.

'Well?' Seth asked, looking amused.

'I'm sorry – what?'

For a moment Seth's gaze followed where Cord's had just come from, and a knowing smile touched his handsome face. 'Maybe I picked the wrong painter for the job, old buddy.' He laughed gustily. 'With those soft, helpless looks she'll have you doing all the work in no time . . . but you probably wouldn't mind – '

'I'm not interested in Emily,' Cord stated flatly.

For one thing he still felt uncomfortable thinking about how he'd nearly devoured her with his eyes.

He'd startled her and he hated that. Obviously, as a woman painter, she'd had a hard time, and he didn't intend to add to that. And for another the woman wasn't at all what he was usually attracted to. In fact he'd never met a woman like her before.

She was petite, yet strong. Fragile-looking, yet level-headed. Practical, yet he could sense a subtle sense of humor. A bundle of contradictions. Purposely he turned his back against her. He wanted tall, lush and a serious lack of inhibition. No complications.

'She's just the painter.'

'Really?' Seth watched as Emily smiled at something her worker said. 'Hmm . . .'

Cord knew that look and he tensed. 'She's not your type. She has a brain that works.'

'Ouch,' Seth winced. 'Normally I'd have to hurt you for that one. But it would take too much energy.' He pushed away from the counter and headed toward the back door. Cord followed him to his car.

'I'll be in tomorrow,' he promised. 'Tell Sheri.'

'You'll make our day,' Seth said, folding himself into his Ferrari. 'The office is a wreck without you.'

A noise shifted Cord's attention. Absently he waved Seth off, watching as Emily climbed agilely up the high scaffolding anchored against the house. Her taller, stronger worker stood at the bottom. Cord became uneasy. He'd never thought of painting as a particularly dangerous occupation – until now.

He moved closer to the house, uneasily aware of how feeble the scaffolding seemed as it swayed gently in the breeze. As a contractor who was afraid of heights, he'd taken more than his fair share of ribbing. Still, it was exactly that fear which drove him now.

'Just a little higher,' her worker called.

'I can see, Josh,' came Emily's caustic reply.

Cord bit back a grin. So she was equally disagreeable and bad-natured to everyone. His grin faded when another gust of wind knocked the scaffolding against the house and Emily grabbed for support.

'Emily!' the worker called nervously, holding onto the bottom of the scaffolding. 'Come down. It's too windy.'

'I have to get this part sanded today,' came the stubborn reply. 'We would have had this done, but – '

'Yeah, yeah – I know. I haven't been here.' Josh gripped the scaffolding tight as Emily hopped up one more story until she stood over twenty feet above them.

'Do you always hire people who aren't reliable?' Cord called up to Emily as he came to stand next to the scaffolding. He felt the color drain from his face when she had to grapple again for balance against the next gust of wind.

She didn't look surprised to see him. Nor did she even bother to look his way, but instead lifted her sander and flipped it on, effectively drowning him out with the noise.

His eyes narrowed but he said nothing. Nor did he yank her down himself, as he was tempted to do. She was the most stubborn creature he'd ever met, he thought irritably as he struggled with dizziness just from watching her.

When the sander finally flipped off, Cord pushed away from the house where he'd been waiting tensely. And when Emily's booted feet hit the earth again, he was there.

She turned and stared up at him, her eyes lit with turbulence and defiance. For a minute he just looked at her, feeling his anger dissolve in the face of her obvious restlessness. It was an emotion he doubted she knew she was showing, but he recognized it well. He felt it himself. And the unexpected sharing of it made her a sort of kindred spirit.

Their eyes met. Her face flushed and he wished he knew if it was because of the physical exertion – or something else. Her helper said nothing.

'Your scaffolding is old,' he said casually.

'Yes.'

'And it's getting pretty windy.'

She glanced around as if noticing that fact for the first time. 'Yes, it is.'

Cord gave her a long look. 'There's a lot of other things you could be doing today.'

Emily set the sander down and squatted before a toolbox. 'Your point being . . .?' She smiled up at him politely.

'Damn it, you know what my point is. It's dangerous to be doing that now. And you're not properly staffed for – '

Emily stood abruptly, a sharp gleam coming into

her pale eyes. 'I'm perfectly aware of the conditions, just as I'm perfectly aware of what I'm doing. And as far as my staff goes, no one but I will decide if they're adequate.'

'He doesn't even show up for work regularly, Emily.' It wasn't his business, true enough, but Cord felt he had to say it.

She flicked a glance back to the worker in question, who at the beginning of their conversation had backed up and remained silent but now moved closer, watching carefully with narrowed eyes.

Cord's angry gaze settled on him then, and he froze. He was looking at Emily's twin, or if not he was damned close. Both had those unsettlingly light green eyes and the matching dark red hair that he'd never seen Emily wear in anything but a rigid braid, and the same stubborn, defiantly set features.

'You're out of line,' the person who looked so familiar said now. He stepped forward and stared at Cord.

'Mr Harrison,' Emily said stiffly, 'this is Joshua. He works for me. Joshua, this is Mr Harrison – the general contractor that I told you about.'

Cord stuck his hand out, half expecting it to be refused. Joshua shook it, and met his stare with a steadiness that Cord had to admire. 'And Emily's brother,' Cord said.

'Yes,' Joshua said coolly; 'I'm her brother. And you're way out of bounds.'

Cord knew it, but he couldn't help it. Josh moved closer to Emily and swung an arm around her shoulders. That they were close was obvious. That he'd only make things worse by pressing the point was equally apparent. Cord held up his hands in a show of truce and forced himself to smile. 'Have at it, guys, I'm going inside. Just try not to get yourselves killed on my job.'

He could feel Emily's eyes on him until he quietly shut the front door behind him.

Damn her, he thought, glancing at his watch. He'd put himself on a strict schedule and she'd taken up far too much of his time.

So he forced her from his mind.

Which lasted all of about three minutes. It didn't matter that he had other, more pressing things to deal with, that he didn't want to think about her – he couldn't stop.

Emily could feel her brother's curious stare on her, but she refused to give in. Besides, what was there to say? Yes, the contractor is a little pushy. Yes, he seems overly involved in aspects of the job that should be solely my responsibility. Yes, he watches me carefully.

She couldn't help but be certain that it wasn't because he doubted her abilities as his subcontractor. She'd seen his brief flash of fear as he'd looked up the scaffolding at her precarious, endangered position, but that fear had eased when he'd seen how easily she managed herself.

No, she was certain he acted strangely because he was as uncomfortably aware of her as she was of him.

And she didn't like it. Okay, that was a big, fat lie. She shifted uncomfortably, knowing that she, for the first time in recent history, felt a teeny, tiny surge of – something. Attraction, she supposed. Whatever it was, it was dangerous and unacceptable. This was going to be her job site for the next couple of months and she didn't want any complications. Especially male ones.

'I don't like him,' Josh said softly as she leaned over to inspect his work. He was preparing the window ledges for staining – work he hated, but would do for her.

'Well, you don't have to like him.'

'It's strange.'

Carefully Emily wound up the long extension cord she'd used earlier, looping it through itself so that it wouldn't tangle. 'What's strange?'

'Lake Tahoe isn't all that big, especially our area, and I've never heard of Cord Harrison, the general contractor.'

She tossed the cord aside and reached in the toolbox, looking for the taper so that she could protect the windows against the spray. 'That hardly qualifies him as strange. Just relatively unknown.'

'He's not in the phone book under contractors.'

Emily leaned back and looked at her brother. 'You've been checking on him.'

'It's weird, Sis.'

'We've certainly heard of the owner – HT Designs. They're famous.'

Josh jammed his hands into his pockets. 'So why is

44

this nobody doing work for them? Out in the middle of nowhere?'

'Maybe it's a favor,' she suggested evenly. 'It doesn't matter, Josh. It isn't our problem. All we have to do is paint it.'

'I still think something's off,' he insisted, straightening and peering over her shoulder. 'And the plot seems to be thickening. Look.'

A car was pulling up next to the house. Out of it came a nun carrying a basket. But a nun forty miles from nowhere wasn't as strange as watching Cord Harrison come out of the house and warmly pull the nun into his arms. His low voice and soft laugh carried on the breeze across the clearing.

'Now, what do you suppose a guy like him has in common with a woman like that?' Josh leaned negligently against the side of the house, slanting a long look at his sister.

She was wondering the same thing, but wasn't about to admit it. It didn't matter. What Cord did, and with whom he did it, was his own business.

Cord would have laughed at the interest Katherine Snow had generated amongst his painters, if he'd known. For Katherine, sister of St Mary's Holy Church of God, had raised Cord, and thought of him as no other than her true son.

As he led Katherine in the house he smiled down at her formal attire. 'I haven't seen you dressed like that in some years, Kath. What's up?'

She sent him a mock frown. 'If you showed up for church once in a while, you'd know. Father Patrick is

45

back for an extended visit and, unlike his more modern peers, he prefers the traditional dress.'

The resigned frustration in her voice had him laughing. 'Does the man know you prefer your jeans?'

'Of course not.' She smiled then, a lovely, secret smile that brought out her natural beauty, despite her short gray hair, complete lack of make-up and rounded figure. 'In his eyes I'm the perfectly content traditional nun.'

Cord had a time trying to picture Katherine as the typical old-fashioned nun. From as far back as he could remember, she, and the others in her order, had taken care of local orphans. He'd been one of their first. He'd learned young that Katherine, unlike the others, tended to be more liberal, more independent, and willing to indulge those same qualities. While that made her an oddity in her order, it was her other, more favorable qualities that made her indispensable. As for Cord, he knew Katherine's fierce loyalty and intense love had sustained him in his earlier troubled years.

Even now he was perfectly aware that the loving, carefree childhood he'd received, despite the fact he was an orphan, was entirely Katherine's doing. And he'd never forget it.

'You're grieving over that woman,' Katherine said softly, cupping Cord's face.

'Women,' he corrected.

'Tayna's death was months ago, Cord. Let it go,' she pleaded softly.

'Lacey's wasn't.'

'But she didn't mean anything to you.'

He bit back the frustration. 'Not in the sense you mean, no. But I cared for her.'

'I know you did. You should.' Katherine sighed. 'I've been working with the city, trying to plan a shelter for the homeless. Their numbers grow every year.'

'I can help.'

She smiled, her eyes full of love. 'I know you will. But you're busy. Seth says you're going to try to find her family and let them know.'

'Yes.' He had to do something for her.

'Won't the authorities do that?'

He shook his head. 'You know they won't. If I don't do this, Katherine, no one will. And she'll just be forgotten. That easily. No human being should be so disposable.'

'No,' she agreed. 'They shouldn't. To hear you speak that way . . . you make me so proud.'

'It's just common decency. You taught me that, Katherine. It comes from you.'

'It's much more than common decency. Look at you – you're even going to spend your own money to find her family. Not very many would do that, go to those lengths.'

'I don't know about that.' As always he was uncomfortable with her praise, her high expectations.

'That will be expensive, I imagine.' She looked at him, her heart in her eyes. 'Won't it?'

He nearly laughed. Katherine absolutely refused to believe he had money – in fact had enough of it never to give it another thought. She still thought of him as that penniless orphan he'd once been – and she probably always would. It didn't matter how many times he and Seth tried to explain it to her, she couldn't accept it.

He had to admit it was hard to believe, even for him. It felt strange, after a lifetime of poverty, not to pause over every purchase. To buy whatever he pleased, no matter when the next paycheck was due.

'I can afford it,' he assured her. 'Please don't worry about money. Okay?' How many times had they had this discussion? Certainly every time he gave money for the church. Much as the donations pleased her, she fretted that he gave too much. But he knew he could never give too much.

'I can't just stop worrying,' she said, a little annoyed. 'It's a lifelong habit of mine. And it scares me to see you down like this.'

'Don't.' He couldn't handle the sympathy welling in her soft eyes.

'You've lost so much,' she whispered. 'I don't like to see you sad.'

'So let's talk of something else, then.' He shifted restlessly beneath her touch.

She let go of him, turned away. 'Your painter – she's a woman.'

'Yes.' He found he was able to smile. 'She's a woman.'

'Is she . . . someone you're interested in?'

Cord glanced at her. 'There you go, being a mother again.'

'I can't help it,' Katherine said. 'So –?'

'Katherine,' he said firmly.

'Oh, all right.' She tilted her head, studying him. 'I'll drop it. I was offered a position teaching at St James's.'

His shoulders relaxed at the change of subject, but he raised his eyebrows at the name. St James's was an exclusive girls' school not far from his house. The teaching position was one Katherine had long hoped for, so he didn't understand her apparent hesitation. 'That's wonderful. Isn't it?'

She looked at him over her shoulder. 'I won't be working with the orphans any longer. I wondered how you'd feel about that.'

He watched her, uncomfortably aware of how much his opinion meant to her. 'I just want you to be happy, Katherine. You know that.'

Her stare was unblinking, her soft eyes needy. '*Your* happiness is what makes me happy.'

Cord knew that. It was what bothered him. As much as he loved Katherine, he didn't like feeling responsible for her feelings. Besides, he knew from experience that you couldn't *make* someone happy. They had to do it for themselves. 'Katherine . . .'

'I know,' she interrupted quietly. 'I know. You have your own life now, and you're a very busy man. And a successful one,' she added with some pride. 'I need my own life. I just didn't want to disappoint you.'

49

'That you could never do,' he assured her. 'The other nuns will still be there, so, whether you leave the orphanage or stay, the kids will be all right. Just do what's right for you.'

'And if I stopped being a nun, Cord?' she asked, her voice wavering slightly. 'What would you think of that?'

He started to laugh, then realized she was serious. Even he knew enough about the Catholic religion to know that leaving the order was a serious business. 'Why would you do that?'

She shrugged. 'Oh, lots of reasons. I can't – I'm not ready to talk about them yet.' Her breath caught, her eyes filled. 'But would you still . . . feel the same?'

He crossed the room to hug her close, sorry she'd had to ask. 'Yes, Katherine. I'd still feel the same.'

Emily spent the day on her scaffolding, preparing the wood to be stained. This one particular stubborn window casing drove her crazy. It wouldn't come smooth, no matter how she punished the wood.

The cool wind stirred her hair, chilling her damp skin from her third-story perch. She wiped the back of her hand across her forehead, wishing Joshua hadn't had to go and finish a term paper. He hadn't exactly been reliable lately.

That he was a junior in high school and loving every minute of it was the only reason Emily didn't raise the issue with him. This would be his last year to be carefree and she would do nothing to spoil it for him. Her own senior year had been radically altered by the sudden and tragic death of her parents, and she knew she'd never really gotten over it.

She had been thrust into the role of mother, father and caretaker of her six-year-old brother at the tender age of seventeen. She had not experienced her senior prom, the excitement of a wild summer fling, nor the carefree and unrestrained feeling of freedom after graduating.

It had been everything she could do to muddle through after the horror of her parents' death – to figure their tenuous financial affairs, earn enough money to feed her and Josh, *and* keep from falling apart from the immense pressure. If she had thought too much about how they had died, she would truly have lost it, but she had put it so firmly out of her mind that even now it was difficult to remember.

There was one thing she recalled clearly about those times. James Wheeler, whom she had thought of as the love of her life since she was thirteen, had chosen that inopportune time in her life to break her heart *and* their engagement.

It had been hard on her, in many ways, but she'd become a stronger person for it. And if that stronger person inside her didn't easily let people in, didn't like to share control of her life – well, then that was something they had to live with.

There weren't too many people in her life anyway. Just Josh and a few scattered casual friends. At first that had been because between caring for Josh, working and school there had been not a spare second in her long day. Now it was by choice. It was easier that way.

Because the past was exactly that. The past. And she intended to keep it that way.

Looking down at herself now in Cord's yard, she had to laugh. Her white overalls were dirty, her hands white and chalky from the dust of sanding. The braid that rested over her shoulder was no longer a dark red, but a lighter, grittier version. Thank goodness she hadn't bothered with make-up because she could feel a layer of grime on her face, knew that if her skin could talk it would be begging for a bar of soap.

If she could only tame this window casing, she'd pack up and go home.

'Hey, Red – punishing the wood for any crime in particular?'

Mentally groaning, and rolling her eyes for effect, Emily stilled at the deep voice that was beginning to become so familiar. Slowly she straightened and looked down at the irritating man she was doomed to spend the next three months with.

He stood far below her, holding the basket she recognized as the one the nun had handed him in the yard the day before. Even with the distance between them she could see the tautness that seized him, the intensely dark expression he wore, despite the lightness to his voice.

'This wood is in terrible shape,' she called down to him. 'It wasn't properly protected against the weather.'

He tilted his head, narrowed his eyes, looking at something beneath her. 'Emily,' he said in a quiet voice of steel, 'come down.'

'When I'm finished – '

'Emily.' He tossed the basket aside, shading his eyes from the sun. He took a step closer, reaching for the scaffolding. 'Come down here. Now.'

She stood, hands on her hips, and stared down at him. No one told her what to do in a tone like that, not even the boss. 'Listen here, Cord – '

He gripped the equipment with both hands, muscles straining beneath his shirt, and sent her a sharp, dangerous look. 'No, damn you. Now. Come down *now*.'

Before she could so much as give him a look, the bottom of the scaffolding collapsed, sending Emily to her bottom on her perch at the top layer. 'Ouch –!'

'Dammit!' Cord exclaimed, yanking his hands back just in time to avoid having his fingers amputated between the sharp metal levels. 'Hang on.'

Emily tentatively placed a hand on either side of her and peered over the edge. Only ten feet above Cord now, she had no problem detecting exactly how furious he was. And those glaring eyes were directed at her. 'What –?'

'Come down here,' he grated, emphasizing each word carefully through clenched teeth. 'Do it now and do it slowly.' He stepped forward again and reached for the scaffolding. 'I'll hold it steady.'

The words were no sooner out of his mouth when the second of the three layers of scaffolding collapsed. Two gallons of paint flew off, narrowly missing him. 'Jump! Emily, jump!' The sander came down, as well as a screwdriver, and Cord ducked with another curse. But he didn't let go. 'Now, Emily!'

She hesitated, but only because she didn't want Cord to get hurt by the collapsing equipment when she kicked away from it. Her steel-tipped hammer slid off and clipped Cord on the shoulder.

'Would you *jump*?' he yelled.

She did.

CHAPTER 3

Flying through the air toward Cord's outstretched arms, two things occurred to Emily.

One, she was going to be mighty embarrassed if she made it alive, and two, Cord Harrison looked damn cute when he got scared.

Her luck – she landed right on him, hard. She heard the air whoosh out of him and winced when she banged her chin against his shoulder, but he wrapped his arms tight around her, cushioning her fall with his own body. The scaffolding folded upon itself, landing in a harmless pile beside them, dust lazily rising.

Emily had no idea how long they lay in the dirt, tangled in a heap of limbs, hearts slamming against each other, until she lifted her head and stared down into Cord's face. 'Okay, I'll come down now.'

He didn't open his eyes, but she caught his soft oath which told her exactly what he thought of her.

She tried again. 'Um . . . maybe it *was* too windy today to be up there.'

'You think?' He shook his head, opened those

55

fathomless dark eyes, then ran his hands from her shoulders to her hands. 'You okay?'

'Yeah.' She was clutching his biceps, face only inches from his, sprawled over him. The shock of what had happened hit her and her fingers convulsed, but even in that state she noticed the brawn beneath his shirt didn't give. Disconcerted, she rolled off him, sat cross-legged in the dirt and stared at her perfectly folded scaffolding. She rubbed her aching jaw. 'How about you?'

'Dandy. Lord.' He shoved himself up, groaning and rolling his shoulders. 'For such a tiny thing, you weigh a ton.'

Okay, she'd fallen on the man, she'd give him a break. She'd even forgive him trying to boss her around earlier. Still, the apology stuck in her throat. 'That's . . . never happened before.'

'Good thing.' He walked to her equipment, shook his head. 'You had no business being up there today, Emily. You could have killed yourself.' He kicked the scaffolding. 'This thing is archaic.'

Pride kept her from telling him she'd been saving for a new one. 'The fall wasn't that bad,' she said, shaking off his concern.

'Yeah?' He shot her a level look. 'You should have tried it from my position, lady. It was bad enough.'

For all her flippancy, Emily felt shaken. She'd never fallen before, had never even come close. That she'd done so today, in front of this man, bothered her. There was no excuse except her own damn pride, since she alone had made the decision to hurry the job.

To gain some badly needed composure, Emily dipped her head and brushed at the dust covering her. 'I'm sorry, Cord.'

He ignored her apology and stooped to pick up his forgotten basket. He turned back to her and suddenly a full-fledged grin flashed across his face.

She was immediately wary. 'What?'

Reaching out with one long arm, he tweaked her braid. 'You're not so red anymore, Red.'

She flushed at the reference to her obviously disheveled state, but didn't rise to the bait. Besides, it didn't matter in the least how she looked to him. It would only amuse him to know how self-conscious she was, knowing she looked a mess. She flipped her braid over her shoulder. With hands on her hips, she faced him defiantly.

'Thanks for warning me – ' she started. At his long look, she added, 'And . . . thanks for catching me.'

He bowed his head. 'I'd say anytime, but . . .'

She nearly laughed, but her pride still choked her. And, as always, it made her a little snippy. 'But when you work hard sometimes accidents happen.'

'Are you saying I don't work hard?' His look was challenging, amused.

She shrugged. 'If the shoes fits . . .'

'Well, I see you're your usual charming self today.'

She just stared at him.

He sighed. 'Would you stop waiting for me to turn

into a jerk? I'm not going to, and the sooner you realize that, the sooner you can relax.'

'I just want to do a good job.'

'Good. So do I.'

She didn't know what to say. 'Look – '

' – Just drop it, Emily.' He held out the basket of cookies, waving it enticingly. 'I came bearing gifts.'

It was hard to let down her guard. So she didn't. 'Another person's gifts, you mean.'

His unbearably knowing grin didn't fade. 'Jealous, my love?'

'Right.'

'Come on,' Cord cajoled, in a soft voice that Emily was sure had melted thousands of hearts. 'Have a cookie. They're scrumptious.'

'I'll bet.' But they smelled heavenly. She took one and eyed him attentively. 'So tell me, how did you convince a nun that you were worthy to cook for?'

'I happen to be a saint.'

'Hmm, right,' she said, around a chocolate chip cookie that was so soft and delicious she nearly moaned with pleasure.

'Do you have any idea how sinful you look eating that thing?'

She jerked her head up to find him staring at her mouth. He was *flirting* with her – her the plain-Jane painter. She'd never thought of herself as particularly sensual. In fact, her experience in that area was vastly limited – so limited she felt greatly uncertain as to what she was supposed to do. Brushing it off seemed the best way. 'You just said you're a saint. Now why do I find that difficult to believe?'

'I don't know. Why do you?'

Gone from his face was the smug grin, leaving a soft, genuine smile. There was no sign of the arrogant, slightly sexist man that she had made him out to be in her mind. Maybe he didn't even exist. It was possible, very possible, that she had Cord Harrison all wrong.

Maybe he *was* some sort of saint. Maybe he'd built a church or something. Maybe . . . maybe he gave regularly to the nun's favorite charity.

'Okay,' she begrudgingly admitted, grabbing another cookie. 'Maybe you're not as bad as I thought.'

He laughed, a deep, rich sound that vibrated through her, leaving her feeling strangely giddy. 'Just maybe, Red?'

'Yeah. Just maybe.' She took stock of his appreciative smile, his relaxed stance and felt a quick thrill rush through her.

He shook his head, his eyes still twinkling. 'That's a start.' He handed her the entire basket, then took advantage of her full hands to touch the growing bruise on her jaw. 'You're *not* okay.'

His touch was disturbingly intimate. Turning her head away, she mumbled, 'I'm fine. You have a hard shoulder, that's all.'

'And I'm thinking you have a hard head, Emily McKay.' With one last brief caress to her jaw, he turned and walked back into the house, his soft laugh once again carrying across the yard, echoing through the woods surrounding her and seeping through the cracks in the wall around her heart.

And late that night, alone with her sketches, she thought of his laugh. It had sounded rusty, but genuine. As if he hadn't done it in a long time. That she had caused it at all brought a smile to her own lips.

For a week, Cord tried to get from his office back to his house before dark so he could work. He didn't make it, not once.

He might have on Thursday, except for the visit with Lacey's sister. Seth went with him, and in their brief few minutes they learned exactly why Lacey had risked homelessness rather than stay with family.

'That woman was a bitch.' Agitated, Seth slammed a fist down on Cord's car dashboard.

'Yes, she was.' He navigated the narrow mountain roads with a speed that might have been illegal but soothed his tense nerves.

'She knew Lacey was manic-depressive and needed regular medicine – '

'– And knew too that Lacey would forget to take it, but didn't try to help her.'

Seth rubbed his eyes. 'She was sitting pretty in that apartment too. Lacey said her father died last year, left a bundle. Betcha her sister encouraged Lacey to forget to take her pills so she'd look crazy *and* homeless. Two strikes.'

'And the father would leave everything to her, none to Lacey,' Cord finished. He believed it too.

And it infuriated him. But what could he do? Lacey was gone. The helplessness hurt.

'You did everything you could, Cord. Stop blaming yourself.'

'I don't.'

Seth gave him a look. 'I've known you forever, remember? Right now you're sitting there thinking, If only I'd gotten her a place, if only I'd taken her to a doctor, if only, if only, if only.'

He shrugged, caught. 'It's hard not to think that way when someone dies. It's so . . .'

'Permanent?' Seth's smile was grim. 'I wouldn't put it past that woman to have given Lacey the overdose herself.'

Cord wouldn't have either.

He didn't get home early on Friday either.

That day Sheri set up a large luncheon with many of their biggest clients for HT Designs' birthday bash. All their employees worked on it. Their entire set of offices manifested themselves into a party for society's finest and no work got done.

Everyone wanted to toast him and Seth, congratulate them on their success, their outstanding reputation. Cord found himself surrounded by clients, acquaintances and associates – and wondering what Emily was doing at that moment.

Probably standing on a ladder wearing that scowl of hers and painting his house. The house he wanted to be in at this very moment.

He hoped she was being careful – that woman courted disaster. He spent some time picturing all the trouble she could get into and hoped her brother was with her.

And that was how he found himself, standing in his own office, with several of local society's most beautiful women at his side, and wishing . . .

Wishing for his home in the woods.

He caught Sheri's curious gaze and knew she wondered what was wrong with him. She nodded her head toward the guests, hoping, he knew, to nudge him into at the least the pretense of mingling.

He tried.

Keith, one of his draftsmen, came up to him. 'What's up, Boss?'

Cord forced a smile. He liked Keith. Though he was a young, ambitious, up-and-coming architect, they shared a strong, fun competition. Often, Keith teased him and Seth about HT Designs becoming his someday.

And, just as often, Seth and Cord teased Keith about being demoted back to pencil sharpener. It wouldn't happen; Keith was simply too good.

'Nothing's up,' Cord told Keith now. 'Just thinking.'

'About our next job?' Keith leaned in eagerly. 'What is it? Something I can work on?'

He recognized the fierce ambition, he felt it himself. But now, Cord knew, he channeled that energy into his house. 'Maybe.' That decision would have to be made by Seth too.

'Let me know.' Then Keith shrugged. 'Sorry, didn't mean to push. I just love the work.'

How well Cord could understand.

As soon as the last guest had left, Sheri came up to Cord and took his still full flute of champagne.

'You didn't have one sip,' she chided. 'I saw you fake at least five different toasts.'

'I'm not thirsty.'

Seth looked up from the design he was studying and lifted one brow. 'You didn't have to be thirsty to enjoy the party, Cord. I have a date every night for a week and didn't even have to try.'

'That's disgusting,' Sheri said, wrinkling her nose and skimming left-over cheese and crackers into the trash. Her gaze fell back to Cord, and he couldn't miss the curiosity there. 'But you could have too,' she said. 'There were women here today clamoring for your attention and you hardly said a word.'

He shrugged, wandered to the window. From where he stood he could see the shimmering lake, parts of the city, the majestic mountains. The view had always pleased him in the past, but now he felt hedged in. He wanted his woods, his solitude.

'Well?' Sheri came close and squeezed his arm. 'Are you going to give us the scoop? Tell us why you all but turned down at least ten of society's hottest woman?'

Seth set down his papers and eyed him with interest. 'This ought to be interesting.'

How did he tell them that none of that had any appeal for him anymore? 'I'm just . . . not in the mood,' he said, sounding prim.

Seth laughed. Sheri smiled too, but there was

something else in her gaze that disturbed Cord. Relief.

'If I didn't know you were a regular red-blooded American male, I'd start to worry,' Seth said, still grinning. 'But I happen to know you enjoy sex as much as the next guy.'

Sheri made a sound of disgust and turned away.

'I know also,' Seth continued, unperturbed, 'that you are rumored to be *almost* as good as me.'

Cord had to laugh, knowing Seth's twisted sense of humor. 'Almost?'

Sheri turned back, her eyes suddenly speculative. Seth tweaked her hair and teased, 'I thought this was disgusting you.'

'It is, it is.' She started to scoop up empty glasses, but she kept glancing back at Cord in a way he couldn't miss.

He swallowed his sigh and moved out of her way. 'Leave that stuff, Sheri. The cleaning crew will get it.'

She nodded, but still collected crumpled napkins and discarded plates. Cord would have had to be an idiot to miss the longing in her gaze. Even Seth – usually oblivious to subtletly – noticed, and Cord caught his silent question, which he returned with a dirty, thanks-a-lot look.

Cord knew that Sheri harbored hopes for them, despite the fact he'd never encouraged her. He cared for her; she was a loyal friend and terrific worker. But there was simply nothing else, and he couldn't fake it to save her feelings.

A casual affair had never been his thing and he had no wish for one now, not even with his beautiful and caring secretary. Especially not with her.

He never mixed business and pleasure. But that didn't mean he enjoyed hurting her feelings. He didn't. He just didn't know how to avoid it.

'Cord,' Sheri said, with a quick glance at Seth, 'I'd hoped you could give me a ride home tonight. If that wouldn't be a problem, that is.'

'I'll take you, Sheri,' Seth offered suddenly, looking up. He didn't meet Cord's glance, but Cord knew. Seth was giving him a break – and trying to atone for his earlier racy remarks.

'Oh.' Sheri's smile didn't reach her eyes. 'Okay, thanks, Seth.'

And Cord breathed a silent breath of relief. He left before them, pretending not to see Sheri's hurt eyes.

He felt so tired.

Not the kind of tired one could sleep off, but something much deeper. The kind that came from pushing too hard without respite, working nonstop without giving his mind time to rejuvenate itself. He was completely burnt out.

Driving up his long driveway, Cord suddenly felt a sense of anticipation that cheered him. He didn't even realize he was smiling.

Stopping his truck, he slowly got out, his eyes on his house. The spring sun hadn't completely set, yet the air was deliciously cool. But the house – it was like a miracle. He'd seen the progress day by day, worked on it with his own hands, and yet he hadn't realized how much had been accomplished. It was the fresh coat of stain on the exterior that did it.

It was perfect.

Emily must have sprayed the stain on the front of the house while he'd been gone. He wondered if she'd had anymore problems with her scaffolding. God, the house looked great. No longer was the siding dark and dingy, it looked bright, beautiful and shiny. The new windows he'd installed still had to be trimmed, but with the new brickwork he'd done, and the fresh coat of stain on the wood, it was a different house.

It was his home.

'You like it?'

He turned. Emily was standing off to his right a few feet from him, where she'd been loading her truck. She watched him with a solemn, hesitant expression, as if she wasn't sure how he would react.

'I'll do the back of the house tomorrow,' she said quickly, 'then trim the windows.' She slipped her stained hands into her pockets in a gesture he was beginning to recognize. He'd bet that those hands were fisted with nervousness. 'You'll get a better idea then.'

'I . . . like it. Very much,' he told her in a great understatement. 'It's a masterpiece.'

She smiled unexpectedly at him . . . and he stopped breathing. Covered with paint, faintly smudged with what looked like sweat and dirt, and wearing those overalls that hid her every curve; her smile transformed her.

Cord found himself simply staring at her.

Then suddenly she laughed, the sound as light and as musical as a chime, and some of the weight eased from Cord's shoulders.

'I think the house is a masterpiece too,' she said. 'Almost as good as my mur – ' She slammed her lips together quickly, then said weakly, 'My others. Almost as good as my others.'

Still staring at her, remembering her glorious smile, Cord managed to speak. 'It's better than I expected.' She stiffened and he could have slapped his own forehead. 'I mean, despite my greatest visions for this house, it's turned out better than I could have dreamed.' Fascinated, he watched as some of the tension seemed to drain from her taut body.

'Oh. Well . . . good.'

'What did you start to say before? When you said it's almost as good as your others?'

The stiffness came back instantly. 'Nothing,' she said. 'I'll just finish packing up.' She turned back toward her truck and bent to the ground for a load of tools.

Curious to see if he could make her smile again, Cord followed. For a woman so seemingly in control, the back of her truck was a disaster. Though clean enough, tools were scattered haphazardly around so that he didn't know how she ever found a thing. Obviously it wasn't easy, because he could hear her muttering to herself about finding something.

It was just his unfortunate luck that had him

leaning in over her shoulder as she straightened and turned . . . with a ladder in her hands.

It hit him directly in the stomach and the next thing he knew he was sitting in the dirt, trying to catch a gulp of air into his lungs.

Slowly, so slowly, Cord was able to work some air back into his lungs. When he could breathe again, he blinked a horrified-looking Emily into focus.

'Oh, Cord,' she said in a low voice, dropping to her knees to grip his shoulders in her hands. 'I'm so sorry – are you all right?'

He wasn't entirely sure, though he no longer felt as if he was going to lose his lunch on her shoes. But having her kneeling in front of him, still holding him, was kind of nice. So was the unusually subdued, concerned gaze in those eyes of hers.

'So,' he managed, 'you *can* be nice.'

Irritation replaced the worried expression more quickly than he could blink. She released him and stood quickly. 'I'm *always* nice.'

He snorted and carefully pushed himself upright. Lifting his shirt, he studied his stomach for signs of injury, half expecting to see blood and guts spilling out. When he found nothing obvious he dropped the shirt back into place and ruefully rubbed his already sore muscles. 'Why are you packing up alone? Where's your brother?'

Her eyes were on the hand holding his stomach, and it took a minute for them to rise to his face. She flushed, and he realized with a start that she'd been staring at him. *At his stomach*. He wanted to grin, but managed to contain it, knowing how it would set her off. 'Your brother?' he asked patiently.

'Oh,' she mumbled, still embarrassed. 'He had to go early.'

'Leaving you to do all the work,' he guessed.

And for the second time in as many minutes he was witness to the quickest change of mood in history.

'What happens between my brother and I doesn't affect this job or you,' she said stiffly. She slammed the tailgate of her truck. At the driver's door she paused. 'Sorry about the ladder.'

He'd insulted her. Hell, it wasn't hard. She was as defensive as a porcupine. And as temperamental. He had no idea why he now sought to make amends, except that he was mightily intrigued by the fact that she'd shown a first small sign of attraction toward him. 'Emily?'

She hesitated, not looking at him.

'You mentioned you paint, and I don't mean houses. Won't you tell me about it?'

She said nothing and he raised an eyebrow. 'It'll take my mind off the ladder you planted in my stomach.'

She rolled her eyes. 'It couldn't have hurt that badly. You've managed to recover rather quickly.'

'Oh, it hurt,' he assured her, bringing his hand to the hem of his shirt. 'Want to see –?'

'No!' She held out her hand and backed up a step, looking nervous and horrified. He fought his grin and let his shirt fall back into place.

'Tell me about your paintings.'

'Oh, all right,' she said, ungraciously. 'I paint sometimes. Okay?'

'Are you any good?'

A reluctant smile touched her lips. 'Yeah. I'm good.'

'Maybe you'll let me see them sometime.'

She looked at him then, as if trying to decide whether it was genuine curiosity that compelled the question. 'They're big.'

'Big?'

'My last one was eight feet high.'

'Murals?'

She nodded, but said nothing more.

Getting information from the woman was like pulling teeth. 'Like . . . on walls?'

'Yeah.'

'So, you'll show me?'

She shrugged, as if it didn't matter in the least. 'Maybe.'

Which was the strangest thing, he thought as he absently rubbed his still aching stomach. Her eyes were lit like a sunrise at his interest yet her face remained stubbornly cool, detached.

She wasn't used to people showing an interest in her work.

And, in truth, he was a little surprised at his own interest in her. It was unwarranted; it was unplanned. But there was something about her that drew him. He didn't want to be curious about her but he couldn't seem to help himself. Why was she so introverted, so seemingly unused to getting close to people?

She turned from him, started to get into her crotchety old truck, and he was left searching for a way to detain her. 'Leaving so early?'

It didn't exactly work like magic, though she didn't get in the truck. 'It's not early,' Emily said with a defensive glance at the watch on her wrist. 'I've put in ten hours today.'

And she looked it. Delicate circles of fatigue lined her eyes, giving her an unexpected look of vulnerability. Her shoulders were slightly slumped, gaping the overalls away from her chest in an interesting way that drew his eyes. Her small hands rested at her sides, as if she were too tired to do anything else with them.

'You've worked hard,' he conceded gently. 'And it's a long drive. I'm going to barbecue steaks, why don't you join me first?' Now where the hell had that offer come from?

'No,' she said too quickly. 'I mean, I have to go home and check on my brother.'

'He's a big boy.'

'I don't expect you to understand.'

He studied her profile as she glanced inside her truck. She wanted to escape him and it was an altogether unpleasant realization. 'So help me understand.'

'I'm the only family he has.'

So she felt a tremendous responsibility for family. An odd combination of jealousy and yearning twisted his insides at that. He couldn't relate – he had no family other than a group of nuns who'd been

71

obligated to raise him. Okay, he thought, that wasn't fair to Katherine. But his deepest fantasy had been to have siblings. A blood-tie that couldn't be denied. 'So you let him work for you, even though he takes advantage of you?'

'He does not.' Anger flared in the green swirling depths of her eyes, intriguing him, so he stepped closer.

She stood between the open door of her truck and the truck itself, and when he came closer he could see her fight not to back up. He wondered if it was because he had inadvertently intimidated her or if because, like him, she was wary of the inexplicable attraction between them. Either way, he paused.

'I know, I know,' he said easily. 'It's between you and him.'

'That's right,' she agreed. 'And I really have to go.'

He was tempted to kiss her. Really tempted, as he hadn't been with another woman in a very long time. But then, if she'd been another woman, he might not have wanted to so very badly. Unable to think of any other reason to keep her, or why he even wanted to, he backed up. 'Drive safe.' He didn't like to think of her on the road alone, especially with all that was going on in the news lately.

The quick confusion in her eyes told him she wasn't as indifferent as she wanted him to believe. 'I always drive safe. A little fast, but safe.'

It took her three tries to start her grumpy truck and she glanced at him as she reached to shut the door. He was in her way.

Feigning a wary look and clutching his injured stomach, he leaped back.

He was rewarded with a crooked smile that warmed him the rest of the night.

Until Seth's phone call.

'What is it?' Cord demanded, his heart starting to pound at the familiarly heartsick tone to Seth's voice.

'It's Sheri,' Seth answered. 'She was attacked on her way out of the office tonight.'

'Oh, hell. Is she –?'

'She's alive,' Seth said tersely. 'But she's going to have a hell of a headache. She was hit from behind as she locked the doors. She's got a concussion and a hairline fracture.'

Cord sank onto a kitchen chair. Again, he thought. It's happened again. 'I thought you were taking her home. What happened?'

'She didn't want me to take her home. Apparently she decided to take a cab.'

He'd thought it couldn't get worse, that he couldn't feel more responsible. How wrong he'd been. 'She wanted me to take her home, damn it. Why the hell didn't I?'

He knew the answer to that one, so did Seth. 'Cord, don't do that to yourself. I offered because I knew you didn't want to hurt her feelings and I should have insisted – even when she later changed her mind. If it's anyone's fault, it's mine. Not yours.'

No, Cord thought. He had no one to blame for Sheri getting hurt other than himself. It had been such a small request, why couldn't he have just driven her? He should have, just as he should have told Sheri immediately he wasn't interested in her in that way.

He hadn't wanted to hurt her, but she'd gotten hurt anyway.

'What the hell did the police say?'

'They're working on it,' Seth said grimly. 'But they're paying attention now. They want to talk to us.'

'They can wait. I'll meet you at the hospital.'

As he drove down the mountain at breakneck speed Cord vowed that no one else would be hurt. Because somehow, some way, he'd find out what was going on and stop it. He wouldn't give up until he did.

Once at the hospital, he ran into the emergency rooms. But to his great frustration – and the police's – Sheri was deemed too ill to hold up to any questioning.

Maybe not so surprising was the police car out at the front of his home when he drove back up the mountain a little while later. Of course, he thought bitterly as he agreed to answer a few questions, it was only natural. They figured him as a prime suspect.

CHAPTER 4

Emily became aware of the attack on one of HT Design's secretaries the next morning. It horrified her, not only by the very nature of the crime but because of what one of the subcontractors had said about Cord being upset. Apparently he'd known her personally.

Despite her inner resolve to maintain her distance, she found herself worrying about how he was holding up. When he appeared in the morning out of nowhere, to help her unload, she glanced at him curiously. She wanted to demand to know why he helped her and not any of the other subcontractors. She didn't want preferential treatment or to be thought as a helpless female.

But one glance at his face told her it was far more than that. He did it because he thought of them as friends and he wanted to make things easier for her if he could.

His welcoming smile seemed wan and it made her feel small to see how tired and tense he looked. 'You okay?'

He paused in the act of lifting a box and looked at her. Her breath caught. Never could she remember anyone looking at her like *that*. It was a look that shot right through to her soul. Her heart hammered its response.

'You heard, then,' he said. 'I'm on my way to visit her right now.'

'Do they know what happened? Or who –?'

'No,' he said flatly. 'Not yet. And she's fuzzy on the details still.'

The rage fairly vibrated off him, and it touched her, this anger he felt in the name of someone else. She was beginning to understand that he was a man who felt freely and deeply for others. 'She doesn't know me,' Emily said, feeling self-conscious. 'But . . . send my best.'

His smile was slow to come, but sweet. Emily found herself returning it.

'Emily!'

She looked up as one of the flooring workers called to her from the door.

'Your supplier just called. Your inside paints are in. They said you can pick them up.'

'Thanks,' she called back, then glanced at Cord. He was looking at the house.

'What you've done looks fantastic.' He lifted a box from the back of her truck. 'You've been busy this week.'

'So have you.'

Together they reached for the same box, and when their hands brushed against each other Emily experienced a sharp pang of . . . longing. It surprised her into letting go of the box and staring down at her hands. Determined to forget it, she reached for her ladder, and so did Cord.

One brow quirked as they looked at each other over the ladder. 'I think,' he said in that half-amused tone of his, 'we'd be safer if you let me handle this one.'

She could feel the red flood her face as she remembered jamming him in the stomach. Then her breath stopped as well, because he reached across the ladder and ran a rough finger over one hot cheek. 'Don't fret, I recovered.'

Just his words conjured the image of him lifting his shirt to examine the damage, exposing the lean, flat planes of his fantastic stomach.

'Well, it's a good thing you've been gone so much,' she joked. 'Or I'd probably have hurt you worse by now.'

'We haven't seen much of each other this week.'

'No.'

'I've missed you these past few days, Emily McKay.'

Being stunned into muteness definitely had its good points. Even if she were capable of talking, she had nothing intelligent to say. It shouldn't feel so good, she chided herself, to have a man say those words while looking at her as if she were the only woman on the earth. 'You don't get around much, do you?'

His eyes lit as his finger ran over the fading bruise on her jaw. 'Certainly nobody's fallen on me before.'

She glared at him and he laughed. But her silence

didn't seem to disturb him. He just smiled that damn sexy smile and finished unloading her truck, tactfully not commenting on the fact that she let him do the rest of the work.

'Thanks for helping me unload,' she said, feeling awkward.

'Thanks for letting me.' One corner of his mouth quirked. 'Though it was hard for you.'

'I – uh – have to go back into town now. To pick up my paints.'

'Good,' he said, nodding and taking her arm. He moved toward his own truck. 'I have to go to town too. I'll drive you.'

'No, I can't,' she said, appalled, trying to pull back. He stopped. 'Why not?'

She looked at him. *Why not?* Because it would be at least an hour there and an hour back, alone with him in an enclosed space. 'I like to drive,' she said lamely. She liked to drive? *Oh, that was good, McKay. Real good.*

He shrugged, a half-smile crossing his face. 'Okay.' And he simply changed direction and walked back to her truck. He slid into the passenger seat. 'I'm easy. You drive.'

She stood there, staring at him like a half-wit. Her heart had absolutely no business doing that slow roll in her chest just because he wanted to be with her. She had no business being even slightly attracted to him – they worked together. 'I meant I like to drive alone.'

His easy smile faded. 'I see.' He looked down at his

clenched hands for a minute, then raised his head. The neediness in his eyes terrified her. 'I guess I just wanted company on the way to the hospital.'

She chewed her lip as she studied him. Did he have to be so compassionate? So sensitive? 'Oh, all right, damn it. Come along. I don't care.' She plopped into the driver's seat, then relented. 'I am really sorry about her, Cord. And I'll be happy to wait for you at the hospital, as long as you want.'

His smile warmed places inside her that she hadn't known existed. And she had to forcibly remind herself that this man was mourning not one but two good friends – and now another, maybe even his girlfriend, had just been attacked. Nope, she definitely had no business thinking about that smile of his.

None at all.

They picked up her paints without fanfare, and at the hospital parking lot she sat back, prepared to wait.

Cord got out of the truck and came around to her side, holding out his hand.

She looked at him in surprise. 'I'll wait here. Take your time.'

'Come in,' he said, tugging her out. 'I don't want you waiting in the car like my cab driver.'

His stress was back, she noted as she sat outside Sheri's room. She waited, reading a magazine, and when a nurse came out of the room the door didn't completely close.

She heard the soft sound of weeping. And Cord's low voice, murmuring.

Emily turned her head and caught sight of him sitting on the edge of the hospital bed, a dark-haired woman in his arms, sobbing.

Something within her tightened, in sympathy, certainly, but it seemed more complicated than that. Emily forced her gaze away, but not before she wondered . . . what would it be like to be held by warm, comforting arms? There'd been a time in her life, long ago now, that she'd needed to be held. She hadn't had anyone to do that – then or now.

With a small, disparaging sound, Emily yanked the magazine open again. But she still couldn't help but hear Cord and Sheri's conversation.

'I wish I would have driven you home like you wanted, Sheri,' he said, his voice sounding tortured. 'I'm so sorry I didn't. None of this would have happened.'

'It still might have,' she answered, her voice muffled by his chest. 'And you might have gotten hurt too. I'm glad you didn't.'

'Sheri.' He cupped her face and tilted it up to him, kissing her cheek softly. 'Seth told me. You're going home to your parents in Texas.'

She nodded, her eyes spilling over. 'I don't want to stay here.'

Emily flipped a page of the magazine, trying not to hear. Trying not to care that Cord had someone in his life.

'We'll get a guard,' he told Sheri. 'I'll make sure you're never alone in the office again. I'll – '

'Don't, Cord,' she whispered. 'It's not your fault.

But I have to go. I can't stay here. I just can't. Do you understand? I'm too afraid.'

He nodded slowly, looking so worried, so sad. 'I understand. We'll – I'll miss you, Sheri.'

Emily closed her eyes and stood abruptly, the magazine falling to the floor. She hadn't meant to listen, to eavesdrop, she really hadn't. Blindly she rushed down the hall, feeling . . . she didn't know what she felt.

Touched by Cord's concern, and Cord and Sheri's mutual pain, certainly. Also saddened, to know how much he cared for Sheri and that she was going to leave him.

And greatly embarrassed to have seen something she shouldn't.

Cord found her waiting in her truck. He didn't say much on the ride back, just stared thoughtfully out of the window at the passing forest.

Before Emily knew it, and far before she was ready for it, she was done with the outside of Cord's house and ready to move to the interior. This was where the bulk of the work was, for every room had an amazing amount of detailed woodwork that needed her attention.

The work didn't worry her. But she would have given anything to know that her next job wouldn't be painting a house. She'd contacted the county because she'd noticed that all their buildings were being prepped for sandblasting. She was hoping that she would be given permission to paint a mural on one of them. She was sure enough of her work to know that people would like it. And want more.

No, it wasn't the work bothering her. It was her general contractor.

She was uncomfortably aware of the fact that Cord was, for some unknown reason, attracted to her. He'd done nothing out of line. In fact they'd hardly spoken all week. But she often felt him watching her and he'd always materialize out of nowhere to help her load and unload. Each time, if they inadvertently touched, Emily felt a strange shock vibrate through her, and she knew he felt the same.

She didn't like it.

On the following Monday she drove to the house, looking forward to working on the interior. She'd been surprised at the brilliant craftsmanship of the house, though she shouldn't have been. She was beginning to know Cord enough to realize he took great pride in his work, no matter what that work was. Everything, down to the smallest detail, was beautifully done. Simple pleasure in her surroundings made her work go by fast.

But finding herself happily working in the presence of Cord Harrison was unsettling. She didn't like how easy it was, and she held her mistrust of him close to her heart. She trusted no one other than her brother. It was an old habit, born too many years ago to change now. But it was impossible not to react to his slow, easy smile that contracted her stomach muscles every single time he flashed it. Oh, well, she thought. She was preoccupied, stressed, busy –

but not dead. And she'd have to be not to react to the vital, rugged, breathtaking Cord Harrison.

When she let herself in the house, she got a surprise.

A man and a woman stood in the foyer, talking softly. Emily recognized the casually dressed woman as the nun who'd given Cord cookies. The man turned toward her and smiled pleasantly. Emily blinked. Dressed liked someone off the pages of a glossy men's magazine, and carrying the tall, blond elegance to go with it, the man exuded an easy charm mixed with a devastating measure of good looks.

'Well, hello,' he said. 'We meet at last. I'm Seth Thompson from HT Designs.'

The man who'd hired her. The owner. She didn't know what she'd expected. An older man, maybe, one who'd worked for years in order to assemble the amount of money it must have cost to buy this place and its land. Instead, Seth Thompson couldn't have been older than thirty-five and was quite simply one of the most gorgeous men she'd ever met.

He shoved his sunglasses on top of his head and offered his hand, smiling as if he knew the world's greatest joke. 'And this is Katherine Snow,' he said, turning to the woman beside him. She was a kind-looking woman, who generously filled out her clothes, at least fifty, maybe more. Not a speck of make-up dusted her even features, yet she was almost unearthly beautiful.

Katherine smiled warmly. 'A woman painter. That's very unusual. Do you enjoy it?'

It kept her electricity from being cut off. 'Yes, I do. I prefer painting murals, but this works for me.'

'Cord is pleased with your work,' Katherine told her, in a voice that spoke of how she valued Cord's opinion. She watched Emily carefully, as if measuring her for her worth. With her hands carefully folded in front of her skirt, her light brown eyes settled with direct intent on Emily's customary outfit of painter's overalls.

Emily felt the strange impulse to squirm and confess her every sin. 'I'm glad Cord likes what I've done.' She struggled for something nice to say. 'Your cookies were delicious.'

Katherine's smile turned to surprise. 'He shared?'

Seth laughed. 'He must like you indeed, Emily. He never shares his cookies. Especially Katherine's.'

Not for the first time, Emily wondered at this relationship between Katherine and Cord.

'Now, come,' Seth said, taking Emily's arm and companionably tucking it into his own. 'Come show me what you're doing inside. We'll leave Katherine to Cord, since she came to see him anyway. She bought him some ridiculously expensive set of something or another.'

'Chisels,' Katherine supplied, laughing. 'And how you got to be such a great architect without a basic knowledge of working tools is beyond me.'

'Good luck, darling – nothing but good luck.'

Katherine smiled warmly at Seth as he took Emily into the large living room. 'I love this room.'

The May sun filled the room through the windows, and even with bare wood, drywall and no furniture, it was breathtaking.

'Me too,' she admitted, bending to pick up a tarp. She wanted to protect the floors the best she could, even though they were as yet unfinished.

Seth came forward and took two corners from her, then backed up to help her spread the tarp. 'You know, you're the most unusual house-painter I've ever seen.'

Emily's head flew up, then she relaxed. He didn't mean it; he was just the type of man for whom flirting came naturally. His pretty eyes shone with speculation as he pondered the ease of his conquest, and she decided right then and there that he was harmless enough.

He grinned wickedly. 'And definitely the most beautiful.'

She tilted her head and forced herself not to laugh. Beautiful she wasn't – and she well knew it. Add her big painter's clothes and wild hair and you got downright frumpy, no way around it. 'Uh-huh,' she said easily. 'And exactly how many female painters have you encountered?'

He hesitated, slightly sheepish. 'None. But you could be the first.'

Knowing his come-on was all in fun, she took it as such. And to her surprise she played right back, as though adept at harmless flirtation. 'You brought one woman up here and you're flirting with another. Very dangerous, Mr Thompson, very dangerous indeed.' Nodding to her tarp, she put him to work.

'Seth,' he corrected, bending to the tarp. 'And Katherine's here to see Cord, not me.'

'Oh.' She didn't know what to make of that. 'Are you going to be here all day?' She thought about the list of questions she had about the job. And the fact that she needed her first payment.

Again that meant-to-be devastating grin. 'Want me to be?'

She put a hand on her hip and studied him. 'Don't count on it.'

'Hmm, a woman who can resist my charms. A challenge I can't pass up. Have dinner with me?'

'No.' She nearly laughed at his absolutely crest-fallen expression that she knew perfectly well was feigned. But she had no reason to purposely insult the man. Especially before she'd gotten paid. And he was even now on his hands and knees spreading out her tarp for her.

'Why not?' he asked, looking up at her. 'I'll be good.'

She bet. 'I'm cooking for my brother tonight.'

He came up off his hands, still on his knees, and nodded. 'Ahh . . . a woman who can cook *and* paint. I think I'm in love.' He surprised her by walking to her on his knees across the spread tarp. 'Marry me?'

'Kind of sudden, isn't it?'

They both jumped and stared at Cord, who stood in the doorway with a startled-looking Katherine at his side.

'Oh, please,' Cord said, lifting a hand. 'Don't let us interrupt.'

He spoke casually enough, but Emily could feel herself flush regardless. The situation was ridiculously embarrassing, though she'd done nothing but speak with the owner of the property she worked on.

Seth, still on one knee before her, released the hand that he'd taken in his and stood. He winked at Emily, then grinned broadly at Cord's unreadable face – not put out at all. 'I'm stealing your painter.'

'Oh, really? Well, be prepared, buddy. She packs a loaded scaffolding unit and a mean ladder.'

More heat flooded Emily's face as everyone looked at her curiously, obviously wondering at the private joke between her and Cord.

'I can handle it.' Seth brushed dust from his pants then ruefully rubbed his chin, glancing at the suddenly and inexplicably tense Cord. 'Oh, relax. She won't have me anyway.' He tossed a grin back to Emily. 'And my heart's broken.'

Emily snickered at that and Cord looked at her, his surprise obvious. Only she hadn't the foggiest idea why. And, looking back and forth between the blond, gorgeous architect Seth and the dark, more rugged contractor Cord, Emily felt more than a little uncomfortable, bosses or not. They exchanged a long, silent look that Emily didn't understand.

Katherine cleared her throat and, in Emily's eyes, saved the day.

'Why don't we let Emily get to work, boys?' she inquired sweetly, maneuvering Cord out and waiting with infinite patience for Seth to follow.

In the ensuing silence Emily breathed a sigh of

relief. She sensed Cord's disapproval, but had no idea what it stemmed from. He was a man not easily read. Seth, on the other hand, was an open book. A little outrageous, but charming. She knew the two to be close friends, yet the way they had eyed each other made her wary.

It didn't matter, she told herself. She was here to work, and work she would.

Cord settled Katherine on the unfinished second-floor terrace with a glass of iced tea.

'Where's mine?' Seth asked.

'Get it yourself.'

'Uh-oh, somebody's mad at me.'

Cord thrust some tea at Seth, narrowly avoiding sloshing the cold liquid over the side and all over his partner's clean clothes. 'Drop it,' he nearly growled. What the hell was wrong with him? Snapping at his best friend, and for what? Because he'd harmlessly flirted with Emily? It made no sense.

Seth grinned that insufferable, knowing grin. 'What's the matter, Cord? Your painter got you in knots?'

Katherine eyed them both with distaste. 'You're acting like two little kids fighting over a Tonka truck.'

'Seth – ' Cord started, inexplicably tense.

The humor faded from Seth's eyes. He clamped a hand on his friend's shoulder. 'Cord, man, relax. I'm just playing with you.'

Cord hesitated, then nodded. 'I know, I'm sorry.

God.' He rubbed his hands over his face. 'This thing with Sheri's really ... got to me. The police hounded me again this morning with questions.'

Katherine lifted her head. 'They don't think it's you?' Her hand lifted to her chest; her mouth went tight with worry.

'It would make it easy for them if they *could* think it's me.' Cord rubbed his neck, feeling the knotted tension. 'But apparently my alibi holds for each attack. But they do think Seth or I might be a link between all the women somehow.'

'Yeah,' Seth added quietly. 'They came to see me again at the office. I worry about every woman we know now.'

'Especially you, Katherine,' Cord said. 'You've got to be careful.'

'I'll be fine,' Katherine said, with a confidence that didn't ease Cord's nerves one bit. 'I went to see Sheri this morning. She's going to recover, Cord.'

He nodded. 'I know. I saw her again yesterday. She can't tell us what happened because she was hit from behind.' Cord's jaw tightened. 'The police are finally trying to put a connection together between Tayna, Lacey and Sheri.'

Seth sighed. 'Thank God Sheri's injuries will fade.'

'But she's pretty shaken up.' Cord ran agitated hands through his hair. There'd been no witnesses and Sheri had seen nothing. Yet he couldn't shake the feeling that this thing wasn't over. It made him sick. First Tayna, then Lacey, now Sheri.

'She says she's going home to Texas. And I don't blame her.' Seth's grim expression matched Cord's.

'I'd do the same,' Katherine admitted. Her face wrinkled with a mother's worry as she looked at Cord. 'I'm worried about you.'

'What?' He was distracted, thinking about the attacks. It bothered him that he'd known each victim. He felt distinctly uneasy. Would someone else he cared about be next? He looked at Katherine and his worry increased. Next to Seth, she was the only family he had. He couldn't bear it if something happened to her. 'It's not me you should be worried about.'

'Well, we are,' Seth said, keeping his eyes on Cord even though Cord did his best to stare him down.

'I'm fine.' He walked to the edge of the deck and leaned against it. The valley below was, as always, a balm to his soul. Lush green forest lay below, framed by the distant view of the sparkling water of Lake Tahoe. 'You're both wasting your time.'

'Cord,' Katherine said gently, setting down her iced tea, 'I've known you for a long time – '

'Longer than anyone.' Cord forced himself to relax his tense shoulders and turned to face the woman who'd raised him.

'I want you to be happy, that's all.'

'I am,' he told her. It was an old habit. Easing Katherine's mind. She'd made it a lifetime habit of hers to worry about him. Besides, he wasn't *un*happy.

She studied him quietly, obviously not believing him but unwilling to push too hard. 'Seth told me how hard you're working. You're pushing yourself, Cord, trying to do too much. How can you be happy?'

It was funny, but when he thought about it, really thought about it, he was the closest thing to happy he'd ever been. Being here, surrounded by the home he loved and the wilderness he craved, he was – well, if not happy, then content. For too many years now he had pushed himself, pushed and pushed. It left him feeling as though he had nothing left to give. But here, at the house, he could feel himself reviving. He could feel his soul stirring and healing.

Cord crouched before Katherine and took her hands in his. 'I'm fine. You worry too much. It's not necessary to use your free time to drive up here every other day. I'm okay.'

She smiled. 'All right.' She patted his hands. 'I'm glad. I just wanted to see you and decide for myself.'

'You're welcome here anytime, you know that.'

Katherine smiled tenderly. 'Did I tell you how much the orphans loved the circus you set up? Making it just for them was a gift they'll never forget. I know how much it cost and – '

'It was nothing,' Cord told her, and meant it.

'It was.' She hesitated. 'You've given so much, Cord. Sometimes I think too much.'

'I could never give too much.' It was true. Cord gave away a good part of his fortune every year. He'd have given it all if he'd thought it would help. Some commended him for his great generosity. Some criticized him – though his critics were mostly all of greater wealth than he. They said he did it for the publicity. They said he did it for the women. They said he did it to give himself a name.

It was for none of that, but then he didn't really expect anyone to understand. Not even Katherine.

He did it because it was easy for him, because underneath it all he had a great tug of social conscience and a guilty heart. Oh, he supposed he was generous. He could afford to be. But it hadn't always been that way. Never would he forget that he'd been born with nothing. Less than nothing. No family and no one to care. Except the system. He'd been one of the lucky ones. Raised in Katherine's order, he'd been tenderly and lovingly brought up. Others were not so lucky, and he knew it.

So he gave time and money, desperately wanting things to be different for others like him.

Cord downed his drink before turning to the unusually silent Seth. 'I need to talk to you.'

'I thought you might,' Seth answered, with an insufferable grin. Silently he followed Cord back into the bedroom, watching with wry amusement as Cord slid the glass door shut.

Cord kicked a loose piece of forgotten drywall and bent to inspect the taped seam on the wall. 'I got a call from Marty. He's worried about you.'

'Tell me why our stockbroker would be worried,' Seth said lightly. 'Haven't we kept the guy busy enough?'

Cord glanced at Seth. 'Apparently too busy. He thinks you've gotten in too deep.'

'He had no right to say anything to you.'

Cord sighed and straightened. He walked to Seth. 'Maybe not, but I'm glad he did. Seth, are you in some kind of trouble?'

Seth's eyes darted away, and he chewed his bottom lip. 'Me? *Trouble*? Never.' He sauntered to the far side of the room, ran his clean hand down the smooth drywall. 'I'll deal with Marty.'

Cord glanced at the stiff spine of his best friend. 'You could tell me, if you wanted to. Maybe I could help.'

Seth was silent so long, Cord thought Seth had forgotten he was there. 'No, thanks. I'll handle it.'

'Where's the Ferrari?' Cord had noticed Katherine's car out front, not Seth's.

'Out for repairs,' came the surprisingly terse reply.

'A brand-new car, out for repairs? Come on, Seth.'

Seth inhaled deeply, closed his eyes briefly. 'All right, it got repossessed last night. Happy now?'

'Oh, yeah, real happy. Come on, Seth. What the hell happened?'

'I told you, I got a little short on cash.'

Cord stared at him. 'Seth, this is serious. Are –?' He glanced through the glass at Katherine, then lowered his voice. 'Is it drugs?'

'No!' Seth looked appalled. 'I hate the stuff, you know that.' His shoulders slumped. 'I told you, I just overextended myself a bit with the investing thing, that's all. I got cocky, thought I could do better than Marty was doing with our money. But it's addictive, to tell you the truth, and I'm lousy at it.'

93

'You've got to stop.'

'I have,' Seth said dryly. 'I don't have a penny left to my name.' He caught Cord's look. 'I know, I know, I went through a ton of it.' He shrugged. 'I've been poor before, remember? It's not going to bother me. Besides, this time I know I can earn more. We've got some big accounts coming up.'

'Let me help you.'

'No,' he said adamantly. 'Thanks, but no. I got myself into this and I'll get myself out.'

Cord sighed. They'd been together since those penniless days in college, when sometimes they'd been lucky to eat at night.

'I'll get myself out,' Seth repeated stubbornly.

Cord understood pride well. 'Fair enough.'

Seth turned, obviously relieved. 'Now let's get back out there and check on your painter. I've never seen anyone look so good in overalls before – '

'Uh, yeah,' Cord said quickly. 'Hey, when was the last time I asked you for something?'

Seth raised his eyebrows. 'I can't remember. Maybe never. Why?'

'Because I'm about to ask. For something.' Cord hesitated.

'Anything. You know that.'

'Good,' Cord said with some relief. 'Stay away from Emily.'

'Anything but that,' Seth amended, a small smile playing about his lips. He crossed his arms over his chest.

Cord sighed as he studied his only close friend.

They'd been through thick and thin. Together, poor as dirt, they'd made names for themselves, and he alone had now amassed more money than his grandchildren could ever spend. In all that time, they'd stuck by each other – no matter what.

'Ask me something else,' Seth suggested, that same irritating smile still in place.

'All right, then,' Cord said, feeling ridiculous. 'I won't ask.'

'Good. Because – '

'I'm *telling*.'

Seth studied Cord thoughtfully. With feigned patience, Cord waited. He didn't understand why he was doing this, why it meant so much to him. But it did.

Then Seth grinned. A huge, face-splitting grin that seemed two feet wide.

'What the hell is so funny?'

'Oh, man. I never thought I'd see the day.' He chortled with delight, slapping his thigh. 'You've got it bad. You're hooked on her.'

'Am not.' Cord straightened, fighting his growing irritation. 'You don't know what the hell you're talking about.'

'Oh, yes, I do.'

No, he didn't. There was no way that he felt anything but a passing curiosity for Emily. Okay, maybe a tad more than that, but there was no way he was 'hooked'. 'You going to back off or not?'

Looking amused, Seth shrugged. 'Maybe.'

'Yes or no,' Cord managed through gritted teeth.

'Yeah.' Seth laughed. 'Of course. You want her, you got her. I'm officially backing off.'

Cord released his breath. Seth was a 'love 'em and leave 'em' type of guy. He told himself his interest stemmed from not wanting Emily hurt – not because of any personal interest.

Seth gave him one last amused glance and headed toward the terrace where Katherine sat, primly drinking her tea. 'Hey.' He stopped before opening the door. 'Want me to ask Emily if she likes you?'

'Seth?'

'Yeah?'

'Shut up.'

Katherine looked up in surprise as the door opened, letting Cord's last words escape. 'Cord!'

He smiled grimly as he helped her off the lawn chair he'd placed so he could watch what he was beginning to think of as *his* valley. 'Sorry. Seth is being . . . Seth.'

'He started it,' Seth laughed. 'But I've definitely outworn my welcome, Katherine. Shall we go?'

Katherine fondly cupped Cord's face. 'Take care. You look a little stressed, dear. Are you going to be all right?'

'Take lover-boy out of here and I'll be just fine.'

'I'm going, I'm going,' Seth assured him. 'Just give me those drawings I need and you won't see me the rest of the weekend.'

Cord handed over the drawings and watched Seth and Katherine leave. He didn't want to think about why he was suddenly so fiercely protective of his redheaded painter, nor did he want to think about why he'd turned on his only true friend.

None of it made any sense, no sense at all.

And neither did the conversation he accidentally overheard between Emily and Joshua late that afternoon.

He hadn't meant to eavesdrop. But it was hard to avoid with the majority of the house empty and every little sound echoing off the walls.

Straightening from where he'd been bent over the kitchen sink, struggling with the ridiculously stubborn plumbing, he heard the low rattle of angry voices. And when he heard Emily whisper furiously, 'It's none of your business!' his curiosity got the better of him.

Dropping his wrench, he moved to the double swinging doors that led to the connecting dining room. On the far end was another set of swinging doors leading to the large living room where Emily and Joshua were.

'Remember James,' Joshua told her in a hushed voice. And even from this distance Cord could hear the rough concern in his voice.

'How can I forget, with you constantly reminding me?'

'Then you'll remember how badly he hurt you. How you cried . . .' His voice faded away and Cord knew they'd moved from the room. He stood there a long moment, rooted by rage at the thought of someone hurting Emily.

Eventually Cord moved back to his work, unable

to forget what he'd heard. The minute he heard Joshua's old VW ramble down the hill, he went in search of his elusive painter.

He found her on the stairwell, and his heart stumbled a little at the sight of her, painstakingly staining the lovely old wood. She was sitting on a stair, her slender white neck stretched as she reached, her stained hands moving elegantly. She was so intent on what she was doing that she didn't notice him, and he was so mesmerized by the rhythmic, sure motions of her hands that it was a long minute before he noticed her expression. It brought him up short.

Never in his life had he seen anyone look sadder and more alone, and he felt a catch deep within him. And he knew he was about to break the never-mix-business-with-pleasure rule. He couldn't help it. He leaned against the doorjamb. 'I thought you loved to paint.'

She jumped, then cursed under her breath as her brush dripped. 'I do.'

Her eyes met his and he saw the veil slip into place, masking her true expression. He felt a keen disappointment. 'So why, then, do you look like someone stole your puppy?'

'I don't,' she denied. Turning away from him, she dipped her brush and painted. Her braid fell over one shoulder and her overalls were speckled with various colors of paint. It shouldn't have been a provocative scene and yet he was suddenly more aware of her than he would have been if a nude model had walked through the room.

It was a new experience for him, being attracted to a woman without having the slightest idea what shape her body was. But this attraction wasn't necessarily sexual – another new experience. He wished he knew whether she felt the same. It was hard to tell with her. She was so cool, so poised, so completely in control. He came closer, standing below the staircase where she sat, stopping when they were at eye level with each other.

He knew he should go, just go, before he started something that neither of them could stop. He didn't want this. But he didn't go because the truth was something had already started between them. And it had a life of its own, whatever it was.

Emily glanced at him, then quickly back to her work. After a second, her head lifted again. Her eyes filled with what might have been exasperated amusement. 'Why do you always look at me like that?'

'Like what?'

'Like you're . . . hungry.'

Cord let out a short, harsh laugh. 'I didn't realize I was being so obvious.'

Emily's arm dropped with a start, directly onto the tray filled with stain, and it popped up, splattering brown liquid down the front of her with a wet, smacking sound.

With a soft curse, Emily looked wildly around, found a rag tucked into her pocket and swiped at the front of her clothes, her face flushed a delicious red. He flustered her, and he decided he liked that because it was a very encouraging sign.

'Are you laughing at me?' she asked, her voice brittle, her eyes icy. 'Because if you are – '

'I'm not,' he said softly, feeling very optimistic. 'I wouldn't dream of it.'

When she picked up her brush again, Cord reached through the railing and took the paint brush from her hands, dropping it onto the tray. He rubbed his thumb across her knuckles, watching with fascination when her eyes darkened with pleasure, panic and God knew what else. 'You looked so unhappy before, Emily. Is it the job? Is it me?'

She shook her head, maybe in denial – he didn't know. All he did know was that she was going to retreat again, and he didn't want that. 'Talk to me, Em.' He reached for her other hand through the wood, watching the emotions war across her face. 'Come on, talk to me.'

'I can't,' she whispered, trying to pull her hands back.

Holding firm, he pressed closer, his body leaning against the wood railing. He leaned his forehead against the wood, wishing there wasn't the barrier between them. 'You can do anything you want to, Red. You just have to want it bad enough.'

'Well, then . . . maybe I don't want to talk to you.'

'I'm a good listener.'

She sagged against the step behind her and he thought he'd won. But then that shutter came down over her eyes again and she straightened, yanking her hands from his. 'Okay, you want to talk.' She wiped her stained hands on the thighs of her overalls and came down the stairs. 'Let's talk about the color the owner picked out for the hallway upstairs.'

It wasn't exactly what he'd had in mind, but at least she was talking. She needed to be in control, and for now that was fine with him. 'Okay. What about the color?'

'It's all wrong. It should be cream, not pure white.'

'What's wrong with pure white?' He'd picked it himself. 'I happen to think it's a fine color.'

'Maybe,' she conceded. 'But not for that wall. Can you check with the owner on it and make sure I have it right? Maybe suggest a change?'

Cord's easy smile faded some. He wasn't sure what kind of game she was playing. The owner was standing right in front of her. Why was she acting as if he wasn't? 'I think I know exactly what the owner wants,' he said slowly.

'That's quite a gift.'

'What?'

'Reading minds like that. You know exactly what the owner wants without a consultation?'

'Actually, I do.' Cord rubbed his chin as he studied Emily. Was it possible that she didn't know who he was? 'And white is it.'

'It can't be,' she insisted. 'It's all wrong.'

'No, it's not.'

She gave him a long, frustrated look that he imagined matched the one on his own face. She obviously wasn't playing with him, and that meant she didn't know who he really was. How in the world had that happened?

And then he saw a golden opportunity that even a saint – which he definitely wasn't – couldn't resist. 'Care to bet on that color?'

'Bet?'

'Yeah. On which color the owner will pick.'

Her eyes narrowed. 'No.'

'What's wrong?' he taunted softly. 'Afraid? I never figured you for a coward.'

'What do you get if you win?' Her eyes were sharp, and wary.

He spoke quickly, to ease her fear. 'If I'm right you have to be nice to me.'

'Nice how?'

Now she looked so downright suspicious he wanted to laugh, but he didn't dare. 'You're a distrustful little thing, aren't you?' he asked mildly, wondering if this James person he'd over-heard about had anything to do with it. 'All I want from you is a friendly attitude and a smile once in a while. No waspishness, no sarcastic remarks. Just niceness. That is, if you think you can handle it.'

He wondered if the challenge would work. She stared at him, pulled out two pieces of pink candy from her pocket and offered him one. She chewed on her piece for a minute, totally distracting him with that soft sucking noise her tongue made. 'All right,' she said finally, with a quick gleam in her green eyes. She pushed at her hair and smiled suddenly. 'We'll bet.'

It took him a minute to realize what she'd said, he'd got so side-tracked by her beautiful smile. He wanted her to keep on doing it. 'Name your stakes,' he said.

'If I'm right – and I will be – you have to get the owner to agree to let me paint a mural here.'

'A mural?'

'That's right,' she said, raising her chin, looking so defiant and . . . smug that he wanted to smile. When he didn't answer immediately some of her confidence faded, and he knew he would do anything to get it back.

'Okay,' he said.

'Okay?' Emily's hands dropped to her sides as she stared at him in wonder. 'Really?' she breathed softly. 'You mean it?'

Oh, he meant it. And if she would always look so happy, he would agree to giving her the moon. 'Of course, you still have to convince the owner that white is ridiculous and cream is the only way to go.' He was kidding. He'd decided immediately that it would be done her way and look the better for it.

'When will Seth be back?' she asked suddenly.

Now he was confused. 'Seth? What does he have to do with this?'

Emily looked at him as if he were an imbecile. 'He's HT Designs. The owner.'

She didn't know the truth – she really didn't. He thought back, to that very first day weeks ago. Hadn't he told her who he was? No, he'd said he was the contractor. He'd only assumed when she heard his name she would know. But her contract said HT Designs, not Cord Harrison. He took a deep breath, anticipating a quick mood-change for his painter. Yep, she was going to be furious. She would feel like a fool and he didn't want that.

'Em,' he said quietly, quickly, 'I am the owner. I purchased this house using my company name. HT Designs.'

She said nothing, but her huge eyes spoke volumes.

'I'm sorry, really I am. I thought you knew this whole time.'

'I didn't.'

'I'm sorry,' he said again, waiting for the rage.

It never came. Calmly, too calmly, she stared at him. 'Well, then, since you cheated on your bet by not making your position clear, you have to forfeit. I win. And I get to paint that mural, *Mr Harrison, the owner.*' She backed up toward the door, only her high color giving away her distress. 'Now if you'll excuse me, I'm wet.' She pulled the stained overalls away from her skin. 'And it's late,' she said flatly. 'I've got to run.'

Nearly tripping at the door in her haste to escape him, she ran down the walk toward her truck.

CHAPTER 5

Good Lord, Emily thought as she hurried toward her truck, for early May in the Sierras, it was hot. Or was it just her? She bent and stripped off her wet overalls, leaving in their place her usual ribbed tank top and bike shorts. Her mind was whirling, but she refused to let the thoughts assemble. She hesitated, debating whether she could escape or if she had to swallow pride and go back in to rinse off her brushes.

She never left her brushes dirty overnight; it was a cardinal rule with her. It ruined them. But she'd made her dramatic exit and didn't want to look any more foolish than she'd already done.

In the end it was the cost of the new brushes that decided her. Turning, with a sigh, she plowed directly into the solid wall that was Cord Harrison's chest.

He gripped her shoulders. 'Hey, Red.'

Emily felt herself go rigid under his cool hands and wished that she hadn't removed her overalls so quickly. She felt naked and vulnerable. But Cord's eyes didn't leave her face. 'Would you stop calling me that?' she asked, surprised at how cool she managed to make her voice sound.

'It's a compliment,' he insisted, grinning. 'Besides, every time I say it, you turn the loveliest color.' His eyes twinkled. 'Like now. Your hair matches your face perfectly.'

She could feel the heat in her face and had to laugh. 'It's the redhead's curse to blush.'

'I like it.' In a strangely tender voice that made her swallow hard, he said, 'Don't run from me, Em. I didn't mean to hurt you. I thought you knew.'

The reminder of her humiliation was painful. All along she'd assumed he was just the contractor . . . and all along he was the rich owner that her brother held in such contempt. 'I didn't know.'

'I can see that.' His fingers moved against her shoulder, tightening gently.

'I've got to go,' she said, not understanding the welling panic his strong fingers and soft voice evoked.

His work-roughened hands moved to her neck, soothing. 'You're upset. And it's a long drive.'

'The drive doesn't bother me.' She thought about the uproar the town was in over the recent murders. 'That was *your* secretary who was attacked.'

'Yeah.'

'And your girlfriend.' Where had that come from? She didn't care – wouldn't let herself care.

'No,' he said. 'Just my secretary.'

She didn't believe him – wouldn't allow herself to. So, instead, she wondered what her quiet, safe world had come to.

He must have been thinking the same thing. His face was tight with honest concern. 'I don't like thinking about you driving those roads after dark alone.'

At that moment, with his warm, comforting hands on her, Emily knew any danger was standing immediately in front of her. 'I'll be fine.'

'I don't want to scare you . . . but the sheriff told me today they suspect the link between the two murders and Sheri's attack might be HT Designs. If that's true, then anyone I know could be in danger.'

'I thought you didn't want to scare me,' she said shakily. She considered herself braver than most, but dead was dead.

'We're all scared.'

She looked at him, knowing he might well be the murderer himself. But her heart told her he wasn't.

'Come inside,' he said gently. 'I'll make you dinner and then follow you into town. I have to go to the office to pick up some papers anyway.'

He was only being kind, of course. He'd be worried about anyone's safety. But this was the second time he'd offered to cook for her and the idea was novel. Her own father had been helpless in the kitchen. So had James. But somehow she couldn't picture Cord Harrison being helpless anywhere.

He waited patiently, not pushing, and the panic receded. Cord's finger stroked her cheek, evoking a shudder she couldn't explain since she'd been so hot a minute before.

'You can cook?'

He looked insulted. 'Of course.'

'Of course,' she repeated, with a choked, self-deprecatory laugh. 'Well, then, Mr Contractor/Owner/Architect, or whatever you are, lead the way.'

He did, first taking her hand in a gesture which she suspected had more to do with keeping her from changing her mind than anything else. It was starting to get dark, and the forest around them was noisy. Trees rustled, birds called their young home. She loved that pleasant hum. It told her the woods were alive, and that life was precious indeed.

There were no memories of death here. So why, then, did she think of her parents at that moment? She'd noticed that kept happening lately. She thought of the past more and more – in dreams, working, driving.

It didn't take a shrink to figure that out, she thought grimly. For the first time in ten years she was attracted to someone and she felt threatened by it. She was afraid to take the next step, afraid it would be taken from her, afraid she'd get hurt. Again.

She wanted to avoid that at any cost.

Cord squeezed her hand gently, as if he could sense her melodramatic thoughts, and the silent walk became more comfortable in that moment, filled with a strange sense of companionship and content.

Inside the bare, unfinished kitchen, Cord headed straight for the refrigerator. She perched on one of two stools against the tile counter Cord had just put in. 'You've been sleeping here?'

He laughed, a rich full sound. 'Camping is more like it. My house in town is on the market.'

'You sleep here because you own this place, not because you're working.'

He glanced at her. 'I never meant to deceive you.'

'I know.'

He started chopping carrots and celery and tossing them into a salad bowl. 'There's wine in the cabinet or soda in the fridge.' He gestured with his head. 'Help yourself.'

Though the offer of wine was tempting, Emily thought of the long drive she still had to make. She opted for a soda and tossed one to Cord, watching him expertly wield a paring knife. And then she wondered what it was about a man chopping vegetables that made him so attractive.

'Will Joshua worry?'

'No.' Josh was eating at Monica's house – she was his sometime girlfriend. Emily knew that Joshua was attracted to Monica more for her normal family than anything else. The lure of a mother, father and lots of siblings was too much to resist.

Cord turned to look at her carefully. 'Will anyone worry?'

'That was subtle.'

His eyes didn't leave her face. 'Will they, Emily?'

'Are you asking me if I'm involved with someone?' she asked, disturbed at how low and husky her voice sounded.

'I guess I am.'

The soda she'd been sipping backed up in her

throat. She shouldn't be doing this, she thought. She really shouldn't. Because though she was not in a relationship, she had absolutely no intention of getting into one. Especially with someone like Cord Harrison. He was entirely too sure of himself. Pushing off the stool, she set down her drink and nervously took a few steps toward the door. 'I'm sorry,' she murmured. 'I shouldn't be staying – '

He caught her with a gentle hand as she reached the doorway. 'It was just a simple question, Em. You don't have to answer. You don't have to do anything.'

She studied the door as if it held the greatest interest. God, she felt like a nit-wit. She felt clumsy, dowdy and awkward – and she hated that. 'Look,' she said slowly, still talking to the door, 'I'm not like the kind of woman you're used to.'

'What kind of woman is that?' he asked gently.

'You know – sophisticated.' And beautiful. And fast. She was none of those things, and never could be. She was an artist who had to make a living painting houses. 'At this very moment I have paint in my hair, stain under my fingernails, work-roughened hands and no make-up on.' Plus she smelled like turpentine. And she wasn't wearing nearly enough clothing to suit her.

'Do you really think any of that matters to me?' he asked quietly. His hand slipped from her arm to her hand and he tugged gently. Slowly she turned to face him and he stepped closer. Here it comes, she thought grimly. *His move.* She should have known it would happen sooner or later. It always did.

'Em?' His deep, low voice had her stomach quivering.

'What?' She couldn't help but grate the word out through gritted teeth. If he so much as ran his eyes down her body she was going to slug him.

He was so close she could feel his warm breath fanning her hair. She wanted to scream, to ask him to come even closer. When he ran his cool fingers down her bare arm, her breath hitched. And it wasn't from fear.

His sleepy eyes were glued to hers. 'I have an important question for you,' he said huskily.

Here it was, she thought, wishing he hadn't rushed her. Wishing he didn't look so utterly at ease in a kitchen. Wishing he didn't smell so damn good, even after an entire day of working.

'I want you to tell me the truth,' he drawled lazily.

Those amazingly seductive fingers ran back up her arm, leaving a trail of goosebumps. Suddenly she didn't feel so plain and unattractive. He did that so effortlessly – made her feel . . . special.

'Can you do that?' he asked, his voice low. 'Be honest?'

'Yes.' And, as soon as she could put a thought together, she'd let him down as kindly as possible.

Cord leaned close, his lips inches from her ear. Emily just barely resisted the impulse to tilt her head and give him better access. Her eyelids fluttered closed.

'I just wanted to know . . .' He trailed off as he

111

inhaled her hair. 'Mmm, you smell good. I love your hair. I wish you'd let it loose sometimes.'

'*What?*' she practically screamed. 'You wanted to know *what?*'

Straightening, he smiled at her. A sexy, dangerous, wicked, very bad man smile. 'I just wanted to know if you want chicken or steak.'

Her mouth fell open and she practically sputtered in disbelief. Until she saw the amusement swirling in his eyes. The man had just reduced her to limp jello with nothing more than words and he had the gall to be laughing at her. 'Steak,' she said primly, lifting her chin. And she sauntered past him, getting back on the stool. She was not going to lift a finger to help him.

Behind her, he laughed. 'A red-meat-eating woman. I like that.' Totally unperturbed at her sulking attitude, he continued to cook.

She watched, suddenly remembering him holding Sheri in those capable arms at the hospital. 'How's Sheri?' she asked, striving to be casual.

'She's going.' He looked at her. 'She wants to go back to her home in Texas.'

'I'm sorry, Cord.'

He started to nod, then stopped. 'You still think she and I were involved.'

She started as the image conjured up by 'involved' flitted across her mind. 'It's none of my business.'

'I see.' He stirred something on the stove. 'I told you we weren't. I never lie, Emily,' he said, turning back to her and rubbing his hands on a dishtowel.

'And I've never wanted to be with someone I worked with. Before.'

She nearly choked on the sip of drink she'd taken. Slowly she put it down. 'I see.' And she was deathly afraid she did.

They fell silent.

He served them. 'You're really good at this,' Emily said with some surprise as she tasted the delicious meal.

'You don't have to sound so amazed.' He took a bite of steak and grinned. 'I do a lot of things pretty good.'

She bet he did. Including looking like a pure innocent with those midnight-blue eyes of his. But it didn't answer her questions. 'So, why are you doing this?'

'Cooking? 'Cos I'm hungry.'

'No.' She gave him a long look. 'Why are you rebuilding this house by yourself? A famous architect must be a pretty busy guy. Why aren't you paying someone to do this for you?'

He shrugged noncommittally.

She couldn't let it go, driven by some strange need to understand the only man in ten years to have fascinated her. 'I guess I don't understand why a person like you would want to do this.'

'"A person like me,"' he repeated slowly, pushing away his plate and looking at her. 'Tell me, Red. What does "a person like me" like to do?'

'Pay someone to do the work.'

One side of his mouth lifted, but the smile was

grim. He rose from his chair and cleared both their plates to the sink. She followed, carrying their glasses, knowing she'd inadvertently insulted him.

At the sink, Cord surprised her by grabbing her hands. 'You know, Em, you've assumed any number of things about me, most of them dead wrong.' He touched her cheek, further smudging the dusting of paint she had smattered there earlier. 'Try it the old-fashioned way,' he suggested.

His touch had funny sensations swimming in her stomach. His words brought her chin up and she fought the urge to back up and yank her hands away. 'Which is what?'

'Getting to know me before you judge me. I'm not so bad, you know.'

Emily smiled weakly and did pull her hands free then. 'I didn't say you were.' She put as much distance between him and her as the kitchen would allow.

'I'm here because I wanted time off from my life,' he told her quietly.

She didn't want to think about what his low, sexy voice did to her nerves. 'Time off?'

'The business really took off a couple of years ago and Seth and I have been working like fiends ever since.' He shrugged and smiled, almost sadly. 'People think it's all glamor, traveling, sophisticated parties and people . . . things like that. And it was, for a while. But it got familiar and I found myself bored, a little jaded, and feeling far too old. It scared me enough that I just wanted to be alone for a while. At least, I hoped that was all I needed.'

'Is it working?'

'It was.' He stepped forward, his eyes on her. 'I love working with my hands, whether I'm designing or hammering.' He smiled. 'And I found that I still have the knack. I worked my way through college doing construction.'

She thought of the incredible craftsmanship in every part of the house he'd touched. 'I'd say you definitely have the knack.'

'It helps when you're working on something you love.'

She thought of her murals and had to agree. 'You still spend a lot of time at your office.' Not, as she'd assumed, his construction office, but at HT Designs.

'That's to keep Seth happy. He thinks he can't do it without me, but he's every bit as good as I am.'

Emily had seen the two of them together. She'd seen them pore over a set of plans, deep in thought. She'd seen them tackle each other to the floor just for the fun of it. 'You're friends as well as business partners.'

'The best. It was Seth's idea to start the business. We didn't have a dime to our collective names, nor a reputation to speak of. It still surprises me, sometimes, to see what we've accomplished.' His eyes shone with mischief.

Good God, the man had a set of eyes that could set the North Pole on fire. They were certainly heating her up in an uncomfortable way that left her hands clammy and her knees wobbly. In her limited experience, a man had never made her feel this way.

Well, she reminded herself, she had only James for comparison. And she'd been a kid then.

She was definitely out of her league. Way out. How long, she thought desperately, did one have to linger after dinner? Was it rude to leave immediately?

'Don't run yet, Red.' Cord spoke softly and approached her slowly. There were two fresh drinks in his hand and a fresh, open smile playing about his lips. 'Come on.' And then he left the room.

He took her to his favorite nightspot. The patio deck off the upstairs landing.

'Out here.' The French doors were softly lit from the light within. He put the drinks down on the thick wooden railing and turned to Emily. 'I love it out here.'

She looked over the edge and he knew what she would see. There were no city lights shining in the valley below, just an occasional flicker from a nearby cabin. It was the sky that commanded all the attention. It was pitch-black, sparkling with millions and millions of stars that shimmered like diamonds. It was a beautiful night, the kind made for secret whispers, stolen kisses of passion, deep promises of love.

Emily's face was sadly whimsical, almost as if she thought a night like this wasn't for a woman like her. He wanted to kiss that look away and keep kissing until she replaced it with another, happier one.

The air was still, occasionally vented by the sharp hoot of an owl. Cord stepped closer and asked her the question that had been haunting him. 'Who's James?'

She paled. 'What?'

'The jerk who hurt you. Tell me about him.'

'You – you eavesdropped.' He could practically see the smoke come out of her ears.

He shrugged, unapologetic. 'Voices carry in this house. Won't you tell me, Em?'

She moved away from him. 'It's nothing. He's nobody.' Cord just looked at her and she sighed. 'It was a long time ago. Ten years.'

'So you were, what? Maybe thirteen, fourteen?'

Emily let out a short laugh. 'I'm not that young. I was seventeen.' She stared out into the dark valley below. 'And we were going to be married.'

That shocked him. 'Married?' He came back to the railing, leaning on it so that they stood side by side, staring out into the night. 'What happened?'

'He decided I was too much trouble.'

That he could believe. 'Seventeen is awfully young, Em. Maybe it was for the best.'

She let out a harsh, choked laugh that had him turning to stare at her. 'There's more?' he said quietly.

'Yeah. There's more.'

She sighed again and his chest brushed up against her bare arm, reminding him of what she was wearing. It had been a struggle to keep his eyes on hers ever since she'd removed her coveralls, for Emily had a tight, nifty little body on her that could tempt a saint. And a saint he was not.

He cleared his throat and forced his gaze back out on the night. 'Tell me.'

117

'My parents died that year.' She spoke softly, her eyes never leaving the deep valley below.

'That must have been rough. How?'

She bit her lip and didn't look at him. 'An accident.' Her eyes clouded over and she closed them briefly, but not before Cord saw the slash of pain. 'Joshua was six,' she said. 'I wanted to keep him with me rather than give him to a foster home, but we had no money.'

Horrified by what she had gone through, and fascinated by this first glimpse of the real Emily McKay, Cord touched her shoulder. 'What did you do?'

She shrugged off his obvious concern and his hand. 'The state tried to take him, but I fought back. I couldn't lose him, not after what we'd been through.'

'Did they give you much trouble?'

'Yes.'

She stood silent for a long moment and he knew she was lost in her memories. Her eyes were dry, but her expression was so tight and grim he wanted to pull her to him. Only the fact that he knew she would resent the offer of comfort stopped him.

'Finally they agreed he could stay with me, but only because he was raising such holy hell with the foster parents.' She smiled sadly. 'It wasn't that he was a bad kid – he wasn't. Just very sensitive and very scared.'

'You must have been scared too,' he said gently. 'So it was circumstances that made you so independent and strong-willed. I was wondering.'

'Were you?' Her smile was brief and hard. 'Some think I'm just stubborn.'

'That too. I think a lesser woman would have given up, fallen apart. But not you, Emily. You'd fight for what you want, every time.'

'You think so?'

'Yeah.' He smiled. 'I like that. I like you.' The admission startled the both of them.

'Well, you wouldn't have liked me back then. I didn't think about fighting back, I was just scared,' she whispered. 'But I wanted Josh with me. He was all I had left besides James. So I got a job and tried to balance college with caring for Joshua and seeing James. It should have been perfect.'

'So what happened?'

She grimaced. 'It didn't work.'

'You were only a kid,' he said easily, thinking she was far too hard on herself. 'And that was a huge responsibility. Did James help?'

Another strangled laugh escaped her. 'No. He didn't help. He decided that an instant family – meaning caring for Joshua – was too much for him to handle. And since I couldn't give him the attention he seemed to think he deserved, he called it off.'

Bastard. He'd just deserted her, leaving her at seventeen with an overwhelming responsibility that would have crushed another woman. 'So what did you do?'

'Worked a lot, mostly. But we managed.'

'Did you get to finish college?'

'Yes.' Her lips twitched in the first sign of amusement he'd seen all evening. 'Barely.'

Cord didn't see the humor in her situation at all. He pictured her, a young woman, struggling to keep her brother with her. Struggling to make enough money. Struggling to stay in college. He looked over at her as she studied the stars and he began to understand the woman she'd become. She was cool and distant because that was how she'd trained herself to be in order to survive. She'd been responsible for so long she didn't remember what it was like to let someone else in, to share herself, to relinquish her stiff control.

'James was a fool, Red.'

She grinned then, and turned to him. 'Yeah?'

'Yeah. So why aren't you painting for a living?'

Her smile froze. 'I am.'

'I mean the kind of painting that you love. Not that you aren't great at house painting.'

'Much as I love it, I can't feed us on my murals.'

He heard her wistful sigh and wished her dreams would come true. 'Maybe someday.'

'Yeah, someday.' She smiled that heart-stopping smile and looked at him speculatively. 'So, now that I've told you all about me, it's your turn.'

He watched her a minute, enjoying her smile. He had trouble keeping a train of thought when she smiled at him like that. 'What do you want to know?'

'Oh, I don't know. The nun.'

He looked surprised. 'What about her?'

'Tell me why a nun bakes for you.'

120

'Katherine?' He laughed. 'That's a long story.'

'I'm listening.'

'I grew up at St Mary's Holy Orphanage near State Line.'

'Oh,' she breathed quietly. She stepped close again. He could feel her eyes on him. 'What happened to your family?'

'It was rumored my mother got pregnant when she was fourteen. The guy – my father – ' his lips curled with distaste '– apparently found the prospect of having a child too offensive. He took off.'

She made a sound of distress and he shrugged. 'Don't. The ending is happy enough.'

'Is it?' she asked softly. 'I hope so.'

'Her father deserted her, rather than face her shame. And at fourteen she was completely alone. The nuns took her in, as they did any orphan who came their way, and they cared for her. They gave her clothes and food, helped her until I was born. She was shy, lonely and nursing a heartache, they often told me. But she was strong and brave. And she loved me very much.'

'She sounds lovely.'

'I have a picture of her, she was . . . too young.'

'That's so sad,' Emily breathed. 'Her family should have helped her. She was just a child herself! What happened?'

'She left me with the orphanage so she could finish school. And one week before she graduated nursing school she was killed by a crazed drug addict raiding the clinic where she studied. The nuns raised me.' He turned to her and caught the soft sympathy and pity he didn't want. 'It was a long time ago, Emily.'

'Still,' she murmured. 'It must hurt. I had my parents until I was nearly eighteen. I never thought about it like this before, but I guess I was lucky to have had them so long.'

In some ways, he agreed. Though he couldn't remember the woman who'd given him birth, he couldn't help but wonder how his life would have been different if she'd lived.

'To think about growing up in an orphanage – ' She stopped and hugged herself. 'It sounds so cold and lonely.'

'It wasn't. I was happy and loved. The other kids were great, the nuns cared – my childhood was memorable enough, Emily. Not the nightmare it could have been. I was spoiled rotten, actually.'

'By Katherine?'

'Yes, among others.' He grinned. 'But Katherine never could resist me.'

She smiled then and he saw more than a little relief in her eyes. He was oddly touched that she cared enough to worry about the child he'd once been.

'What was it like, having a bunch of nuns care for you? Anything like having a troop of angels look over you?'

He tipped his head back to the night sky, remembering. 'You'd think it would have been a strict upbringing, wouldn't you? Catholic nuns and babies.' He smiled gratefully. 'But it wasn't. Not one of them had the heart to deny us much, especially considering our circumstances.'

'So they did spoil you.'

He couldn't help but smile at his memories: Katherine beaming proudly from the sidelines of the annual second grade bike-athon when he'd earned fifteen dollars for the orphanage. The nuns pooling their very limited resources to send him to Texas for a national spelling bee that he'd made finalist in. Their collective approval when he'd managed to maintain an excellent grade average *and* play every sport available. Their collective and very obvious *dis*approval when he'd been caught necking with Darla Lyons. He'd had to hug a tree for an hour and his arms ached just remembering. 'Yeah, they spoiled me.'

Her glance was speculative. 'Tell the truth, you were a troublemaker.'

'No.' Her eyebrows disappeared into her hair and he laughed. 'Okay, maybe a little.'

'Tell me.'

He couldn't resist, knowing that with every passing moment James got further and further from her mind. 'Well, there was the time I sneaked into mass, crawled along the pews and tied everyone's shoes together in a nice, neat straight row.'

Her laughter warmed his heart. 'You didn't.'

'I did,' he assured her. 'And you should have seen the priest's face when he asked everyone to stand and half of them fell over.'

She slapped a hand over her mouth. 'Cord!'

His grin was sheepish. 'Katherine had to hide herself in her office so I couldn't see her laugh.'

'What happened?'

'It only took an hour to untangle everyone.' He sighed with forgotten pleasure. He didn't often think of those days, but he really had been very lucky. He knew that he might very well have been fostered into multiple homes – and multiple problems. Thankfully, he'd had Katherine and the others, the one constant in his life. 'They all loved me very much, but I still got in big trouble.'

'I can imagine.' She shook her head. 'Do you keep in touch with all of them?'

'Not so much anymore. In spite of growing up with Catholic nuns, religion never seemed to take with me. And when I got older, and moved away, I didn't go to church as often as they probably thought I should.'

'Were they upset?'

'No, I believe they honestly cared for me whether I went or not. Disappointed, maybe.' He smiled sadly. 'So I drifted away. I still see Katherine frequently, though she usually comes to me. She came today to tell me she's moving to a nearby girls' school to teach. She won't be at the church with the orphans any longer.'

'Does that make you sad?'

'No. For some reason she's not been happy at the church for some time. This will be better for her.' He grinned crookedly. 'There was a time she had great visions of me becoming a priest.'

That startled a laugh out of her, one that he thoroughly enjoyed. 'That,' she chuckled, 'I have a hard time picturing.'

'Laugh if you must,' he told her, smiling, thinking she should laugh more often. 'But Katherine kept her hopes high all through college. It wasn't until then that she realized it was . . . well, impossible.' That was about the time Katherine had understood he was hooked, not on God, but on women.

Her laughing eyes settled on him, warm and appraising. He watched her bare, creamy skin shimmer in the moonlight and all thoughts of priesthood flew out of his mind while his fingers itched to touch.

Emily's smile faded abruptly and she stepped back away from him. A line appeared between her watchful eyes. 'You're looking at me like that again.'

'Like how?'

'Like I'm a five-course meal and you're a starving man.' She backed up another step and crossed her arms over herself. 'Stop it.' Then she shivered.

'I can't.' He moved forward. Gently and ever so slowly he pushed a stray tendril of hair from her cheek. 'There's something happening between us, Em. Can't you feel it?'

'No.' She shook her head emphatically as she stepped back. 'No, I can't. And . . .' She looked desperately around her, but for what he didn't know. 'I've got to go now.'

'Don't. Don't go.' He took one of her arms from around her middle and pulled her toward him. Then he reached for her other arm and wrapped it around his neck. She moved as if in a trance, her gaze centered on his chest. 'Em, look at me.'

She shook her head.

'Why not?' He ducked his head down to try to see her face.

She averted it further. 'If I do, you'll kiss me.'

He laughed and hugged her. 'I guess you're right. Would it be so awful?'

'No,' she whispered. 'Not awful at all.'

Her words had his blood pumping. 'Then why not try it?' he suggested, moving his hands up and down her slim back and wanting so much more. 'Come on – if you don't like it, we'll stop.'

'I've got to go.'

She sounded desperate, but not afraid or angry. He nibbled her ear and her body went rigid. 'Oh, God,' she mumbled, shuddering. 'Don't do that.'

'Then kiss me. You want to.'

'No.' But under his hands her body quivered, and he nudged her chin up with his face, loving the light scent of her, the sweet texture of her skin. His lips touched hers once, twice, in a gentle sweep, cautious, testing, giving her the chance to back away.

She didn't. Instead, she tightened her arms around his neck and pulled his head back down, her mouth recklessly seeking his. Unexpected need slammed through him like a gloved fist.

God, he wanted her – only her. It showed in the desperate, groping, wild kiss. He felt her straining against him, her hands fighting with his for leverage, and his mind went blank. He could think of nothing except how good she tasted, how incredibly arousing those little whimpery sounds coming from her throat were.

He had to touch her. His hands streaked down her back and over her hips, his breath quickening at the smooth, tight material of her bike shorts – the only thing separating him from her. He skimmed up her front, feeling the outline of her ribs through her thin top –

She jerked free and stared at him, her breathing uneven. 'Don't.'

He reached for her, only to soothe, but she backed up a step, her eyes wide. 'Don't touch me. Please.'

It was that last plea that broke through, and he forced an easy smile, though he felt far from steady himself and had to fight for air. 'I would never do anything you don't want, Emily.'

She just looked at him. 'I don't want you to kiss me.'

'But I'd ask that you don't lie.'

She blinked, then flushed. 'I'm sorry, you're right. I practically kissed you, didn't I? That makes it okay to . . . to – '

' – It doesn't matter who kissed who,' he said slowly, trying to figure out how to get back on track – difficult when his brain was still mush. 'The point is . . .' What the hell was the point? 'I want you, Emily.'

She stared at him in growing dismay. 'I've got to go.' She whirled and ran and he knew enough about her not to try to stop her at that moment. She'd only run all that much faster. Besides, his body still reeled from that kiss, a kiss unlike anything he'd known. He'd wanted women before, so he understood the punch of arousal, but still, he'd been knocked out.

When Emily dashed through the house, he sighed, even as he followed her. Much as she might deny it, she *did* feel something between them. He was as sure of that as he was his own name. He didn't want it anymore than she did, but it was there.

She made it to her truck before he caught up with her. 'What are you doing?' she asked him as he held the door to her truck, blocking the entrance.

She looked so panic-stricken, he stopped short. 'Emily, please wait.'

'No,' she said quickly. 'I really can't.'

'I didn't mean to frighten you off.'

'You – you didn't.' Her gaze didn't meet his.

'Emily, at least be truthful with me.'

She looked at him, twisting her bottom lip between her teeth. 'Okay,' she said finally, letting out a deep breath of air. 'I got scared . . . a little.' When he would have stepped closer, she held out a hand. 'But it's not you, it's me. You're . . . looking for more than I – I've never just – ' A soft sound escaped her. 'I'm just not the right person for you, Cord. I'm sorry.'

'I never asked you to be anything other than who you are.'

'I know.' She looked away and he became aware of the dark night around them. Somewhere in the far distance an owl called for its mate. 'That kiss . . .'

128

She trailed off, studying her toe which traced circles in the dirt drive. 'It was something.'

He laughed at the understatement. 'Yes, it was. Want another?'

Her head jerked up and her eyes narrowed in on his smiling face. 'You're teasing me.'

He shook his head, enjoying the flush that crept into her cheeks. 'No, I'm not. I'll be happy to kiss you again. There's no joke to that.'

'I think I want to go home. Now,' she clarified.

'Okay.' He knew she wouldn't let him drive her home so he stepped near his own truck.

'What are you doing?'

He glanced at her. 'I'm following you down the mountain.'

'I'll be fine.'

'I'm going to follow you, Emily.' He swore when he saw her shiver. Pulling off his sweatshirt, he walked toward her and yanked it over her head. It fell to her thighs, embracing her neat little curves, and he told himself it was ridiculous to be jealous of a sweatshirt.

'I said I'll be fine.' Her voice sounded weak as he straightened the sweatshirt around her.

He understood perfectly. His own knees felt wobbly, just from touching her again. Had he ever wanted a woman so badly? If so, he couldn't remember. 'I know you will. But I'm going to follow you anyway.'

Instead of refusing the sweatshirt, as he'd half thought she would, she hugged it closer to her body. It looked good on her – too damn good. He'd never wanted to share his clothes before, but he was suddenly willing to rethink that.

He wanted to kiss her again, just once more. 'Emily – '

'Thanks for dinner,' she said quickly, leaning away from him.

He smiled wryly. Nope, no more kisses tonight. 'Goodnight, Em. Stay warm.'

She fingered his sweatshirt. 'I will.' And for just the briefest second her light eyes softened, warmed. Then the moment was gone and she shut the door.

Oh, she felt something all right, he thought as he followed her old truck down the long, windy road. She was just too stubborn to admit it. Too afraid to let go of herself long enough to give in to it.

He'd have to change that.

Then he laughed at himself. Why the hell should he? He wasn't looking for any sort of relationship with her. *He absolutely wasn't.* Or was he?

He was so busy following Emily down the windy road and convincing himself that he wasn't attracted to her, he almost missed it.

It happened part-way down the mountain. Suddenly Emily's truck swerved sharply in front of him, narrowly missing the sharp curve that would have sent her spiraling down the steep embankment.

Cord cursed loudly, helplessly, as he watched the truck veer away – directly toward the solid rock cliff on the other side of the road. The truck angled away in time, then wobbled dangerously back and forth between the drop-off and the rock wall. While he watched in terror, Emily seemed to recover the wheel and slowed to a grinding halt at the side of the road.

Cord's truck had barely skidded to a halt when he ran out into the night and slammed open her truck door. He yanked a stricken-looking Emily out of her truck. 'Are you all right? What the hell happened? You almost went over – ' He stopped abruptly, his hands flexing on her shoulders. She was pale and shaking and staring down at her flat tire.

She'd had a blow-out.

But something seemed odd. Cord released Emily and crouched down. He pulled at the sagging tire and it was then that he saw it. Sticking out of the side was a large tack. It wasn't on the part of the tire that had touched the road, but on the side, by the rim. There was no way it could have gotten there by accident.

Cord's blood chilled.

It had been purposely placed there, in the knowledge that it would be at least several miles before the tire gave.

Just enough so that Emily would be alone on a dark mountain road with no help in sight.

CHAPTER 6

'What?' Emily demanded from above him as Cord crouched, studying her tire. 'What is it?'

He looked up at her. 'Emily – '

'Oh, my God,' she said softly, her eyes searching his. 'You think this was done on purpose.' She backed up a step, shaking her head in denial. 'That's ridiculous. No one would – ' She trailed off shakily.

He hadn't planned to take her into his arms. But that was exactly what he did. For an all too brief moment she sagged against him and he held her tight, closing his eyes. The soft scent of her hair, her pale face and the slight tremble of her tiny body against his all packed a wallop the size of a Mac truck and he pulled her closer.

Quite simply, he didn't want to let go. His hand came up under her braid to cup her head and he lowered his face, nuzzling it against her cheek. The thought of someone trying to hurt her had his arms tightening around her, pulling her closer.

Then she shoved him. Hard enough so that his

head came up in surprise. She wagged a finger in his face. 'That was . . . disgusting, Harrison.' She paused to drag in air past her lungs. 'And desperate.'

'Wait a minute, Red. Just hold on.' He stared at her, unable to digest that this wide-eyed, hot-tempered woman was the same soft, terrified one he'd held just seconds ago. Hell, his heart was still ricocheting off his ribs from the scare she'd given him. 'What the hell are you talking about?'

'Taking advantage at a time like this is sick – really sick.' She whirled from him and knelt by her very flat tire.

Okay, add paranoid to his list of hot-tempered and terrified. But he thought he understood what was happening to her, since he was feeling a little paranoid himself. Quickly he glanced around into the dark night. So far another car hadn't come by, but he expected one soon. Someone would be coming by to check out their handiwork on Emily's tire. The thought unnerved him enough that he wanted nothing more than to get her far away – and quickly. Hell of a night to forget his car phone.

'I should have expected no less.' Her voice was harsh, her breathing rapid.

She wasn't going to go willingly, he thought. He stepped toward her where she knelt facing her truck, wishing she'd turn to him. 'Em, it's okay to be scared. You handled the truck like a pro, but it's over now.'

'I'm not scared. What I am is furious at you.'

He dared another step, his eyes still scanning the

133

road for any sign of approaching headlights. 'We've got to get out of here, Em.'

'I'm not leaving my truck,' she said stubbornly. 'I've got a spare; I'll change it myself.'

There was no way he was going to risk changing the tire himself, with Emily standing defenseless at the side of the road. Maybe he was overreacting, but the feeling of danger was stronger now. He had to get her away. 'I'll drive you home, then come back and do it.'

A short laugh escaped her and it scraped at his raw nerves. He couldn't shake the feeling that they needed to hurry. He tried a different approach – making her madder. 'What are you really so angry at, Red? That I tried to comfort you or that you liked it?'

'How about that my tire is blown apart?'

It was just dark enough that he couldn't see her clearly. That fact only further irritated him, as did talking to her back. 'Emily, look at me.'

She didn't move, but studied her tire as if her life depended on it.

'Emily.' Gently he reached for her arm to pull her up. She threw him off and turned on him, her temper flaring in her eyes. 'Don't.'

'Don't what?'

'Don't . . . I don't know.' She sighed and pushed her hair away from her eyes. 'I don't need comforting or protecting, Cord. I'm fine.'

She didn't look fine. Her body was so tight it was practically vibrating like a plucked string, and those magnificent eyes looked huge and dilated. Her breath came in shallow, shocked pants.

'Okay, you're fine,' he said quietly, slowly, trying to soothe and not show his own fear. 'But your truck isn't.'

'I can see that.'

'I'm going to drive you home now and then come back and change your tire. All right?'

She wanted to refuse him; he could see that in her stubborn, beautiful face. 'Joshua can do it.'

There was no nice way to put it and he was afraid they were running out of time. They were alone on a dark road, on an equally dark night, far from help. He didn't want to think about how vulnerable they were, totally unarmed. 'Emily, someone wrecked this tire on purpose.' Her eyes widened and her breath stopped, yet there wasn't even time to curse himself.

Far in the distance he could see the dim lights of an approaching car. Fear and anticipation tingled up his spine. He turned to the back of his truck and grabbed the first thing that he came to. A wrench.

Emily's eyes flew from the quickly approaching lights, to the tool in his hand, to his own heavy gaze. 'Oh, my God, Cord. Are you going to need that?'

'I don't know,' he answered grimly, taking her wrist so that she couldn't argue. 'Let's go. Now.' He pushed her gently into the driver's side of his truck. While he waited for her to scoot over he looked back. The lights were closer now, much closer. Quickly he got in, pushed Emily's head down and ignored her squeak of muffled protest. He locked the door.

The car coming up on them slowed nearly to a crawl just before his car.

'My equipment,' Emily hissed, struggling to rise and fighting the hand he used to hold her head down.

'Stop it,' he whispered harshly. 'Just hold on a second.'

But it was too late. The car did stop, then was roughly shoved in reverse and suddenly disappeared back around the previous turn. Cord loudly swore at the moonless night that had made it impossible to clearly see the car or the driver, before quickly starting his truck and making a sharp U-turn.

'Wait,' Emily cried, taking advantage of Cord's concentration to straighten up. She craned her neck to see her rapidly disappearing truck. 'I didn't lock it up.'

He didn't know how to tell her that a lock wasn't going to stop whoever had purposely sabotaged her tire. With one eye on the treacherous road in front of them and one on the rearview mirror for any un-planned surprises, he hit the gas.

But it was too late. The car – and he wasn't even sure of the color – had been small but fast.

And it was long gone.

He couldn't say for certain why he felt so strongly that the destruction of the tire had been deliberate. But it had practically been confirmed now. He pressed a hand to his forehead, trying to rub out the sharp pounding that had settled there.

The pounding only increased over his next thought. Tayna was dead. Lacey was dead. Sheri had been attacked. All women he knew and cared about.

It seemed Emily was next.

Emily sat silently in the car, as she had for the entire drive to her apartment building. Now Cord's engine was off and he was staring at the flickering light that lit the path to her building as if it were the most interesting thing he'd ever seen. 'What's going on, Cord?'

'I'm going to walk you inside and then go back to fix your truck.' His voice was tight, weighed down with something she didn't understand.

'Are you going to tell me what's going on?'

'I just did.'

She snorted. 'So much for being truthful with one another.'

He swore at that.

'Why didn't we just fix the truck while we were there?' He glanced at her then, and she got a good look at the tension and anxiety on his face. 'Cord, you're scaring me. Tell me. Tell me why someone would do that to my tire on purpose. Tell me why you thought you needed a weapon to get us off that mountain safely.'

That roused him. He opened his door and pulled her out with him. He glanced around, then, appearing satisfied, walked her toward the building. 'There's no security gate here,' he said.

'The cockroaches keep guard.'

He looked at her, horrified.

'Jeez, I'm kidding.' She stopped at the third door on the right and pulled out her keys.

He took them from her and put them in the lock. 'You live on the ground floor too close to the street. I don't like it.'

'I've never had a problem before. You know that this town rarely has crime.'

'This town,' he said in a low, unnerved voice, his hand still on the closed door, 'is hiding a maniac. There's been two murders, an attack and now this. You need to be more careful, if not for yourself then for the people who care about you.'

He was *not* going to get away with a cryptic statement like that one. Her stomach turned suddenly. 'Oh, my God,' she whispered. 'You told me tonight that those other woman all knew you. The police think they're connected.' She reached a hand out to the wall to steady herself. 'Was this the next attempt?'

His expression was bleak. 'Let's go inside.'

'I want to know.' The same person who had done those hideous things had attacked *her*? Looking into his dark, somber eyes, she realized that was exactly what he was suggesting. 'Tell me, damn you. I – '

The door opened suddenly and a sleepy-looking Josh smiled at Emily, then frowned sharply when he saw Cord. 'What's he doing here?'

Cord stepped forward, but Josh didn't move aside. 'Mind if we come in?' He pushed his way through without waiting for an answer.

'You'll have to excuse his wonderful mood, Josh,'

138

Emily told her brother, trying to keep her voice light. 'But we've had quite a night.'

'Really?' Josh looked from Cord to Emily.

'I want to talk to you – alone,' Cord said, turning to Emily.

'Whatever you have to say to her, you can say in front of me,' Josh said firmly. 'So say what you have to say and go.'

Emily rolled her eyes at the high level of testosterone hanging in the air. Josh's 'protective brother' routine was real enough, and Emily well understood where it came from – they had only each other, and they always stuck together – only this time she didn't need it. 'Josh,' Emily started, 'I – '

'I mean it, Emily,' Cord interrupted. 'We need to talk. Now.'

'So talk.' Josh folded his arms over his chest in a stubborn stance that on any other night might have made Emily smile. Cord was not only much bigger and much stronger, he had a street-smart attitude about him that spoke volumes of his ability to take care of himself. She'd seen that firsthand tonight. The way he'd gripped that wrench in his strong, capable hand had made it clear that he was prepared for anything.

'Cord,' she said evenly, 'I'm going to tell Josh about tonight anyway.'

'Tell me what?' Josh demanded.

Cord stared hard at Emily and Emily stared right back. She wasn't going to let him intimidate her, nor was she going to back down. Because, God help her, if she stopped long enough to think about what had happened tonight she'd fall apart. And there was no way that she would let herself do that in front of Cord. No way at all.

Oh, she'd come close, she had to admit. From the second Cord had pulled her from her truck and wrapped his long, warm arms around her, she'd wanted nothing more than to give in to her growing fear and cling to him. And for a short minute she'd allowed herself to do just that. Her only excuse was that it had been a very long time since someone had held her. Too long.

And even longer since she'd been kissed – and never like he had tonight.

She was strong enough not to need him. Or anyone.

'Someone tell me what's going on,' Josh said tightly.

'Emily had a blow out on I-9 tonight and nearly got herself killed,' Cord said bluntly, his eyes never leaving Emily's.

'I did not,' she corrected. 'I didn't go that close to the edge of the embankment.'

Cord snorted, shook his head and turned away.

Josh backed to a chair and shakily sat, sending Emily a look that nearly broke her heart. 'You almost went over?'

'I didn't – '

'You could have died,' he whispered in a little voice, all bravado draining abruptly.

'That's right,' Cord said quietly, turning back to

them and eyeing them both. 'She could have, and if not then, then later, when she was alone on the side of the road.'

'*What*?' Josh's devastated eyes rose to Cord's.

'Her tire was purposely sabotaged.

'You think,' Emily said quickly. 'You don't know that for sure.'

'Fine,' Cord said. 'You're right, we don't know that for sure. That's why I'm going to call the sheriff, who happens to be a close friend of mine. We'll go back for your truck and he'll call someone to watch over you until we know what's going on.'

Josh's eyes just got wider and wider, and Emily's heart twisted at the sight. Suddenly he looked like nothing more than a scared little boy – a forcible reminder of how young he really was and how much he'd already faced in his short life.

She looked to Cord. 'I want this to be just an accident.'

His eyes softened when they moved to her. 'Believe me, so do I.' Her fear must have conveyed itself. 'You'll be safe from now on, I promise.'

'That's a promise you can't keep.'

His gaze slid over her features slowly, then rose back to hers. 'Please, Emily, trust me.'

If she closed her eyes she could still feel the fierce pounding of his heart as it had rocketed against hers when she'd been pressed against him. He'd been as terrified as she after her close call. But she sensed he was holding back, and trust had never come naturally to her. 'I can't unless you tell me everything.'

Cord glanced once at Josh, who was still sitting stunned in the chair. 'The police think they're dealing with a serial killer.'

Emily watched his face twist with grief, bitterness and an unfamiliar rage and her uneasiness doubled. 'Oh, no.'

'And that, somehow, I'm the catalyst,' he said. 'They were all my friends, Emily.' The muscle in his jaw spasmed. 'And two of them are gone forever. Sheri got lucky.'

Emily's legs felt like water. 'And . . . so did I.'

He nodded miserably and Josh closed his eyes.

'What's it all about?' she whispered. 'Why?'

Cord shook his head. 'I don't know. Yet.' He added that last word with grim resolution. 'But we will.' He moved from the small living room toward the kitchen. 'I need your phone.'

When they were alone, Josh opened his eyes and looked at her. 'Emily,' he said, his voice wavering, 'if something had happened to you tonight – '

'But nothing did,' she said, kneeling in front of him and taking his ice-cold hands in hers. 'I'm here.'

He gripped her hands tight. 'I couldn't have handled it if you'd been hurt or . . .' He swallowed hard. 'What would happen to me if you were suddenly gone?'

'Oh, Josh,' she whispered, hugging him tight. 'I'm not gone. I'm right here.'

'I still miss them, Emily. Real bad.'

A vivid memory of their parents' faces, pale in death, and her own terrified screams made her jerk.

She forced herself to remember them as they were before that, remember them as beautiful, loving parents. It was hard, but she had to do it for Josh's sake. He'd been too young to know the truth, and the guilt shamed her. She swallowed a lump the size of a soccer ball. 'Me too, Josh. Me too.'

'You'll quit this job now, won't you?'

She couldn't do that. They needed the money and there was no other job in sight. 'I'm safe now.'

'What if what he says is true? Then you're not safe at all.'

'It's nonsense.' She smiled reassuringly as her heart did flip-flops. 'Those women were all his . . . friends.' She blushed furiously and hated herself for it. 'And I'm not.'

'But what if someone thinks you are?'

She forced a laugh. 'Why would anyone think that?'

Josh gripped her shoulders. 'Even worse, what if he's the one offing everybody?'

Her laugh was genuine this time. That simply wasn't a possibility. He was too . . . what? Too kind and gentle to be a psychopath? Too thoughtful and sensitive to brutally murder people? She closed her eyes. It was too awful to contemplate. Besides, she was inexplicably, absolutely, positively certain. 'He's not.'

'How can you be so sure?'

The memory of Cord's arms wrapped in terror around her was so real she could still feel his warmth. 'I just am.'

'Sheriff Stone is on his way,' Cord said from the doorway.

When Emily looked up, she knew by the speck of relief in his cobalt eyes that he'd heard her. A brief but tender smile touched his lips. Directed at her. Her stomach flip-flopped again, but this time it wasn't from nerves.

Their gazes locked for an eternal moment. Then Cord squared his broad shoulders and pushed away from the kitchen, moving toward her with that long, purposeful stride of his. In a tender and moving gesture, he cupped her face in his wide, gentle hands and kissed her forehead, his lips lingering. 'Thanks for trusting me enough to believe in me.'

She tilted her face to his; her gaze strayed to his lips.

He made a small sound, then, with a soft, whispery touch, he moved his lips across hers, his unwavering stare holding hers.

She actually leaned forward for another, in awe of the flood of emotions the short kiss had caused, but he didn't do it again. His fingers caressed her face as he lifted his head.

'Stay safe,' he whispered. 'I'll be back.'

Long after he was gone she stood still, one hand to the cheek he'd touched.

Patience didn't happen to be one of Emily's virtues. The waiting killed her. For the tenth time in as many minutes, she peeked out her front window. Yep, the police car was still there. She was still being guarded.

It should have been comforting, but the fact that she needed it at all was slightly horrifying.

She turned at the low, soft snore emitting from her brother, who was crashed out on the couch. She didn't blame him; it was late. Her body demanded that she too get some sleep, but her mind wouldn't co-operate.

She wanted answers. Lots of them. It had been nearly two hours since Cord and the sheriff had left – plenty of time to change a tire. What was keeping them?

The small stack of mail on the table caught her eye. Well, if nothing else, opening some more bills might take her mind off her current trouble.

She froze at the return address on an official-looking envelope. The County Planner's Office. Her heart galloped as she opened it, hoping for a response to her request to paint a mural for them.

She sank to the couch, sitting on her brother's feet. Josh didn't budge. At the end of the letter she laughed aloud and hugged herself. And for one long, blessed moment her other problems were forgotten.

They wanted to see some of her sketches. Yes! It was going to work out, she promised herself, giggling. It would.

She desperately wanted to wake Josh and share the news, but she didn't have the heart. He needed his sleep. He'd be just as happy for her tomorrow morning. So she danced around the small apartment, a secret, pleased, smug smile on her face.

A half-hour later some of her elation had faded. Cord still hadn't returned.

Just when she'd paced the small living room enough to groove a path in her worn carpet, just when she thought she'd scream in frustration, she finally heard her truck drive up.

Less than a minute later, the police car was gone and Cord was standing in her doorway, his expression carefully masked.

'Hi,' he said.

'Hi yourself.' She searched his face for a clue as to what he'd found, but he was adept at hiding his feelings.

Emily had long since changed out of her shorts and put on leggings, but for some reason she hadn't been able to part with his sweatshirt. His eyes ran hungrily down the length of her, warming at the sight of his clothing on her.

'You okay?' His fingers stroked her face, and erotic pictures danced through her head, shocking her. She wasn't used to such casual affection. For hours she had been impatiently waiting for his return for information, and yet now all she could think about was how he made her feel. It had to stop.

'What did the sheriff think?' she demanded. She firmly ignored how her heart was racing from his simple touch, how good he looked in his loose black T-shirt and well-worn jeans, how sexy he was with his dark, concerned eyes and tight jaw.

His hand dropped to take hers, squeezing lightly. 'He thought you had a blow-out.'

She took in his careful choice of words, hooded eyes. 'And that's all?'

'That's all.'

His mouth was grim, his body taut with tension. He was angry and trying to keep it from her. 'Maybe he's right.' God, she hoped so.

'Maybe.'

'You still don't think so?'

His answer was a long time coming. 'No, I don't. It's too coincidental.'

'But I'm not . . .' How was she supposed to say this? *I'm not in a relationship with you, like the others?* 'I'm not like the other women . . . to you.'

'No,' he agreed, his warm, appraising eyes on her. 'You're not like them at all. Emily, Lacey was a friend, someone I cared about, but we weren't in a relationship. And Sheri – '

'You don't have to tell me this, Cord.'

'I want you to know. Sheri was a co-worker and my friend. Just like I already told you. And Tayna, well . . . I'd only dated her a few times before her death.'

'Oh.' It didn't make it any easier to deal with the deaths. 'It's awful to lose people you care about so suddenly.' That was something she understood all too well.

'At least Sheri was spared. Obviously, it's all connected. And that's what scares me – that maybe somehow I've put you in danger.'

She said nothing and he winced. 'I know. I sound paranoid.'

'No, you don't.' For the first time in her adult life,

147

Emily reached out to a man. She touched his chest and looked deep into his eyes. And for the first time, despite the danger, maybe even because of it, she *wanted* to be kissed. *Desperately.* 'I'll be all right, Cord.'

'Yeah,' he said, grabbing her hand on his chest and holding it against him. His intense eyes told her he knew exactly how difficult the move had been for her. His heavy heartbeat beneath her hand told her how much he liked it. 'You *will* be all right.' He leaned down and gave her one quick, hard kiss. 'Because I'll make sure of it.'

Their eyes caught and held each other like a soft caress. Emily didn't have to time to wonder at the longing flowing through her veins like hot lava, all she could do was lower her gaze to his beautiful, sexy mouth and wish he'd settle it against hers like he had before.

He did. She went limp with pleasure as his lips brushed over hers. She would have melted into a boneless heap on the floor right then and there if Josh hadn't chosen that very inopportune time to snort loudly.

Emily jumped back, breaking the contact as Josh sat straight up and rubbed his eyes. 'You're back,' he grumbled at Cord.

Regret and frustration raged a battle and wry amusement won. Cord smiled despite Josh's scowl. 'Yep. I'm back.' He dropped a small black leather case into Emily's hand.

'What's this?'

'A portable phone. I want you to have it in your truck.'

She looked at the expensive-looking phone. 'I can't take this.'

'Then borrow it. I don't care what you call it, just keep it in your truck for now. Please?'

She nodded reluctantly. 'I don't know what to say.'

'Just say you'll be careful.'

'I'll be careful.'

Though his eyes remained solemn, the look he gave her was hot enough to melt any lingering resolve, and full of promise of things to come. She didn't want him to look at her like that – did she? She looked away and caught Josh's watchful and distrustful gaze from the couch. It was uncomfortably grounding. No, she didn't want anyone to look at her like that. She didn't want anyone to look at her like that ever again.

On his way back up the mountain, Cord stopped at Seth's house.

'It happened again, Seth,' he said, pushing past his friend the second the door opened. With familiar ease, he went directly to the living room and plopped down on the black leather couch.

Seth still stood at the front door, wearing nothing but sweat pants. 'Come on in,' Seth told the empty space. 'No, don't worry. It's not too late. Who needs sleep?' He rubbed his chest sleepily and yawned.

'Seth, would you wake up and listen?' Cord

149

growled. '*It happened again*. And this time it was Emily.'

Seth blinked, then sank next to Cord as if his legs would no longer hold him. 'What happened? Is she –?'

'She's shaken, but okay. Her tire blew out on the mountain. She nearly went over the side.'

'The sheriff?'

'Stone's not sure it's another attempt. He's working on it.' Cord sighed and shoved two hands through his hair. 'I should have known, Seth. I should have figured she'd be in danger.'

'No, don't do that to yourself. No one could know what this psycho is going to do next. No one.'

'They'll question you too,' Cord said. 'They still won't discount either one of us.'

'Fine,' Seth said tightly. 'Let them. We have nothing to hide. What about Katherine? Doesn't it seem logical that she could attract this guy too?'

'Yeah. I thought of that.' And it had made him absolutely sick. 'Stone says he'll send a car by periodically to check on her. I'll call her.'

'She should be safe there at the church.'

'I didn't tell you,' Cord said. 'In all the excitement, I forgot. She accepted a teaching position. She's living at the school with the girls instead of at the church.' He shook his head, unable to let go of the overwhelming guilt that he was causing this. 'And it's not over with this guy – I can feel it. Until it is, everyone we know and care about is in danger.'

* * *

Emily found Katherine waiting for her the next morning. The older woman sat on the steps to the large house, sipping coffee and looking so utterly serene and at home that Emily had to smile. Her own mother had often looked like that, satisfied in her own little world, happy to simply watch over her children.

After what Cord had told her about Katherine, Emily thought of the woman as his true mother.

Katherine stood the minute she saw her, some of the serenity vanishing to be replaced by an urgency that touched Emily. 'You're okay? You're really okay?'

'You know already, then.' Emily sighed and re-settled the box she carried at her hip. 'Yes, I'm fine.' The obvious concern both embarrassed and touched her. 'Thank you.'

'I made coffee. Would you like some?'

Katherine stared at her hopefully, but Emily had to decline. She never had developed the taste for coffee, and she really wanted to paint. She'd intended to work the second floor of Cord's house this morning, but the mural he'd won by forfeit beckoned her – and it wouldn't wait for anyone, even Katherine.

'I'm sorry, Katherine. I've got tons of work.' She preferred to work alone, especially when painting a mural, but her strange and inexplicable attraction to Cord had her curious about the woman who'd raised him. 'Would you like to keep me company?'

Katherine studied her silently a moment, as if making sure she really seemed okay. Again, Emily felt a mix of embarrassment and warmth over the concern. 'No, thanks. If you're anything like my Cord, you want to work alone.'

The simple understanding, the easy acceptance seemed overwhelming. 'Most people don't understand.'

'I do,' Katherine said simply. 'Believe me, I do. Have a good day, dear. And take care. We all have to take care.'

Emily shivered, suddenly cold. How easily she'd forgotten.

She climbed the stairs and went to the room she wanted. She contemplated the white, open space waiting for her. Yes, the bet had been just a farce, but she was so thankful for the opportunity to do something she loved with all her heart, she didn't care. She knew that Cord didn't really want or need a mural, but she planned on dazzling him so much with her talent that he wouldn't mind.

Besides, it would be practice for when she got the job for the county building. Not *if*, she told herself firmly, but *when*. She made a mental note to have the sketches to the Planning Office by the end of the week. If she was lucky – very lucky – then she could line up that mural job directly after she finished Cord's house. And maybe she could get another job – a paying one – immediately after if they saw how good she was.

She had picked an out-of-the-way room on the third floor for her mural, and in a rare move chose to paint the ceiling instead of a wall. Yes, it would be more difficult to do, but it would be perfect for the room. Windows covered two walls and the light in the morning was spectacular. Emily planned to paint the sky and the heavens – a pure fantasy piece. She couldn't wait.

She started sketching, mostly to keep her mind off the night before. Cord had kissed her, had wanted to do it again. She had told him she didn't, but she'd lied.

No matter what she wanted him to believe, she had liked it. That was scary, almost more scary than what had happened to her on the mountain. A blow-out she could handle. Even a crazed lunatic stalking her was easier to accept than the fact that she was attracted to a man she hardly knew.

She didn't want to feel like this. She wasn't ready for this.

It's all right, she told herself. *Just keep your distance and everything will be fine.* Besides, last night's kiss had probably been just a fluke. Being terrified always led people to seek comfort; it was just a fact.

She wouldn't kiss him again.

She knew Cord was in the house; she'd heard water running when she'd first arrived and thought maybe he was in the shower. She stopped suddenly, standing in the empty room, her sketching pencil in her hand. An unbidden picture of Cord standing nude, hot water sluicing off his hard, powerful body, caused her to lean weakly against the wall. Her mouth went dry.

With a helpless sound she looked out of the

window at the bright morning. Birds were singing, the sky was brilliant . . . everything was normal.

Except her heart rate.

Then she knew. She was no longer alone in the room.

She turned slowly and he was standing right there. He was staring at her when he stepped closer, so close she could feel his warm breath on her forehead. His dark hair was wet and he smelled like soap, so much more appealing than any cologne could ever be. His eyes scanned her face slowly, then lowered to take in her body. At the sight of her overalls a small smile touched his lips.

When his eyes came back to hers, she stopped breathing. Oh, God, she thought desperately, she wanted him to kiss her again.

He must have read her mind, because without a word he bent and kissed her neck, stopping to nuzzle the skin with his lips and teeth in a way that made her moan softly with pleasure. She tilted her head to make more room, feeling one solid arm curl around her waist. The other hand came up to tip her head back and their eyes met in a scorching, provocative gaze. He molded her body to his, the tenderness staggering, the possessiveness thrilling. Then he lowered his head and kissed her mouth.

CHAPTER 7

Slowly Cord pulled back, pausing to kiss each side of Emily's full lips. Desire pounded through him. He'd felt it before, of course, with other women. But this was different – so much more potent, so much more dangerous. Because he couldn't resist, he kissed her again, and only when his heart hammered fiercely against his chest did he pull back. He wanted her, quite desperately, but there was something else, something deeper than a physical need. He wanted all of her, her mind, her soul, her heart as well. So simply taking – as incredible as that would be – couldn't be enough. And until he'd sorted that out he could be patient and wait.

Emily's beautiful eyes fluttered open, staring in wonder at his mouth.

'Good morning,' he murmured with a soft smile, dipping his head to nibble the racing pulse at the base of her neck. For now, this was enough, he reminded himself. But he savored and lingered, with more than a hint of the promise of what was to come between them.

'Uh . . . good morning,' she whispered in a husky voice, her answering smile wobbly. Her hands grasped his shoulders as if she needed the support.

To please himself, and her, he trailed his lips to the spot where her neck merged with her shoulder. She shivered and drew in a sharp breath, intoxicating him. She smelled heavenly and he couldn't get enough. 'Sleep okay?' he asked, his lips still against her. He could almost feel how it would be to really be with her, to feel her bare skin against his, feel her moving and writhing beneath him.

'Um . . . yeah.' She sighed as his mouth traveled back up her neck to the sensitive skin beneath her ear.

Though he couldn't keep his hands and lips off her, talking seemed to keep his body in control. 'Everything all right on the drive up here?' His teeth closed over her earlobe and he heard her breath stop short.

'Oh, God,' she murmured. She leaned her forehead against his chest and took a deep breath. 'Cord, stop. I can't think.'

He smiled. 'That's okay.'

She laughed shakily, backing up a step. 'No, it's not. I have lots of work. I think you should go away now so I can get to it.' She smiled nervously at him, then picked up her sketchpad. She twirled the pencil in her hands.

She was nervous, he realized with a sweet pang. He made her nervous. To make her at ease, he leaned against the window ledge, thankful that at least that delectable body of hers was covered from head to toe.

'Was there something you wanted?' she asked.

'Another kiss?' he asked hopefully.

Her teeth raked across her lower lip as she contemplated him. 'Cord . . . we shouldn't have done that.'

'Why?' He didn't see what was wrong with going with what felt right. And kissing her felt right. Okay, so he had a policy against seeing women he worked with. And he definitely hadn't been looking for this. But he was willing to make an exception here, willing to concede that he no longer wanted to fight his attraction to her. All he could think of was kissing her again, kissing her until they were both senseless. His body was aching and begging for more just at the thought. Of course he'd been awake most of the night thinking about her, and that last, incredible kiss hadn't helped.

'Why shouldn't we have done that?' she repeated carefully. 'Because I don't want to complicate anything. Because I like working on this house. Because . . . well, maybe I don't want to.'

That last was a lie, and they both knew it, but he let it go. He wasn't about to push himself on her for a quick make-out session, enjoyable as it would be. With regret, he would give. At least until she got more used to the idea that there was something happening between them. After all, he had barely accepted it himself. Never before had he allowed a woman to get so under his skin that he couldn't work, couldn't relax, couldn't get her out of his mind.

That he was attracted didn't shock him nearly as

much as how immediate that attraction had been. It was much more than sexual. The way she kept herself covered, he hadn't even known what a fantastic figure she had until yesterday. No, it was much more than physical. He admired her strength and resolve. And, after last night, he admired her courage as well.

'Okay,' he said easily. 'You don't want to kiss now. But promise me something.'

She looked at him warily, as if unable to believe he'd drop it so easily. It made him all the more determined not to push. 'What?'

'Promise you'll consider it for later.'

'Consider what?'

'Kissing.'

'Oh.' Her eyes darted from his. She concentrated on her pad, her pencil flying over the paper.

'Emily?'

Her pencil stilled. 'Maybe.'

'Maybe, what?'

She shot him an exasperated, defensive look. 'Maybe, okay? Maybe I'll *consider* considering it.'

He nearly laughed at her prickly tone. Back to her temperamental self. '*It*?'

She threw down her pad. 'Us! Kissing! Okay? Now go away and let me work.'

He grinned like a teenage fool; he couldn't help it. 'Yes, ma'am. What are you working on?'

'The mural.'

Again that defensive look. It almost, but not quite, hid the hesitant, unsure flicker in her eyes. 'In here?' he asked.

'Is that a problem?'

'Nope. But this room won't be used much. It might not get noticed.'

She smiled that smile he was beginning to crave. 'Oh, it will get noticed. I'm putting it on the ceiling.'

'The ceiling?'

'You do have a problem,' she stated flatly.

'I have a feeling that even if I did it wouldn't matter much,' he assured her. 'Have at it, Red.' He stopped at the door. 'Oh, I'll be in my office in town tomorrow, and for the rest of the week. There'll be a flooring contractor on the job every day and also a roofer – Raymond Roofing. The guy there says he knows you.'

'Yes, we've worked together lots of times. He'll do a good job for you.'

'I know, I'm familiar with his work.' He hesitated, not sure how she would take what he had to say next. But he was going to be adamant about this. He'd spent all last night thinking about her and her safety, and all this morning making plans. 'That's why I asked him to co-ordinate his arrival and leaving times with you so that he can follow you up and down the mountain.'

For a long minute she just stared at him. He could see each emotion cross her face. Stunned surprise, anger, embarrassment. 'No,' she said finally. 'Absolutely not.'

'Why?'

'I can't believe you planned all this without consulting me! I'm not your responsibility, Cord

159

Harrison. I can take care of myself and I don't want you interfering in my life like this.'

She was going to make this difficult. God, she was a beautiful, stubborn woman. 'I know how independent you are, Em. But – '

'But nothing.' She flashed angry, hurt eyes at him before she turned away. 'Please go away. I have work to do.'

He'd checked out both the subcontractors' references well, making sure that the men were well-known, well-liked and respected in the community. It helped that they were older, and both happily married. He wasn't taking any more chances with her safety. 'Do you have a problem with either contractor? Because if you do, just say so and I'll get another. I want you to be comfortable – '

A disbelieving squeak escaped her before she found her tongue. 'My problem is with you.'

'Emily – '

'*Go away*, Cord.' She turned and worked her pencil across her pad.

'I'll go,' he said, in a low, frustrated voice. 'But first you'll listen. Three women have been viciously attacked. Two are now dead. *Dead*, Emily. I'll bet if you could offer them a second chance, with added precautions, they would take it.'

He saw her pause from her furious sketching. 'Just think about it, Emily. I only want you safe. I'm not trying to run your life or tell you what to do. I'm trying to help you protect yourself.'

'What if it's nothing?'

'Then it's nothing, and the worst that's happened is a little inconvenience.' He had to tell her the truth. 'But, Red, agree to this or I'll follow you up and down that mountain myself.'

Her eyes narrowed angrily at his words and her mouth opened. Then closed. She looked at him defiantly, but he didn't back down. He had to do this, he thought. He had to find a way to make sure she'd be okay.

'*You'll* follow me,' she said dubiously.

'Believe it.'

'You're too busy for that.'

'I'll do it. Trust me.'

'It's not necessary.'

'I hope not. But if I do nothing, and you get hurt, it'll be my fault.'

'So this is guilt talking?'

'It's not guilt talking! I care about you; I want you safe. Why won't you believe that?'

As he'd expected, she didn't answer. He gave up in exasperation. 'I'm going to get to work now. But one way or another someone is going to follow you home tonight.' The door was nearly shut behind him when her soft voice reached him.

'I'll caravan with Raymond.'

Relief filled him as he flicked a glance at her. She was no longer spitting defiance, but stood looking at him with quiet apology.

'Thanks,' she added softly. 'You know . . . for caring.'

He nodded, accepting the wordless apology that

161

was so evident in those amazing green eyes. He knew how hard it was for her to admit she needed help, especially protection. She was used to fending for herself.

For the next few hours, as he laid tiles in the kitchen, he thought about the perplexing woman two flights up. What sort of woman was it that couldn't trust, couldn't let herself open up, couldn't easily accept anything from another human being?

The sort of woman who had been hurt and betrayed. The sort of woman who had schooled herself to need nothing and no one but herself. He wondered what would happen to a woman like that if she were shown a little patience, some compassion – shown how wonderful it could be to lean on someone who wanted to be leaned on.

He was being absurd, of course. He didn't have time for all that. He positively didn't. Not even for a gorgeous but aloof painter, whose very presence in his house was distracting him beyond reason.

The front door opened and a minute later Josh poked his head into the kitchen. 'Where's Emily?'

'Hello to you, too.'

Josh frowned. 'Where is she?'

Cord sighed and straightened, stretching. His back ached from the hours bent over on the floor. 'Couldn't you have gotten up early for once? You could at least have followed her in today, especially after last night.'

Josh's frown turned into a fierce scowl. 'She rigged my clock, if it's any of your business – which it isn't.'

'She rigged your clock?'

'Yeah.' Josh eyed the tiles that Cord had been working on for the past few hours with interest. They were incredible, Cord himself had to modestly admit. Twelve-inch by twelve-inch stark white tiles were surrounded by tiny midnight-blue squares in an exquisite design that Cord had worked out himself.

'Why would she do such a thing?' he asked, pleased by Josh's mute reaction to his work.

'I don't know – maybe she knew how tired I was, how much homework I had. She shut off the volume on my alarm and sneaked out without me.' Agitated, he ran a hand through his mop of red hair. 'I would have come with her.'

'She was trying to be considerate, then.'

'Yeah.' He eyed Cord with such a familiar look of suspicion that Cord wanted to smile. Brother and sister were alike indeed. 'Where is she?'

'Upstairs.' Josh nodded and started out. 'Josh?'

He stopped, but didn't turn back.

'I'm not so bad, you know.'

'You're rich, aren't you?'

'So?'

'So, you're all alike.'

'You're poor, aren't you?' He hated that pale, proud look that flashed across Josh's face, but he had a point to prove to a kid who thought he knew it all. 'You all alike?'

'Of course not,' Josh said furiously.

Cord just smiled gently. 'No, of course not. Give me a chance, Josh. Maybe I'm all right.'

Josh shifted his weight. 'I – I want you to leave my sister alone.'

He raised his eyebrows. 'I'm not bothering her.'

'You're bothering *me*.'

'I see.' Cord straightened, feeling a link to the boy that went beyond Emily. Despite the nuns and his friends at the orphanage, Cord well remembered what it felt like to be completely alone at a very young age. At least Josh and Emily had each other. 'Well, much as I'd like to accommodate you, I can't.'

'Why not?' Josh demanded.

'I like her.'

'Well, like someone else. My sister isn't – '

'Isn't what?'

Joshua scowled. 'She's not used to . . . Oh, forget it. You'll do what you want anyway.' He turned abruptly, headed to the door.

'I won't hurt her, Josh.'

Josh stopped. 'Better not.'

Cord watched thoughtfully as Josh left. He could hear his heavy footsteps stomping up the stairs. He was an angry, bitter kid. But proud and protective of his sister. He liked that.

His portable phone rang, startling him from his thoughts.

Sheriff Stone didn't beat around the bush. 'Did you know about your partner's financial difficulties?'

They might have known each other a long time, but Cord knew Stone wouldn't let that get in the way of his investigation. Just as he wouldn't let it get between his and Seth's friendship. 'What's the point, Sheriff?'

'Ever consider the fact maybe you're being set up? Set up by someone who needs you out of the picture?'

'Not by Seth. Absolutely not.'

'His alibi is shaky, Cord.'

Cord let out a wobbly breath, leaned against the closest wall. 'You're wasting your time there. Seth wouldn't hurt a soul.' Lord, the guy actually caught spiders and took them outside rather than kill them. 'He's had money trouble, I know. But it isn't getting to him. He just figures he'll make more – no big deal. That's how he is.'

'Stay available.'

Cord hung up and for a very long time stayed on the floor, staring at the phone.

He got into his truck and drove straight to the office. Keith was at the reception desk, looking ruffled.

He slammed a line on hold and shot Cord a look. 'These phones are ringing off the hook and the temp is at lunch. Phillips wants to know when his design is going to be ready and what you're buying him for dinner if he signs for three more restaurants. Some lady named Karen – ' At Cord's blank look, Kevin shook his head and sighed. 'You met her at the party here – the hot babe in the pink clingy dress. – She wants to know if you're free tomorrow night to look over some . . . plans.' The last word was exaggerated in an affected breathy voice Cord could only assume meant Keith was imitating the woman he couldn't remember.

'Great. Been busy, huh?'

'Busy isn't the word.'

Cord sighed. 'I'm sorry, Keith. We'll hire someone permanent soon.'

Keith shoved a file drawer closed. 'I miss Sheri.'

'So do I, believe me.' The office was a wreck without Sheri's smooth competence. And, he realized with some regret, he'd spent too much time away from the office.

'I came here to be an architect, Cord. Not an expensive receptionist.'

'With Sheri gone,' Cord said carefully, 'there's bound to be some adjustments. We're well known, Keith, because we're good. But we're still relatively small – small enough that we all pitch in and help however it's needed. If that's too much for you, let me know.'

A muscle in Keith's jaw worked as he studied his boss. Finally, he gave a little smile. 'It's not. I'm just not good at this front desk stuff. It got to me.' He plopped back in the chair to wait for the returning temporary receptionist. 'Well, at least she's got a comfy chair, meant for sitting.' He scooted in, plopped his elbows on the desk and sighed. 'Sorry for the tantrum. If you need me I'll be here, trying to look pretty and sound friendly.'

'Great,' said Cord. 'I need to see Seth.' He grinned as Keith pulled out a nail file from the desk drawer and pretended to file his nails. 'Hold our calls, could you?'

Seth was interviewing new secretaries, and looking mighty thrilled to be doing so. He excused himself from the current interviewee – who happened to be leggy, curvaceous and very blonde – and met Cord in his office.

'What's up, buddy?' Seth rubbed his hands together. 'If I'd known how much fun it was to interview prospective secretaries, I'd have fired Sheri long ago.'

Cord didn't break a smile.

'I'm kidding. Really.' Seth looked at him strangely. 'I loved Sheri.'

'I know that,' Cord told him. He was losing it. 'Sit down.'

'I mean, I know Margo in there is a looker, but she's perfectly qualified. I like her best, actually, out of all the others I saw today. Want to meet her?'

'Later. Seth, I got a call from Stone.' He told Seth the conversation he'd had. His friend paled, but remained calm.

'They can't pin any of it on me.'

'We're getting you a lawyer. Today,' Cord said, stalking around the office. 'And don't answer any questions without him.'

'All right. Avoiding Stone will be a pleasure.'

'This sounds bad, but we need to have all our draftsmen investigated.'

'God.' Seth whistled. 'They're our friends, Cord. Keith, Tom, Lance – all of them.'

'We hope.' The thought sickened him, really sickened him. Their staff was small, but a tight-

167

knit group. A family. He couldn't stand the thought that someone in their midst was doing these terrible things. He thought of Keith and his strange behavior earlier, then shrugged it off.

He was getting paranoid.

'Cord,' Seth said, leaning back against the desk, his arms crossed over his chest, 'you're wearing a path in the carpet, buddy. Sit down.'

'I can't.' He looked over at Seth in confused amazement. 'And how you can be so . . . resigned is beyond me.' *Unless, of course –*

'I didn't do it, Cord.' Seth's words were deadly quiet.

God, what had he almost thought? That Seth could possibly have murdered in cold blood? And for what? Simply so that his partner would *maybe* go to jail for it? It was insane, and he closed his eyes, shaking his head. He had no reason to doubt his best friend, none at all. 'Then at least help me help you.'

'You worry about keeping Emily and Katherine safe. I'll worry about myself.'

Emily. That thought brought him up short. If anything happened to her, it would be all his fault.

To help the flooring contractor, Emily agreed the next day to have the floorboards for the downstairs completely finished by mid-morning. She tried not to resent the interruption of her mural, tried to remember that she was really there to paint the house, but it was difficult.

She wanted to work on her mural. Early, just after

sunrise, she spread the floorboards out on a drop cloth in the backyard and bent to prepare her airless sprayer. It was her pride and joy. She'd saved for months for one, and now it would save her countless hours of work. She carefully filled the pump with the bright white high-gloss paint and lifted the hose, with its handle-operated nozzle, in her hand.

Straightening, she aimed the nozzle at the long row of floorboards and started to spray them, concentrating on getting a nice even flow. Twice she had to bend down to move a board and once to straighten the hose, but just as she rose again the last time her arm was grabbed.

She gasped, and whirled, her hand convulsing on the control of the spray.

When she blinked, she was staring in horror at Cord, whose beautiful and very expensive-looking dark blue shirt sported a wet white streak across the middle.

'Oh, no.' She dropped the sprayer and covered her mouth with her hands, unsure whether to run or cry. 'Oh, Cord, I'm so sorry.'

Slowly he let go of her arm and looked down at himself in disbelief. She waited for his anger, but he only pulled the wet shirt from his skin and sighed. 'Never liked this shirt much, anyway.'

Her desire to weep dissolved into helpless giggles.

He lifted his head and stared at her, his brow lifted. 'You think this is funny?'

He didn't fool her, not for a minute. His eyes were smiling. 'You should never grab a painting woman,' she pointed out, slipping her hands into her pockets to keep them off the man she'd just painted.

'I'll keep that in mind.' A different light entered his eyes and he stepped toward her. She backed up, prepared, not trusting that stalking, predatory look he'd taken on.

'You should go change,' she said quickly.

'I should. But that can wait.' He grabbed her arms, held her still, a foot away from him.

She could read his mind, and retribution was first and foremost in it. 'Don't!'

'Oh, but why not?' he asked innocently, his grip made of iron. 'After all, you're wearing overalls. You're prepared for any sort of . . . painting accident.'

He yanked her close and she gasped as she stuck to him, streaking her overalls with the paint from his shirt. 'Cord!'

He swallowed her gasp with his hot, greedy mouth. Any thoughts were sapped by his mind-draining kiss, proving once and for all that their sizzling attraction was not a one-time fluke.

There was something about his mouth, something that tore through her defenses and left her bare. She clung to him, plunged her hands through his hair, and kissed him back until the sounds around them faded into a dull blur.

'Emily,' he whispered against her mouth, his voice low and urgent. 'How much longer are you going to make us wait?'

'I don't know.' Carefully she stepped back, raked her hair off her hot forehead. 'I don't know.' She looked down at herself. Paint had smeared across the front of her, adding just one more layer to the already battered overalls. She thought absently that it just might be time to indulge herself and buy a new pair.

'Em – '

'You'd better change, Cord. The paint will irritate your skin.'

He glanced at his watch, cursed. 'I've got a meeting.' He looked at her, his gaze hot and so full of longing that her mouth went dry. 'We'll finish this thing, Emily. We both want to.'

She could say nothing.

But she thought of him the entire day through. Especially when Katherine called, just to check in on her.

'Did Cord ask you to call me?' Emily asked, balancing the cordless phone on her shoulder as she sketched her mural.

'Now, dear, we all have to stick together through this.' Katherine laughed lightly. 'And, as Cord will tell you, I like to mother everyone I know. I hope you don't mind too much. I think of you as one of us now.'

The words warmed, more than Emily could have believed. How long since she'd had a mother figure? 'I appreciate the thought, Katherine. But I'm fine. I'm not alone up here.'

'No?'

'Are you kidding? Cord's got an entire schedule planned. I'm not even allowed to drive up and down the mountain by myself.'

'It's for the best,' Katherine said. 'Until we know who's terrorizing us all, it's for the best.'

Emily wasn't so sure they weren't all over-exaggerating their problems, but she said nothing. Her mural was on her mind and, as with most artists, she was single-minded during a project.

The first problem with caravaning came the next night. Raymond wanted to leave earlier than Emily did. She was beginning to sketch in the mural and absolutely refused to leave. The adrenaline was flowing through her in tune to the wonderful ideas she had and she couldn't possibly think of stopping now. Not when the creative juices were so hot. So what if her neck was stiff and her hand cramped? She wouldn't leave.

'Josh.' Raymond looked to Emily's brother for support. 'Help me out here. I know you just got here from school, but I can't leave the two of you up here.'

Josh looked uncomfortably from Raymond to Emily, but his first loyalty was and always would be to his sister. 'Sis? Come on, you can finish tomorrow.'

'Ask him why he can't leave us up here,' Emily said around the pencil in her mouth. Her eyes didn't leave the ceiling and her sketching. She didn't want to be interrupted – couldn't they see that? With a quick swivel of her hips she managed to scoot the ladder she stood on over a good two feet.

Josh looked at Raymond.

Raymond rolled his eyes and Emily pretended not to notice. They'd known each other for years and had worked together many times before. The rapport between them had always been friendly. But Emily's stubbornness was well known.

'I promised Cord,' Raymond said, appealing to Joshua. 'He didn't want me to leave Emily alone up here.'

Emily bit back a smile as Josh's eyes narrowed. She knew all too well that stubbornness ran in her family, and that Josh had certainly gotten his share. If he thought that his very frail seventeen-year-old ego was in question here, he wouldn't budge an inch.

She was right. 'She's not alone,' Josh said a little crossly. 'We'll be fine.'

'Yep,' Emily agreed absently, her attention already turning back to her work. It was going so well. All she wanted was a few more minutes. 'Don't worry, Raymond. We'll leave soon enough.'

Raymond made a face. 'All right, all right. But make sure that you do leave soon. Okay?'

Too busy drawing, Emily didn't answer.

'Emily? Okay?'

'Yeah, yeah, Raymond. We'll leave soon.' The mural was going to be incredible, she thought, dismissing everyone and everything from her mind as her aching hands flew across the ceiling. She wasn't a complete idiot, and Raymond did have a point. They'd leave before Cord got home. Though she was entirely uncertain if the danger came from some mysterious sicko or from one of Cord's searing kisses. Either way, they'd leave. In just a few minutes.

Of course she did no such thing.

Two hours later Josh was checking his watch every three minutes and shifting his weight impatiently. 'Come on, Sis. I told Monica I'd see her tonight. We've got homework. Let's go.'

Emily couldn't possibly stop now. The entire mural was coming together right before her eyes. She hadn't actually started painting yet, but her sketching was nearly complete. If she could just have a few more minutes –

'No,' Josh said firmly. 'I can see it in your eyes. You want more time. Well, you can't have it! It's nearly six o'clock, Emily. We've got to go.'

'You're right,' she said easily, tucking her pencil behind her ear and backing down the ladder. 'I'll be right behind you.'

His shoulders slumped with relief. 'Good. Don't forget, I'm not going straight home. I'll be at Monica's till late.'

'No problem.' Emily smiled sweetly. 'Drive safe. 'Kay?'

''Kay.' Josh smiled back. 'You crack me up when you're working, you know that? You lose track of absolutely everything. I don't know how you do that. I'm sorry I got impatient.'

'No problem.' She laughed, feeling a sense of euphoria overcome her. This mural was going to be brilliant.

A minute later she heard Josh's VW start and she

stood, undecided. She should definitely keep her word and go. Now. Sighing, she glanced up. And smiled from ear to ear. Just one more minute, she promised herself as she climbed back up the ladder. Just one more minute was all she needed.

'Just one more game,' Cord gasped, sliding to the floor and leaning back against the racquetball court.

'Hell.' Seth was already flat on the floor, sweat pouring off him. 'No.'

Cord's lungs were going to burst, his legs were screaming in pain and his arms were leaden weights. 'Come on. One more game. Wimp,' he added for extra incentive, when Seth didn't move.

Seth had another short, choice epithet for him, accompanied by a weak hand gesture, but he didn't so much as open an eye.

'All right,' Cord managed. 'If you're sure you don't want to play anymore, I'm going to run a few laps.'

One of Seth's eyes slitted open. 'You're insane.'

Cord just smiled and let his own eyes drift shut. He thought about standing, but his legs were still quivering.

'Or in love . . .'

Cord's eyes shot open. 'That's not funny.'

'Well, I don't know, buddy.' Seth pushed up to sit, groaned noisily and then stood. He stared cockily down at Cord from his considerable height. 'You had that certain look to you today at work.'

Cord eyed him warily. 'Certain look?'

'That very preoccupied look, if you know what I mean.'

'Maybe that look was stress. Stress from worrying about certain people who get themselves in stupid predicaments . . .' He slid Seth a long look.

'Nope,' Seth said with certainty. 'This look has nothing to do with me. It comes from thinking about a woman.'

Okay, so Cord couldn't get yesterday's kiss from his mind. But that was only because it had been so long since he'd kissed like that, been kissed like that.

'Maybe that was satisfaction from our new account. The one that's going to make us a ton of money – and get you out of a hole.'

'Hell, you're already stinking rich, Cord.' Seth stretched and winced. Then the eagle eye he was well known for honed in on his best friend. Cord squirmed. He knew that look. 'It's more than the new account; it's more than worry over me. And now you're out to kill yourself – *and me* – with exercise. What's up?'

Cord shrugged.

'You're not going to tell me a damn thing about it, are you?'

'There's nothing to tell.'

Seth looked disappointed. 'You mean to tell me you've been spending all that time alone up in that huge place of yours with the sexiest painter around – and there's nothing to tell? You're walking around today with a stupid grin on your face and *there's nothing to tell*?' He shook his head solemnly. 'She's the best thing to come along in . . . forever. And you're going to let her get away, aren't you?'

Cord sighed and rubbed his tired eyes.

Seth looked disgusted. 'If you do, she's fair game, bud. And believe me, I'll know what to do with her when *I* get her.'

And that gave Cord something to think about on his long drive home. He wasn't sure exactly what it was about Emily that drew him, but something definitely did. So why did he hesitate?

He hesitated because no one – ever – had made him feel the way that Emily McKay did. Was it love? He honestly didn't know, having had little or no experience in that department. But he liked her a whole lot more than he would have thought possible.

The night was dark, the moon a thin sliver of light that cast a cool glow over the tall pines and narrow road. It was comfortably cool, not cold – a sure sign that summer was indeed close.

Summer was his favorite season. This year would be different. He had purposely not made his usual plans with his usual crowd. No houseboat on the lake with twenty of his and Seth's friends. No water skiing tournament that he'd won three years in a row. No big summer bash at Seth's condo. He had wanted time off from all that, time to be alone.

Now all he wanted was to be with Emily. On the surface she could be difficult and moody, but there was so much more to her than that. He had been amazed at how much she had given up to raise her brother. Underneath that temperamental and tough exterior lay a sensitive, fiercely loyal, giving woman.

A woman he wanted to know better.

The sound of a car coming up the driveway pulled Emily out of her reverie. She'd been frantically sketching, lost in time just a second ago. Now she stood in the center of the third-floor room, slightly disoriented. She rubbed her charcoal-covered hands absently on her overalls, ignoring the rag hanging from her pocket.

A glance at her watch told her it was nearly seven o'clock. Oh, well, she thought, straightening her shoulders. It was her life and she'd do as she pleased. Just the same, she hurried now, not completely oblivious to the possibility of danger.

Shutting the door behind her, Emily dashed down the steps, knowing Cord would be furious to find her alone.

She skidded to a stop, the sound of the front doorknob turning in place freezing her to the spot. In growing horror she watched it click back and forth. It was locked.

Cord would have had a key.

Oh, God, she'd been so stupid to stay here alone. She found her legs and raced toward the kitchen, her heart stuck in her throat, her sobbing breath too noisy to her own ears.

Why hadn't she listened? Why had she allowed herself to get so caught up in her work that nothing else mattered?

Throwing herself at the back kitchen door, she held her breath and tried to yank it open. It wouldn't budge. With a soft noise of frustration and fear she pulled harder, until she realized it was locked too – and she didn't have the key.

From where she stood, struck dumb by terror, she heard the front door give and squeak open.

CHAPTER 8

Emily stood, completely still, in the center of the kitchen, shaking, legs locked in place. She wondered if she'd be killed, like Tayna and Lacey, or if she'd be lucky enough to escape like Sheri. Footsteps! They came toward the kitchen. Her head flew up and the strangled gasp escaped her before she could muffle it.

She had time to whirl around – no knife in sight, damn it – and grab a heavy serving spoon off the counter. But then she hesitated, spoon in her damp palm, debating whether to hide under the table or under the sink.

The door flew open.

Cord strode in and Emily was so relieved her legs almost buckled. But the fury emanating from his every pore shocked her into silence. The man looked ready for battle.

'Well, you're alive at least.' Cord dropped his briefcase on the floor and shrugged out of his light parka, tossing it carelessly aside. 'Why are you alone?'

'It's you,' she said stupidly, her heart tripping.

His gaze blazed. 'Of course it's me.'

'I wasn't sure, because I heard the door rattle like you didn't have a key, and – well . . .' She laughed nervously and rattled on, aware she was babbling hopelessly. 'You can imagine what I thought. Maybe you can't, but you really startled me. I began to picture exactly what could happen to a person all the way up here alone and it wasn't a pretty thought.'

He eyed her strangely. 'The lock's broken . . . You thought I was – ' He broke off with a sharp oath. 'Where the hell is Raymond?'

Emily swallowed hard, flipped her braid over her shoulder and tilted her chin up. 'He had to go. Josh was here.'

Dark eyebrows rose and his startling blue eyes leveled on her then deliberately lowered to the flat spoon in her hand. 'Was?' he inquired in a polite tone that didn't fool her – he barely had his temper in check. 'And what the hell did you think you were going to do with that? Offer to stir my soup?'

'Look,' she said, with more defiance then she felt – her heart was still hammering. 'I could have protected myself if I had to.' She dropped the utensil on the counter. 'Raymond had to go and I promised Josh I was right behind him, all right?' There was nothing she hated more than doing something stupid – like staying up here alone – and then having someone else point it out. She accounted only to herself, not this man. 'And – '

'Stop, Emily.' He held up a hand and shook his head. 'You don't have to explain yourself to me.' He

181

shoved his hair back and placed his hands low on his hips, staring at her. He was wearing a T-shirt and snug gym shorts with worn high tops sneakers; looking more fit than any man had a right to look. 'I'm just the guy you have a contract with, that's all.'

His statement knocked the air out of her. 'Yes, that's right,' she said slowly, surprised at the pain his words caused. 'I don't answer to you at all, do I?' She walked deliberately around him, out of the kitchen, through the foyer and reached for the door.

'Damn you,' he breathed over her head, slamming a hand on the solid oak of the door in front of her. She tugged at it anyway, to no avail. 'Do you have any idea how annoying it is when you completely shut me out like that? You must, or you wouldn't do it.'

'I'm just trying to go home.'

'Well, forget it. You had your chance hours ago.'

'You can't stop me.'

His eyes shone with the challenge and he straightened to his full height. 'Really? I've had a hell of a day, Emily. Believe me, I'm in the mood to take you on – and win. So don't tempt me unless you mean it.' He paused, letting his words sink in, while Emily felt her own temper rise.

She looked at the locked door, felt him directly behind her, so close the warmth of his legs seeped through her overalls. She could see the veins and the tight, sinewy strength in the hand and arm that held the door closed. 'Don't bully me, Cord. Or I'll show you exactly how much damage I could have caused with that spoon.'

'As tempting as that offer is,' he said in a bland voice, 'I just got here. And I'm starving – I'm *not* driving back down that mountain again until I eat.' He turned her toward him, skimming his eyes over her. The anger drained, to be replaced by something hotter, more intense. 'God, Emily. Do you have any idea what the hell you're doing to me?'

Well, if it was even half of what she felt with his strong hands at her waist, his hungry eyes on her and that strange liquid feeling where her bones had been only seconds ago, she thought maybe she understood.

'I went crazy when I realized you were here alone,' he whispered, pulling her close.

'You scared me half to death.' She snuggled close, just for a minute, because it felt so good to have him hold her.

'I'm sorry.' He ran a hand up her spine, causing a shiver. 'You're too stubborn for your own good, Emily. And you don't listen worth a damn.'

She shoved back. 'I'm not a little kid that you're responsible for.'

His eyes ran over her. 'No,' he said slowly. 'You're definitely not a little kid.'

She crossed her arms over her chest. 'Stop that. Stop looking at me like that. I'm mad at you.'

'You're always mad at me.' He tried to pull her back, but she slapped his hands away.

He sighed and looked at her. 'I suppose a good-evening kiss is out of the question.'

She let her breath out slowly. Just his low, husky

suggestion had her insides humming and every one of her senses working overtime. From anger to attraction. She'd never gone from one emotion to another so quickly with anyone else. 'I thought you were mad at me too.'

'I am.' He shook her gently, until her head tipped back and their eyes met. 'I've just never met anyone quite so set on being independent, so infuriatingly beautiful – '

'Don't.' She turned her head as his mouth descended, his kiss grazing her cheek.

'Don't what, Em? Tell you the truth?' His mouth moved hotly down her jaw and it took every ounce of will she had to push him away. 'You are beautiful.'

She turned, not wanting him to see her face. She didn't need a mirror to know her skin was flaming red, her eyes conflicted.

'I hate this, Cord. I hate knowing that I need to be watched.'

'And I hate it for you. But until we know – '

She sighed and looked at him over her shoulder. 'I'm sorry about tonight. The time just got away from me.' She thought about the mural upstairs that she wasn't ready for him to see, and how she would have loved to work through the night, putting color to her pencil sketch. 'I should go.'

He shook his head slowly and took her arm, leading her into the large kitchen. 'Not until we eat.'

'Who's cooking?'

Cord stopped in the center of the kitchen and glanced at her with interest. 'Can you cook?'

She knew where this was leading. 'Why?'

"Cos it's your turn.' He shot her a smile meant to charm candy from a baby. 'Unless, of course, you don't know how – then I guess I will.'

The challenge was meant to irritate, but it only amused. 'I can cook, Cord,' she said, and laughed. He blinked at her, looking surprised. And in truth she was a little shocked herself. *Laughing at ease with a man?* It was new and it felt . . . good.

'That's great, because I'm beat.' With an easy grace for one so large, he hopped up on the counter, put his hands behind his head and leaned back against a cabinet. Idly he crossed his long legs. 'I'll supervise.'

'Long day?' She opened the refrigerator and inspected his supply. Every food was in place and perfectly organized. It was the same in his cabinets. She thought of her own comfortably messy kitchen, knowing she couldn't manage to put anything away in the same spot twice.

'Mmm. Very,' he said as she started a pot of water on the range.

Something in his voice told her exactly how long his day had been. She glanced at him as she pulled a bag of fresh vegetables from the refrigerator. His eyes were half closed, though he still watched with that familiar intensity. 'What's happened?'

'Nothing.'

'No?' she said carefully, studying him. Every muscle seemed coiled, and his face was tight with concern, fatigue. 'Something's wrong.' Her eyes

185

widened. 'The sheriff. Has he found anything, any-one?'

Cord's mouth tightened. 'Emily – '

'He has, hasn't he?' She could see the answer in his troubled eyes. 'Oh, my God, he thinks it's you. Doesn't he?'

'Not exactly.' He grimaced. 'But it's just as bad. He thinks it could be Seth.' Before she could speak, he said quickly. 'But it's not. There's no way it's him.'

'Why would Seth be a suspect?'

'The sheriff is under the misguided impression that Seth would actually try to frame me for the murders so he could have one hundred percent control of HT Designs.'

She didn't understand. 'Why would someone kill to be in charge of a company like that?'

His mouth curved wryly. 'Because it's worth . . . a lot. But that's not the point. *Seth wouldn't do it.*'

'Of course not,' she said indignantly. 'You couldn't know someone all their life and miss the fact they're a serial killer.'

'I like it when you do that,' he said quietly.

'What?' She opened the vegetables. But it was difficult to concentrate when he stared at her like that, approval and warmth and friendship there for the offering.

A heavy thud told her he'd pushed off the counter. Every part of her being told her he was directly behind her. 'When you stand up for me. When you show me how much you care.'

She dropped the vegetables and hunched down to

retrieve them. But he was quicker. They met, nose to nose, on the tile floor, both reaching. A current ran through Emily when their hands touched. Cord grinned slowly.

'Come on, Em. I'm still waiting for my hello kiss.'

It had been much, much easier to maintain her distance when he'd been angry. It had also been far more simple to concentrate when he'd been sitting on the other side of the room. Close proximity with this man made her lose her every thought. 'Don't hold your breath,' she muttered, standing.

His eyes gleaming, he rose and took a raw carrot, biting off the end with strong white teeth. 'You want to kiss me.'

'Are you always so sure of yourself?' Irritation had her chopping hard at the vegetables. She'd never admit now that he was right, that she did want to kiss him. Desperately. 'It's really annoying.'

He grinned as she peeled a carrot into mush. 'You sure you can cook?'

'Yes,' she said tersely, peeling another carrot. She saw no need to mention that she hated cooking and always had. The only reason she had learned in the first place was because she'd had to feed Josh. There was also no need to mention that Josh had learned to cook at a very early age simply to protect himself from his sister's efforts.

She peeled another carrot viciously. Why had she agreed to do this? What did she think she was doing? Playing with fire was what she was doing. And she needed the fire department.

She belonged back at home with her brother, with her paints, where she was comfortable and everything was familiar. This was new territory. It was scary – and exciting. She attacked another carrot with the peeler, chewing down on her lip.

'Do you always concentrate so hard when you're cooking?' he asked in his deep, soft voice.

She did if she wanted to cook something edible. But concentration was difficult. He was standing right next to her now, so close she could feel the warmth radiating from him. His chest was brushing up against her arm every time she stroked the peeler over the carrot. 'Yes, I always concentrate. Now back up and give me some room.'

'Why? Will you mess up your recipe if I don't? What are we having anyway?'

'Chicken and veggies over rice. And no, I won't lose track of what I'm doing because of you, thank you very much. I happen to be an excellent cook and you aren't all that great a distraction.' She tossed the abused carrot in the pot and reached for another, wondering when it had gotten so hot in the room.

She nearly jumped out of her skin when she felt the cool, hard edge of a carrot run softly down her bare arm.

'You have the most beautiful skin, Em,' he whispered near her ear. The carrot ran slowly back up her arm, giving her the chills in a room she had been hot in only a second before. 'So creamy smooth. Makes me want to taste it.'

She jumped when the carrot rose up and over her

188

bare shoulder and her hands faltered at their task. Cord leaned in close and brought his lips to the spot behind her ear. Her stomach tightened. She dropped the carrot.

'I bet you taste real good, Em.' He licked the sensitive spot at the base of her neck where her pulse raced and Em felt flooded by heat. 'Mmm,' was the only sound he made. The blessedly cool carrot he held followed his hot tongue and her hands gave up the pretense of work.

Her insides were vibrating now, and when he trailed the carrot provocatively across her collarbone she nearly sank to the floor. Instead, she grasped onto the countertop, locked her knees and dropped her head, giving him greater access to nuzzle at her neck.

She made a little gasping sound when he lightly bit her ear and the carrot stroked her jaw. Eyes closed, she felt the unfamiliar wave of arousal in every clenched muscle and tingling nerve-end.

'God, you are sexy,' he murmured in a thick voice, tossing the carrot over his shoulder and pulling her close.

Unbelievably she went, her body like mush and her mind not far behind. *More*, was all she could think. *I want more.*

'Em?' he said in his low, husky voice.

'Hmm?' She left her eyes closed and waited for a new wave of sensation to hit.

He kissed her earlobe. 'Your water's boiling over.'

'Oh!' Her eyes flew open and she ran to the range

to turn it down, ignoring his low chuckle. Her face flaming from embarrassment, anger and who knew what else, she turned slowly back to him.

His grin was broad and insufferable. 'Not much of a distraction, huh?'

He'd done it to her on purpose. He'd purposely stood there and schemed to make her lose her control. It was reprehensible. It was manipulative. It was . . . thrilling. That he could do it at all was amazing.

'I'm shocked you can fit your ego through that front door of yours.' She forced herself to calmly pick up the peeler she'd dropped.

He laughed good-naturedly, not insulted in the least. And she was powerless not to return the smile.

It was pure revenge that had her refusing to give him a goodnight kiss two hours later, when he had followed her home and walked her to her door.

But in the end it seemed she'd cut off her nose to spite her face. As she watched him walk away every part of her wanted to call him back. Every part of her wanted a kiss goodnight from Cord Harrison.

For days Cord remained torn between lust for his painter and real concern for his partner. Seth, despite his protestations that he wasn't concerned about the sheriff, slunk about the office, neither working nor talking. And nothing Cord said made any difference.

His investigation was shaky at best. To consider his employees made him sick, as did the fact that he couldn't one hundred percent dismiss any of them as suspects. Nearly all of them had been to the party at his office, and many had still been on their way home, alone in their cars, at the time of Sheri's attack. Not a great alibi, but he believed in them. And then, to add to the trouble, there was Seth's continuing money trouble.

'I got myself into this,' he continued to protest when Cord tried to offer financial help, 'and I'll get myself out.'

When Katherine called, Cord felt desperate enough to ask her to try to talk some sense into his friend. 'He needs our help,' he told her. 'He's just too stubborn to accept it.'

'It's pride,' Katherine said, a smile in her voice. 'You should know about that, you have enough of it. But I'll talk to him. Don't fret, dear. Have some faith. He didn't commit the crimes. They can't charge him for something he didn't do.'

Logically, Cord knew that. Yet, he couldn't help but feel he was missing something. Something important.

'How's the house coming?'

'It looks great.'

'Emily seems to be doing a fine job.' Her voice was light and casual, but Cord smiled at the thinly veiled curiosity.

'She's doing better than fine. Right now she's working on a mural for one of the upstairs rooms.'

Something in his voice must have tipped her off. 'She's a beautiful woman, isn't she?'

'Katherine.' Unlike most mothers, who pushed their sons to marry, Katherine had always been the opposite. No woman had ever met with her approval. 'Are you actually playing matchmaker?'

'No,' she said quickly. 'No, I'm not. She's a lovely woman, really. But . . . well, you aren't well suited, are you? You come from two different worlds.'

Ah, here was the Katherine he expected. The one who instantly disliked anyone he looked twice at. 'Yes, we do. But the fact is not many people come from my world, do they?'

'I'm sorry, Cord. This isn't any of my business, and I know it, but I worry about you. You've made so much for yourself, you're a target for women looking for material things. You know that.'

How well he did. 'Katherine, Emily isn't looking for anything from me.'

'Just be careful, Cord. She seems lovely, but you just can't tell.'

'I'm careful. And so far you have nothing to worry about.'

'You sound disappointed.'

'A little.' He laughed. 'I'm working on it.'

'You're smitten.'

Smitten? Maybe. Yeah, likely.

'You've never been really serious before,' she pointed out correctly. 'Is this different?'

'I don't know.' That, at least, was honest.

'Is she . . . a good muralist?'

'Yes,' he said confidently. 'The best.'

'Well, maybe she'd be interested in doing a mural for St James's.'

'I'm sure she would,' Cord said, giving the phone a surprised glance. 'You feeling all right?'

Katherine laughed. 'Maybe I'm just getting mellow in my old age.'

'You're not old,' he said automatically. 'But mellowing? Sounds like it.'

'I just want you to be happy,' she whispered, as she had so many times before.

She cared deeply. He knew that, and he counted on it. Yet sometimes, as now, her fierce protectiveness disturbed him. And, as he'd also thought many times before, he wished her happiness weren't quite so dependent on his.

For days Emily worked nonstop on her mural, completely forgetting about taking time off. The only break she took was when she dropped off her sketches to the County Planner's Office.

At Cord's, the flooring contractor was in her way in every room she hadn't completed, giving her the perfect excuse to do nothing else but work on her mural. As always when she worked on her own painting – she forgot about everything else. Sleeping, eating and anything of equal importance always came second to painting.

Josh had become used to that, and he was busy with school anyway. In two days his entire class would be taking a field trip to Washington, DC for a week. Between getting ready for that and being with his girlfriend he was more than a little distracted himself.

She hadn't seen Cord. He was gone each day at his office, leaving early and returning late. She was sure he'd not given her another thought and she told herself she was glad. Then Raymond mentioned that Cord called him each day to verify he would follow her up and down the mountain.

She didn't know what to think then. Anger that he was checking on her alternated with embarrassment that he thought she couldn't handle herself. All that was mixed in with relief that he still cared, concocting a brew of emotions like nothing she'd ever had before. Whatever it was, it was difficult to swallow. Never could she remember feeling so . . . out of sorts.

It was the way he kissed, as if she were all that mattered. It had left her yearning for something she couldn't quite put a name to. Yet she was terrified to go after that elusive something.

So she painted. Almost finished, she knew without a doubt it was the most glorious, wondrous mural she'd ever done.

In mostly soft but deep colors, in order to preserve the lightness in the room, she'd created a midsummer's sky as she envisioned it, complete with her interpretation of the heavens. White puffy clouds played peek-a-boo with angels, the sun smiled upon a rainbow that ended with a luscious, sparkling pot of swirling gold, and in a corner a mischievous moon was just waiting its turn to leap out.

Emily fell a little in love with each of her paintings, and she knew all too well the dangers. It became so much a part of her it was like letting go of her own child, and it was made all the more painful because this one wasn't in a public place she could easily visit at the end.

If this was even half of what true love felt like, she wanted nothing to do with it.

'Emily, we gotta get going soon – wow!'

She turned to see Raymond standing in the doorway, neck craned to study the mural, a forgotten bag of open potato chips in his hand.

He stepped in to get a better view. 'This is incredible, Emily. I had no idea you were so talented.' Absently he brought a handful of chips to his mouth.

The praise was ego-boosting. But more than that it was reaffirming, and a balm to the soul. Slightly uncomfortable, as she always was when someone studied her work, she reached a hand up to her aching neck. Painting ceilings tweaked her neck. 'I'm glad you like it.'

Around a mouthful of chips Raymond said enthusiastically, 'It's fantastic. This room feels . . . alive.' He shook his head in admiration. 'Look how the fading light from the windows streaks the sky as if your painted sun is setting also. It's so real.'

Startled, she looked out the window at the setting sun. She'd had no idea it was that late. No wonder her neck hurt. She'd been painting all day without stopping. She felt suddenly exhausted. 'I'd better clean up.' She looked in dismay at the messy array of opened paints she still had to clear.

Raymond held out the bag of chips in silent offering and she grabbed a handful. This time he finished chewing before speaking. 'Yeah, we've got to hurry if we want to get home before dark.'

Emily grinned and reached for more chips. They tasted wonderful, reminding her that she had forgotten to eat again. 'What's the matter? You turn into a pumpkin after dark?'

'Funny,' he smirked. 'No, your guardian angel left orders.'

Her smiled faded quickly and she brushed salt from her fingers. 'Orders?'

'We're to be off the mountain by nightfall. And I'm not to leave you again if I want to get paid.'

It was pure pride that kept her smiling evenly and assuring poor Raymond she'd be ready in a minute. Okay, maybe she hadn't entirely believed she faced any real danger. The burst tire could well have been an accident.

But she remembered the terror she'd felt the other night, when Cord had come upon her alone in his house. Her fear had been real, not imagined. In that brief instant she'd believed she was being stalked. It was a memory that wouldn't fade any time soon.

She also understood that Cord shared her fear, and he only did now what he felt was right. He wanted her safe. But he didn't trust her enough to leave her in charge.

Which was why it made it hard to swallow his bossiness now. Another time, perhaps, she'd have stayed just to be stubborn and had it out with him. But not this time.

She wasn't ready to face his reaction to her mural.

Yes, it was a purely cowardly thing. But she'd practically forced it on him, leaving him no choice but to accept it – and now she had to face the very real possibility he might not like it.

Her heart constricted when she glanced up once more. She loved this painting. And she simply couldn't stand it that he probably wouldn't feel the same.

With a heavy, nervous heart she raced through clean-up and hurried down the stairs, unwilling to stay too long and run into him. As she dashed through the kitchen she caught quick sight of a note and stopped. Thinking it was for her, she read it.

Cord, hope you enjoy this new recipe! I called you at the office, but you were already at lunch with Margo. Seth told me about your new account – congrats! (You work too hard!!) Lots of love, Katherine.

Emily snorted derisively as she stole a cookie. 'Margo,' she muttered. So what if Cord had kissed her until her bones were the consistency of jello and now was taking Margo to lunch? She didn't care. She didn't even like him.

Okay, that was a big, fat lie, but she didn't have time to dwell on it. One glance at her watch had her cursing the late hour and running out to meet Raymond. She couldn't run into him now, not when she felt so raw and . . . exposed. Painting did that to her. And Cord would only make it worse.

Her legs couldn't carry her fast enough, and her sense of urgency increased. She was opening her truck door when the sound of a smooth-running truck driving up the road made her groan.

Cord was home.

CHAPTER 9

A light film of sweat broke out over Emily's body as she silently prayed that Raymond would just hurry and start his truck. Cord hadn't yet seen them. If they drove away from his front yard right now they could pretend they didn't see him and – It was too late. She slumped in dismay as Raymond got out of his truck and waved at Cord.

Emily bit her lip, hating the panic that welled through her stiff body. There was no rational reason for it.

Cord pushed himself out of his truck, pausing to reach back in for his briefcase and jacket, and for a long second Emily forgot her hurry. She hadn't seen him in over a week. And she'd never seen him in anything but jeans or shorts.

While he filled denim out better than anyone she'd ever known, in a suit he was an impressive sight. The expensive-looking black shirt tucked into smooth and equally expensive-looking charcoal-gray trousers suited his dark coloring perfectly. He seemed even taller and broader than ever, and Emily wondered how she had ever thought Seth was the more elegant half of HT Designs. Cord exuded charisma, power, confidence . . . and sex appeal. She hardly recognized him as the easy-going, warm man she'd worked with for nearly a month.

It was frightening.

For a minute he simply stood there, and even from her distance Emily could see the hard eyes and the tension in his lean form. He was almost unrecognizable – until he looked at his house. Instantly his shoulders relaxed and the stress seemed to drain from him, making him seem more like himself. He turned slightly and she knew the minute those electric-blue eyes found her. She had a crazy impulse to run.

Until the smile. It was instantaneous, warm, genuine – and directed right at her.

How could anyone resist that damn smile? Without meaning to, she answered with her own helplessly inevitable smile, standing still as he walked toward her. She ignored the sudden racing of her heart, and the mush where her joints used to be.

'Hey, Red.' Cord ran his eyes down the length of her, as if he were hungry for the first sight of her he'd had in days.

She knew what he would see. Her braid was loose, her hair ruffled and spiked from shoving at it all day. Her favorite overalls were speckled with every color of paint in the rainbow and her hands matched. She shoved them into her front pockets, knowing her smile had long since faded and she was now scowling. In comparison to him, she was a mess. And she just bet that Margo hadn't been.

'We're just leaving,' she said.

A corner of his mouth turned up. 'I can see that.' His eyes moved over her lips, as if he would have loved to kiss the frown from her face, but thankfully Raymond was moving toward them. So, instead, he tugged on her braid. There was something in the way that he looked at her that took away her self-consciousness about her appearance. It was as if he looked deeper, past the exterior. And once again her resolve to keep him at bay melted – because he made her feel different. Alive. Beautiful.

He reached into his pocket and held out a package of the watermelon candy she loved. 'I saw these at lunch and thought of you.'

She didn't recognize the flare of pure green emotion for what it was. 'That must have thrilled Margo.' She snapped her mouth shut and wished for a hole to swallow her up. She couldn't believe she'd said that.

He looked at her strangely. 'What does my new secretary have to do with anything?'

Not just any hole, she thought. A huge, gigantic hole. One that she could never crawl out of. 'Nothing,' she mumbled. She was an idiot.

'Been working hard?'

She thought of her mural and shot her truck a desperate glance. 'Um, yeah.'

'Cord, I'm just about finished,' Raymond said, coming up behind them. 'Probably be completely done by tomorrow.'

While the two men discussed the roof Emily started to move away, hoping for an unnoticed escape. Cord's hand shot out and grabbed her wrist, trapping her. While answering a question of Raymond's he slanted her an amused glance, knowing damn well that she couldn't yank away her hand without making a scene.

It didn't improve her mood.

Finally Raymond moved toward his own truck, and Emily tried to pull her hand away.

Cord held onto it tight, leaning in close so that she could see nothing past his broad shoulders. His lips brushed her neck before moving to her ear. 'Do you have any idea how long it's been since I kissed you?' Cord whispered.

God, what just his words did to her. 'I – Uh – '

'Too long.' He reached for her, but she ducked him.

'Don't.'

Cord's easy smile faded and his face turned rough with concern. 'What's the matter?'

'Nothing. I've got to go – '

'Raymond isn't leaving without you.' Sure enough Raymond had started his truck, but didn't move. 'Something bothering you?'

You, she wanted to scream. Up close, he was the picture of authority, success, affluence. 'No,' she replied, surprised at how evenly she answered. 'I've just got to go.'

'Em,' he sighed, looking frustrated. 'I thought we'd gotten past this.'

'Past what?'

He flicked a finger at her bangs to see clearly into her eyes, then ran his thumb across her cheek. 'Your wall.'

'What wall?'

He softly tapped at her temple. 'The one in here.'

She refused to give in to that look, the one that could melt her resolve. It was the only thing holding her together. 'I gotta go.'

He knew she was lying; she could read it in his face. But he didn't try to stop her again.

On the drive home she absently ate three of the watermelon candies. *I thought we'd gotten past this . . . your wall*, Cord had said. It was scary how well he knew her. She *had* put up a wall. Only she didn't know if she wanted to tear it down or build it higher.

By the time she drove into her parking space at home her head was pounding fiercely. Too much thinking, she told herself, and forced a smile when she entered the apartment.

'Hey, Sis, can I borrow your camera?'

She stared in surprise at Josh, stuffing things into his duffel bag. 'You aren't leaving for two days.'

He looked at her strangely. 'I'm leaving first thing in the morning.' He smiled affectionately. 'You've lost track of the days again, haven't you? It's Friday.'

Friday. The night she'd promised to take him and Monica out for pizza before their trip. She sighed and headed for the kitchen to gulp down aspirin. It was going to be a long week without Joshua around.

And lonely. She stood at the sink, staring sightlessly out the window.

'Hey, you okay?'

She blinked furiously at the unaccustomed wetness behind her eyes. 'Of course.'

'You don't look it.' He moved into the room, tried to look at her face, but she turned away. 'Emily?'

'I just don't feel well, that's all. A little headache. I took aspirin – I'll be fine enough to go for pizza.'

'Sure?'

She forced herself to nod, then turned to face him. 'Do you have everything you need for your trip?'

'Yeah. Gonna enjoy your week of quiet?'

She smiled then, a genuine one. 'It *will* be quiet, without Pearl Jam rattling the windows at all hours.'

He laughed, looking the picture of a carefree teen about to embark on his first trip of freedom. Again she felt overcome by a bitter sweetness. Despite their tragic beginning, he'd turned out okay. She'd done that, she realized with some surprise. She'd raised him all by herself, and she'd done a good job.

Without her parents.

Guilt pummeled her, in relentless waves that the years hadn't allayed. They didn't have parents because of *her*. Nothing, not even time, could change that fact.

And now the job of raising Josh had nearly come to an end.

She wouldn't – couldn't – think of it now, or she'd start to cry. After all, he would be leaving for college soon enough, and she'd really be alone then. He was growing up and she had to let him. It was time.

Seth and Cord stood in the room on the third floor, silently surveying the mural.

'Wow,' Seth finally said.

'Yeah. Wow,' Cord echoed, reeling.

'Did you have any idea how talented she was?'

Cord couldn't take his eyes off the mesmerizing painting. 'Absolutely none.' It was the most amazing thing, he thought. He almost believed that he was looking at the actual sky, it was that real.

'I feel like those angels are moving,' Seth said in awe. 'They're actually smiling and looking *at* me. Cord – '

'No.'

Seth dropped his eyes from the picture and looked at Cord in exasperation. 'You don't even know what I was going to say.'

'If it has anything to do with keeping Emily around any longer than this job, forget it.'

Seth looked at him as if he were crazy. 'What's the matter with you? You were the one who told me to back off. You even threatened to remove my limbs one by one.'

That made Cord laugh, just as he knew Seth had intended. 'I *never* said that.'

'All right, maybe not. But it was definitely implied.'

'She's different.'

'Different like she speaks in tongues? Or different

like she eats crackers in bed? Because – '

'Would you knock it off? I thought you were serious.'

Seth stopped. 'I am serious. I just want to understand why you're willing to walk away from the best thing that's ever happened to you.'

'I think – I'm beginning to have feelings for her.'

Seth looked at Cord as if he were crazy. 'And this is a problem because . . .?'

'No.' How could he expect anyone else to understand something *he* didn't even get? '*Real* feelings. You know, the ones that come from here.' Cord rubbed his chest over his heart. Then sighed. 'That sounded stupid.'

'What's stupid is not doing anything about it.'

Cord agreed, but some things were easier said than done. 'She's not exactly eager to start anything.'

'When did that ever stop you?' Seth grinned, then sobered. 'Oh. I get it. You're not backing off because of her – you're terrified.'

Cord took a deep breath. 'I just can't stop thinking about the things that have happened to the others. And then there was Emily's tire.'

'But that might have just been a coincidence.'

Cord shot him a look. 'You don't really believe that.'

Seth's mouth tightened. 'No, I guess I don't. I wish I could have the guy doing this. I hate being set up.'

'You and me both. I don't want anything to happen to Emily.'

Seth studied the mural, shook his head. 'So you'll give her up rather than have her near you and possibly get hurt.' He glanced at Cord. 'Noble gesture, but if these things really are connected, don't you think it's too late? That Emily is threatened regardless?'

It was what he was afraid of. 'I don't know. I hope to God not.'

'I'm taking Margo out for pizza tonight,' Seth said. 'She's a little unnerved at all the attention this thing is getting in the local papers.'

'I'm surprised she agreed to the job after we told about Sheri.'

Seth lifted his eyebrows meaningfully. 'Yeah, it's amazing what money'll do. Still, she's good and we do need her. I figure a few beers should help keep my mind off my troubles. Keith and some of the others are meeting us there.'

Cord looked at him. 'This new account we got should help you. Will it be enough?'

'For now,' Seth replied evenly. 'Stop worrying about me.' He laughed. 'I'd been so long without money that when I got too much I went into overload. It'll work out.'

'Plan to stay away from investing, I hope?'

'Yep,' Seth assured him. 'A plain old checking account is all I'm going to need for a while. God, I'm starved. Come with us?'

'I have work.'

'The work will wait. You've put in a jillion hours already this week. Let it rest. Have some fun.'

'Really, I can't.'

'You can do whatever you want to. Try being happy.'

Cord forced a smile. 'Now you're beginning to sound like Katherine.'

The local pizza parlor was jammed. It seemed as if just about everyone in town was there celebrating a birthday or an anniversary, or just the week's end.

All of Joshua's friends were there, playing the jukebox at an ear-splitting level and shouting to be heard. Emily knew just about everyone else there as well, including Raymond and several of the other subcontractors she'd seen coming and going over the week at Cord's.

Normally Emily would have relaxed and enjoyed herself, but her headache had come back with a vengeance.

She was wondering how long it would be before she could drag Josh and Monica home when Seth entered with a graceful, polished blonde. She smiled, thinking a couple as good-looking as that belonged anywhere but a pizza joint. They joined several others at a table already full of laughing, happy people.

A few minutes later Seth came over alone and sat down at Emily's table. He handed her a tall glass of iced tea. 'You look like you could use a real drink, but the bartender didn't think you were old enough.'

She smiled. 'Remind me to kiss him.' She sipped her tea and sighed. 'Thanks.'

'The mural is incredible, Emily.'

Her head shot up in surprise. 'You saw it.'

'Earlier. You're wasting talent painting houses.'

The compliment was embarrassingly flattering, as was his frank appraisal and warm smile. But all she wanted to know was what Cord thought. It shouldn't matter, but it did. She cringed, thinking how she'd run out on him earlier. Her only excuse was fear, fueled by how he made her feel.

'I have a proposal for you.'

She laughed and glanced at his date across the room. 'Another one? Won't your friend be upset?'

He chuckled and shook his head. 'That's Margo, our new secretary. Besides, this proposal is different.' His smile lingered. 'And probably much more appealing to you. I want to commission you to do our office walls.'

Considering HT Designs had a three-story office building, that was some offer. But it was more than that; it was a chance to do what she *loved*. 'I don't know what to say.'

'Well, why don't you think about it?' Seth stood up. 'I'm sure Cord would agree with me that there's no one else around that could do it better.'

'You haven't discussed this with Cord?'

'Not exactly.' Seth's gorgeous smile turned ironic. 'Let's just say it's a surprise.' Then he laughed, as if he'd told the funniest joke he'd ever heard, and went back to Margo.

Emily's headache didn't improve. By the time she had dropped Monica back off at her house and driven home, her body was aching and she had the chills.

Then the stomach cramps started, kicking in with a vengeance that had her gasping for breath. She started sweating getting out of the truck and barely made it to the bathroom in time to throw up everything she'd just eaten.

Joshua hovered on the other side of the locked door, sounding worried. 'Emily? You've got the flu or something?'

Or something, she thought, still on her knees, arms clasped around the piercing pain in her abdomen. 'I don't know.'

'Great,' he muttered to himself. 'I'm calling the doctor.'

'Don't,' she called out, weakly leaning her head against the wall as she slumped back. 'I'm fine.'

Or she was for about five more seconds.

'I can't leave when you're this sick,' Josh said to Emily through the bathroom door some moments later, when she still hadn't come out. 'Let me in.'

She couldn't move, much less make it across the cold floor to unlock the door. 'You can still go,' she managed to call out. 'I'll be fine.'

But she wasn't. She was violently sick most of the night and by morning she lay trembling on the bathroom floor, alternating between freezing and burning up so hot she thought her skin would melt off.

'Emily?' Josh's concerned voice once again filtered through the door as he tried the lock. 'Have you been in there all night?'

It was an effort to answer. 'No,' she lied. She had hours ago stripped off her sweat-drenched clothes. *For Joshua*, she told herself. *Do this for him.* Somehow she found the energy to stand and wrapped herself in a towel. Slowly and painfully she opened the door. 'It's all yours. I'm going . . . back to bed.' She dragged herself down the hall and pulled an oversized – shirt over her head. She fell into her bed, fast asleep by the time her head hit the pillow.

'Emily.' Josh's voice called. She felt him gently shake her, and reluctantly she slid from peaceful, dreamless sleep to the painful state of awareness. 'I've got to go,' he said. 'Are you *sure* you're all right?'

She forced an eyelid open against the immense torment radiating through her head. 'I'm fine,' she promised, barely able to get the words out through her chattering teeth. 'Just . . . the flu.'

He looked uncertain. 'It's nine o'clock. My ride will be here any second. I'm going to cancel.'

'Nine o'clock,' she repeated dumbly. She was vaguely aware that she was late for work, but her head hurt so bad it didn't matter. At least the cramping had eased. 'Don't, Josh. Really. Just . . . call me . . . okay?'

She felt him squeeze her hand. 'Emily?'

'It's just the flu. Geez, you'd think I was dying or something.'

He smiled. 'You sounded like it last night.'

'I'm better now.'

'Okay, if you're sure?' he said, drawing out the last

word like a question. She managed to nod assuringly one more time, collapsing back against the pillow the instant he turned away.

Less than five minutes after Josh had left, the cramping returned. And she bolted into the bathroom in the nick of time.

'Say that again,' Cord said to Raymond, feeling an inkling of dread fill him.

Raymond got out of his truck. Cord stood, hands on his hips, waiting impatiently. He'd been waiting an hour already, concerned.

'Her truck's there, but no one answered my knock.' Raymond shrugged. 'It's Saturday, and since we hadn't made definite plans I figured she was sleeping in. I waited a little while, then came here. Sorry if you were waiting for me.'

Forget the damn wait; he wanted to know about Emily. 'She didn't plan to come to work today?' Cord asked.

'I don't know for sure. I saw her last night at the pizza parlor, but I didn't ask her.'

It wasn't right. Something wasn't right. She *always* worked on Saturdays. He thought about the incredible mural upstairs. Maybe she was nervous about his reaction. Without another word, he whipped out his phone and dialed her apartment.

The machine picked up.

'Emily,' he said to the recorder, 'call me.'

But she didn't.

* * *

212

Two hours later, Cord could no longer stand the not knowing. Emily had failed to show up or return his call, and no amount of work could take him mind off one thing.

Something was wrong.

Even Raymond was shaking his head and saying how unlike her it was not to return a phone call.

Cord made it down the mountain in record time, cursing his own stupidity for ever letting her go, cursing her own bull-headedness that had them in this predicament in the first place.

His clammy hands stuck to the steering wheel as he thought about all the things that could have happened to her. Tayna's and Lacey's faces haunted him. Then Sheri's. God, she could at this very minute be hurt or – It didn't bear thinking about.

But if something had indeed happened to her, he personally would tear the town apart to find the culprit. Amazingly enough, he didn't get pulled over for speeding – because he had to have broken every record as he whipped into Emily's apartment complex.

Her truck sat in its spot, looking helplessly normal. He felt the quick spurt of irritation. So it was the mural, damn it. She had painted it, but didn't have the guts to see what he thought. He wasn't surprised when she didn't answer his knock.

It took only a minute to find the key hidden under Emily's mat. He didn't know whether to be furious that she had hidden it so poorly, or relieved that he could get in without force. Still shaking his head, he opened the door and called her name.

The kitchen and living room, though comfortably cluttered, were empty. So was the first bedroom which, given the black walls and wild posters, was obviously Josh's room.

His relief began to fade. Still calling her name, he went down the hall to the second bedroom. At first he thought it, too, was empty. Clothes and shoes, thrown randomly around the room, appeared to be the only occupants. The bed had a haphazard pile of blankets thrown across it.

But then the lump beneath them groaned softly. Cord stepped closer, seeing for the first time a mass of dark red hair sticking out of the heap. Some of the tension left him, but concern immediately filled the spot.

'Emily?'

She didn't move. Cord smoothed back the tangled hair and touched her head. No temperature. 'Emily?'

He got no reaction.

Her unnatural stillness had him pushing the covers back, exposing pale skin that glistened with dampness. Her eyes remained closed; her breathing was too deep for comfort. Feeling panicky, he rested a knee on the bed and took her shoulders in his trembling hands. 'Emily. Wake up.'

She still didn't budge.

CHAPTER 10

Cord shook Emily harder, shoving away the rest of her blankets. 'Emily! Come on, baby, wake up.'

'No,' she mumbled and rolled away from him.

He studied her dull hair and pasty profile. 'Are you sick?' She didn't answer. He sank down beside her, frowning when she shivered. At least six thick blankets had been piled on her and the nights were no longer all that cold. 'Emily, what's the matter?'

She flinched and covered her ears. 'Shh.'

Cord rolled her to her back and held her shoulders. 'Emily.'

Her eyes opened, unseeing at first. When they focused on him, she moaned and slammed them shut. 'Cord. Go away.'

Relief that he'd found her sharpened his voice. 'Not until you tell me what's wrong.'

Her eyes flew open again. 'What are you doing here?'

'It's noon. You didn't show up and you didn't call me back. I got worried. You're sick?'

She shut her eyes again and brought her hands up

215

to her head. 'The flu. I didn't go to bed until a couple of hours ago.'

'Does your stomach hurt or just your head?'

'Both,' she said through gritted teeth. 'Please . . . just go.'

'Where's Joshua?'

'He left on his trip.'

Before he could comment, she groaned and clutched her stomach. 'Not again,' she moaned, rolling onto her side in a tight ball.

He had time to drag her hair from her face before she jerked to an upright position. With a horrified expression, she shoved him out of her way and bolted down the hall into the bathroom. He followed her, getting a quick glimpse of bare, lean legs.

In the bathroom, he kneeled beside her, holding her hair off her face. When she'd finished throwing up, he carried her back to bed. She was so weak she couldn't protest, and he was so concerned that he found himself rambling.

'It's going to be okay, Em,' he whispered, lying her in the bed. 'You're cold; I'm going to pile the blankets back on.' He spread the last one out and touched her cheek. She lay still with her eyes closed. She hated being helpless, he knew.

His pent-up fear for her had him rushing into speech. 'I saw your mural today, Em. It's magnificent. I love it.' Still she didn't move. 'Seth loved it too. We both looked at it and felt something – something wonderful. It was a good feeling, Em. You did that for us.' Worried, he leaned close. 'Em?'

She didn't budge. Her breathing was low, steady and even. Fast asleep.

He mopped her sticky face with a wet washcloth and straightened out her bedding, and still she didn't stir. Then he called his doctor for advice and learned how little one could do for the flu.

He found some juice and crackers in the messy kitchen, brought them into Emily's bedroom. And waited.

When she shifted and moaned softly, he leaned over her. 'Em? Is your stomach cramping again?'

She nodded miserably. He slipped his hand under the covers and massaged her tight stomach, wishing he could take away the pain. 'Here, press this close.' And he replaced his hand with a hot water bottle he'd found under the sink.

'Please . . . go away,' she whispered, burying her face into the pillow.

He knew by the high spots of color staining her cheeks she was mortified, but he couldn't help it. He wasn't leaving her. 'Em, you're really sick. I can't leave you alone.'

'I'm fine –' She stopped abruptly, white as cotton, and threw the covers off. With a hand clamped tight over her mouth she ran down the hallway.

This time when she was done she collapsed on the floor, out cold. He scooped her into his arms and once again carried her back to bed. She was shivering uncontrollably, even when he placed all six blankets on her. For about half a second he debated, but when he heard her teeth clatter together the decision was made for him. He kicked off his shoes and crawled into the bed with her, pulling her small, chilled body close.

His body warmth seemed to slowly seep into her limbs. She pressed against him in her sleep, one slim arm clutching his thigh to keep him close. He closed his eyes at the intimate touch, forcing himself to recite telephone numbers in order to put out the flaming lust shooting through him. When that didn't work he shifted to multiplication tables, but that too proved ineffective.

Giving in to the irresistible urge, he ran a hand down the length of her, telling himself he was simply trying to absorb her chill. Instead, he got a handful of the softest skin he could remember. She was thin, but curvy every place it mattered, and he shifted uncomfortably, painfully erect against his jeans.

She was sick, he told himself with disgust. And asleep. Still, his body responded. When Emily shivered violently, he felt like the lowest form on earth even as he pulled her closer and half beneath him. Eventually she stopped shaking, but her skin grew warmer too and she became restless in her sleep.

For several tortured hours Cord held her tight, even when she tried to toss and turn. When her knee connected painfully with his swollen groin, he winced before managing to pin her legs between his.

'No!' she gasped suddenly in a terrified voice. 'It's not true – it can't be true. Oh, my God, Mom, no! Dad . . . no!' She choked back a sob and buried her face in his shoulder.

'Em?' He smoothed her hair back from her face, relieved she wasn't feverish. 'It's a dream. It's just a dream.'

'No!'

'Come on, baby. Wake up.' He cupped her warm face in his hands. 'Emily, wake up.'

'Don't die,' she cried. 'Not because of me!'

'Emily, it's okay,' he murmured reassuringly, frowning at the raw emotion in her voice. 'You're safe.' He couldn't say the same for her parents and he wondered exactly how they'd died.

Her body tensed and her eyes opened. She blinked, her eyes wide, her heart going wild against his.

'You okay now?' he asked, still holding her. For a minute she was so transparent Cord knew exactly what she was thinking. She was wrapped around him, scantily dressed, and she didn't know how she had gotten there. When she blushed, he knew she was remembering how she'd thrown up in front of him earlier and how he'd matter-of-factly cleaned up. 'Emily? It was just a dream.'

'I know.' Her voice was soft and raspy.

'It was a bad one. Tell me?'

'No.' She shook her head quickly. 'It was nothing.'

He could still feel the quick drumming of her heart, the slight tremble of her limbs, and sincerely doubted it had been nothing. He ran warm fingers up and down her arm, wishing she wasn't so sick, wishing her bare legs didn't feel so good against his.

'How did . . . we get here?'

'You passed out in the bathroom. I carried you.'

She sighed and pulled out of his arms. 'Cord, this is really embarrassing.'

'Stop it.' He sat up and touched her face. 'Do you feel any better?'

'I don't know.' She took silent inventory. 'My stomach doesn't hurt.'

'That's a start.'

She gave him a wary look, reminding him that she was fighting this crazy attraction between them every step of the way. 'Why are you in bed with me?'

'You were cold and there were no more blankets.' *And because he hadn't been able to resist holding her.*

'Please,' she said, her eyes darting away as if she had read his thoughts. 'Please, just go.'

'Not until I'm sure you're going to be all right.'

'I'm fine. I'll probably be at work in a little while.'

Cord glanced out the window where dusk was rapidly turning into night. 'The day is gone, Emily.'

Her eyes widened in dismay. 'I slept all day.'

'Here.' He reached out for the glass of clear juice he'd brought into the bedroom. 'You need to drink something.'

She took a sip and turned her head away.

'More,' he demanded. 'You'll get dehydrated.'

Emily wrinkled her nose and drank more before pushing the glass away.

'A cracker?'

'No way.' Her face turned green at the thought. She touched her matted, tangled hair. 'I want a shower.' She looked down the hall, probably wondering how she was going to get there wearing what she was wearing without him seeing her.

Cord stood. 'Where's your robe?'

She gestured to the hook on her door. He brought it to her and held it while she pushed her arms through, thinking she looked as if she might topple over. Even as he thought it she slumped back to the bed, completely worn out.

'Wait until morning.' Her color had him worried. She would drown herself if she tried now.

'No.' Stubborn as ever, she pushed herself to a stand, then wobbled to the door. He wrapped a supporting arm around her waist, and it was a sign of just how weary she was that she let him practically carry her to the bathroom.

Cord started the water for her and turned to take off her robe. She shoved his hands away. 'I can do it. I'm fine now.'

He could see the pure misery and humiliation in her face and was torn. He didn't want to rob her of her tenuously held control – she needed that – and yet he was afraid to leave her alone. But being in charge meant everything to Emily and he knew he couldn't bring himself to take it from her.

'Okay. But I'll wait right outside the door.'

She stared mutinously at him, and he would have laughed if she hadn't looked so wan and listless. 'I'm fine,' she repeated, then, as if to prove it, she moved deliberately toward the shower.

'Call me if you need me,' he said easily. He waited right outside the door, listening to every sound.

When twenty minutes had passed and the water was still on, he pounded on the door. 'Emily?'

She didn't answer and he could no longer hear her moving.

'Emily!' He tried the door, cursing when he discovered it locked. 'Emily!'

The water turned off and he sighed in relief. 'Emily, let me in.'

Two very long minutes later, she opened the door a crack. 'Sweatsuit,' she whispered. 'In the top drawer.'

Her drawer was empty. Probably because most of her clothes were scattered across the floor. How did the woman find anything in this mess? He slammed another drawer, frustrated, picturing Emily shivering in the bathroom. Finally he found a nightgown in the next drawer over and rushed down the hall. Emily, wrapped in a towel that dwarfed her, leaned listlessly against the sink, her face pale and wan, her hair dripping all over her.

Torn between wanting to shake some sense into her and needing to wrap his arms around her, he settled for thrusting out the nightgown.

She frowned.

'It's all there was,' he said quickly, out of breath from his search. 'Do you ever do laundry?'

Her frown deepened. 'I – '

'Never mind,' he said quickly, sensing a fight. 'Here, let me help you.'

'No.' She shook her head, then slumped down onto the toilet, too weak to stand any longer. 'Go away.'

Cord didn't bother to ask again. He pulled the white cotton gown over her head, holding his hand out for the towel that she pulled out from beneath the gown, keeping her head averted. Ignoring her flaming face, he pulled her back into his arms and carried her back to her bedroom, berating himself the entire way for getting turned on by the quick glimpse of soft curves he'd gotten.

'I hate this,' she whispered, turning her face into his chest.

He looked down at her, tenderness for her flaring through him. 'I know you do.' He set her gently on the bed, then towel-dried her long, wet, glorious hair the best he could. Never having seen it loose before, he couldn't resist touching it. 'But I want to be here. I want to help you.' He continued the long strokes on her hair. 'Why does it have to be so hard to let me?'

She lifted a shoulder. 'I'm not used to it.' She closed her eyes. 'Mmm. That feels good,' she mumbled.

He wanted to tell her to get used to accepting his help, but knew it would only scare her. So he sighed, stifled his own raging desires and continued to work on her hair.

'I got the flu once when I was little,' he began, talking more to soothe his own nerves than anything else. He loved playing with her hair. 'I must have been about eight or nine. I wouldn't eat dinner and one of the nuns was bugging me, trying to get me to finish my plate. But I didn't want to; I had a stomach ache. She made me eat it all.' He laughed. 'But was she sorry when I stood up at the end of the meal and lost every last bite all over her shoes.'

'She never should have made you eat it,' Emily muttered slowly, her words slurred from exhaustion. 'I think that's mean.'

Her quick defense warmed his heart. 'I know. Katherine gave her hell – Well, maybe not hell, but she did cut into her. They babied me for days, and I dragged out that flu as long as I could. And wouldn't you know, I never caught it again? Did you get the flu when you were little?'

She didn't answer. Her chest rose and fell with her deep and even breathing. Fast asleep, he thought, relieved. He could stop jabbering like an idiot now. And she was going to be fine, he assured himself, because he wasn't going to leave until she was. He glanced at the only chair in the room, tossed the books and clothes that covered it to the floor, and settled in to watch her sleep.

He awoke with a start and a kinked neck some time later. He could hear Emily in the bathroom, getting sick. This time Cord didn't mess around. She was violently, deathly ill. When she'd finished, he wrapped her up the best he could and took her to the local emergency care, with Emily protesting weakly the entire way.

Due to the late hour, Emily didn't have a long wait. But, to his vast irritation, she refused to let him come into the examining room with her. She emerged half an hour later, looking as if a small breeze could blow her over.

He didn't have to stand; he'd been wearing a path in the waiting room. 'What is it?' He moved anxiously toward her.

She shrugged, her shoulders sagging. 'Let's go.'

His eyes narrowed. She wasn't going to tell him a thing. Wordlessly, he helped her into his truck.

'I hope Josh isn't sick,' she mused quietly on the drive back to her apartment.

'The flu?'

She didn't answer and one quick glance told him why. She'd fallen fast asleep, her head resting against the window. Even in sleep he could see the strain in her features and the light shadows beneath her eyes. Her hair fell past her shoulders in wild, unconfined curls, and he decided that Emily-the-Painter had been hiding that stunning hair.

He'd never seen anyone so sick. That it was Emily only made it worse. He hated the powerless feeling, and knew he would gladly have taken on the flu for her if he could. Another quick glance showed him that, while her color still looked bad, she no longer gripped her stomach as though in pain.

It was difficult to be helpless, difficult to watch her suffer. He wanted her healthy and he wanted her safe. But it wasn't as if the flu were terminal; she'd live. And he'd make sure she stayed safe.

He pulled into Emily's apartment complex and had to laugh at himself, hovering over her like a mother hen. Never before had he worried so much over another human being. Never before had he been so protective, so possessive.

The fact that he couldn't always keep her happy and well was a surprising blow. The fact that she didn't need him much was another. Emily McKay was like no other woman he'd ever known. Shy and unsure, yet fiercely independent and proud. She had an amazingly strong will, but was loyal to the bone about the people she cared about.

He wanted to protect her – and, to make it worse, he wanted her to need him.

That either made him a macho fool – or a very human male falling in love.

No, not him.

Scoffing at the very idea, he carried Emily into the house and set her on the chair by the bed. Plenty of times before he'd thought himself in love and it had never proven to be true. There was no reason to believe it now.

With the fresh linens he found in the hall, he changed her bed. Then he turned to where Emily half-sat, half-lay in the chair, deep asleep. While carrying her to the bed he noticed the wild tangles in her hair, so he sat next to her with a brush and struggled with the knots. When he'd gotten most of them out, he simply brushed the long strands. He'd completely lost it, he thought. Brushing a woman's hair. Just as he was about to toss the brush aside with self-disgust, she hummed with pleasure.

Because he had to, he touched her, running his fingers along the side of her face and over a covered shoulder.

She tossed herself onto her back in her sleep, her

face tense. He swiped her hair off her hot forehead, then forced more liquid down her. She mumbled, shivered and turned over.

He couldn't leave her. She might get worse or have another nightmare. Tucking her in as tightly as he could, Cord settled into the chair. The hard, small, uncomfortable chair.

He looked at Emily.

If he climbed back into that bed with her and she settled against him, there was no way he could control his body's reaction to her. He'd stay in the chair.

For five long minutes he struggled to get comfortable and failed miserably. He was simply too long for the damn thing. He glanced at Emily, saw her shiver. She already had all the blankets. With a fatalistic shrug, he peeled off his shirt, kicked off his shoes, then slipped into the bed and pulled her close.

Her nightgown was tangled up high on her legs and the white cotton only enhanced her every curve. She snuggled close in her sleep and the gown gaped away from her, teasing him with little glimpses of her breasts.

'Mmm,' she murmured quietly, pressing even closer. 'You're warm.'

There was a long moment of pained silence while his body reacted to the huskiness in her voice and the heat of her body. One of her legs slipped between his, rubbing against his thigh, and he slammed his eyes shut, barely stifling a moan.

The bed was a very bad idea.

Helpless to resist, he ran his hands along her body. 'Cord?'

'Shh. Go to sleep,' he told her, hearing the strain in his voice.

She lifted her face and settled it in the crook of his neck, her hair tickling his face and chin. Fresh from her earlier shower, it smelled like a summer rain.

It was going to be a long night.

Emily came awake in slow degrees. Warm and toasty and very comfortable, she left her eyes closed, enjoying it. Things were good. Her head didn't hurt and her stomach didn't cramp, though her entire body ached as if she'd been run through a wringer.

Then, quite suddenly, she became aware of several things.

One, her face was resting against a bare, fuzzy chest. And two, her legs were comfortably trapped between two powerful thighs.

Cord's.

Oh, God. She leapt up and was promptly grabbed by two strong arms.

'Em, it's all right. Another dream?'

'No.'

He looked at her doubtfully, eyes heavy with sleep, his hair mussed, a light growth of stubble running along his jaw.

He looked gorgeous, even in the morning.

'You sure?' he asked, still holding her.

She pushed at him, then unsteadily backed up against the headboard. Not because she wanted to stay in bed with him, but because she'd faint if she moved that fast again. Cautiously she raised her hands to her spinning head, but it wasn't pounding. She didn't even feel nauseous. She sighed in relief.

'Em? Are you going to be sick?'

That made her smile ruefully. 'Scared?'

'Hardly.' He sat next to her, scanning her face carefully, as if trying to judge for himself how she was. 'But, seeing as I've changed these sheets twice already, I do have a vested interest.'

She dropped her hands from her head. 'Twice?'

'You sweat a lot in your sleep.'

She wanted to die right there. The man had watched her throw up countless times, had seen her semi-conscious *and* drenched in sweat. It was too much.

The sheet fell to Cord's flat belly and Emily found her eyes traveling down the length of him. He had a great stomach – not that she'd seen many. As embarrassing as it was to admit, James's anatomy was all she had for comparison.

Cord rubbed his chest and stretched, and for the life of her she couldn't tear her eyes away from the fascinating movement of muscle and skin. She had no idea what he looked like below the covers, but she bet it was equally impressive. Just the thought made her swallow, hard.

'Oh, wait,' Cord said into her silence. 'I read

somewhere that it's not politically correct to accuse a woman of sweating.' He smiled. 'You *perspired.*'

'I was sick,' she said weakly. 'People sweat when they're sick.'

'You're kind of cute when you're embarrassed,' he said, his smile widening to an insufferable grin. He touched her flaming cheeks softly.

'Oh, shut up.' Emily yanked the sheet up to her chin and forced her gaze from Cord's broad chest. She had the uncomfortable feeling he was enjoying her roaming eyes.

'You also dream a lot,' he said evenly.

Okay, she wouldn't panic. She strove for casual. 'So?'

'You know, Emily, you can trust me,' he said gently, turning on his side and reaching a hand across to touch her shoulder. 'I mean it. If there's something bothering you, you could tell me. You could tell me anything.'

What the hell had she said in her sleep?

'You talked about your parents,' he said quietly, with that strange knack he had for reading her mind. 'Talk to me, Em. Maybe I can help.'

'I don't need any help.' She definitely wasn't ready for that. Besides, it was his fault she was even thinking about her parents' tragic deaths in the first place. Okay, maybe that wasn't exactly fair, but she was still far from ready to share that experience with anyone. 'I know I asked you this before, but *why* are you in bed with me?'

'You were cold.'

'Uh-huh,' she said agreeably, pushing his hand away. 'And you decided to become my personal electric blanket.'

'Something like that.'

His dark blue eyes touched on the hands that clenched the sheet to her. They didn't hold disgust, or even concern, but something much more devastating – burning fire, passion and sheer longing. Something funny happened to her insides, just watching him watch her, leaving her warm and flushed with excitement.

For the first time in years she actually felt a tug of pure lust. She shifted uncomfortably, wondering if she could give in to it without losing anything more vital. Like her heart.

Nope. Not a chance. Not with this man.

'I'm not familiar with morning-after etiquette,' she ventured, making a move to leave the bed. 'But I imagine brushing my teeth would help.'

Cord grabbed her arm, smiling softly. 'What do you mean, "morning-after etiquette"?'

Was he going to make her spell it out for him? 'You know.'

He shook his head. 'I'm afraid I don't.'

She rolled her eyes and tried to look away, but he gently caught her jaw and forced her to look at him. 'Emily.'

'I've never – I mean, I haven't – ' She clamped her mouth shut before she could make a further fool of herself.

His fingers brushed her jaw while his eyes went

soft and tender. 'You've never slept with a man before?'

'Well, yes. I mean, no,' she corrected. She felt her skin flame again. Would she forever feel tongue-tied around this man? She sighed, loudly. 'I've never *slept* with anyone before. You know . . . really *sleep* . . . in a bed for the entire night.' James had never been interested in that.

He smile grew. 'So I'm your first.'

She purposely fueled her irritation. It helped keep her mental distance. 'You know,' she said, pulling her head back, 'it's pretty arrogant to be so damned amused.'

'I'm not amused,' he corrected quickly. He sat up and leaned a muscled arm on either side of her, lowering his lips to hers in a quick, soft caress. 'It's just that I'm incredibly touched.'

'Well,' she managed breathlessly, 'I guess it's a good thing you can't catch food poisoning, huh?'

He went utterly still. 'What?' he asked against her lips.

'I'd feel awful if you got sick because of me.'

He grabbed her shoulders and, so quickly her head spun, pulled her upright so they knelt on the bed facing each other. Her aching body protested the quick movement, but at the look on his face she swallowed her remark.

'*Food poisoning?*' he demanded. 'Not the flu?'

She stared at his tense face and hard, flashing eyes. 'That's what the doctor said. It was too volatile to be the flu – and I didn't get a fever.'

He muttered one, short expletive that told her exactly how upset he was. Then he surprised her again by yanking her into his arms and pressing his face in her hair. His hands molded her against him. 'Thank God,' he mumbled, but even with his mouth muffled against her hair she could hear the deep emotion. 'Thank God it wasn't worse.'

She tried to pull back. 'Cord?'

'What did you eat before you got sick?' he demanded, not letting her go. 'Who did you see?'

It was difficult to think with her face plastered against his hard chest, her hands trapped at their sides, his jeans scraping her. He hadn't completely stripped down and she knew instinctively that he'd slept all night uncomfortable – for her. It was oddly touching.

'I ate a lot of things,' she said when he pulled her away to look at her face. 'No, wait.' She stopped, thinking. 'I had nothing but the liquids you gave me yesterday. The day before I had only pizza – because I painted all day and I forgot – ' She stopped and gasped, his horrified expression sinking in. 'You think I was poisoned.'

CHAPTER 11

Cord nodded grimly as they stared at each other on the bed. 'Yeah. I think you were poisoned.'

Emily sat back on her heels, dizziness overwhelming her. 'But . . . why?' It was a stupid question, they both knew why.

'Tell me everything you ate and where it came from.'

Thankful he still held her shoulders, because she felt unsteady, Emily struggled to remember. 'Just pizza. From town. And – '

The phone rang, startling them both. Emily rose shakily, grabbed the phone and promptly sat – weakly – back on the bed. 'Hello?'

'Hey, Sis. How are you feeling?'

'Josh.' Her heart was still racing from Cord's announcement, her limbs still quivering from her illness. 'I'm . . .' She looked helplessly at Cord. 'I'm better.'

'I'm sorry,' he said, the long distance giving his voice a pingy sound. 'I just realized it's still early there. Did I wake you?'

She glanced at Cord as he stood and stretched, his muscles bunching and pulling in a way that had her mouth watering. 'No, you didn't wake me. Josh, you didn't get sick, did you?'

'Nope. Healthy as a horse. Hey, you sure everything's all right?'

She convinced Josh she was fine, hung up the phone and turned to Cord. His eyes roamed over her, reminding her that she was wearing nothing more than a thin white gown that was doing nothing to hide the fact she was suddenly cold.

He came to her and wrapped her robe around her, his hands lingering on her waist as he tied the belt. 'There's nothing I'd like more than to warm you up the old-fashioned way,' he said in a low, husky voice that told her he'd noticed her chill. He pulled her hair out of the collar of her robe by the fistful. 'But I want to take you back to the doctor and see if they can do a blood test to check for poison.'

She shivered, whether from the mention of poison or from the feel of his fingers on her neck, she didn't know. He brought her hands up to his lips, then kissed them softly. 'If it turns out you were purposely poisoned, I promise you, I'll find out who did it.'

Emily thought about the others who had been hurt, then her near miss on the mountain road, and knew he was thinking the same. It hurt to see such sorrow and guilt in his eyes. 'It isn't your fault.'

He squeezed her hands gently, then released her. 'We need to go. Can I use your shower?'

She waited for him in her kitchen, leaning against

the counter and staring down at her now lukewarm tea. Already showered and dressed, she felt completely wiped out. She didn't even have the energy to heat her tea. Every muscle still hurt, but the worst of it came from being as weak as a baby.

Even her mind hurt – from thinking too much.

It'd been easy to convince herself the danger wasn't real – until now. If it was true, if someone had tried to poison her, then she couldn't possibly attribute her blow-out to an accident. And either time she could have died.

Like her parents.

No, she corrected – not like them at all. Again the macabre image shimmered through her mind, as clear as a movie. The image she'd been denying for ten years. They'd left her, just as James had. Just as Josh would. At times like these, when she was feeling too vulnerable, the hurt seeped through her barricades.

And if she let herself care too much about Cord, he too would have that power to hurt her.

She couldn't allow it.

'Em? You okay?'

She turned quickly at the familiar sexy voice. Cord came into the kitchen, looking completely at ease in the small room. He was all too quickly becoming a part of her life – which was more terrifying than the prospect of someone trying to kill her.

She didn't think she could stand another loss.

'Em?' He moved close, gently drew her to him. 'You have that same horrified look on your face as you did after your nightmare.'

236

'It's the prospect of a blood test,' she said, pushing the other thoughts from her head. 'I hate needles.' But she clung to him – just for a minute.

He looked very sorry and very sympathetic. 'I'll hold your hand.'

Which, Emily thought as they drove, was even more dangerous. Because every minute she spent with Cord, every time he did something for her, the barrier around her heart lowered. Pretty soon she'd have no protection left against him. None at all.

Sunday night became tense. Cord insisted on staying with Emily because she still seemed so weak – and because they didn't have her blood test results back. He'd paged both Seth and Katherine. To their collective relief, Katherine had promised not to leave her school unless calling first. Seth had yet to return the call.

He didn't want to think what that could mean.

'Tell me again, and start from the beginning,' Cord demanded, leaning forward on the chair in her bedroom.

Emily sighed and, from where she lay on the bed, stared at the ceiling. She'd never felt so tired. 'I went all day without eating.'

'Why?' A quick glance at him told her he looked stern and uncompromising – the perfect picture of the interrogating officer. 'How could you go all day without feeding yourself?' he wanted to know.

'I told you,' she said quietly, wishing for the sweet oblivion of sleep. 'Sometimes I lose track of time.

When Raymond told me it was time to go, I was surprised at how late it was.'

'Emily,' he said, his eyes softening, 'you've got to take better care of yourself.'

She didn't want to think about why his concern reassured her – she was far too weary for that now. 'I was in a hurry then, and I ran outside. You know this because that's when you drove – ' She stopped abruptly.

He sat up straight in the car, frowning. 'I drove up and what?'

'And . . .' She hesitated, saw the exact moment it occurred to him.

'And I gave you candy, didn't I?' he said in a low, strangled voice. He shot up. 'Lord, Emily. You don't think –?'

'No.' She streaked out of bed, heedless of her aching body and her light nightgown, and gripped his tense hands in hers. She met his horrified gaze. 'No, Cord, I don't think you poisoned the watermelon candy.'

He turned his hands over so their palms faced each other, and entwined his fingers with hers. For an eternal minute he stared at their hands. 'That's good,' he said slowly. 'Because the thought of you believing otherwise makes me sick.'

She started to smile, but the effort seemed too much. If she had the energy, she'd crawl back into bed, but she couldn't manage even that.

Slowly, keeping his eyes on hers, he sat, then pulled her to his lap. 'You're cold.' And then he set about doing his best to remedy it. When his hands slipped around her waist she let herself sag against him, thankful for his warmth.

'Tell me the rest,' he said against her ear, his soft, warm breath tickling her skin.

'Uh . . . I – ' She stopped with a whispery sigh when he tugged at her earlobe with his teeth.

'Go ahead,' he murmured, his incredibly warm, sure hands rubbing circles along her spine. 'You . . .?'

Thinking became a chore. Between his caresses and her own exhaustion, she'd become languorous and incapable of movement. 'I . . . went for pizza with Josh.'

'Uh-huh.' One hand cupped her neck, tilting her head closer to his. 'Pizza.'

'Before I ate, Seth brought me an iced tea.' His hands brought her to that fuzzy line between being awake and asleep, and she slurred her words sleepily. 'I saw Margo . . . I guess being pretty and sophisticated is a requirement for working at HT Designs.'

Cord went completely still and she jerked fully awake. God, had she really called him pretty?

'I'm sorry,' she mumbled, sitting straight up in his lap and covering her face with her hands. 'I'm – '

'Emily.' Cord's rough hands brought her own hands down from her face, forcing her to look at him. 'Say that again.'

'No.'

She tried to rise, but he held her still. 'Please, Emily,' he said hoarsely. 'The thing about the tea. Say it again.'

'Seth brought me a tea,' she said slowly, blinking at the wrenching anguish on his face. 'Cord?'

'He brought you a tea,' he repeated. 'God, no.'

'Wait a minute,' Emily said, grabbing his shoulders. 'You think he . . .? No. You said yourself, Seth couldn't ever – '

'Who, then?'

'I don't know, but not Seth. He couldn't – anymore than you could.'

'Don't you think I want to believe that? But Sheriff Stone is going to have a field-day with this.' He closed his eyes. 'I've got to think.'

'Nothing makes any sense,' she said, climbing off Cord's lap, emotions riding over her as she watched Cord struggle with his own. 'And we don't even know for sure I was poisoned. It could have just been the flu.'

'Maybe.' He didn't look convinced.

'Let's wait and see. Okay?'

He looked at her. 'I'm not leaving your side.'

'Cord.'

'I mean it, Emily.' He turned away. 'My gut tells me Seth is innocent, but I can't take the chance. Not with you.'

She backed to the bed and, before her legs could give out, sat. 'I don't think you need to stay here.' She couldn't let him do that. Panic welled, because for her the danger came from losing her heart, not from the unknown stalker. 'I can take care of myself.'

'Of course you can,' he said easily, watching her carefully. 'And you're going to be fine. I just want to stay until we know the results.'

'I want to go to bed.' She crawled to the head of the bed, slipped under the covers. It was all she could do to pull another blanket over her, but she caught the look on his face. 'Alone.'

'Relax,' Cord told her. 'I don't ravish sick maidens.' He made a face of self-disgust. 'I'm going to call the sheriff and then I'm getting you something to eat.' And he stalked from the room.

But Emily didn't have the energy to worry about his mood; she was just too damned tired.

He brought her soup, and told her with some discouragement that the sheriff couldn't make a move until the doctor's report came in. She wasn't hungry, but he was watching her with a quiet intensity that made her nervous, so she ate. The food gave her some strength, allowing her defiance to peek out.

'You don't need to stay here,' she said, playing with the carrots floating in her vegetable soup.

He frowned, his eyes glinting. 'So you've said.'

'I'll be fine.'

He rose from the chair, took her bowl. With his back to her, he said quietly, 'I can't leave, Emily. I'm sorry if my company upsets you, but unless there's someone else you can call that I trust, you really don't have a choice.'

'Someone *you* trust?' She could feel her temper flaring at his none too subtle controlling tactic. She had been on her own too long to allow it. 'You don't *have* to stay. I can call the police if I want protection.'

He turned to her, his expression still tense and

241

angry. 'And tell them what? You heard what Sheriff Stone said when I called him. He needs the doctor's report before they'll do anything.' His voice softened. 'Em, it's better to be safe than sorry. Why are you fighting me on this?'

She didn't know. But the thought of him spending another night with her was unnerving. Maybe because she knew without a doubt that if she woke up in his arms again her body would betray her. She wanted him, damn it, and it was hard to accept. She, Emily McKay, the woman who didn't need anyone in her life except Joshua, needed him. Badly. It was reason enough to kick him out, slam and bolt the door and run for cover.

But looking at him now, seeing the hurt and anger on his face that she'd put there, was hard. All he had ever tried to do was help her, and all she'd ever done in return was complain and hurt his feelings.

She licked her lips, feeling hesitant. 'I never thanked you.'

He scowled. 'Forget it.'

'I can't.' She shrugged. 'Staying here when I was sick . . . it's the nicest thing anyone has ever done for me.'

He looked at her then – really looked. His anger drained and something akin to understanding filled his eyes. 'Good,' he said. He straightened those broad shoulders and came toward her. 'Get used to it because there's more where that came from.'

'That sounds like a command.' She was ridiculously touched in spite of herself. It had been a very long time since someone had looked out for her – since anyone had even wanted to.

'Emily.' He laughed softly. The bed shifted and creaked when he lowered his weight down to sit next to her. 'I wouldn't dare try to command you. You don't take it so well.' He cupped the nape of her neck in one strong, warm hand, drawing her close. 'We'll work this all out yet, Red. You'll see.'

'Cord – '

'Look, you wanted to thank me. You can do that by letting me care about you. Stop fighting me. Stop fighting this.'

He lowered his mouth to hers, fisting one hand in her hair and holding her head steady. With sweet torment he kissed away her resistance, and when she heard a soft moan she was startled to realize it was her own.

They kissed until she couldn't remember exactly why she was fighting him, fighting this. It was too strong for her. Besides, she wanted and needed it. She deserved it. A little immediate gratification never hurt anyone, she thought, and pulled him closer.

He reacted immediately, pulling her across him so that her bottom settled against his lap. She could feel the hardness of him beneath her, could feel the heat of it even with his jeans and her nightgown between them. He made a soft, rough sound of need and she slid herself over him, just to hear him make it again.

She could give him this. She could give him this part of herself and still keep her heart safe. And separate.

Couldn't she?

The answer was a big, fat, resounding no. When her knees wobbled and her blood raced desperately, she knew she couldn't. This wasn't something she could continue and still control. She unwound her arms from where they'd been clinging around his neck and pushed at his chest.

Cord pulled back slowly, reluctantly, his breathing uneven, opening his glazed eyes on hers.

'I – I'd like to go to bed. Now,' she added shakily.

His gaze cleared and he grimaced. 'I take it that's not an invitation.'

Emily raised an unsteady hand to her head, where a dull ache had started. 'I'm not ready for this, Cord. I'm sorry. It's just too fast. Way too fast. I know it sounds silly and a cliché, but . . . I just want to be friends.'

Though his voice was thick and gravelly, he dropped his arms and his sexy mouth curved in a warm smile. 'Emily, I don't want to rush you. But you've got to give me a minute after a kiss like that.' She moved over and he ran his hands through his thick hair. 'We've known each other a month. We've become good friends, or at least I'd like to think so.'

Relief filled her. 'Yes.' That's all, she promised herself. More would kill her. Hell, another kiss like the last one and she'd explode.

His eyes bored into her as he took her shoulders. 'Then accept this. I'm staying – on the couch if you want. I just don't want to leave you alone. Not yet. Not until – '

'You can't always protect me.' Though, she had to admit, the thought wasn't as awful as she would have believed.

His face had a hard, determined look that scared her. His hands slipped down her arms to hers. 'You're freezing.' He lifted them to his lips, rubbing them gently over her skin. Then, his blue eyes holding hers, he blew on them softly, causing a tingling from deep within her.

'I'm not cold. I'm scared.' She pulled her hands from his and turned away.

'Nothing else is going to happen to you.'

He sounded so sure, though what she was afraid of wasn't the sort of thing that went bump in the night – what she was scared of sat next to her. 'I'm afraid of you,' she admitted softly. 'I'm afraid of what you make me feel.' She laughed once, turning away. 'Isn't that funny? I've never been afraid of anything or anyone before. But I am now.'

She felt his fingers on her jaw. Felt them turn her gently toward him.

'It's not funny,' he agreed. 'I should know – you scare me too.'

'Me? Why?'

He cupped her face with his large hands, his thumbs tracing her lower lip until she ached for another kiss. But instead of answering he said, 'You're so tired a small breeze could blow you over. Come on.'

She let him help her back under the covers, watched as he flipped off the light. Her eyes drifted closed, not even opening when he leaned over her and kissed her full on the mouth.

'Goodnight,' he whispered. 'I'll be here.'

For a time she could hear him pattering about in the living room. He hadn't tried to persuade her to let him stay in her bed. She wasn't sure if she was relieved or disappointed.

Blood everywhere. Screams, high-pitched and screeching, rent the air.

They were her own, but Emily couldn't stop.

'No!' She collapsed in a heap at her parents' feet, closing her eyes against the broken, bleeding bodies. 'Don't die. Not because of me! You can't!'

Hands tried to pull her away from them, but she fought back, opening her eyes, gasping and drenched in sweat.

Cord's face was the first thing she focused on.

'Another dream?'

She nodded and he moved from the doorway to the bed, holding her wide-eyed stare. Her thoughts scrambled at the sight of him. Hair disheveled, wearing nothing but jeans. Hard, smooth chest glimmering in the faint light from the hallway. Skin stretched tight over sinew and bone. Eyes dark with concern – for her.

He was easily the sexiest man she'd ever known.

He didn't sit, nor touch her, and Emily thought it was almost as if he didn't trust himself to. But suddenly there was nothing she wanted or needed more than to be held. The remnants of the nastiest

246

nightmare yet had left her cold and shivery. She shifted over and lifted the covers.

Cord's eyes dropped from hers to the invitingly turned down blanket, to the long, bare length of thigh she was exposing and back up to her face. He didn't say a word.

'Please?' she whispered. 'I – I want to be held. I want you to hold me.'

He slipped wordlessly in beside her and turned, taking her in his warm, long arms. Emily sighed and pressed closer, closing her eyes and leaning her face against his bare chest. He smelled heavenly. Gradually her heart rate changed tempo from wildly racing to merely thundering. Beneath her ear, Cord's own heart thudded steadily. It was settling, soothing.

'Emily,' he said in a low voice. 'Tell me what happened to you that you have such nightmares.'

In a movement she recognized as childish, she buried her face deeper against him.

'Em,' he said softly, stroking her back. 'It's okay now. I'm here. Tell me.'

'I haven't had them in so long. Not since . . .'

'Since what?'

'Since my parents' deaths.'

'You were calling for them in your sleep.' She felt him kiss her temple, her hair. 'How did they die?'

Emily's eyes slammed shut, but she knew it was time, past time, to share it with someone. With Cord. 'My parents were great. They loved us, wanted the best for us, even though times were hard. My mother was a seamstress, my father a tool and dye maker.'

She smiled fondly. 'He loved craft, though even then computers and machinery were making his work a thing of the past. Work was hard to come by.' Yet he'd always remained positive.

'They encouraged Josh and I to be the best we could be, convinced us we could do anything we wanted. And, even though we never had enough money, they wanted me to go to university to study art.'

'Did you want to?' Cord asked, stroking her hair in the dark room.

'Oh, yes,' she breathed. 'Very, very much. But it was so expensive. I intended to go to a local, inexpensive college but my dream was Stanford. There was no way we could afford it, but I applied anyway. And I got accepted.' She smiled bitterly, remembering. 'I wanted to go so badly that I forgot how we couldn't afford it. God, it seems so selfish now.'

'Wanting the best for yourself isn't selfish,' Cord said quietly.

Desperately she wanted to believe him. But remembering that part of her life was hard, so very hard. 'I knew we didn't have the money to go.'

'Did you get a scholarship?' Cord asked.

His voice was low and steady, his skin warm against hers. She couldn't see his expression, it was too dark, but she could feel the concern in his hands as they skimmed over her, and there in the dark she clung to him. For the first time she wasn't alone with the horror, and, while it didn't fade away completely, the companionship made it slightly easier.

'Yeah, I got a scholarship.' She could taste the

bitter disgust. 'And I left as soon as I could. I got caught up in it, in the whole thing, and I didn't get home for Thanksgiving.' Her breath hitched, and she could hear the strain and breathiness in her voice, but couldn't control it. 'So Mom and Dad decided to come see me. They missed me, Josh told me.'

Whether he sensed the tears threatening, or maybe just reacted to what she'd said, she didn't know, but he tightened his arms. What surprised her was that she could take his comfort at all. 'So they got into the car and drove – just like that.' She swallowed hard. 'They missed me – and that was all that mattered to them, even though their selfish daughter hadn't bothered to call or visit.'

Emily gulped in air, then let it out slowly through her teeth. Though he hadn't moved or made a sound, Emily realized her fingers were digging painfully into Cord's shoulders.

'Em?' His fingers squeezed her waist gently. 'What happened?'

'They . . . never made it. A drunk driver hit them head-on, going fifty-five miles an hour. It was all over in a blink of an eye.'

'Lord.' His arms tightened and he pressed her face against his neck. 'Oh, Em, I'm so sorry.'

'Dead,' she went on dully, not acknowledging his soft words of sympathy. 'Because of me.'

'Wait a minute.' She felt Cord lift his head, searching for her face in the dark. 'Wait – not because of you, Emily. You don't blame yourself for that?'

She turned her head away.

'You do,' he breathed. 'God, Emily, it wasn't your fault. It was the fault of the stupid drunk driver.'

'No,' she whispered. 'If I had come home sooner, or called more, or – '

'Bullshit.'

'I killed them,' she choked out.

Cord swiftly rose up and over her, capturing her head between his large hands. 'No, you didn't. Don't do this to yourself.'

'But they're gone.'

'Josh survived.'

'Without a scratch. Stroke of luck, the doctor said.' She took another deep breath. 'Whew,' she said, letting out the air slowly. 'Nice bedtime story, huh?' She tried to turn away, embarrassed at her show of emotion, but he held tight.

'What happened afterward?'

She shrugged. 'We were alone.'

'Wasn't there anyone to help you? No other relatives? No close friends of the family?'

'There was James,' she said wryly.

His muttered curse let her know exactly what he thought of that. 'There was no one else? God, you must have been so scared and alone.' He sounded angry and she realized it was for her. He was angry *for* her.

No, there had been no one else. No one who had wanted to hold and love and comfort the terrified and guilt-ridden girl forced into womanhood too early.

No one but Josh, and he had been a child – a child who had desperately needed *her*. The few people that she'd trusted in her life – James and a handful of friends – had quickly disappeared. And there had been no one since.

'We were alone,' she said quietly. 'There was no one to take care of us. No one who really cared all that much. So I took care of both of us.'

Cord fell silent, and Emily was forcibly reminded about something Josh had once said. '*We have only fair-weather friends, Emily. Even after you think you know someone, they'll disappear when the going gets rough.*' Cord would too, she thought. It was all a matter of time.

And she was wrapped around the man in her bed as if she planned to stay there the rest of her life. The familiar distrust took over and she struggled to disentangle herself.

Cord wasn't having it. 'Let me go,' she whispered furiously, shoving at his broad chest.

Cord sighed, easily captured her flailing legs between his powerful thighs, then sank his fingers in her hair to tip her head up. 'You know why you're having the dreams again, after all this time. Don't you?'

Of course she did, but instead of answering she closed her eyes.

Cord Harrison was a patient man. 'You do know.'

'I don't want to talk about it.'

'You're having the dreams now because after all this time there's someone in your life besides Josh that you care about.' He shook her gently. 'You care about *me* and it's scaring you to death.'

Emily opened her eyes. 'I already told you I was scared, no need to rub it in. Please. Go away.'

'You don't have to be alone anymore, Em.' The tenderness in his hands, in the rough scrape of his voice made her eyes burn and her throat clog. 'You have me,' he said. 'And I care about you too, very much.'

She shook her head in denial, as much as his hands would allow. 'No. I don't want you to. And I *never* said I cared about you.'

He smiled, a bittersweet smile that tore at her heart, and rested his chin on her head as he loosened his grip to hold her gently. 'It's too late, sweetheart. The damage is done. We both care.' A short laugh puffed against her hair. 'And for what it's worth, I've been fighting it as hard as you. I didn't want any complications, and what's between us certainly qualifies as that. I can't say I've ever been attracted to someone I worked with before.'

'You mean one of your laborers.'

'I mean,' he corrected mildly, 'a beautiful artist with the temperament to match – '

'I'm not beautiful.'

He flipped on her bedside lamp, casting them in a soft gold glow. His eyes, hot with longing and something else she couldn't name, roamed over her, warming her every place they touched and in places they didn't. 'Yes, you are beautiful,' he told her. His hands skimmed over her, eliciting responses

252

she didn't know she had. 'And that body . . . it should be a sin to cover it in those overalls of yours.'

She didn't want to think about why his words were so very thrilling. 'I'm short.'

He smiled. 'Petite, Red, not short. And I like it. I like you.'

'I'm a grouch.'

His grin widened. 'Moody, prickly. A little grumpy, maybe. Stubborn as hell, too.' He kissed each eyelid. 'But those eyes, Red. They tell your secrets. They tell me what you're really feeling.' He kissed her flaming cheek. 'And you're so cute when you're embarrassed.'

'Don't. I'm not cute.'

'And sweet.' He licked the tip of her nose. 'Mmm. Definitely sweet.'

She covered her face with her hands, mortified that she'd been fishing for more compliments and that she'd gotten them. She'd never –

He peeled her hands away and held them against his chest, his easy grin gone. 'I think that you are an amazing woman, Emily. You were forced into a position where you had to be strong and in control for your brother, and you did it without a thought of yourself or a backward glance. I don't know very many people who could have handled all that you did. And no one who could have survived it to become the incredible woman you've become.'

She looked away, but he brought her face back around. 'What I'm saying is that I've never been

253

attracted to that because I never met anyone like you before.'

It was hard to think, surrounded by him as she was. His steady heartbeat had picked up considerably beneath her hands. 'I thought you weren't up for any complications.'

He flashed a very wicked grin. 'Oh, I'm *up* for it all right.' He grimaced and shifted, leaving her in no doubt just how 'up' he was.

She was suddenly warm from the inside out, only this time it wasn't from her illness. She looked at him in the soft light and held her breath. He was so remarkably attractive, with his soulful eyes and rough hands working magic on her body. Their bare feet intermingled, sharing the heat. It would take no effort to give in to this. A flutter worked inside her belly. Cord Harrison was turning her on – big time – and it wasn't easy to accept or rationalize.

But Cord dipped down and kissed her then, leaving little room for more thought, much less rationale. Another flutter, this time from deep within. Long, hot and wet, the kiss went on and the flutters inside Emily intensified wildly. Cord caught her up closer against him and the contact made her melt further into the kiss, into him. He was so large and strong and hard, and he felt so good under her restless hands, against her body. With trembling hands she reached for him, fumbling uncertainly, drowning in the whirling emotions he evoked.

She could lose herself in these feelings. She could lose herself in him. She heard her own groan of pleasure when his tongue stroked hers in tune with his hands stroking her sides, her back, her thighs, and her own hands moved restlessly over his taut back and shoulders. She grew hot and cold, shivery and sweaty, as needs welled up from deep within – needs she hadn't even known she had.

She became dizzy with passion, impatient for his touch, and felt as though they floated above the bed. When his hands slid around and up her ribcage her back arched and she writhed beneath him, waiting for his touch. Needing his touch. 'Cord.' God, was that husky voice hers?

He dipped his head, planting kisses along her throat, feeding the desire that grew within her. 'Shh,' he murmured, running his open mouth down her neck, letting his rough, clever hands and heaving breath speak for him.

Arousal clouded her thoughts, tripled her pulse. When his fingers cupped her breast through the cotton of her gown, and his tongue flickered over the pebbled point, she let out a little cry that was part panic, part desire. 'Wait!' she cried, pulling back. She nearly let out a hysterical laugh when he lifted his head and gazed at her, his eyes half-wild. 'I – I . . . uh . . .' She paused, raking her teeth along her lip.

His gaze cleared quickly. 'Em?' He cupped her face. 'What's the matter?'

'It's been a . . . long time,' she said breathlessly, closing her eyes on the humiliation.

He stroked her jaw with a soft touch that had her

leaning into him. 'That's okay, we're doing just fine.'

'I think . . . I forgot how.'

'We'll make it up as we go along,' he promised, one hand moving down over her to cup her breast, his fingers stroking, teasing, tormenting. His gaze dropped to watch his own fingers move over her. He slid a thigh between hers, and slowly raised the hem of her gown.

His questing fingers got to her mid-thigh and her breath rasped as if she'd climbed a mountain. When he played with the edge of her panties, she bit her lip to keep from begging him to hurry. He didn't, but slid his fingers under them with a slow languor that had her lifting her hips without realizing it. He stroked her with a knowing finger and she grasped the sheets with clenched fists, crying out when he dipped into her.

'God, Em,' he moaned. 'You're ready for me, baby, so ready.'

He took her mouth again, his tongue and fingers moving together inside her with a slow, sure motion that had her writhing and bucking desperately beneath him in a hot, urgent need. She gasped in surprise and panic when her body tightened, trembled, then exploded. She sank back, limp, but he continued to touch her, patiently, quietly, with a sureness that had her unbelievably panting with desire and need again, far before she thought it could be possible.

She tried to pull him over her then, but he whispered gently, 'Not yet.' He pushed her back, those magic hands of his skimming over her, back to the source of her heat to start over. Her last coherent thought was that she'd never had anyone touch her there like that, with that light but deliberate movement that had her moaning unintelligible words of encouragement. Each time she climaxed he calmly and lovingly soothed her, touched her, and drove her back up again before she could catch her breath.

Finally, while she still trembled from his last assault on her senses, he pulled himself up to straddle her, looking down at her with a searing gaze that stole her breath. Through his jeans, his erection nudged at her still pulsing heat. He took her hands in his and curled them around him, jerking beneath her fingers. She wanted him, wanted him with a desperation she'd never felt, but even as she thought that reality encroached on the fuzzy edges of her vision.

What the hell did she think she was doing? She'd get hurt. Again. She sighed, tensed, and let her fingers fall from him.

Cord's hands stilled on her instantly. Silently he studied her stiff body, his own breathing still ragged. One long finger smoothed over her cheek while within his eyes she could see the struggle to bank the fire she'd created. 'Cord – '

He shook his head. Without a word, he rose from the bed and left the room, shutting the door softly behind him.

CHAPTER 12

Without a thought of modesty, Emily kicked off the covers and dashed to the door after Cord, yanking it open. He turned, his eyes carefully blank.

'What – where are you going?' she asked breathlessly, her mouth still wet from his kisses, her body aching.

He drew an uneven breath, shoved his hands in his pockets. 'To the couch.'

'Don't be mad at me,' she whispered, voicing her greatest fear.

He made a sound. 'I'm not,' he said. 'I promise, I'm not. His mouth curved slightly, though his eyes remained solemn. 'I told you once I'd never ask you to do something you don't want. You don't want this, Red, not really. And no matter how much I do, it's no good for me if you don't trust me.'

It didn't make it any less disturbing to know that at that moment she could easily have thrown herself down at his feet and begged for more. 'You're . . . leaving?'

'No. I'll be here if you need me.' He turned and went to the living room, leaving Emily staring after him, needing him so desperately that it hurt but unable to do anything about it.

Which only told her how unprepared for this she was, she thought wearily as she climbed back into the bed. The sheets were still warm from their shared body heat, and she could smell Cord's wonderful, utterly masculine scent.

She'd let him touch her, let him do things to her, for her, that she'd never done before. Then, without returning any of it, she'd turned him away. She closed her eyes on the overwhelming humiliation.

God help her, but she wanted him. Yet it was one thing to think these things about someone, it was another entirely to admit it to them.

The bottom line was, she wasn't ready – and didn't think she ever would be.

Emily insisted on working Monday and, short of brute force, Cord couldn't stop her. But he could forgo the office to keep an eye on her.

He followed her up the mountain, the drive long enough that he could roll down his window and try to use the gorgeous weather to clear his head. He slid sunglasses over his eyes to shade them from the painfully brilliant blue sky, then shifted uncomfortably. The sky wasn't the only thing painful this morning, but he had only himself to blame.

He'd kept his promise to himself, and, as difficult as it'd been, he'd remained on the couch the rest of the night, a room away from the only woman ever to drive him crazy.

God, he wanted her.

To keep his mind off the amazing, irritating woman in front of him, he pulled out his phone and dialed Seth, relieved to catch him at the office. There were no casual banalities.

'Hell's teeth, Cord. I've been paging you all morning.'

'Why didn't you call me back last night?'

'Stone paid me a little visit this morning, Cord. So I can understand why you're mad. Is she okay?'

'Where were you?'

Seth sighed. 'I had planned on bragging about my latest conquest, but now it doesn't seem so appropriate. Let's just say I was indisposed and leave it at that. Now tell me how she is.'

He thought of how Emily's hands had trembled at breakfast, how pale she still looked, how her eyes reflected her growing fear. 'She's better. Seth – '

'I didn't do it, Cord.'

'I know.' Cord let out a heavy breath. Cord was well aware that if he was wrong, his loyalty for his longtime friend had put Emily in danger. He *couldn't* be wrong. 'But somebody is trying to set you up, buddy.' He slammed a hand on the steering wheel. 'Who?'

'I wish I knew.'

'What did Stone say to you?'

It was Seth's turn to take a deep breath. 'They can't charge me without lab reports. They don't have them yet.'

Another call came in on Cord's line. 'Hang tight, Seth. I'll get back to you.'

The other call was Katherine, her voice high and nervous. 'Cord, any word yet?'

'None. Are you being careful?'

'As promised. I guess it's a mixed blessing that this school is so far out of the way. I have nowhere to go unless I want to go all the way into town, which I don't.'

'I'm hoping this will be over soon, Katherine,' Cord told her, trying to soothe the nerves she wouldn't admit to, but that he could tell plagued her. 'Stone seems sure it will be. He thinks the guy is getting scared, and scared means sloppy. He'll make another move and he'll get caught.'

'Just stay safe,' she whispered, letting her fear show. 'Keep safe.'

'I will.' It wasn't himself he worried about.

'Are . . . are you with Emily?'

He had to smile at the not-so-subtle mothering tones. 'I'm on my way home now. I'll be there all week.'

'Okay, dear. Is she better now?'

'Much.'

'Well, maybe she'd be interested in painting that mural for me. Say, this weekend?'

'I'll ask her.' He pulled in his driveway right behind Emily and said goodbye.

The flooring crew had already arrived, as well as the plumber he'd hired. Cord got out and stopped to look at his house, feeling the familiar burst of satisfaction. It was a long way from finished, but pride of ownership had him beaming anyway.

Emily's frown surprised him. 'That's strange,' he heard her mutter as he came up beside her.

'What's strange?'

'That top window – the one in the attic,' she said, pointing. 'See it?'

Part of her job had been to paint over one hundred removable wooden window grids that graced the large house. The one she referred to was small, round, and absolutely the perfect touch to accent the roofline. It was also the only grid that wasn't painted. 'Looks like you missed something,' he teased.

Her frown deepened, reminding him of how distant she'd been all morning. 'I never miss anything. I *know* I painted that. Damn.' She shook her head, muttered some more, tossed her braid over her shoulder and started toward the house.

'Emily.' He knew what she was going to do, and if she hadn't still seemed so pale and frail from her illness he might have let it go. 'Don't climb all the way up there. It can wait.' He didn't bother to add that it required four flights of stairs, then a dangerous walk balancing across the attic ceiling joists.

'Cord.' She stopped and turned in exasperation. 'I have a job to do, please let me do it.'

She'd been politely civil since he'd walked out of her bedroom the night before, and he wasn't sure how to bridge the gap. Wasn't sure if it was even possible. 'Fine. Start with the den, like you'd planned, and I'll remove the casing and bring it to you to paint.'

She agreed so easily that he was left staring at the dust her boots kicked up as she entered the house ahead of him. Either she was weaker than he'd thought or she was trying hard to compromise.

All he knew was that he couldn't let her make the treacherous walk across an open-beamed attic while she was not one hundred percent. Hell, he thought as he climbed the stairs, *he* didn't wanted to make this walk. He could ask one of the guys to do it and that would be the end of it. But he didn't.

He hesitated on the small, floored area in the attic. He stood on the edge of an expanse of loose, fluffy white insulation material that covered the joists and lay between him and the attic window. It looked like a vast expanse of cloudy sky. Never a man to waste time on regrets, he started the tenuous, cautious walk over the joists to the window.

But that didn't mean he couldn't grumble. And it wasn't the precarious position he found himself in that made him do it. It was Emily herself. Despite their amazing chemistry and deepening friendship, she didn't want a relationship with him. No, scratch that – she was *terrified* of having a relationship with him.

He thought he understood why. Her fear of losing the people she loved had left a mark on the fiery, talented, sensitive woman he cared so much for. Even Josh was going to leave her eventually, and he had every right, but it would hurt Emily just the same because she thought he was all she had left. She needed someone else in her life, and he intended to be that person, but he didn't think she would see it that way.

Emily McKay was one beautiful but stubborn woman. Strangely enough, her dig-in-her-heels attitude was one of the things that attracted him. That, too, was new – a woman who didn't need him to protect, cherish and pamper.

The change was welcome only because he genuinely liked Emily exactly as she was, no matter how much she seemed to believe otherwise. What worried him was that he was beginning to think not of having time off to be alone, but of time off to be with Emily. Permanently.

The thought scared him enough that he nearly missed his step. He broke out in a light sweat, not knowing if it was from the impending relationship or his fear of heights. Definitely his fear of heights, he thought as he glanced down through the white puffy insulation. It was a long way to fall to the floor below him. The hammering and sawing of the workers far below drifted up. It was a pleasant sound that meant things were getting done.

It was also a sickening reminder of how high up he was. He felt sweat pool at the base of his spine.

He stepped cautiously closer to the window, ignoring his hammering heart and the fact that all he could see out the window were the tops of pine trees.

Pine trees were very, very tall, and at this moment he was far too high above them for comfort. Quickly he reached out, resisting the urge to close his eyes, removed the window grid and then turned to make the long walk back.

He hadn't taken a step when the ominous crack of wood giving sounded beneath his foot. Before he could register surprise, the wood sank several inches beneath him. He nearly lost his balance as he clung to the grid. He carefully shifted his weight, preparing to leap to the next beam, but it was too late.

He plunged through the insulation, between the joists, through the hard, brittle plaster ceiling underneath, then on through to the floor far below.

CHAPTER 13

Cord fell through the ceiling hard. The landing was even harder. The noise was incredible. For a minute he simply lay there, stunned, while plaster continued to rain down heavily around him.

He'd actually missed his step and fallen like a novice. Hell. It was unbelievable. Dumbfounding. He started to remember something else, something about the sound he'd heard as he fell, but his head hurt and the heavy sound of feet on the steps side-tracked him.

The door to the room was flung open. Raymond stood there panting, as if he'd run up all three flights, staring at him. Two of the other crew members pushed their way past, all breathing heavily. Each stared at him as he lay sprawled flat, in his greatest moment of mortification.

Cord sat up slowly, gingerly, covered in white puffy insulation that stuck to his hair and clothes. It clung to the stubble on his face – he hadn't shaved at Emily's because he hadn't a razor. He imagined he looked like a dark-haired Santa. Pieces of broken plaster surrounded him like snow. Raymond picked insulation out of his hair, clicking his tongue, while Cord took stock of his injuries. Relieved to find that they were limited to badly bruised legs and a shattered ego, he sighed. And waited in painful silence.

He expected snickers, maybe a snide remark or a joke, but no one spoke. He couldn't imagine what they were going to say, but his misery must have been apparent, even through the layers of insulation, because no one even muttered.

Then Raymond started to chuckle. Which gave way to peals of laughter that everyone else joined, including Cord. When you took a dive through an expensive ceiling in an expensive house, the reaction was either laughing or crying.

Laughing was better.

Then he realized. Not all of the plaster surrounding him was white. Much of it was blue, yellow, orange – and his stomach clenched.

With dread icing his veins, he looked up, then wished he hadn't. Jagged pieces of plaster hung from the huge, gaping hole in the ceiling while insulation still fell from the attic like lazy snowflakes.

Emily's mural was destroyed.

He must have made a sound. In unison every head tipped up to study the demolished ceiling, then back to Cord. The laughter died.

'Well, hell,' Raymond said, scratching his head.

Cord couldn't have said it better himself.

Everyone flinched as a huge chunk of plaster crashed down, three inches from Cord. It was part of a cloud with a beautiful angel's face peering over the edge. She still smiled sweetly.

It began to sink into his befuddled head. The mural he loved, the one that meant so much because Emily had painted it for him, was gone. In order to fix the enormous hole, the entire ceiling would have to be redone. That would require removing what little remained of Emily's painting.

How the hell could he tell her?

They heard footsteps pounding up the stairs and Cord held his breath.

'What was that crash?' Emily pushed her way into the room, saw Cord and gasped. She glanced around, as if looking for the source of the crash, before looking up. When she did, Cord cringed at the look on her face.

She took an involuntary step back, her eyes widening, and swallowed hard. Her eyes darted back to him and his condition, then back up again. She shook her head and covered her mouth with her hand.

Raymond cleared his throat, and in less than three seconds the men were gone, leaving just Emily and Cord.

He struggled to stand. His legs were beginning to feel pain. Dust flew off him, got caught in the sunlight streaming through the windows, giving the room a hazy, surreal feeling. 'Emily. God, I'm so sorry. I – '

She held up a hand, her eyes bright. 'You fell. Are you all right?'

He stepped toward her, brushing more dust off him, wanting to comfort. 'I'm okay. But – '

'Good, then.' She took another step. 'I'm glad you're not hurt.' She backed to the door, not looking up again. 'I've – I've got to go.' She turned, stumbled.

He caught up with her and turned her to face him. 'Emily, please wait. Your painting – '

She shrugged free with amazing strength. 'Don't worry about it.' She touched a finger to his lip. 'You're bleeding.'

He brought his hand up to his lip, looked at the bright red spot of blood in surprise. 'I must have bitten my lip.' All he could taste was plaster, insulation. He tried to pull her back to him, but she backed out of his way. Her eyes shimmered with devastation, disappointment. He'd put that look there and he could feel her pain as if it were his, but he didn't know how to reach her. 'Tell me what I can do,' he whispered, wanting to hold her. 'I'm so sorry.'

'You're covered in plaster and paint.'

'Emily, please.'

She shrugged, her face colorless. 'It's done.'

God, he'd never felt so helpless in his entire life. 'Emily – '

'No,' she whispered, violently shaking her head. 'Don't say anything else; you'll make it worse.' And she turned to leave again.

He grabbed for her, though his legs were two sticks of fire now. Nearly missing, he knocked them both against the door. 'Damn it,' he gasped, but she used his pain to her advantage and ran. He caught her on the third step and, gritting his teeth, held her tight.

Still fighting him, she opened her mouth, and because he was afraid she was going to start screaming, he clamped a hand over it.

Fury filled her face and she struggled anew. It became difficult to hold her because his entire body was aching, but he was afraid to let go. If he did, she'd leave, and then she might be in danger. 'I can't let you go,' he told her quickly. 'You know that.'

She struggled wordlessly, her face twisted. He dragged her back into the room, shut the door. The minute he let her go she straightened and said calmly, 'I want to leave.'

'Emily.' He shook her once, gently, until she looked at him. Twin pools of sea-green stared mistily at him. 'You're mad – furious, even. And you have every right to be. God, you do, and I know it. But I can't let you leave. I'm afraid something will happen to you.'

She clamped her mouth shut tight and whirled from him. There was silence while she looked out the window at the ridiculously bright and sunny morning.

He expected temper, was prepared for it, even, so that when the sudden torrent of tears came he was stunned. Sobs shook her shoulders, racked her body, and he was completely unmanned. Every shuddering cry she made ripped at his heart and there was nothing he could do or say to make her feel better. He had thought he couldn't feel more helpless, but he'd been wrong. Very wrong.

'I'm so sorry,' he whispered, his voice hoarse.

There'd been very few female tears in his life, leaving him at a loss as to how to deal with them. 'God, Em, don't cry. Please, don't cry.' He touched her, touched her shoulders, her hair, pulled her back against him, trying to soothe. Was there anything more humbling than causing a strong woman to cry? 'I'm so sorry, Em. Really I am. I didn't mean to destroy your painting.' She cried quietly and he turned her in his arms, holding her close. He was surprised she let him. For long minutes he simply held her, hating himself.

'It's just the stupid painting,' she said eventually. She hiccuped against his chest while her words had his heart slipping heavily to the floor at his feet. Her hands were balled at her sides, her face hidden against him. 'I – I loved it beyond reason.'

'I did too.'

She stiffened. 'Don't, Cord. Don't lie. It's insulting.'

While he was relieved that her voice sounded calmer, her words didn't make sense. 'I didn't lie. The mural was beautiful – I've never seen anything like it.'

Sniffling, she moved away from him and swiped at her eyes. 'Right. Look, I'm going . . . for supplies.' She opened the door. 'Be back later.'

He reached around her and shut the door before she could get out. Slowly she turned, her wet red eyes flashing temper. 'Look,' she said carefully, 'I've just noticed something about you. You give orders and I don't like it. Now you've stopped me for the last time. I'm leaving here or I'll start screaming. Got it?'

'Yeah, I get it,' he said softly, not making a move toward her. He was a quick study. When faced with Emily's temper, it was best to back off and let it wind down. 'I just want to say something. Your mural *was* special. It *was* a masterpiece. I already told you that, but I figure with what you've been through lately you deserve a little slack, so I'll tell you again. I loved every single stroke of color on that ceiling because it was beautiful, it was amazing, and most of all because it had been painted by you. For me. It was irreplaceable, and with one careless step I ruined it. I can't get it back nor can I apologize enough, but I can promise you that I have the bruises to pay for it.'

Her eyes didn't leave his face. 'You *never* told me.'

He wanted to finish this conversation because it was very important to make her understand. But if he didn't sit down his screaming legs were going to give, and he'd be humiliated for the second time in an hour. He leaned against the window casing with a barely muffled sigh. 'Yes, I did tell you. When you were sick.'

She shook her head. 'I would definitely have remembered.' She blushed and closed her eyes. 'When I think of how much I wanted to hear what you thought of it and how I couldn't ask – '

'Silly, stubborn woman.' Slowly, testing his ground, he put his hands on her hips. He pulled her closer until she stood nestled between his thighs. 'God, Em, don't you get it yet? I don't want it to be awkward between us. I don't want you to fight us every step of the way. I want you to be able to say anything, ask anything. Even if all we are is friends, I want you to be that comfortable.'

Her hands fell to his legs and her head dropped between her shoulders. Lightly, he kissed the top of her head, and, when her hands squeezed his thighs, skimmed his lips to her temple. Just that small touch sent his senses reeling.

He nudged closer to kiss her jaw, fully intending to work his way to those luscious lips of hers. She was all he could think about, all he wanted. And though what she said next doused the fire within him somewhat, it endeared her to him forever.

'You are my only true friend, Cord,' she whispered. She bit her lip and let out a loud gust of air. 'God.'

He smiled and touched her chin, absurdly touched. He understood that, to Emily, the statement was tantamount to an admission of how much she cared. 'Did that hurt to admit?'

Her shy returning smile lit his heart. 'Not too much.'

'Good.' He cupped her face and did what he'd been dying to do. He kissed her.

'Cord.' She put a hand on his chest and lifted her face. He got more than a little satisfaction from her uneven breathing. 'Friends don't kiss like this.'

'Yes, they do.' Okay, he was reaching here. But he was only a man, and a very aroused one. 'We do.'

That lovely mouth curved. 'I have work.' She

moved from him and opened the door. 'I really do have to get some supplies.'

'Did you hear from the doctor yet?'

'No.'

'Then I'll drive you.'

She sighed and looked at him. 'Raymond will go; you're busy.'

'I'm not.'

'Okay, then, but you're filthy.' She gave him a pointed look.

'You're still upset.'

She shrugged, then nodded slowly. 'I'd be lying if I said I wasn't.' She glanced sadly up at the destroyed mural. 'I put a little of myself into each painting. I fall a little in love with every single one. It's painful enough to let go when I'm finished, even more painful when I know I'll never see one of them again. But this one . . . this one was different. I think it was my favorite.' Still looking up at the wrecked ceiling, she sighed. 'But I'm not an unreasonable woman, Cord. It obviously was an accident.'

'Still mad?'

Her lips quirked upward. 'Not anymore.'

'So let me take you to the store.'

She studied him thoughtfully. 'You're not a nineties kind of guy, are you?'

'I – What does that mean?'

She leaned on the door with her hands deep in her pockets and continued to stare at him bemusedly. 'I never would have guessed. But you're old-fashioned. You open doors, you always let women go first, the idea of going Dutch on a date would horrify you. You want to protect, you like to be leaned on, needed.' Her lips twitched. 'You know, a man like that is considered a little sexist in today's world.'

'I'm not sexist.' He tried not to be insulted. He enjoyed women, recreationally and professionally, and for the most part thought of them as his equal. Yes, he liked women, even cherished them. He'd been brought up by the nuns to respect and admire them, though to their constant dismay he had yet to incorporate one into his lifestyle.

She raised her eyebrows, obviously expecting him to deny each charge. How the hell had this gotten so turned around? 'All right,' he said, surprised at how defensive he suddenly felt. 'Maybe I expect to take care of a woman, but what's wrong with that? It's important to treat people right, with respect. And if I tend to protect and fuss a little, it's only because I care.'

'We're very different, Cord,' she said softly, seriously. 'I don't want or need someone to take care of me. I can do that by myself.'

'I know that.' With effort, he stood and walked toward her, admiring her strength, her resolve, her honesty. And if a teeny little part of him just wanted to protect her, hide her away somewhere so she'd be safe, he didn't quite dare say so. 'But, in truth, we're not all that different, Em. Look what you've done for Joshua.'

'That was different.'

'Was it? How?'

275

'I love Joshua.'

Well, he'd asked for it, hadn't he? If she could read his mind now, she'd start running and never stop. For the first time in his entire life he thought he just might have found the woman he could invite into his heart and ask to share his life. Only she wanted no part of it. It was more than a little deflating. Definitely worth fighting for. He changed tactics. 'In some ways, Emily, we're very much alike.'

Her hands were jammed in her pockets again, probably fisted. She had plaster smudged on one cheek, tearstained eyes and insulation stuck to her overalls. Her thick hair was braided lopsided and he thought she'd never looked so small, so vulnerable nor more exquisitely beautiful.

She took a deep breath. 'What I'm trying to say here is that I . . . appreciate our friendship.'

He didn't think he wanted to hear the next part. 'But?'

Her eyes flickered with what he would have sworn was uncertainty. 'But there can't be more.'

'Because we're so different,' he said evenly.

Her shoulders slumped and her wary eyes filled with relief. 'Yes, that's right.'

Moving closer, he managed a smile. 'So what do we do about the other thing between us?'

'What thing?'

'This,' he whispered, and kissed her.

His lips were their only connection, and to Emily it was the sweetest, warmest kiss she'd ever had. She could have left it at that forever. Just a kiss.

Until he touched her.

Cupping her face in his rough hands, with a tenderness that overwhelmed her, he deepened the kiss. Fierce, insistent hungry demand slammed into her, leaving her limp, shell-shocked.

It would be so easy to give in to this desperate, urgent need, but she knew she couldn't. Wouldn't.

With her hands covering his, she pulled back. '*This* can be controlled, Cord.'

He looked at her. 'Did I mention that you are a very stubborn woman?'

She felt herself smile. 'You might have.'

He brushed her knuckles across his lips. 'I'm a patient man, Red.'

His rangy body was close, his rugged face smiling. His expression held understanding, a trace of laughter and a touch of frustration that made her smile grow.

'What?' he asked.

How could she explain? Never had such a gorgeous, charismatic man been so physically attracted to her. James had been handsome, but it was hard to remember ever feeling weak-kneed after his kisses. She'd certainly never gotten such a heady rush of power from the realization that he wanted her. But there was more. With Cord, she wasn't the plain, unsophisticated house painter. She felt as if she was so much more – *he* made her feel as if she was so much more. She felt . . . beautiful.

'You're attracted to me,' she stated, feeling awed.

The sound he made was part laughter, part sigh. 'Isn't that what this is all about?'

'But – why?'

'I thought we'd covered that.'

'You could have anyone,' she pointed out. 'Why me?'

'That's flattering, Em. But I don't want just *anyone*. I want *you*.' His long fingers traced the delicate line of her throat. 'I'm drawn to you unlike anyone else. For a lot of reasons. Right time, right place. Because I like you. Because I think you are rare and different, intelligent, lovely and so incredibly talented. You're warm and caring.'

He smiled at her sniff of doubt, letting his fingers linger at the frantic pulse at the base of her neck. 'Even when you're being your difficult old ornery self you still have a deep concern for others, and you have a twisted sense of humor . . .' She smiled at that. 'I like that, too. You're a lot of things, Emily McKay, and they all excite me.' He moved closer and looked into her eyes. '*You* excite me. But you keep pushing me away. I want to be closer, as close as we can be. I want to – '

A lone piece of plaster crashed to the floor. Emily flinched. Her mural, the one she'd loved above all the others, was gone. Gone with one careless step. She took a deep breath, then stilled.

Cord was an exceptionally graceful, elegant man. 'How did you lose your balance?'

His eyebrows drew together and he straightened. 'Have you ever tried to balance across those joists when you can't even see them? It's impossible. And high up too.'

'But if you couldn't see because of the insulation cover, how did the height bother you?'

He looked insulted. 'Just because you can't see down doesn't mean you don't know how bad the fall is. I should have used a ladder from the outside – '

Emily chewed her lip to hide her sudden amusement. 'Uh-huh. You're afraid of heights.'

'Anyone would be afraid of that height.'

She gave up hiding her grin. 'You *are* afraid of heights.'

'And that's funny?'

She nodded. 'Very.'

'You're a sick woman, Emily.' He bent to retrieve the grid and barely contained his moan. His body was killing him.

'Are you sure you're okay?'

His grin was sudden and wicked. 'No. Want to kiss it better?'

Her eyes narrowed. 'And you think *I'm* sick.' She took the grid and started to leave the room.

'Em?' When she paused, he hesitated. 'If I promise not to fall through it, will you paint me another mural?'

Emily thought about Cord's question for the next few days. Would she paint him another mural? As she stepped into his attic she admitted to herself she probably would. In her hands was the painted grid that in all the excitement of Cord's fall she'd forgotten to replace. She looked down onto the white cloud of insulation as no doubt Cord had, days earlier.

A grin split her face as she imagined him sweating at the height as he crossed the nearly invisible joists. That smug grin faded when she remembered how costly Cord's fall had been. Forget the high cost of repairing the ceiling – her mural was gone.

Her sigh rent the air. God, she had loved that painting.

Holding a grudge was impossible, as tempting as the thought was. First of all, it wasn't in her nature, and, second, it truly was a balancing act from joist to joist.

She came to the second to last joist, her eyes on the window. When she glanced down for her footing, she nearly lost it. 'Oh, my God.' The skin at the back of her neck prickled.

Squatting down, she leaned in for a better look, but couldn't deny what she saw.

A joist was missing a large chunk of wood. The missing piece must have been where Cord had set his weight – and then fallen. But joists were made for strength, and didn't just break. This one certainly hadn't, she thought grimly as she ran a finger along the smooth edge of the wood.

It had been cut.

CHAPTER 14

Emily had the long drive into town to decide exactly what she would tell Cord. He'd gone into his office the past few days, but only because Seth had seemed to need him to. And only after extracting promises from Emily that she would stay put on the jobsite until either Raymond left and could follow her, or Cord himself returned.

She knew how frustrated he felt over the lab's lack of response to their request to hurry her test results. She knew, too, that Sheriff Stone felt that frustration as well. He'd been by every day to see her, just as she knew he checked on Katherine.

Raymond followed her down the mountain, then left her in Cord's office parking lot to go pick up some supplies. She'd never been in HT Design's cosmopolitan building before. Silly as it was, Emily's tongue tied itself in knots, and she fumbled nervously for a few minutes, locking up her car.

The feeling increased dramatically when she entered the sleek, posh office. A sophisticated-looking blonde woman, who was dressed to kill, smiled politely from behind a glass and chrome desk.

The sense of danger receded in the face of self-consciousness. She didn't fit in here. Pride overtook common sense as she smoothed a hand down her wrinkled overalls.

Well, she thought a bit defensively, she might as well make this a business trip. The contract she'd signed with HT Designs allowed her three draws of payment. She'd collected the first check before she'd started. The last would be collected upon completion of the job. She might as well get the second one now. Heaven knew, she could use it.

For the minute she refused to think about what had really caused her to come running here. Refused to think about her sabotaged tire, her illness, Cord's fall that had been meant for her. Refused to think about how she'd turned to Cord without hesitation when she'd gotten scared. In fact, she outright denied it.

She had not come running to Cord the minute she felt threatened, she had absolutely not.

Okay, she had. But no one had to know it.

'Can I help you?' the woman asked, her eyes cool.

She asked to see Cord and the woman flipped open a large calendar. 'Do you have an appointment?'

Cord would overreact if he thought she was in danger. She knew it and forced herself to get a grip. 'No,' she told the woman. 'I'm Emily McKay – McKay Painting.'

The woman looked up. 'A subcontractor?'

'Yes.'

'Which job?'

'Cord's – the hunting lodge.'

'Okay.' She stood. 'Let me check your file. Did you need a draw?'

'Yes.' Emily watched as the woman left the room, vaguely aware of the envy she felt for the sleek, polished clothes and perfect make-up. Ridiculous, she reminded herself. As a painter, she was rarely in anything but jeans or overalls. Make-up and beautiful clothes played no part in her world and were as alien as the sophistication and glitz that went with them.

'Emily.'

She started violently at Cord's low, sexy voice. If she lived to be one hundred and ten, she'd never get used to how her heart reacted to the way he said her name. Slowly she turned toward him. And if she lived to be that old, she'd never get used to the way his smile affected her pulse.

That heart-warming smile of his, she noted as she turned, was tinged with more than a bit of frustration.

He glanced through the glass door behind her, then around the beautiful reception area. 'You came alone. Of course.' He sighed and came closer. 'You worry me.'

'Raymond followed me. He'll be back.'

Cord the contractor was gone. In his place lived and breathed the architect – beautifully dressed and looking good enough to steal her breath.

She backed up a step, suddenly conflicted. She'd panicked at his house and had desperately needed to see him. But now that she was here she hesitated to do the one thing she so badly wanted – to throw herself in his very capable arms.

'I – I wanted to see you,' she stammered.

His eyes heated. The pretty receptionist walked back into the room, but he didn't appear to notice. He slipped a work-roughened hand behind her neck and drew her close. 'Did you?'

Emily put a hand against his chest, whether to gain her distance or to gain her desperately needed balance she didn't know.

'Here's your check,' the woman said behind them, and Emily jolted.

Cord's eyes never left Emily. 'Thanks, Margo. Hold my calls, please.' He took Emily's hand and pulled her down a wide hallway. 'You should have told me you needed more money.' He spoke quietly. 'I'm sorry.'

'It wasn't that – '

He pulled her into the last office.

It was huge. One wall, filled with windows, afforded them an incredible view of Lake Tahoe. The others were filled with pictures of impressive buildings, gorgeous houses and local scenery. The oak desk was an antique – and in excellent condition. Before she could open her mouth to comment on the lovely room she was backed against the closed door and held there by Cord's powerful body.

The kiss took her breath.

When she was dizzy, hot and aroused beyond belief, he lifted his head, his body still imprisoning hers. 'I couldn't wait to do that again,' he told her, his voice rough.

Before she could answer, his mouth was taking hers again, drowning out any thoughts except, *more. She had to have more.*

He gave it. Warm hands slipped in the sides of her overalls and under her shirt, stroking her sides and back.

'I should be furious that you're alone,' he told her, his mouth open and wet on her neck. 'But, God, am I glad you're here. You feel so good, Em.'

She forgot the danger that seemed to be lurking around her. She forgot the loss of her mural. She forgot the vast differences between her and this incredible man pressed against her from lips to curling toes.

She forgot she didn't want to need him – because she did.

His thumbs rubbed slow, tortuous circles just beneath her breasts, and she quivered, closing her eyes. His strong thigh rose between her legs, rubbing against the core of her, and she moaned.

'Tell me you came here because you missed me.' His lips caressed her jaw, her ear, everywhere they could reach, while his fingers trailed over her breasts. Her knees threatened to give. She heard his low voice, but couldn't put meaning to the words. Her head was buzzing, her heart drumming, her blood pumping, and she would have fallen if he hadn't been holding her up.

'Tell me,' he urged, using his hands and fingers to

tease until her head flopped uselessly back against the door.

She couldn't think; it was useless to try. 'Tell you what?' She gasped when he raised his leg higher, his thigh causing friction in all the right places. She felt hot, moist and unbelievably ready.

'Tell me you missed me as much as I missed you.'

'I missed you.' Her eyes opened to stare deep into eyes so blue she could drown. 'I can't believe I'm telling you, but I missed you.'

His smile was slow, sexy and a little smug. 'Good.' His eyes still on hers, he moved his thigh suggestively. Her body reacted immediately, and she barely contained her small, needy whimper.

'Don't hold back with me, Em. I want it all.' When he withdrew his leg, she protested with a sigh and clutched at him. 'Don't worry.' He lifted her. 'I'm not going anywhere.' He turned and set her on his desk, leaned around her to shove a handful of files aside. They hit the floor with a loud thud and Emily laughed.

'Love that sound,' he murmured, shoving another pile off.

She glanced down at the last pile and her eyes widened. On top of the stack was a check written to Cord. All the zeros caught her attention, and had the effect of a very cold bucket of water. 'My God.'

'I'm hurrying, Red.' With a careless flick of his wrist the last stack of files hit the floor, including the check. Slowly it fluttered through the air before landing just as his wet mouth claimed her neck.

'Cord, your check – it's on the floor. I think it's your paycheck.'

'Yeah,' he said against her skin. 'I'll get it later.' He reached for her, but she twisted to look at the check on the floor. He gave a choked laugh. 'Em, forget it for now. Let's finish what we started.' He leaned toward her, then paused at the look on her face. Slowly he straightened. 'Why do I get the feeling there's a problem?'

He had just dropped an incredible amount of money on the floor with a careless attitude that disturbed her. It had been easy to forget what kind of world he belonged to when he was wearing ragged jeans and boots. She thought of the painting equipment she'd been saving all year to buy, of Josh's education, of the stack of bills at home she'd been avoiding – including the second notice from the gas company. Cord could pay for all that with pocket change.

'Emily?' He took her chin in his hand and turned her face to him.

'Your paycheck. It's . . .' It's what? More money than she dreamed of? 'Do you get them . . . often?'

He glanced down at the check. 'Every week or so.'

She nearly fell off the desk. 'Every *week*?'

'Crazy, isn't it? Seth and I can't believe it either, but they just keep paying us.' With a grin, he shrugged.

Emily's shoulders drooped and she looked away. He was so casual about it, so callous. Yet she knew he had come from nothing once. 'It's a lot of money, Cord.'

His easy smile faded and once again he captured her chin, gently forcing her to look at him. 'So it is. Is that a problem?'

'Maybe.'

'I don't understand.'

Humiliating as it was, she had to be direct. 'I guess I can't figure out what a guy like you would want with someone like me. I mean, you could have anyone.'

'That's flattering,' he said wryly. 'But we've been through this. I only want you.'

'Why?' She leaned her hands on his desk for support.

'You don't think I want you?' His voice was incredulous.

'I don't know.'

He muttered something under his breath about the strange and alien workings of a woman's mind, then stepped in front of her where she still sat on his desk. The zipper of his trousers lightly touched her closed knees. Strong fingers pushed her thighs apart and he pressed himself closer, pulling her hard against him. His hands lifted her legs higher, then gripped her hips and ground them against his, making it painfully clear how much he wanted her.

'Does this feel like I don't want you, Emily?' He kissed her again and she braced herself for the onslaught of powerful, overwhelming passion. But there was no defense against his devastating tenderness, the incredible emotion and sensitivity he poured into that one kiss. 'No other woman can 'make me feel this way,' he whispered softly, before kissing her again.

She surrendered with a quiet sigh before melting against him.

When he lifted his head, it was to stare deep in her eyes. They each breathed raggedly, the only sound in the room.

'Is that all there is?' she asked when she could speak again. 'A physical attraction?'

The minute the words were out, she wished them back. If there was more, she didn't want to hear it. Yet.

'Oh, that's just the beginning,' he promised, touching her face. He smiled sadly at the look of exposed panic she knew was written all over her. 'Though I can see that idea just thrills the hell out of you.'

He pulled back and offered her a hand. She jumped down on wobbly legs, torn between asking for another kiss and running as far as her legs would carry her. She started to move away. He stopped her with a hand on her arm. 'It's hard, Em. Knowing you still don't trust me. After all this time, you still can't let yourself believe in me.'

'I trust you.' The sentence was simple and it was the plain truth.

'But you don't *believe* in me. I have so much I want to give to you, Em.' He traced her lower lip with his thumb, causing a pure, sensual curl from deep within her. She swallowed hard. His intense eyes watched his fingers move on her. 'But I'm selfish,' he said. 'I want you to give the same back. And you're not willing.'

She closed her mouth. Very unsure of herself, and even more uncertain of what he meant, she didn't quite trust herself to speak.

'Since that subject is obviously closed, let's start another.' He waited until she looked at him. 'I don't like you driving up and down that highway. I've told you that.'

Knowing what she did about his fall, she suddenly couldn't agree with him more. 'I came for a good reason.'

His smile was back. 'Yeah. Because you missed me.'

'Well, there was that,' she admitted with a little smile.

'I wish you could have asked me for the money, Red.'

'I didn't come for the money.' She took a deep breath, then let it out in one loud whoosh. 'The fall you took in the attic was meant for me.'

He opened his mouth and she rushed on, explaining how she'd climbed into the attic and seen the cut beam herself. 'The unpainted grid must have been a lure. Whoever did it knew I would see it right away and take out the grid.' She shivered, remembering.

Immediately he was there, running warm, sure hands up and down her arms. 'It could have been you,' he breathed. He pulled her close and hugged her tight, slowly rocking them back and forth. 'It could have been you to take that fall.'

'Yeah. And my head isn't as hard as yours,' she tried to joke.

He didn't laugh. 'You know what this means, don't you?'

'That I'm the most popular girl on your job?'

'Em, stop it.' He pulled back, his hands on her shoulders. 'You're being stalked. Because of me.' He swore again and hugged her to him fiercely. 'Because of me, damn it. But now we finally have proof it wasn't Seth.'

'The cut wood?'

'Yeah, the cut wood. Seth wouldn't know a bandsaw from a screwdriver. He couldn't possibly have figured out how to cut that wood without killing himself.' He took her hand, kissed her lightly. 'If I catch you driving alone, I'm going to be mighty unhappy with you.' He kissed her again, harder, and for just long enough that her head spun dizzily. 'Let's go tell Seth and Stone.'

Cord brought a tray of three iced teas to his porch. Katherine smiled her thanks and took one.

'Were you waiting for me long?' he asked her as he set an iced tea before Emily.

'Not too long.' The worry was evident in her face, as it had been ever since Cord had told her about Emily's possible poisoning and the cut wood. 'I can't believe everything that's happened.'

'It's pretty unbelievable.' Cord glanced at Emily and frowned. Pale, shaky and distant, she hadn't spoken much since they'd come from his office to find Katherine waiting. It was as if it had just hit her – the danger was real. Together the three of them had studied the cut joist, then called the sheriff.

'It's warm today, isn't it?' Emily pulled her tea close and stared into it. 'I can't believe summer's just around the corner already.'

'Emily.' Cord hunkered down before her and touched her arm, recognizing delayed shock.

'And the days are getting longer.' Emily sipped her tea and avoided his gaze. 'Josh'll be home on Sunday.'

Katherine shot Cord a concerned look.

'Em, stop.' He squeezed her arm gently. 'You're scared. It's going to be all right.'

'Of course it is, dear,' Katherine echoed softly. 'Everything will be fine. You'll see.'

'When?' She raised gorgeous, fear-filled eyes. 'When will it be all right? When whoever it is succeeds in killing me? Or someone else?'

Cord fingered the silky strands of her braid. 'The sheriff – '

'Is here.' Sheriff Stone stepped up on the porch. He was a tall man built like a heavyweight boxer. Good at his job and well liked in their small community, Stone had a reputation that was invincible. Once a New York cop, he knew the ropes, respected the danger and appreciated the relative slow life that this town afforded him. But he hated crime. 'Katherine. Ms McKay.' He tipped his hat.

'Hello, Sheriff,' Emily said. Katherine managed a smile.

Cord rose from Emily's side and took a chair next to her. The fact that the sheriff didn't look at him was telling.

Stone sat. 'I got a message from the lab today.'

'And?' Cord asked.

Stone turned to him then, and nodded. 'Cord.'

'The message?' Cord repeated, frowning. Stone and he were friends from way back, but neither would let it interfere with business. 'From the lab. What did they say?'

The sheriff sighed and leaned back. 'You called me earlier. Something about a cut joist and a fall.'

'Yes. I already told you what happened,' Cord said impatiently. 'The lab, Stone. What did they say?'

Stone studied Cord carefully before answering. 'She was poisoned.'

Katherine closed her eyes and moved her lips in a silent prayer. Emily gasped and covered her mouth with a shaking hand.

Before Cord could rise to go to Emily, Stone stopped him. 'Cord. I have to do this.' He flipped open a notepad. 'I have some questions for you.'

He'd been waiting for this. 'Let me guess,' Cord said calmly. 'About Tayna's death. And Lacey. Maybe even Sheri. All questions you've already asked me a hundred times.'

'That's right,' Stone said evenly, meeting his eyes honestly. It didn't help Cord to see the repressed pain there. 'And about Emily's problems. Her tire. The poisoning. And now your fall.'

'No!'

They all turned in surprise at Emily's outburst. 'You can't think Cord's responsible!'

'Absolutely not!' Katherine echoed with her own adamant response.

Stone twirled his pen for a long moment, then sent Cord an apologetic glance. 'Maybe we should handle this at the station, Cord?'

'No!' Emily said again, sitting up straight. 'He couldn't have done anything to hurt anyone. You must know that. And he certainly didn't plan his own fall.'

'Emily – ' Cord started.

'No, wait.' Emily whirled to the sheriff. 'I don't believe this. Someone's stalking me, I mean *really* stalking me, and you're wasting time with the wrong man. He didn't do it.'

'I just have a few questions, Emily,' Stone told her quietly. 'Surely you must see that in order to do my job right I have to do this.'

'No, I don't see that at all!' Emily stood, and to Cord's surprise she grabbed his hand, squeezing tight.

'Me neither.' Katherine said, her face tight. 'It's impossible.'

'I still have to ask,' the sheriff said calmly. 'Ladies, you'll have to be quiet or excuse us.'

Katherine tightened her lips and said nothing. But her eyes said it all as they directed darts at the sheriff.

Emily couldn't remain silent. 'Well, then, ask quick, Sheriff. You have a psycho to catch and you're wasting time.'

Cord felt the tremor in the small hand clasping his and his heart twisted. God, she was sweet. She wasn't ready for what was happening between them, she didn't completely trust him – no matter what she said – yet she was standing by him, never doubting his innocence. Besides Katherine, she was the strongest, most loyal woman he'd known in his life, and despite the situation he felt like the luckiest man on earth.

He was in love.

Going still, he ran his eyes over Emily McKay, for a minute doubting his heart. But it was no use. He loved her. For the first time he really understood those words and meant them. He loved a woman and it was all he could do to keep from jumping up and announcing it.

'On second thought,' the sheriff said slowly, dividing a glance between the silent Katherine and not so silent Emily. 'This would be much better done at the station. You'll excuse us ladies. Cord?'

'Cord?' Emily grabbed him, looking panicked.

He stood, touched her shoulders, and shook gently until she looked at him. 'Em, I'll be fine. I'll be back as soon as I can.' He wanted desperately to tell her the feelings he'd just discovered, but there was something more important. Her safety. He looked at Katherine over Emily's head. 'Stay with her?'

'Of course.' Katherine rose, stared hard at the sheriff. 'I imagine you'll be right back. Isn't that right, Sheriff?'

'That's right, ma'am. This won't take long.'

'Emily.' Cord hugged her hard, then held her face,

looking down into her tortured, beautiful green eyes. 'Stay with Katherine, please.'

'Cord – '

'Promise,' he demanded desperately. God, he couldn't leave knowing she might be alone.

'I promise.' She held him tight. 'But hurry.'

He would if he could.

For the countless time in two hours, Emily paced Cord's large living room. Unable to work, unable to hold a simple conversation with Katherine, she felt useless.

How in the world had things gotten so out of control? And how could anyone believe Cord capable of the murders of two people he cared about, a vicious attack on his own secretary and the strange stalking she was going through?

It was simply impossible.

'How're you doing?'

Emily forced a smile and turned. Katherine stood in the doorway, only her eyes reflecting her nerves. 'I'm fine. I'm sure they'll be back anytime now.'

The older woman watched Emily another moment before coming close and squeezing her hand. Her voice was quiet, controlled, and utterly soothing. 'It will be all right, Emily, dear. You'll see. No one will believe Cord could hurt anyone.'

'Of course not.'

Katherine sighed and turned to the window. The view was spectacular. The lush green valley far below was in all its early summer glory. 'I love him, you know. I couldn't love him any more if he were my own son.'

Emily watched Katherine twist her hands together nervously, saw her eyes dart to the long driveway, searching for a car. She'd never seen her be anything but quietly serene, completely at peace, no matter what was happening around her. Emily's heart went out to this woman who meant so much to Cord. 'You raised him. He thinks of you as his mother.'

Katherine's lips curved and she sighed. 'You are kind.' She shifted, still watching the outside world. 'He loves you. Cord loves you.'

Emily felt her mouth fall open.

'Yes, my dear, it's true. Oh, he hasn't said so, of course. He wouldn't. But I can see it in his eyes when he looks at you. Do you have any idea how lucky you are to have a man like that be in love with you?'

Words failed Emily. But for one brief flash she allowed herself the luxury of the thought. Allowed herself to picture someone actually speaking the words, *I love you*, and meaning them. It was a fantasy, of course. And an unbelievable one at that. She simply didn't picture herself as all that lovable. 'I – I think you must be mistaken.'

'No,' Katherine said simply. 'I'm not. I know him better than anyone. Cord's different, special. It's not that there haven't been women before. There've been plenty.' She daintily wrinkled her nose, and Emily nearly smiled at her look of pure distaste. 'Too many. But never have I seen him lose his heart as he has with you.'

Katherine peered at her, her eyes narrowed. She was waiting for a response, some sort of reassurance that Emily wouldn't hurt the man she thought of as her own. But Emily didn't have any reassurances for her. There couldn't be that kind of love between Cord and herself. It was impossible. 'I'm sorry, Katherine. But Cord and I don't have a relationship like that. We're . . .' What were they? 'Just friends.'

There was a quick look of disappointment, then it was carefully masked. 'You don't want to talk about it. That's okay, you don't really know me. You have no reason to trust me.'

'It's not that,' Emily protested quickly, not wanting to insult the woman.

'Then it's because of my chosen profession.'

Emily had to smile at that. 'Well, I have to admit, it's a little disconcerting to discuss a man with a nun – much less the man's mother!'

Katherine touched Emily's hand again, softly. 'I am a woman of God, Emily. But I'm not unaware of the strange and beautiful emotions that can pass between a man and a woman. I care for you both, so, please, if you ever want to talk, I'm available.'

'Thank you.' It was a lovely offer, but one Emily knew she wouldn't accept. There was nothing to discuss. She thought of the way Cord had kissed her in his office and felt the heat flood her face. There was no way she could discuss whatever it was that she felt for Cord with a nun.

'We don't have to talk about Cord,' Katherine said, smiling knowingly. 'Since it's obvious that subject makes you so uncomfortable. Let's talk about your painting.'

'My painting?'

'Yes. Cord says you're extremely talented. I'd like for you to paint a mural for the school where I work – at St James's. On the weekends, the girls all go home. I thought it'd be a wonderful surprise for them if you could paint a mural while they're gone.'

'I'd love to.' And she would, too. It would be a dream come true.

Katherine smiled at her. 'I imagine the profession you've chosen for yourself can get lonely. Especially when your brother's in school.'

It was true. Emily loved to paint. She *lived* to paint. But sometimes she did feel alone. 'I would think your profession could also get lonely.'

Katherine nodded. 'Yes. But I've never regretted my decision.'

'Me either.'

Katherine studied her with interest. 'So, you're interested in doing that mural for me? For the girls?'

'Of course.'

'Well, how about this weekend?'

'You mean . . . tomorrow?' Emily couldn't control the small burst of excitement.

'Yes, tomorrow. It'd be perfect as most of the staff will be on a special retreat and anyone else will be visiting family. I really want to surprise them.'

'Did you have any particular kind of picture in mind?'

'I don't want to take away from your creativity, so

I'll let you use your best judgement. Can you finish in two days?'

'If I do nothing but paint,' Emily said, smiling.

'I don't want to take you away from your brother . . . and Cord.' Katherine's glance was sly – and very interested.

'Once I start a painting,' Emily told her, 'wild horses couldn't drag me away. I'll finish, no problem. And you'll have your surprise to give to the girls.'

'Oh, that'll be wonderful. You know, if you're going to work around the clock, you might as well stay there. We have extra beds. Why don't I come for you in the morning? I'll drive you myself.'

'That would be fine.' Emily absolutely refused to think about the possibility of Cord being held by the sheriff. They couldn't do that, she convinced herself. They couldn't because he was innocent.

Katherine looked at her, then hesitated. 'Emily, please don't take this the wrong way, but you look exhausted. Won't you go upstairs and lie down?'

Emily knew she referred to the only room besides the kitchen that was furnished. Cord's bedroom. She shouldn't, she really shouldn't. Lying in his bed would definitely seem too intimate a thing.

But the thought of a soft bed and a few minutes with her eyes closed was too much to resist.

Katherine left her, claiming she was going to search the kitchen for something good to eat. Emily climbed the stairs and slowly opened the door to Cord's bedroom.

She'd been in the room once before, to paint it. But a desk, a chair and several lamps had been added. The king-size bed seemed huge and took up most of the room. And the sight of the rumpled, hastily straightened blankets turned her mouth dry, but she crawled onto them anyway and closed her eyes.

Her body was exhausted, but, surrounded as she was by Cord's things, all she could do was lie there and think of him. It didn't help that Cord's own wonderful male scent clung to the sheets, or that seeing his clothes folded neatly on the chair brought images of his gorgeous physique to mind.

She wanted him.

It was a fact she couldn't avoid. She also enjoyed talking to him, working with him, even laughing with him – a first for her. She was beginning to think of him as one of her greatest and most important friends.

But did she . . . love him? She honestly didn't know, but just thinking about it terrified her. Nothing but hurt had ever come from love. Which, she knew, made her nothing but a coward.

Sighing, she closed her eyes.

They flew open again. For a minute Emily lay there, uncertain. Had she been sleeping? Disoriented, she sat up, unsure of how much time had gone by since she'd lain down. A quick glance at her watch told her nearly an hour had passed.

What had woken her?

Then came a steady sound she couldn't place. Pushing off the bed, she went to the window.

Katherine's car was gone, but Cord's truck was back.

The house was eerily empty, but she could still hear the regular thudding and she followed it out the door and around to the side of the house. There she found Cord, his back to her, and for a moment she could only stare.

He was chopping wood. Shirtless, he set another large chunk of wood on a stump and lifted the ax. Sleek muscles bunched and coiled under faintly gleaming bronzed skin as he raised it, slamming it down on the wood. Splinters flew as the wood divided itself perfectly. Cord tossed them aside and lifted a new log.

Something about his quick, precise movements drew her attention. She didn't have to see his face to know he was unsettled, upset.

She stepped closer, her attention riveted by the way his splendid body moved. She stopped abruptly when she realized her hand was outstretched, as if to touch him.

He must have sensed her. He turned his head and looked up, directly and unwaveringly at her. She smiled tentatively. His eyes lit, yet he didn't return the smile. After a timeless minute, he tossed aside the ax and stepped toward her.

'Emily.'

'You're back,' she said inanely. God, he was impressive. Dark hair unruly, eyes nearly black with emotion, chest vaguely damp and jeans clinging to his lean and powerful thighs like a second skin. Emily found herself staring like a schoolgirl. She had the sudden and strange urge to throw her arms around him and toss her uncertainties in the wind.

'You're awake.' He still didn't smile, yet she could see clearly in those blue eyes how happy he was to see her.

She pictured him looking in on her sleeping and the thought was oddly arousing. 'Are you okay? What did the sheriff say?'

He shook his head sharply. 'No, not now. Emily –' He closed the last step between them and took her shoulders in his strong hands. 'I can't keep this to myself any longer.'

'You're upset.'

His fingers convulsed on her shoulders, then moved up and down her arms as if warming her. 'I didn't hurt those women.'

'God, Cord. I know that.' She rested her hands on his. 'I told you, I never thought you were responsible.'

'But you're involved in this because of me and I hate that.' His mouth twisted. 'I couldn't stand it if something happened to you.'

Because he seemed to need the reassurance – and because she couldn't stop herself if she tried – she wrapped her arms around his neck and pulled close. 'I'll be all right.' She let her gaze fall to his wonderful full lips, knowing she played with a fire she couldn't control.

He held her tight. 'I want you.'

'Cord – '

'I want you more than I've wanted anything or

anyone in my entire life – and I've wanted a lot. It's killing me, this wanting.' He pulled back to look at her and she could have cried at the amount of emotion pouring from his eyes.

His next words were devastatingly simple and had her heart slamming against her ribs. 'I love you, Emily.'

CHAPTER 15

Emily pulled abruptly out of his arms at his words, her ears roaring. Had he really said it? Or had her over-active imagination been playing tricks on her?

'I just wanted you to know.' His low voice shook, as did his hands when they reached for her again. She dodged him and he shook his head sadly. 'Don't look at me like that, Em. I didn't mean to hurt you. I just had to tell you – it was eating at me.'

'I – ' She stopped, made a disparaging sound, lifting her hands helplessly. Damn him, he'd ruined everything. 'I made a terrible mistake, Cord.' She drew a ragged breath and wrapped her arms around herself, chilled despite the warm afternoon air. 'I shouldn't have let this go so far – I'm sorry.'

'You can't run from this,' he said softly. 'You can't.'

She stared at him wildly. 'I don't want you to love me. I – I don't want you to get hurt, but I can't love you back. I just can't!'

Cord stepped toward her, his heart in his throat at the wide-eyed panic on her face. 'You're frightened.

I understand. You've lost people you loved before, and I understand that too. Love hasn't worked for you, and to tell you the truth it hasn't worked for me either. But I believe in us, Emily. We both have a lot to give and a lot to learn, but we can do it together, you and me. I know you've been hurt – but this time will be different. You've just got to trust us both enough to try it. Please, trust me, Em – '

'No!' She backed up a step, tripping over a piece of wood, her chest heaving with each breath. 'Don't come any closer. When your arms are around me, I can't think. I need to think.' She held her head, massaging her temples. 'God, I just need to think a minute.'

She looked so helplessly miserable he couldn't help but try again. He reached for her.

'Stay away from me. Please.'

'*I can't*. You know I can't.' He backed her to a tree, surrounded her body with his. 'We love each other.'

Panic flared in her eyes. 'No,' she whispered.

His arms held her shoulders when she tried to escape. He hated the hurt, the sorrow in her eyes, but he couldn't stop. Not when he knew he was right. 'Fine. If you can't tell me you love me . . . then tell me you don't.'

Her eyes flew from his and he gripped her head in gentle hands. 'No, no,' he murmured. 'Look at me. Come on. This is your chance, Emily. Tell me you don't love me – tell me to go away.'

Her eyes filled and his heart ached, but there was no room for doubts. He rested his forehead against hers when she tried to lower her gaze, to hide from him. 'Tell me you don't love me,' he whispered. 'Just tell me you don't feel a thing for me and I'll leave you in peace.'

She said nothing, but looked at him in mute misery. 'Can't do it, huh?' he asked after a minute, unable to keep the triumph out of his voice.

A lone tear fell and he swiped at it tenderly with the pad of his thumb. A vise gripped his chest, but he wouldn't tell her not to cry, not to feel. She'd been doing that for too long.

'It hurts,' she whispered.

He tilted her head up, forced their gazes to meet. 'It doesn't have to, Em. Just let it be, let it grow.' He took her small hand and placed it against his chest so that she could feel the solid thump of his heartbeat. 'You're a part of me, a part I don't ever want to be without.'

'Ever? What – what are you saying?'

'I want you to marry me, Emily.'

'Oh, my God.'

He was jumping the gun, he knew, but he wouldn't take the words back. He meant them. If they scared her, he was sorry for it, but he could no longer see himself without her. 'Be mine always, Em. Say you will.'

'Oh, Cord,' she whispered, her voice thick. Her heart was tripping like a trapped rabbit's against his hand.

It was hard, very hard to watch her struggle with something that he was certain of. And, though it was

307

playing dirty, he kissed her. Kissed her senseless –
until she willingly lowered her defenses and reason
escaped her, until she clung to him with a reckless
abandon. He went on a quiet exploration of her face
with his lips: her eyelids, her cheeks, her temples.
And he felt her tremble beneath his hands. She
moved with a quiet desperation against him, driving
him half-insane. He wanted to feel her move under
him, wanted to be deep inside her.

They were both breathless by the time he took her
lips again, deeper and more slowly. Her welcoming
murmur had relief flowing through him, weakening
his knees. Her hands slid up his shoulder to grip,
then went lax, leaving him to support them both
against the tree.

She was everything to him. Holding her like this,
both of them quivering with need, was a kind of
sweet torture he wouldn't give up for anything.

He lifted his head and stared into her glorious
green eyes. He didn't have a single breath left. All
he could think about was how right it felt to hold her,
how long it would take him to peel her out of her
overalls.

They both started violently at the sound of the car
coming up the driveway. Cord swore softly when he
saw his best friend coming toward them.

'Bad timing? Wait – ' Seth laughed good-naturedly
at the scowl on Cord's face. 'Don't answer that.'

'Go away.' Cord reluctantly helped Emily slide out
from between him and the tree.

'Cord!' Emily shot him a look before she smiled

shakily at Seth. 'You'll have to excuse him, Seth. The heat got to him.'

'I'll bet.' Seth eyed Emily's ruffled overalls and shot Cord a knowing look before smiling evenly.

Cord scowled at his friend, then glanced at Emily. She was relieved, he thought, and sighed with frustration. Visions of making slow and thorough love beneath the lazy afternoon sun, surrounded by the lush forest, tormented him.

Seth's ridiculous grin didn't fade. 'Hey, I see you got your hot tub installed.' He gestured to the side patio where a new Jacuzzi sat, surrounded by a beautiful redwood deck.

'Yesterday.' He clamped down on his impatience with his best friend. 'We're kinda busy here, Seth.'

'Oh, I can see that.' Purposely not taking the hint, he turned to Emily. 'I have a friend in the County Planner's Office who told me you're going to be doing some work for them. I guess I'll have to take a number to have our offices done, huh?'

Emily's mouth fell open. 'Excuse me?'

Cord blinked at her. 'You didn't tell me. That's wonderful.'

'I didn't know. I submitted some sketches and had high hopes but . . .' Her smile came and Cord was helpless to respond in kind. 'Between that and Katherine's mural, I may never paint another house again.'

Cord stared at her, realizing just how much of herself Emily had withheld from him. He wanted to know everything about her . . . her hopes, her dreams, her wants, her needs . . . and yet she continually tried to hide those very things from him.

It wasn't comforting, nor was it a good sign of things to come. But it didn't matter. He'd break through and gain her love – or die trying.

Seth looked at him. 'Katherine called me.'

Hence the reason for the visit. Cord knew Seth well enough to read the deep-grained worry and care in his friend's eyes. 'I'm okay, Seth.'

'You sure?'

No. 'Yeah.'

'It just doesn't seem fair that the very thing which got me off the hook may have sunk you.' Seth studied Cord. 'Do you want me to call Mark?'

Their lawyer. He closed his eyes against the wave of sickness he felt. But he thought he just might have convinced Stone he couldn't possibly be charged. 'No.'

Seth held up a foil-lined bag. 'I brought dinner. But I think I'll just leave it for you two.' He handed the bag to Cord, smiled easily at Emily. 'Take care, Emily.' He looked at Cord, hard. 'If you need anything, call me.'

Not quite trusting his voice, Cord nodded. He felt Emily's eyes on him and glanced over. There was still a faint blush to her cheeks, making her even lovelier. 'He's a good friend,' she said.

'The best.' He reached for her. 'Congratulations, Red.' His smile was genuine, as was his happiness for what she'd accomplished for herself. 'We should celebrate.'

'I can't believe it's true.' She wrung her hands together. 'After all this time, it might really happen. I just might get to make a living at it. I've been so nervous about it for so long now.'

'I wish you could have told me about it.' It hurt that she hadn't.

'It didn't have anything to do with you.' She flushed again, a telling sign that she knew how those words would wound. 'Wait.' She rubbed her face and took a deep breath. 'What I meant is –'

'I know what you meant, Emily.' He backed up, suddenly very tired and very close to losing his temper. 'You are in control of your own life, have been for a very long time. You aren't ready to share that life with anyone else, even someone who loves you beyond reason. You'd rather be alone than risk being hurt. Do I have it right?'

'Okay, yes!' she cried, flinging her hands wide. 'I'm scared. Is that so unbelievable? So awful?'

'No.' He took another step away from her, unable, at that moment at least, to try to break through. 'It's not awful to be scared. That's natural. What isn't acceptable is letting your damn pride get in the way of a relationship that was meant, Emily. Yes, it's your pride,' he said roughly when she shook her head in denial. 'You've been in charge of your world so long you can't stand to let go enough to let someone else in. It's not fear, Emily, it's your damn ego – and I'm tired of bashing my head against it.'

He turned, and though it was the hardest thing he'd ever done he walked away. At the new redwood decking, he stepped up, dipped his hand into the new hot tub. Hot. Very hot. Good, he thought angrily. He needed to relax. He needed to be alone to lick the wound that was his heart. Alone. He could almost laugh. Months ago that had been all he wanted when he'd bought this house. To be alone.

But the sad truth was he didn't *really* want to be alone at all. He wanted one redheaded, hot-tempered painter at his side. And he wanted her as hopelessly in love with him as he was with her.

'Cord.'

He tensed at her soft voice, but didn't turn.

'I – I do have feelings for you.'

'Do you?'

'How can you doubt it?' The distress in her voice tore at him, but he still didn't turn. 'I've never seen you so angry.'

'Not angry,' he said, kneeling on one of the redwood benches and letting his hand play in the hot, bubbling water. The noise of the jet was soothing, beckoning. 'You claim to have feelings for me, Emily. But all I see you doing is pushing me away in the name of those elusive feelings. The closer I try to get, the more you push me away. It scares me to death.'

'*You're* afraid?'

God, he wanted to see her, hold her, kiss her. But if he turned and saw the anguish in her eyes that he could hear so clearly in her voice, she'd break him. 'You're cutting me in half, Red. I feel like I'm bleeding to death.'

'Do you –? You think I'm ending it?'

The water churned, matching his emotions. 'Aren't you?'

'No,' she whispered. 'I'm not. But what exactly is it between us?'

He closed his eyes against the hope. 'At this point, that's up to you.'

She didn't speak for a long, painful moment, the only sound was the rushing, turning water. Occasionally a warm drop hit his bare chest. 'You do funny things to me,' she said eventually. He heard her step closer, up on the deck behind him. 'Sometimes I just see you and I get so completely tongue-tied – and it's frustrating and embarrassing because I know you notice. You like it.'

He couldn't deny that, so he said nothing.

'Then you smile or say something to me in that husky voice of yours and my insides get all twisted. And I get upset at myself for being that way. I feel young and hopelessly stupid.'

'You've never been stupid,' he said quietly. 'Never.'

'Well, I'm something, and it drives me crazy. It makes me . . . kinda out-of-sorts.'

'*Kinda*?' But, with his back still to her, he smiled.

'And . . . well . . . okay – irritable. Bad-tempered. Bitchy. Whatever you want to call it.' She came closer. 'I can't work, Cord. I can't eat. Hell,' she sighed. 'I can't even sleep. I'm afraid I'm losing it. I mean, really losing it.'

The anger and frustration were abruptly gone, left in its place was a giddiness he was helpless to control.

'You may be losing it, Emily. But it's a good thing.' He turned to her then, nearly bursting with laughter and love.

'What's so funny?' she demanded as he straightened in front of her. 'I'm pouring my heart out here, and you're laughing – '

'I love you too, Emily.'

Her eyes widened, and she took an involuntary step back. 'I didn't say I love you.'

'Didn't you?' he asked casually, bringing his hands to his belt.

'*What are you doing*?' she squeaked in shock when his belt went flying across the deck.

'I'm getting in my new hot tub,' he explained patiently, undoing his pants.

'You're – Why?' she demanded, eyes riveted to the workings of his hands as they finished their task.

He didn't answer, but had to turn away to hide his smile at her wide-eyed, horrified expression.

'Oh, my God,' she muttered, slapping her hands over her eyes as he dropped the jeans. '*Oh, my God.*'

He hid his laugh as he bent, calmly folded the jeans and tossed them to the bench. God, she was sweet. Stepping around her, he sank into the blessedly hot water and sighed loudly. 'It's heavenly.' Emily hadn't moved, nor uncovered her eyes. 'Come on in.'

'We're talking!' she cried. 'And you just took off your pants – just dropped them, calm as you please – right in the middle of a conversation!'

'You can look now,' he told her mildly. 'I'm all the way in.'

She peeked warily, then lowered her hands. 'I can't believe you did that.' Her gaze moved over his damp chest and he saw her swallow hard. It was a thrill, knowing he had the same effect on her as she did on him. She hadn't removed a stitch of clothing and already he was fully aroused. Hell, he'd been in that painful state since the first time he'd kissed her.

He held out a hand. 'Come on in, Em. It will help relax you.'

'We were talking,' she repeated weakly.

'We can talk in here,' he promised, even though talking was the *last* thing he wanted to do.

'But I'll get wet.'

'That's the idea of this thing, Emily. Getting wet and warm and relaxed. But take off your clothes if it'll make you feel better.' He bit his lip to keep from laughing out loud at the murderous expression on her face.

'You want me to take off all my clothes and just hop in?'

He did laugh then. 'You could leave them on, but it will definitely be more comfortable without them.'

She crossed her arms over her chest and lifted her chin. 'No way. Absolutely not.'

Her shyness amused him, especially since she had the most incredible little body. He should know – it hadn't been far from his mind ever since he'd helped her out of the shower when she'd been poisoned. 'Suit yourself.'

She glared at him.

'Ahh,' he moaned, leaning back, allowing the water

to soothe him. The bubbles rose to his chest, enveloping him in wonderful, powerful heat. 'This is the life. You should really try it.'

'There's no way.'

The woman defined the word stubborn. 'Come in, Emily. You'll enjoy it.' That comment met with silence. Silence was good, he thought. It meant she was mulling it over. One more minute and he'd have her in.

'I don't have a bathing suit.'

He was wise enough to hide his grin. 'I'll close my eyes.'

Her eyes narrowed suspiciously. 'The whole time?'

He looked at her and laughed. He couldn't help it. She stood there with her arms crossed, temper flaring and looking so incredibly tempted he felt a little sorry for her. 'Emily, come on, love. There's nothing to be shy about. After all, we're going to be married.'

Her hands fisted. 'You're impossible. And deaf. I *never* said I was going to marry you.'

Deciding that ignoring that would be the best strategy, Cord closed his eyes and simply enjoyed the jets of water pressing against his aching body.

She sighed, loudly. The steady tapping he knew came from her impatiently moving foot.

Then he heard the sound he'd been waiting for – a rustling which could only be one thing. Her clothes – thank you, God.

'If you peek, Harrison, I swear I'll sock you.'

Staying still, he said nothing. He didn't dare. The water shifted and he heard her delighted gasp. He didn't need to see her to picture how good she'd look naked and soaking wet.

'Will you tell me what the sheriff wanted?'

He opened his eyes. She was sitting opposite him and low in the bubbling water. He could barely make out the outline of the ribbed tank top she'd left on – which meant she most likely had left her panties on too. Knowing she wasn't as nude and as aroused as he was helped him concentrate on the sudden subject change. 'I'll tell you, if you promise to paint me another mural.'

Looking uncertain and disbelieving, she crossed wet arms over her chest. 'Does this have anything to do with me getting the city job?'

He wanted to shake some sense into her. 'Is it so hard to believe that I think you have magnificent talent – regardless of what others think? Is it so hard to believe that I want something you've painted – for me?'

'I'm sorry,' she said, so quietly he almost couldn't hear her over the purr of the jets. She gave her head a little shake that had her long wet braid swinging. 'But sometimes, yes. It's hard to believe – after all this time – that people want me to paint for them.' She looked at him. 'I'd love to make another mural for you – just not on a ceiling.'

That she could joke at all was a good sign, Cord thought.

'Now tell me. What did Stone say?'

'Seth hasn't been completely ruled out, despite

what I told him about Seth and the tools. But I don't think he believes it's Seth, not really. Stone's too smart, and not afraid to go with his instincts.'

'So, what do his instincts tell him about you?'

'He doesn't understand the personal connection I've had to each victim. He thinks it's strange.'

'And?'

Her eyes were glued to his, demanding the truth, no matter how much he wanted to hide it from her. It hurt that he couldn't protect her, not from this. 'And he wanted to know what I was doing each night there was an occurrence.' It wasn't the first time Stone had asked, but it was the first time Cord had felt real fear. He was definitely being set up, and the noose was getting tighter.

'Oh, Cord.'

There was obvious concern and genuine caring in her large, shining eyes. Tendrils of hair clung damply to her face and the steam rose between them, but even so he saw the exact second her expression shifted. Longing, hot and deep, ran between them like a current, and he was powerless to control it. Their feet brushed together and he gave up the effort to try. The last of his frustration over her inability to admit what was happening between them deserted him. Hunger – for her – took over.

They moved at the same time, coming together in a slow dance of tangled arms and legs. Warm water slipped between them, over them, enhancing the feeling of skin against skin, making them weightless as they clung together.

Cord watched Emily's eyes lowered to his lips, her own lips parting, and it was all the invitation he needed. Kissing her gently and softly, his hands went to her face, fingers spread to touch as much of her as he could.

'This doesn't mean anything but what it is,' Emily whispered breathlessly, raising her eyes.

'Shh.' His fingers explored and his lips nibbled.

She gasped when he nipped her ear. 'Cord, wait. I don't want to mislead you.'

'Later, Em. Save it for later. Just *feel*.'

She relinquished her tightly held control with sweet and complete surrender, leaning into a searing kiss that stole Cord's breath, robbed all thought and nearly drowned them both.

'This is crazy,' she said, sputtering as they resurfaced, laughing. She shook the water from her braid. 'We're crazy.'

'This is beautiful,' he corrected, sobering and reaching for her again, smoothing back her hair. 'You're beautiful. No, don't say anything,' he warned her with a soft finger against her lips when she would have spoken. 'Don't think. Just feel.'

He stood and dragged her to her feet in the center of the tub; water was raining off them. She was wearing just her tank top and wispy panties, both of which were hugging her deliciously wet curves in a way that left him aching to touch. Just one more taste, he promised himself. He would use all the finesse and tenderness he had to show her how much he wanted her. Then he'd let her go until she knew her mind. He had to.

So he plundered, and his careful plan went awry, for he'd underestimated her power over him. One touch of her restless hands, the low, encouraging sound from deep in her throat, the insistent movement of her hips against his – and he was completely undone.

Finesse and tenderness flew with the wind as they streaked their hands over each other there in the water, grappling and fumbling to possess.

'God, Emily.' Cord shook, struggling to hold them both upright in the swirling water. 'I can't believe what you do to me.'

Her eyes opened, wild and glazed, her breath heavy. 'Remember what you said – don't think.' She fisted both hands in his hair, pulled his mouth back to hers, tasting warm, sweet and absolutely irresistible. There was no turning back, he knew that now, so he lifted her and stepped from the tub. Water sluiced off them, splashing to the deck.

Emily clung tightly to him and closed her eyes. 'Cord, I feel so strange. Cold, but hot.'

'Me too, Em. Me too.'

'I've never felt this way.'

Neither had he. The day had given way to night. In the growing darkness, her pale, wet skin gleamed, and he lowered his head to kiss her slim neck. 'Come upstairs with me, Emily.' His voice was rough, hoarse, and he hardly recognized it. Her wet, warm body was snuggled up against his chest as if she were

320

made for the spot. So wet and so sheer were her clothes, she might have been wearing nothing at all. 'Please.'

She pressed closer. 'Yes. Hurry.'

They made it as far as the stairs before Emily, her eyes still closed, rooted out with her mouth and placed an open-mouthed kiss on Cord's chest.

She heard his violent oath before he practically dropped her, still dripping wet, on the stairs. His long, hard body followed down on top of hers, with one hard forearm bracing her head. 'You drive me to the brink, Red,' he muttered thickly, his mouth ravishing her neck, shoulders and face so that she didn't feel the discomfort of the hard wood stairs beneath her. 'You always have.'

She opened her eyes to find his upon her. They were deep, intent, and full of such fierce love and longing it humbled her. All she knew was that it felt right and she wanted him. Now – and in a way she'd never wanted anyone else. It didn't change the fact that she didn't understand his claim of love, or the fact that she wasn't prepared to reciprocate the feeling, but she wouldn't think of that now.

Maybe it was simply because she'd denied her body this very thing for so very long, but, whatever it was, she was going to give in to it.

'Emily,' he murmured softly, kissing her until she lay eager and pliant against the arm that supported her. 'You're so lovely.' His lips, those wonderfully talented and greedy lips, smoothed their way from shoulder to shoulder, along the scooped neckline of her tank top. Her body, of its own accord, moved against him, wanting more. When his hot tongue snaked over her cooled skin, under the edge of her top and across the curve of her breast, her back arched off the stairs.

She shivered in anticipation, but Cord lifted his head. 'You're cold.' He started to rise, but she clutched at him.

'No,' she begged him. 'Don't stop.'

'Oh, Em.' His laugh was short, harsh as he stood. 'I couldn't stop now if I wanted to.' He lifted her, pausing to slide her hips hard against his. Her gaze flew up to meet his as she felt exactly how much he wanted her. 'But this time,' he told her, planting kisses over her face, 'this first time, you deserve a bed.'

In his dark bedroom he left her only to flip on the connecting bathroom light and grab a towel to wrap her in. The light in the other room drifted out, enveloping them in soft shadows, but it wasn't dark enough to hide the magnificent body standing before her. He was amazingly unaware of his own beauty, the broad chest that narrowed to a flat stomach, the lean hips and . . . Emily blushed furiously.

How long had it been since she'd stood, practically naked, next to a man? Ten long years – and even then it had never been like this. She'd been a young girl then, and James practically still a boy. Standing before her was at least one hundred and eighty pounds of full-grown man – and a very aroused one at that.

It was easy to hide her sudden shyness – until he lifted her face, his thumb seductively tracing her lower lip. 'Change your mind?'

Those clear blue eyes were mesmerizing. And she wanted him so badly. Badly enough to risk the embarrassment of her inexperience. 'No,' she whispered.

He touched the hands that clutched the towel to her, smiling gently. 'You're nervous.'

She started to deny it with a shake of her head, then shrugged. 'A little.'

'Don't be embarrassed. It's sweet.'

'Being . . . inept is sweet?'

'If you were inept,' he asked thickly, pulling her against his hips, 'would I feel like this?'

She swallowed hard against the pulsing hardness she felt pressed against her belly. 'No,' she whispered, thrilling to the knowledge that she had this kind of power over him. 'But I've . . . only done this once. And . . . I wasn't very good at it.'

'Says who?'

She hesitated. 'James – '

His eyes lit. 'James wasn't only a fool, Em. He was an idiot.' He smoothed back her hair. 'I like knowing this is special to you,' he said. 'As special as it is to me. I want to remember this always.'

There was no doubt she would, she thought hazily as he took her mouth again. The towel dropped, long forgotten, and his hands skimmed lightly over her body, again evoking delicious shivers she couldn't control. He pulled back to slowly tug off her wet

323

clothes, eyes riveted to the skin which he exposed.

Not one to do anything halfway, she shed her modesty to take the last step between them, resting her hands lightly on his shoulders. 'I've dreamed about this,' she admitted.

His gaze lifted to hers. 'I have too, Em.' Taking his time, he slid his hands down her sides and up her back. 'I've dreamed of this every night since that first day you found me on the floor in the bathroom, cursing my pipes.' His fingertips grazed her nipples and her knees nearly buckled, but Cord simply backed her to the bed, then tumbled her down upon it.

One kiss and the powerful passion gripped them again. They rolled heedless across the bed until she lay sprawled over him, hands braced on his chest, her wet braid hanging between them. With intent, purposeful movements, he removed the rubber band at the end and slowly unwound her hair. 'I love it loose like this,' he whispered, running his fingers through it. 'There's so much of it.'

Emily's eyes fluttered closed in the simple pleasure of having someone work on her hair. When he pushed the mass of it back, exposing all of her to him, she couldn't wait for him to touch. Hard palms and gentle fingers teased her mercilessly until she fairly vibrated with tension, ached with the need to be possessed. That unaccustomed inner heat was back, and she raced uncontrollably toward a climax she couldn't live without, yet he held her on the tenuous edge with his teasing fingers. Her hips rocked against his, feeling the velvet steel of his hardness beneath her.

'Cord,' she grated through clenched teeth. 'Now.' She moved against him, ready to take matters into her own hands, but he wasn't finished with her yet.

He gripped her hips, holding her from taking him within her, his eyes shimmering with heat. But, instead of thrusting deep inside as she'd expected, he brought his hand down between their bodies, watching as she arched back and moaned, his fingers continuing their masterful and exquisite torture until she came in one hot, surprised burst.

'Again,' he demanded, rising up and rolling her beneath him, replacing his fingers with his mouth. She cried out in dazed shock and pleasure as her senses ceased to function and he drove her up again, lost in the rolling sensations, locked in ecstasy.

Her thighs were still quivering when he said hoarsely, 'Emily. Look at me.'

Somehow she managed to open her eyes. Cord towered over her, his arms trembling with strain, eyes glittering with passion, hunger. 'I love you,' he said fiercely, on a ragged breath, his hands fisted on either side of her head. 'God, I love you.'

Tears sprang to her eyes, emotion mingling with need. He pressed partly into her then, wrenching a low moan from her. She lifted her hips, desperate for more of him, but he held her still.

'Wait – let me,' he said thickly. 'I don't want to hurt you . . . you're so small.'

She could feel him stretching her, but the intense pleasure far outweighed any discomfort. She wouldn't – couldn't – wait any longer, and she urgently pressed upward, taking the rest of him deep within her. He groaned, and she was lost then while his body tirelessly plunged into her. Mindlessly she pushed him on, gripping his hair and pulling him closer, closer, fighting for air, once again racing for that final burst.

She could feel it building again, unbearably, and she could do nothing, nothing but cling helplessly to him, each breath a sob. She hung on even as he called her name, even as he buried his face in her hair and stiffened, then began to shudder. She exploded right along with him, shattering in a million pieces.

'You okay?'

Still exhilarated, and more than a little shaken, Emily lay with her eyes closed and summoned the energy to answer. 'No. I'm paralyzed.'

Cord's laughter rumbled against her ear. 'That's because I'm still on you. I'll get off when I can move again.'

'No. Don't.' She clutched at him, liking the weight. 'Oh, God, wait. I'm blind too.'

'It got dark while you were busy seducing me in the hot tub, remember? Adjust your eyes; the bathroom light is still on. See?'

'I did not seduce you.' Turning her head, she squinted. She was tucked half against him, half under him, and they faced each other sideways on the bed, their feet hanging off. 'I've never seduced anyone in my life.'

'Then you're a natural.'

So was he, she thought. But she saw no need to tell him so, since it would only stuff his ego. Her muscles spasmed – an aftershock of incredible sex. Then she told him anyway. 'That was . . . wow.'

He laughed again, a magical sound that was beginning to be like food to her brain, and rolled to his side, bringing her with him. 'My thoughts exactly.' He looked down at her with deep, inscrutable eyes. 'It had been a long time.'

She felt herself stiffen and flush and was thankful for the dark. 'I told you that. I warned you.'

He pushed the hair from her face. 'I meant for me.'

'Oh.'

'It made it that much better, Em. For both of us, I hope.'

She didn't know what to say, and awkwardness took over. It had been incredibly special, more than he could ever know. She'd never felt so . . . free, so gloriously sexual as she had in his arms. But now, when the moment had passed, she only felt hopelessly embarrassed. The room had turned cold and the covers were puddled beneath them. She lay on the man's bed, naked as she pleased – as if she belonged there.

But she didn't.

No matter how amazing it had been, they had problems. He loved her and she was still working on getting used to liking him, trusting him. She still wasn't prepared to let Cord slip into her life as if he belonged there. She couldn't. Wouldn't.

And she absolutely didn't want to *love* him – or anyone. Ever.

It was going to hurt him and she hated knowing that. She shivered, anticipating his reaction. He would be civil and cool. And she would lose the best friend she'd ever had.

'Em? What is it?' He stirred, tried to pull her close, but she had sat up. 'What's wrong?'

How to tell him? How to get out of here with some measure of self-respect? 'I made a terrible mistake here tonight, Cord. I'm so sorry.'

His arms dropped. 'What mistake was that?'

She scooted off the bed and reached for the towel, more than a little self-conscious. 'This.' She gestured helplessly to the bed.

'It wasn't a mistake.' With easy grace for one so large, Cord came toward her in the near darkness, either ignoring or forgetting the fact he was completely nude. 'And how you can even think it after what we just shared is beyond me.' His voice was low and controlled, only his eyes reflecting his anger, his pain.

This was possibly the most difficult thing she'd ever done. 'I don't want to hurt you, Cord.'

He took her shoulders. 'Then don't.'

She could see that she would, over and over again, unless she stopped this madness now. Because being this close to him made it very difficult to make her stand. All she wanted to do was throw her arms around him and lose herself in his magic again.

She shrugged off his hands, gripping the towel tight. 'I have to go.'

'No, you don't. You can't run away from this.'

'We can't do this again.'

His eyes went dark, smoldered, but he said nothing.

Bending, she retrieved her wet garments and ran from the room, surprised he didn't stop her. But she had to go. Didn't she?

She stopped on the stairs where they'd dropped eagerly only a short time before, kissing. Her heart twisted.

He'd said he loved her, and she was leaving him because she was scared to let him into her life, to relinquish some of her hard-won control. She was afraid to love.

She was a coward.

She closed her eyes, picturing Cord's heart-stopping smile, hearing his low, sexy voice in her mind. She'd waited too long. It was too late. He'd already insinuated himself into her life, her heart, her soul – all when she wasn't looking. The thick, hefty wall she'd built around her heart and protected for years was crumbling.

Even with her eyes closed she could vividly picture Cord's terror as he'd held her the night her blown tire had nearly sent her over the cliffs to her death. Even now she could hear his gruff concern when she'd been so violently ill. She could see the hot, hungry look in his eyes when she'd stood, drenched, in his hot tub.

And she was leaving him.

He was kind, loving and sweet, with a sense of humor that never failed to bring her out of a foul temper. In return she'd been nothing but irritable, moody and temperamental. He deserved so much more.

She had to leave.

Regardless, her feet wouldn't take her down the stairs and to the door. The reason was simple. *She didn't want to go*.

She whirled around and plowed directly into him.

His warm hands steadied her as she pressed tight against his chest. 'Couldn't do it, huh?'

'Damn you.' Needy, she held on for dear life. 'No. I couldn't go.' Face buried in his neck, she sighed, then clutched him tighter. 'But this doesn't mean I love you. And I'm not going to m-m-marry you.'

He took her shoulders and forced her to look at him. The anger was still simmering in those blue eyes, but mixed in was humor and something much, much more. Love. Enough love to have her swallowing hard against the rush of emotion.

'I rushed you,' he said quietly. 'And for that I'm sorry. But I meant everything I said before. And someday, hopefully soon, you'll be ready to deal with it.'

'What if I'm never ready?'

'I won't push you when you're not ready. It's not fair. But neither will I give up. I believe in us, Emily, whether you do or not. And, for now, I've got enough trust and love for the both of us.'

'Aren't you ever afraid?' she whispered. 'Afraid of getting hurt?'

'Of course I am.' He smiled tightly. 'I was terrified just a minute ago, when you left me in the bedroom. But I came from nothing, Emily. *Nothing.* No family, no background, no heritage. I was taught that it didn't matter, that you could always find more love if you tried, if you were open for it. I want to try with you, Emily. Together we could have family, background, heritage. I want that more than you'll ever know – but you have to want it too. And as much as I do, if this thing is going to work.'

Her eyes narrowed at the stubborn set of his jaw, the endless patience in his expression. 'You had no intentions of letting me leave, did you?'

'Absolutely none.'

She shook her head, then dropped her eyes, moved by his words. And then saw for the first time that he was still stark naked. She would have thought that she couldn't feel such arousal, such longing again – not so soon after the intense experience they'd had – but she was very wrong. His body was beautiful, solid, and sculptured from old-fashioned hard work, not equipment. Her eyes lowered and she gasped.

Even in the low light she could see his injuries clearly. Deep, harsh scratches scored the length of his thighs and calves. From his hips to his toes there were dark blue and purplish bruises, just beginning to turn yellow.

CHAPTER 16

'Cord!' Emily bent, lightly touching his bare, abused legs. 'What happened?'

He pulled back, embarrassed. 'It's nothing. Forget it.'

Damn it, he'd forgotten to keep his legs hidden. Grabbing her hand, he led her back up the stairs. In the darkened bedroom he sat back down on the bed, pulled her beside him and threw the blanket over them.

Something cold and wet brushed against him and he flinched, cursed, then tossed the wet clothes Emily still held to the floor.

Shooting him a stubborn look, Emily drew back the blanket to expose his legs, managing, he noticed with a roll of his eyes, to keep herself covered with that damn towel.

'Tell me how you got hurt,' she demanded.

Sighing, more from the loss of the beautiful view of her delectable body than anything else, Cord leaned back, bracing his head on folded arms. 'It might have been an exceptionally long time, but I'm pretty sure when a man and a woman finish making the most incredible love in recent history they usually make the most of those precious aftermoments.' He leered at her suggestively.

She didn't give an inch. 'Cord. Tell me.'

Well, it'd been worth a try. 'Would you believe I'm unbelievably clumsy?'

Emily's eyes flickered over his body, but she didn't move. 'You're the most agile man I know. *What happened?*'

He watched her eyes linger on his body in spaces he wasn't injured, and it did something to him. God, he wanted her again. And, if she kept her eyes on his body like that, she was soon going to be very aware of it. It would be easy to succumb to that need, to tempt her to feel it also, but he badly wanted her to want it as much as he.

'You need a doctor.'

And he needed a quick change of subject. He'd give anything to protect her from the truth. 'My legs are fine. They're already healing.'

Face white, mouth tight, she scooted off the bed and backed up a step. 'It's from the fall, isn't it? The one that was meant for me.'

Trying to make light of it, Cord smiled. 'Lucky for me, your mural broke my fall.'

'It's not funny.' She looked sick.

His smile vanished. 'No, it's not. Now come over here and make it better.'

Her eyes flew to his. 'Does it hurt very badly?'

'Yes,' he said, rising. God, she was a sight, standing there wrapped in his towel, her lithe body shimmering in the pale light. How could he possibly resist her? 'It needs a kiss.'

Her eyes narrowed and she flipped her loose hair over her shoulder. 'You're teasing me. Someone is trying to kill me and you're teasing – '

Gently he pulled her to the bed before she could finish her sentence, unable to stand the horror in her eyes a second longer. 'Let it go for now, Em. It's just us here and we're safe. It's our time.'

'But it's too much – it's all too much – ' She pushed him aside and tried to leave the bed again, but he was quick. Grabbing her, he wrestled her down and pinned her to the mattress.

Stretched out beneath him and unwilling to play, Emily shook her head. 'I give up.'

'Never give up,' he told her, lowering his mouth to the soft shoulder he'd just bared. He loosened the towel she'd cocooned herself in and tossed it to the floor.

'Cord!' She squirmed, trying to cover herself up again. 'Stop it. I'm worried, we have to talk.'

He wanted the satisfied, salacious Emily back. The one who had been panting and bucking beneath him, begging for more. But he'd settle for a relaxed, happy Emily. So he tickled her.

'Don't make me hurt you,' she said, laughing when he nipped at a rib. 'I will, I promise.'

He ignored her, easily gathering both wrists in one hand over her head, and tickled mercilessly. Enjoying her laughter, he hardly noticed when one of her hands snaked free.

Until she clobbered him on the side of his head with his own pillow. He stared down at her in amazement. 'You got me.'

She smiled, smugly. And smacked him with the pillow again. Hard.

'That's enough!' he shouted, laughing. 'You've called for drastic measures.' He pushed up to his knees, distracted by the sight of her, stretched out before him. Suddenly laughing was the furthest thing on his mind, and he drew her up off the bed and settled her against the largest erection he'd ever had. He watched with satisfaction as her eyes changed from amused to sultry.

When he ran his hands down her body, stopping to play with the sensitive peaks of her breasts, she clutched at him helplessly. 'We should . . . talk,' she insisted with obvious difficulty.

'You talk, I'll listen,' he assured her.

'Did Stone see your legs? Because – ' He pulled a nipple into his mouth, tugging gently. She gasped and held his head. ' – If – if he saw them, he couldn't possibly think you – ' She broke off on a moan when he fingers cupped her, slipping into her wetness.

'Cord, you're not . . . helping,' she struggled to say, breathless.

'No?' he murmured, kissing her neck. 'Then allow me to help.' With one hand around her hips, the other at her back, he pushed into her, then held absolutely still, savoring the moment. 'How's that?'

'Oh,' she whispered, closing her eyes and dropping her head to his chest. 'That's . . . I can't . . . think.'

'Good,' he managed, and felt her smile against him. 'This is . . . better than worrying, isn't it?' All he could think was how gloriously and thoroughly complete he felt inside her.

'Yeah.' She lifted her hips. 'Please . . . now?'

'In a minute,' he whispered against her lips, wanting to hold out as long as he could.

'You make me feel so good, Cord.'

His heart caught. No woman had ever touched him so deeply, no woman had ever felt so right against him, no woman had ever held him with arms that trembled and eyes that spoke what her lips wouldn't. 'That's good, Em, because you do the same for me.'

'Now,' she demanded, insistently pulling at him. 'Move. Now.'

He pushed her back down to the bed, and while her hips rose to meet his he dove into her again and again, managing to hold back only long enough to feel her first quiver before he drove himself to the edge and plunged.

Emily couldn't believe it when she opened her eyes and had to squint against the stream of sunlight pouring in the windows. Morning. A hard body lay spooned behind her, a heavy arm resting over her, holding her tight against a warm chest. Her feet and legs were pinned by a muscular leg.

She turned her head on the pillow and looked into Cord's sleeping face. And then blushed, remembering the incredible things he'd done to her, the things she'd done back to him. Silly to be modest now, she thought, stretching. A few aches and pains made themselves known, a forcible reminder of her inexperience. A smug grin crossed her face. Cord hadn't seemed to mind – and as a result they hadn't gotten much sleep.

The sound of someone running up the stairs jerked her fully awake.

'Emily!'

Startled and disoriented, she sat up, throwing off Cord's arm. Josh. Quickly, she glanced back. Cord mumbled something unintelligible, then rolled over, sprawling face-down across the entire bed. Great. No help there.

'Emily!' Josh called again, his voice echoing strangely in the empty house. 'Where are you?'

She jumped up, then with a very unladylike curse, sat down on the edge of the bed. Her panties and tank top lay haphazardly on the floor at her feet, still damp. Her overalls? Probably laying just where she'd dropped them – on the deck outside by the hot tub. Her incredible night of passion turned into a nightmare before her very eyes.

Still cursing under her breath, she ran to Cord's dresser and got lucky on the first drawer. Sweatsuits, neatly folded. Panicked as she was, she still took a minute to shake her head at the disgustingly perfect piles of clothes. When did he have time for that? She yanked first pants then a sweatshirt on, and dashed to the door just as Cord stirred. He sat up, an unbelievably sexy smile on his face.

'Those look good on you,' he said in a sleep-husky

voice. 'Now come here so I can take them back off.'

'Shh!' She waved wildly at him to keep quiet. She was swimming in the sweatsuit and desperately trying to figure out a way out of this mess. How could she have slept so long? She *never* slept in.

Opening the door a crack, she peeked out. Josh still called her, his voice coming from the floor above. And he sounded worried, damn it. What was she going to do?

Cord pulled her back and she turned to stare at him in surprise. He'd already pulled on his customary work clothes – jeans and T-shirt. Kissing her once, he smiled, touched her cheek and said softly, 'Take your time. I'll stall him.'

The smile on his face said that she'd owe him later. The lump in her throat said she was more touched than she wanted to admit. But Josh was a smart kid – too smart for his own good. It was obvious she'd spent the night here and he'd be upset. She owed it to him to be there.

So she followed Cord up the stairs, finding both of them on the third-floor balcony.

'Where is she?' Josh asked Cord, a heavy scowl on his face.

'I'm right here, Josh.' She held her breath for his reaction to her disheveled appearance, but it never came.

'Thank God.' He ran a hand over his face, then came to her quickly and, in a rare show of affection, hugged her to him.

'I missed you too, Josh,' Emily joked, holding him

close. But when he trembled, her stomach clenched. Pulling back, she looked at him. 'What is it?' His normally laughing young eyes were filled with terror. 'What's happened?'

'You're okay,' Josh said shakily. 'That's what matters.'

'I'm fine,' Emily said, guilt hitting her. 'I'm sorry I didn't leave you a note, but – '

'I don't know what I thought I was going to do if you weren't here.' Josh shook his head. 'I'm just glad I found you.'

'Something else has happened.' Cord spoke calmly enough, but as he stepped forward his tenseness was palpable. 'And it's not just that you didn't find Emily at your apartment. Tell us.'

'Someone messed up our apartment pretty bad – like they were looking for someone.' Josh's voice still shook. 'At first I thought maybe they'd taken you, Emily, and I freaked – but the truck was gone . . . and, *God*, am I glad you're here.'

'Our apartment?' Emily backed up a step, her mind whirling. Cord's eyes met hers and she knew he was thinking about what could have happened to her if she'd been home.

'Did you call the police?' he asked Josh.

'No. I wasn't really thinking about anything except finding Emily.' He hesitated.

'What?' Emily asked, pushing. She knew that look. 'What else?'

'I listened to the machine in case you'd left a message.' He bit his lip in an old familiar gesture that spoke of his nerves. 'Katherine mentioned something about that mural you're supposed to paint for her this weekend, how she'll pick you up and . . .'

'And what?' she demanded, touching his shoulder. 'Josh, just tell me.'

'She said she hoped you felt all better – from your *poisoning*. Geez, Emily – you told me you just had the flu.' He looked sick and Emily's heart twisted. 'I can't believe it. I can't believe you didn't tell me. Why?'

'I was going to tell you as soon as you got home, really I was. I just didn't know how to say it over the phone.'

'You didn't want me to worry,' Josh said, shaking his head. 'I'm not a kid, Emily. You're in big trouble and I think I deserve to know what's going on.' Josh glanced at Cord. 'She also said something about Cord's fall. She thought you'd be shaken up enough to want to get out of town.'

Emily winced at the hurt look on her brother's face. They'd never kept secrets before, never needed to. 'I'm sorry you had to walk into that apartment alone. And I wanted to tell you about the poison and the fall myself, but – '

'Yeah, yeah,' he interrupted, irritated. 'But you wanted to tell me in person.'

'It's the truth,' Cord said firmly. 'No one was trying to hide anything from you.'

'*You* got her into this. Because of you, she's running for her life.'

Emily saw Josh's accusation register on Cord, but he just stood still. 'It's not his fault, Josh. He can't control the person doing this anymore than we can.'

'He's right.' Cord turned to Emily, his eyes reflecting his anger and helpless despair. 'I *did* get you into this, and I'll get you out.'

'You'd better.'

Emily recognized Josh's rising temper. 'The important thing is that we're all still safe,' Emily said quickly, jumping in before he could make another scathing remark.

'I'm just glad you weren't in the apartment last night,' Josh looked at Emily. His eyes took in her wild, untamed hair, the clothes that were obviously Cord's. 'But I don't think I'm so glad about what that means.'

Emily glanced at Cord, and, as amazing as it seemed to her, he still managed to give her that look that said she was all he thought about.

'It's going to be okay, Josh,' Cord said to him. 'It's all going to work out.'

'Yeah,' Josh said, still looking at his sister. 'Whatever.'

'No, I mean it.' Cord grabbed Emily's hand, then included Josh by touching his shoulder. 'Trust me. This will work out, and we'll be okay.'

Josh stood between Cord and Emily, looking young and uncertain and very afraid. But the animosity he'd shown Cord vanished. 'How do you know that?'

'Because I'm going to make damn sure it is.'

Most amazing to Emily was the look that passed between Cord and Josh. She could practically see them silently agree to team together to pull them all through this.

It was perhaps the most heartwarming sight Emily had ever beheld, and somehow she actually believed it. They would get through this – together.

Josh cleared his throat. 'I brought you some stuff. I think you should go paint that mural. Maybe between the police and Cord and I we can figure out what the hell is going on while you're gone. No one but us knows you'll be there, so you'll be safe.'

And just when did he get so grown up? Emily wondered. But she couldn't do it. 'I'm *not* going to just leave for the weekend. Not when all this is going on. And I want to see the apartment.'

'We'll call the police first,' Cord said, taking Emily's shoulders when she would have moved away. 'But Josh is right. With the blown tire incident, this makes at least three attempts.' He squeezed her gently, then spoke carefully. 'And I think that doing the mural is a great idea.'

'No. Absolutely not.'

'Please, Em,' he said, his blue eyes eloquent and pleading.

'I'd be too worried about Josh.' *And you*, she thought.

'He'll stay here. With me. It's only for two days and you'll be safe there. I won't rest until we solve

342

this thing, but I can't concentrate when I'm worried about you getting hurt.'

'*Please*, Emily,' Josh added. 'Please, go.'

'But – '

'Damn it, Red.' Cord shook her lightly, all casual elegance gone. Eyes hard and serious probed into her. 'We're afraid for you. Is that so difficult to understand?'

It was a conspiracy, she thought. But as she looked back and forth between the two people she cared most about in the entire world she caved. 'All right. I'll go. Two days, you guys. You've got two days and I'll be back.'

'We'll find a way to solve this thing,' Cord promised. 'And in the meantime we'll know you're safe.'

But, Emily wondered, how would she know that they were safe?

Cord stood in the driveway, watching Katherine drive off with the only woman who'd ever captured his heart. No one but the three of them and the police would know where she was for the weekend.

Sheriff Stone was on his way to Emily's apartment, and when he was done there Cord was sure he'd pay a visit for more questions. Seth had just called from their office, and planned on being there when Stone came by to question him again as well.

Josh was safely tucked away upstairs, painting.

So why, then, couldn't Cord shake the feeling that danger was closer than ever?

Trying to take his mind off Emily with plumbing

didn't work. Neither did caulking the new bathroom window. Or wiring the upstairs hallway for a three-way light. Visions from the night before crowded his mind, making work near impossible. It had been the most beautiful, passion-filled night he'd ever spent. She'd made love with a sweet fierceness that had taken his breath, made all the more special because he knew how new it all was for her.

She'd made it new for him too, and he knew things would never be the same again.

He was hopelessly in love with her.

But even that was overshadowed by the feeling he just couldn't shake. He suddenly regretted the decision to send her away, wishing she were by his side at this very moment. He'd call her – just to make sure she'd arrived safely.

He would have paged Katherine, but that would take too long. He'd yet to call the new number to the school she'd given him, and it took him long minutes even to find it. No answer. His stomach took a long roll.

He waited five more minutes – with increasing frustration – then waited on the line to Katherine's church while he waited for someone to verify Katherine's new number.

'I could have driven there myself by now,' he muttered, tapping impatiently on the receiver.

'What's the matter?'

Cord watched as Josh came warily into the room. 'Nothing. I'm just calling to make sure of Katherine's number so I can check on your sister.'

'Why? Do you think there's a problem?'

'Uh, no.' Yet the sensation of impending danger was stronger than ever. 'Just want to check, that's all.'

'Mr Harrison?' The clerk came back on the phone. 'I'm sorry to keep you waiting. I can give you the number I have for St James's, if you'd like, but that school isn't open this year due to cutbacks.'

His heart stopped, simply stopped.

'Can I speak to Katherine?' he asked in a voice he didn't recognize.

'Katherine?'

'Katherine Snow. She's in the order there.'

'Just a minute, please.' She came back on a moment later. 'She's no longer here.'

His knees turned to water. 'What do you mean?'

'She left the order eight months ago.'

Katherine lifted her bowed head and smiled at the altar. Candles glowed in the silent church, casting eerie shadows onto the dark stone walls. She was alone. Emily waited for her in the car. She'd believed Katherine's sudden need to stop and give prayer, just as she'd respected Katherine's wish to be alone to do it.

Katherine paused before praying. She should be frightened; she knew it. But she wasn't; she never was. God was on her side.

God loved her. She stood from where she'd been kneeling and made the sign of the cross. As if to purify herself from evil thoughts, she sprinkled holy water down the front of her skirt.

Being a woman of God, such as she was, she sorely regretted that she'd been forced to resort to such a drastic measure as murder. *Murders*, she corrected.

She could still remember the first time, with that Tayna woman, meticulously washing her hands afterward, shivering delicately as the last of the blood came off her skin and swirled down the drain. She had looked in the mirror over the sink that night and smiled, knowing she was indeed a woman of God.

She sighed. It had been very satisfying.

God had seen fit to reward her with Cord – not her biological son, true, but her son nonetheless. She loved him with all the pure abandonment and passion that only another mother could understand.

Or God.

God understood that love. He also understood how she felt every time Cord sullied his soul with a woman not worthy of him. After all, it'd been God who had given her permission to fix things as she saw fit – which she'd done with pleasure.

It was a shame, of course. But then that Lacey woman had settled on *her* Cord, and that couldn't be allowed to continue.

Then there'd been Sheri. The secretary had practically thrown herself at Cord, and, though he hadn't seemed interested, Katherine hadn't wanted to take chances.

Things hadn't gone the way Katherine had

346

planned there. If they had, Sheri's family would have been planning a funeral instead of worrying about her sudden move back home. But the message had been delivered, and Katherine felt confident that Cord was safe from that woman.

Katherine knew she'd do anything – absolutely anything – to keep Cord's soul safe. It wasn't his fault that he was so devastatingly handsome, such a lure to women of all shapes and sizes. He had such a kind heart and a wonderful mind. He didn't understand that women were the path to hell, but she'd help him.

Fingering her rosary beads with one hand, the other holding the heavy cross she wore around her neck, she bowed her head and prayed for guidance. Because there was yet another woman who tempted Cord. And this simply couldn't be allowed to continue.

The painter had to go, that much she knew. She'd seen Cord glance at Emily, his eyes filled with a dark, fierce longing such as she'd never seen before. The thought of him losing his heart to this woman scared her to the bone.

Fisting her hands, she drummed them against her thighs, not feeling the pain. He was hers, she silently screamed, tossing her head back and staring at the dark ceiling as if she could actually see God in his heavens.

Forcing a deep breath, Katherine calmed herself. When she could think calmly, she again bowed her head in prayer.

God had forgiven the mistake with Emily's scaffolding, then her tire, forgiven her the indiscretion with the poison, and now, because she'd been patient, he'd given her another chance.

This time she wouldn't fail. Both God and Cord were counting on her.

Katherine sat, hands folded demurely in her lap, fingering the rosary beads.

She might no longer be a bride of Christ, but old habits died hard. She again felt for her cross, sighed when she felt its reassuring weight around her neck. Glancing around the old historic church, she smiled. She was in a good place these days, in a place not quite so rigid as that order she'd quit. A place that would bring her the ultimate satisfaction.

She was free. She grinned uncontrollably at the power of it all, then prayed briefly for forgiveness for the flash of cockiness.

Of course, she needed God's help, she revised mentally. She couldn't do it without him. She wouldn't even try.

She did feel badly about the lie to Cord about her teaching, but he couldn't understand her need to be free of the church. No one could understand that but God.

All she had left to do to complete her happiness was to ensure Cord's soul was safe. To do that she had to take care of Emily.

Katherine moved about the aisle, lighting candles, chanting softly to herself. Preparing herself for the upcoming ritual of caring for Cord's soul. Emily would have to die. Again she fingered her rosary beads, touched her sacred cross, seeking peace.

It didn't come.

For added protection she again sprinkled herself, and the room, with holy water, then bowed her head in prayer, gripping the small vial tightly in her hands.

She needed a plan and had hoped God would provide one. She squeezed her eyes tight, frustration and fear mingling with the knowledge that her son needed her, and she'd not yet come through for him. His feelings for the woman were deep, too deep, and they had to be stopped – at any cost. She'd lose him if she didn't act fast.

She drummed her fists against her thighs again, screeching when the glass shattered in her hand and water sprayed across her skirt.

Blood dripped slowly from her palm down her leg. Katherine tilted her head and watched the flow, not feeling the pain.

Her failure made her numb.

But God, in his infinite patience and love, forgave her. He always did.

And then he gave her the strength to try yet again. And with that strength came a lovely plan.

This time she wouldn't fail.

Knees weak and bile backing up his throat, Cord hung up the phone with the church and immediately picked it up again.

'What?' Josh demanded, his eyes on Cord's pale face. 'Did you get the number?'

'Sheriff Stone, please,' Cord croaked into the phone when the dispatcher picked up. While he was on hold he turned to Josh as disbelief washed over him. 'Josh, sit down.'

'Why?' he demanded, gripping the counter. 'Spill it, Harrison. You're making me nervous.'

Absolutely sick, and cold with terror, Cord shook his head grimly. How could he not have known that Katherine was no longer a nun? Granted, he had not made church a priority in the past few months, but still – someone should have told him. Certainly one of the few nuns that were still there from when he'd lived at the orphanage.

They probably would have, Cord reminded himself harshly, *if he'd gotten to church this year.*

He'd thought it strange that Katherine had insisted he use her pager if he wanted to get in touch, rather than call the school, but he'd been so busy in his own world he hadn't questioned her.

Emily would pay the price for that.

'First, sit,' he told Josh. 'You're not going to believe this.' He heard the beep indicating he had another call on the line and he punched the receiver, hoping against hope it would be Emily. 'Harrison here.'

'Cord. How are you, darling?'

Relief had him sinking into the closest chair. 'Katherine, thank God. *Where's Emily?*'

'Oh, Cord,' she said, sorrow filling her voice. 'I wanted to save you that pain, but it's too late now, isn't it? You already love her. *Don't you?*'

350

His blood froze. 'Where is she, Katherine?'

Josh jumped to his feet again at the stricken tone in Cord's voice.

'Right here, darling. She's right here. For now. She has to die, you know.'

CHAPTER 17

'No, she doesn't,' Cord said quickly, leaping to his feet, his heart pounding with fear. 'No one has to die.' Josh rushed forward and Cord gripped his arm – whether in comfort or alarm, he didn't know. '*Listen to me*, Katherine. Just tell me where you are and I'll come for you. You need help – I'll make sure you get it. Just tell me *where you are*.'

'It's going to be okay, you know,' she sang, in that same calm voice. 'All along I've been watching out for you. I was your protector against the evil world, Cord. I have to do this, or your soul will be condemned.'

'No. No, you don't have to do anything. Where are you –?'

'You know, you can't keep doing this to me, Cord.' The first tinge of impatience crept into her voice. 'You have to give your life to God, not cheap women. I've tried to overlook it, really I have, but we really need to talk.'

'You're at the school? St James's?' He looked at Josh, who was staring at him, wild-eyed.

'Cord, my son, you're not listening to me. I'm going to take care of this little matter, but you have to promise me this is the last time. You must prepare yourself for the Lord, Cord. He isn't pleased.'

He felt sick. 'Katherine, please,' he said hoarsely. 'Tell me where you are.'

'Come to the school, Cord. I will show you how to prepare yourself.'

'I'll be right there. But first let me talk to Emily –'

'No!' she cried, striking terror in his heart. 'I can't let you talk to her. It's her fault you are contaminating yourself. It's wrong, but I'm going to take care of that, my darling. You'll not be tempted by the likes of her again.'

'I'm leaving right now. But please, wait until I get there. Okay?'

'Oh, I don't think so, Cord. It's going to take you awhile to drive here, and I'm not that patient anymore. But this is going to take some time – don't worry about that.'

The chilling thrill in her voice practically choked him with panic. 'Please, Katherine.' He'd beg if she wanted him to. 'Wait until I get there – do you understand? *Don't do anything until I get there!*' He could only pray that the sheriff's department was still holding on the other line.

'Come alone, Cord. *You must come alone*. I won't tolerate any further tainting of your soul. Goodbye, darling.'

'Katherine, wait!'

'Yes?'

His thoughts were racing with desperation, but he forced his voice to be cool, calm, collected. 'We've been through a lot together, haven't we? I mean, you practically raised me.'

Her voice softened. 'Yes, I did. And it was the greatest pleasure of my life, believe me. That's why I'm doing this, don't you see? God gave you to me, Cord, and I thank Him for it every day. But that's why I have to help you now. He's asked me to.'

'I understand.' He rubbed a hand over his eyes, forcing himself to sound calm. 'That's why I want to ask you a favor, because I know how much you care about me. I know you'll want to do this one last thing – for me.'

'Just ask, dear. What?'

'Will you wait until I get there to . . . to take care of – ' He glanced at Josh, who was hanging carefully on his every word. 'Could you wait before you . . .?' Lord, he was going to lose it right here. 'I – I want to be there with you for this.'

He could almost see Katherine's wide, surprised smile. 'Oh, the Lord is working with you! That's wonderful! But I'm not sure it's a good idea. It will be painful for you.'

He swallowed hard. 'No, it will be fine. I'll hurry, Katherine. Just promise me you'll wait.'

'We'll see,' she said cryptically. 'God speed.' And then she hung up.

'I can't believe it. *We* sent her off with the woman who's been systematically killing people.'

Cord gripped the steering wheel of his truck with white-knuckled hands and sent Josh a look. He didn't have time to worry about him now. The kid was shaken, and white as a ghost, but holding up unbelievably well.

He wished he could say the same for himself.

'The fog is rolling in.' Josh banged a fisted hand on the dash. 'Hell.' He leaned forward and squinted. 'Can't you drive this piece any faster?'

Not only was the fog rolling in, but the late afternoon sun was all but gone. With fear driving him, Cord negotiated a particularly narrow curve on the tight road too closely and all four tires squealed. 'If I drive any faster we won't get there at all.'

'She wanted you to come alone.'

Cord risked another quick glance at him, remembering the fit Josh had pitched when Cord had wanted to leave him at home. 'Yeah. I told you that.'

'But you called Stone – even though she said not to.'

'Stone and his men are in town. It will take them twice as long as us to get there. The damn school is out in the middle of absolutely nowhere.' His heart was hammering at the thought. Cold sweat slicked his hands so that it became hard to hold onto the steering wheel. 'Remember what I told you?'

Josh grumbled. 'Stay down when you start up the drive. Wait in the truck until you get back.'

'What else?' he demanded. God, he hadn't wanted to risk Josh too, but Emily's brother was as stubborn as she was. 'Joshua, what else did I tell you?'

355

'If you're not back in fifteen minutes, drive the truck down the driveway and wait for Stone. Just get my sister back, Harrison. I'll be fine.'

Finally they reached the isolated long driveway of the school. Cord cursed long and fluently at the sight of the dense, thick woods surrounding the three-story building. The place looked deserted.

Terrific.

Details were difficult to see in the misty fog, but the windows of the wooden and brick building all appeared dark. The afternoon fog warmed the air, strangely enough. Even so, a chill ran through Cord.

How the hell would he find Emily?

The sheriff would not be pleased when he found out Cord was moving in by himself, but he didn't care. If he waited for help it would be too late for Emily. It might already be too late, but he refused to think about that.

He glanced once at Josh, who was hunkered down near the floorboards. He nodded in approval, tossed him down the carphone and mouthed the words, '*Stay here.*'

Guilt and concern threatened to paralyze Cord, but sheer will and love for Emily had him moving. By design he'd left on his tool belt, giving the impression he'd been working and had been quickly called away from the job. But, in truth, he felt the need for some sort of weapon. The thought of using the steel hammer that swung against his thigh for self-defense made him sick, but he knew he would kill to protect Emily.

It was that simple and that terrifying.

He'd figured Katherine would be waiting anxiously for him, so he was surprised when he entered and neither saw nor heard a thing.

Standing in the entranceway, surrounded by old stone walls and an eerie silence, panic welled. Maybe he was too late.

He took a step, then paused, glancing at the closet door on his right. Once, when he'd been a little boy, and playing hide-and-go-seek in the rectory, he'd hidden in a similar closet. It had been filled with priest robes and nun habits, a strange combination of black and white clingy material that had scared the daylights out of him. They'd found him, huddled deep in the corner, afraid to come out.

The front doorhandle rattled behind him. Josh's tight, nervous face appeared and with a silent groan Cord yanked him forward and into the closet with him, shutting the door behind them.

'What the hell was that for?' Josh whispered. 'You scared me to death.'

'You were supposed to wait in the truck,' Cord said tersely. A soft rustling from within the closet had them both instantly quiet.

They squinted as a bright flare lit the room, then settled into the soft glow from a small cigarette lighter. The large, dirty hand that held the light was attached to a big, grubby man with nervous eyes. He wore at least five layers of clothes, that hadn't seen a washing machine in this decade, and what looked like rubber boots with holes in them

357

worn over a pair of tennis shoes. Over his thick mane of silver hair were two hats, both crooked, one with long furry flaps that covered his ears and a good portion of his face.

'This is *our* closet,' the man said, then glanced at his smaller companion.

Cord recognized her as a woman, though she certainly wasn't dressed as such. Wearing similar clothing to the man's, she looked equally dirty . . . and equally down on her luck. Sympathy for them both had Cord relaxing his tense features. 'I'm sorry,' he told the homeless couple. 'We didn't know. Have you been here long?'

'Since winter,' the woman said, her face crinkling kindly. 'But if you need a place, we can share.'

Cord had absolutely no idea how old she was; she might have been anywhere from twenty to ninety – it was impossible to tell. 'We're looking for someone,' he told them, reaching into his pocket for his wallet. 'Actually, two women.' He divided whatever bills he had and handed it to them. 'Have you seen anyone?'

The man stared at Cord and Josh in distrust. 'You cops?'

Still holding out the money, Cord shook his head. 'No. We're just – '

'Keep your money,' the man said gruffly. 'Get out.'

'This woman has my sister,' Josh blurted out. 'And she wants to hurt her. We're just trying to get her back safely. Please, help us.'

'How do I know that you're telling the truth?' the

man demanded. 'That it isn't a trick to get us to leave so you can have this space?'

Cord's eyes had accustomed themselves to the dark, and he could see the neat stacks of assorted magazines and papers scattered in the small room. Behind the couple he could see a makeshift bed of rags and paper. The smell of stale food was strong.

His stomach turned, not from disgust, but with heartfelt grief. This might have been him, he thought. Homeless. Except for the grace of the nuns, he could have ended up like this, with nothing.

And now one of those nuns was trying to destroy the only person he'd ever truly loved. 'Please,' he went on desperately, 'believe us. This isn't a trick. If we don't hurry, she may die.'

The woman put her hand on the man's arm. 'I believe him, Ed.' She looked at Josh. 'We haven't seen anyone, son. I'm sorry. And thank you, but we couldn't take your money.' Gently she pushed his outstretched hand away.

Katherine would be expecting him; she might even at this very moment know he had arrived. She'd know exactly what to look for, what to expect.

He glanced at the couple's torn and battered clothes, then down at his own clean jeans and shirt. In comparison, even Josh looked neat in his baggy overalls and loose shirt.

Inspiration struck. 'How attached are you to your clothes?' Cord asked, his eyes shining.

The man and woman looked at each other in confusion.

Cord leaned forward. 'I've got an idea,' he said. 'If you'd be kind enough. Here.' Once again he held out the money. 'An exchange.'

The woman glanced at the money, unable to hide her need.

Cord set it in her lap. 'I'm desperate, really I am. You'd be helping me. It's not a handout, because I need something from you in return.'

The woman hesitated, then scooped up the money, her eyes shimmering as she counted it. 'All right, then. Thank you.' And she reached for her top button.

Josh, catching on, closed his eyes and groaned.

Cold drops splashed Emily's face, awakening her. Her head pounded sickeningly, a forcible reminder of how Katherine had calmly and viciously knocked her out with a golf club. She blinked a blurry Katherine into view, wincing as each breath echoed painfully in her head.

'Just holy water, my child,' Katherine told her, smiling as she watched Emily struggle to move her leaden limbs. She sprinkled Emily yet again from a small vial attached to her skirt and made the sign of the cross. 'Don't bother trying to move. I've been at it again with the poison. But this time, only your motor skills are affected.'

With horror, Emily realized she was perched precariously on a wide wooden window ledge and that the window was open. Through the fog she could barely make out the woodsy yard, three stories below.

There was no screen on the window.

Emily slammed her eyes shut, ignoring her splitting headache, but her eyes flew open again as a terrible languor swept over her. Even as terrified as she was, she could hardly stay awake.

Nothing bound her to the ledge except her white-knuckled fists and her desperate will. But, for the first time in her life, she suffered from a fear of heights – and the unknown. Emily shook her head, trying to clear her misty vision. She couldn't. As she tried to lean into the room a hard rap on her knuckles with the club stopped her.

'Don't get down,' Katherine warned. 'You're still weak enough that I could beat you with this club – and don't think that I wouldn't. Stay right where you are.'

Emily found herself shaking like a leaf. To combat her terrible shaking, she closed her eyes.

'Come on now,' Katherine said evenly, even kindly. 'Open your eyes. We're not finished here. That's a girl. Now hold on tight. I don't want you to fall before I'm ready for you to.' She smiled. 'That would ruin everything.'

'Why?' Emily managed, forcing her eyes off the dizzy view of the woods below and on to the woman she'd thought her friend. She forced her heavy eyelids to stay open.

'Because when you fall – and you will – I want you to know exactly what's happening to you. And I want you to pray for forgiveness beforehand. It's only right.'

Emily stared at the woman in disbelief. It was so incongruous, the insane woman standing there so sweetly discussing God and murder in the same breath.

'This must look like a suicide,' Katherine went on cheerfully. She stood a few feet back, still brandishing the golf club. 'That'll throw the sheriff off and then he'll stop harassing my Cord.'

At the look of disbelief that Emily couldn't suppress, Katherine nodded. 'That's right, he is *my* Cord, Emily. Not yours. God gave him to me and I won't share him. I won't share him with you and I won't share him with any other of your kind.'

The implications of that statement sunk in to Emily's terrified, frozen veins. '*You've* been doing this? The . . . other women?'

'They were evil,' Katherine said simply. 'And they had to be stopped. For Cord's sake.'

'My tire?' Emily asked weakly.

'Now that blow-out was a bust, wasn't it? I thought you'd just get a flat, then I'd come along and finish off the job.' Katherine frowned. 'But you were a slippery thing, weren't you? You escaped that time, thanks to my lovely, kind-hearted son. He never could stand it when someone was in trouble.'

Emily stared at her, remembering how uneasy Cord had been that night, how he'd rushed her into his truck. Through the blazing pain in her head she dimly recalled the car that followed them that night, and she knew that if Cord hadn't been there with her she'd be dead.

The wind stirred the treetops, brushed over Emily's face like chilly fingers. She shivered, and her fingers started to cramp.

'Certainly you remember how I poisoned you,' Katherine said companionably, even gently. 'I left those cookies on Cord's counter. I knew you wouldn't be able to resist them. I knew also Cord wouldn't touch them. He hates peanut butter cookies, but he's far too polite to mention it to me.'

She was going to be sick. Unless she fell first. Her hands ached from gripping the wooden ledge. 'Cord's fall?'

'*That* was a mistake.' Katherine came closer, her face still carefully calm. 'One that you'll pay for, since it was your fault. He took that fall for you, got hurt for you.'

Katherine's eyes were insane. Emily shook her head and looked away.

'How could you have let him do that?'

The dizziness was the worst of it, Emily thought. Her fingers slipped, and with a small whimper she managed to get another grip.

'You don't ask about your scaffolding. That was a simple enough thing, just to pull a steel pin. I can't believe how unsafe those things actually are.'

Emily looked at her, horrified. 'You did that?' It hurt to think, but she remembered enough. 'You almost squished Cord between the layers.'

'Because, even then, you had him under your spell. If he'd been hurt, you'd have had no one to blame but yourself.'

'I don't believe this. I can't believe it's you.'

'I won't share him,' Katherine said again.

'That's why you've done this? So you don't have to share him?' Emily thought of the others, the women who Katherine had obviously already hurt, and knew she was about to be the next statistic. 'That's sick.'

She knew her mistake immediately, and managed to pull her foot back in time to avoid Katherine's angry thrust with the club. Breathing heavily, Katherine looked at her. 'Listen carefully. I . . . won't . . . share . . . him.'

Through the ball of fear lodged in her throat, Emily said, 'Cord loves you, Katherine. You raised him.'

'Of course he does.' Katherine smoothed her skirt, visibly calmed herself. 'He's an angel. My angel.' Her eyes turned to ice and Emily's fear increased tenfold as Katherine again stepped closer. 'And you keep turning his head away from me. Away from God.'

The wind shifted, away from the house. To Emily, who was struggling to keep a hold on the ledge with hands that shook violently, it seemed as if she would be sucked out. Knowing she was about to plunge to her death made it difficult to concentrate.

No one could survive a fall from this height.

Emily gripped the ledge even tighter, feeling the cramps tightening her hands unbearably. The urge to close her eyes and give in to sleep was strong. She managed to move her legs a few inches toward the room, but Katherine was quick with the club. She stabbed at them and Emily tightened every muscle, straining to keep her balance when she could hardly even feel her legs.

'I drugged you with a cloth over your nose,' Katherine explained calmly, satisfied that Emily wasn't going to move again. 'It will wear off soon, but even that will be too late. It's time, my dear. Time to pray for your forgiveness.'

'No!' Emily cried, unable to believe it would all be over like this. 'Cord won't understand this, Katherine. You want his love – this isn't the way to do it!'

'I already have his love.'

Emily closed her eyes. Pain, but not a physical one, slashed through her. She would never again see Cord, never again see his laughing eyes, his beautiful smile. She would never hear that wonderful low voice of his telling her how he loved her. Brick by slow brick he had tumbled down the wall she'd built around her heart until he'd insinuated himself into her soul. It hit her then, with a sharp, piercing stab through her heart.

She loved him.

She loved Cord Harrison completely, as she hadn't allowed herself to love in over ten years. And he would never know.

No! It wasn't going to end like this. It couldn't. For a long time, too long now, she had simply stopped living life to its fullest because she was unwilling to get hurt. But now, in the face of death, she realized how wrong that was. To live the way she wanted to – with love, with passion, in full color like one of her murals – she had to risk a little pain.

She wanted desperately to live. To share her life. To love Cord. To love Joshua. To paint.

'Katherine,' she said suddenly. 'You can't do this. You're a *nun*.'

Katherine laughed harshly, insanity shimmering in her eyes. 'No, I'm not. The order no longer served my purposes.'

Think, Emily, *think*. 'You'll destroy Cord. Think about your son, Katherine.'

'He agrees, my dear. He knows you tempt him, just as he knows this is for the best.' Katherine frowned briefly. 'He'll be upset I didn't wait for him, of course, but I don't think seeing this is in his best interests.'

Wait for him? Heart thundering, Emily blinked in surprise. Could Cord know where she was? Did he know she was in danger? Oh, God, she thought, please let him be on his way. Stalling, she asked, 'Does he know what you are doing for him? What you've done for him?'

'Oh, yes. I called him while you were still out cold. He's got such a kind, warm heart, my Cord. I know he suffers, thinking about what has to be done, but he knows it's for the best.'

'Are – are you sure?' Emily's confidence was lagging, especially as Katherine came toward her with the club. Her head still hurt so much it was difficult to see, and she felt as if she might be sick. Meanwhile the strange languor still inflicted her body, and she had to concentrate hard to keep awake. But knowing Cord was maybe on his way gave her a surge of hope.

'Now,' Katherine said quietly, that same serene smile on her face, 'I want you to dangle your feet over the edge. Like this.' She pushed at Emily's feet with the club, staying back.

Emily gasped in terror as she gripped the ledge, unable to make her muscles work enough even to try to fall back into the room. She resisted the push of the club, biting her lips so hard she tasted blood, but still Katherine persevered. When Emily sat limply, her feet dangling over the edge, Katherine laughed triumphantly. 'Good,' she said. 'Now. *Pray.*'

Emily managed to look up in disbelief. Katherine nodded encouragingly. 'I can't push you over until I know that you've made your peace with God, my child. That would be very unfair of me.'

Emily nearly laughed, but she knew that if she did she would become hysterical. Katherine jammed the club into the small of her back, giving her an incentive.

'Pray,' she demanded. 'You must.'

CHAPTER 18

Feet hanging over the window ledge, vision not blurry enough to hide the hideous three-story height, Emily teetered for one dizzy moment.

'Pray!' Katherine repeated, more sternly, stabbing at her with the club. 'There's no time left for you.'

With the club sharply pushing her, Emily lurched and screamed, nearly falling. She just barely held on, feeling splinters of wood dig painfully into her fingers. Wind tousled her hair, blew softly in her sweat-slicked face. She closed her eyes against the swirling view, but all she could see was Cord's face. 'No,' she sobbed. 'Please, don't.'

'God bless you, child,' Katherine said. Then she shoved at Emily again.

The door to the small room slammed open. Both Katherine and Emily whipped their heads around. And both women gasped.

Standing in the doorway was a dirty, disheveled old man with an equally filthy, disheveled woman. But Emily didn't have much time to digest that fact because Katherine whirled on her, ignoring the vagrant couple,

368

and poked her hard with the club. 'Forget praying,' she said quickly and harshly. 'Jump.'

'*No!*' The old man pushed into the room, grimy hands outstretched, his cap flapping over most of his filthy face. 'Stop.' He took a deep gulp of air, visibly shaken, his voice rough. 'I need to talk to you.'

'I'm on a mission from God and can't help you now,' Katherine said, her eyes on Emily. 'You'll have to wait.'

The old woman started to say something, but stopped at a look from the tall one. 'It can't wait,' she said in a low, strained voice. 'It must be now. Come with us. Please.' She held out her smeared hand, but Katherine ignored the softly spoken plea.

She wildly waved the club, warding them all off, and stood between Emily and the couple. 'Come one step closer and I'll shove her off. I will!'

The man raised his hands in surrender and stopped, then motioned for the woman to stay put. 'Please, Katherine – '

'How did you know my name?' she demanded, waving the club back and forth between the two strangers and Emily. 'Who are you?'

The man tucked his hands into the voluminous folds of the blanket wrapped around his body. With his head tipped respectfully down, his cap covered his expression. 'We've come to help you. We were sent.'

Katherine's lips parted in surprise. Then she smiled. 'Of course. God is good to me.'

The man moved a step closer, his hands still

hidden within the blanket. Emily squinted, struggling to see, but her vision was fading and her head hurt so badly she thought she might get sick. She weaved slowly, unable to control it. Sheer terror alone kept her clinging weakly to the ledge.

But something about the couple caught her attention – something other than the fact she didn't want them to get hurt. The husky, whispery voice, the strangely large hands . . . and then unexpectedly she caught the tall man's eyes. Dark, shimmering blue and startlingly familiar. Swimming with anguish, regret, rage. She was losing it, she thought sleepily as her vision turned gray. Definitely losing it.

The couple moved closer. 'I'm waiting for my son,' Katherine said, a touch of uncertainty in her voice. 'Where's my son?'

The old man hesitated. 'It will be all right,' he said quietly. 'You're going to be all right.' He took another step.

'No. Stay back a minute,' Katherine said, shaking her head. 'I have work left to do. You mustn't interfere. I have to do this for my son – I love him, you know. God told me I could do this for him.'

'Let's wait for him, then,' the woman said, coming up behind the man. And Emily nearly gasped again, even with her eyes closed – for she could have sworn that she sounded like . . . Josh.

'I have to take away the evil temptation from my son. He must remain pure, his soul must be untainted for God. This woman is trying to take him away from me.'

370

Sirens sounded in the distance. Katherine turned from the old man and woman. To Emily she said, 'Time has run out.' Stepping toward the window, she raised the club, preparing to send Emily flying off the ledge.

For Emily, everything happened in slow motion. 'The hammer,' the woman cried.

'I can't.' The man pulled his hands from the blanket, tossing a large hammer aside with a loud clatter that made Emily wince painfully. As Katherine's club came toward her the man shouted, 'No!' and dove at Katherine.

Emily closed her eyes as the club came down, hearing Cord's voice yell, 'Katherine, no!'

That was funny, she thought vaguely, she could hear Cord's voice. She was braced for a blow that never came, but all she could think of was Cord. Tears clogged her throat, stung her eyes, and she was distantly aware of a huge commotion around her. Cord. She could hear him as clearly as if he were right in the room with her.

She forced her eyes open, just as she was rudely yanked from the ledge by the woman – the woman whose hat had fallen off, revealing a short crop of dark red hair. She opened her mouth to complain about the pain in her head as they crashed to the floor of the room, but only a squeak escaped her lips.

The old man was sitting on the floor, cradling Katherine in his arms. Only his head was now bare and it wasn't an old man at all, but Cord. Katherine's eyes were closed and she was mumbling as if lost in prayer.

From downstairs came the sounds of the front door being forced open, then the sounds of pounding footsteps on the stairs below. Emily herself was held by the woman and she tipped her head back to stare into her green eyes. She reached up, and touched the woman's wet cheek. 'Josh,' she said groggily. 'You came.'

Josh swiped his eyes on the sleeve of his shirt, smearing dirt across his cheek, then lowered his forehead to his sister's. His every muscle was quaking. 'Shh,' he said. 'Stay still a minute.'

The door behind them crashed open and three uniformed officers leaped into the room, fully armed. Stone came in next and hunkered down by Cord and Katherine. When Emily opened her eyes again Cord was leading a subdued Katherine out of the room and whispering softly to her, the anguish and shock clear on his face.

'You're bleeding.'

Josh's worried voice made her jump. 'Am I?' She looked down at herself. Blood had dripped from her head wound down her face and her neck, and had soaked her shirt. She hadn't noticed until now. Nausea welled and she pushed away from Josh, sure she would be sick.

A tall figure appeared in front of her, but her vision wavered and grayed. He hunkered down before her, his lips moving, but she couldn't make out the words over the rushing roar of pain in her head.

Cord.

She wanted to speak, but couldn't; her mouth wouldn't work. She reached for him, but the purling clouds of unconsciousness took her first.

Disoriented and afraid to move, Emily forced herself to lie still with her eyes closed. Her heart hammered with the need to run. But she knew; the narrow ledge beneath her, the sharp cramps in her hands, the dizzy view . . . they no longer existed but in her nightmares.

The danger had passed. Vaguely she remembered the ambulance ride off the mountain and into town, the painful stitching of the gash on her head. It still throbbed, making her ill. Imagining the harsh lights, she refused to open her eyes, though hushed voices whispered nearby. She didn't need her eyes to know the voices she loved most.

'I told you to stay in the truck, damn it. You could have been hurt.'

'Oh, that's gratitude for you,' came Josh's whisper. 'If I'd stayed, who would have helped you look like a bum? Who'd have caught Emily from falling off the ledge as you stopped Katherine from smashing her? Huh?'

'Smart-mouthed kid. Can't follow directions worth a damn.'

Emily wondered at Cord's soft, snarling attitude, but couldn't bring herself to open her eyes. It hurt to move.

Josh seemed unperturbed at Cord's tone. 'Well,

the homeless thing *was* a stroke of genius, I'll give you that much. You ought to think about taking a shower.' Then came Josh's soft snicker. 'You're gross.'

'Yeah? Well, you're not so clean yourself. And you should have seen what a great girl you made, McKay,' came Cord's caustic whisper.

'Wonder what that stuff is you streaked over your face?' Josh snickered again. 'Geez, it stinks. I hope it isn't – '

'– Josh?'

'Yeah?'

'Go to hell.'

They fell silent and Emily nearly dozed off again. 'The doctor said she was going to be fine, you know,' Josh said, startling her again. 'Just a concussion.'

'Yeah,' Cord muttered. 'She's got a hard head.'

Emily could hear the heartsick concern and understood his earlier temper. He was probably worried sick. She wanted to reassure them, wanted to see Cord and tell him she loved him, wanted to hug her brother, but her eyes wouldn't work. She felt so incredibly tired . . .

To her disappointment, when she awoke again Josh was alone.

'I'm fine,' she said, when Josh jumped up out of his chair, his worried eyes roaming over her. He was just a kid, she thought, and he'd been through so much in his short life. 'Really, Josh. I'm okay.'

'You have a bump on your head the size of a football.'

'So I'm not going to win any beauty contests.'

'Twelve stitches.'

'Are you trying to make me feel better?' she said with a choked laugh. 'You're doing a poor job of it.'

He fiddled with her braid before raising his gaze to hers. 'I can't believe it, you know?'

'I wonder what'll happen to Katherine now.'

'She's earned a trip to the loony bin without passing go.'

'Josh!'

He had the good grace to look sheepish. 'She's nutso, Emily. Completely wacko. Did you know she wasn't even a nun anymore? She'd left the convent eight months ago.'

'Right before the first murder.'

'Yeah.' He was silent a minute. 'She'll probably never go to prison.'

From all of the victims' standpoint, it was grossly unfair. And yet the woman was truly ill. She hadn't thought it possible after what she'd been through, but Emily found she had the compassion to wish Katherine the right care and support. She didn't hate her; she couldn't. The woman had raised the man she loved. Cord. He must be devastated.

'Where's Cord?'

She'd thought her question casual enough but her brother's eyes sharpened on her. 'He left a little while ago. Said he'd arrange for our ride home when you were released.'

'Oh.'

'Your concussion is minor.'

'Great.' It didn't *feel* minor.

'They're not going to keep you overnight, so I guess they'll let us go soon.'

'Oh.'

Silently, Josh watched her. He fumbled with her covers. 'He's a wreck, Sis. Don't be upset.'

She looked at him, a little surprised by his intuitiveness. 'I'm not,' she said, lying.

'Yeah, you are.' He sighed, flicked her braid. 'I didn't want to like him, you know.'

'Didn't? As in past tense?' She could well remember the animosity between the two men when they'd first met. One thinking he had to protect her from all men, the other thinking she was being taken advantage of.

'He didn't know about Katherine leaving the order. I think he's beating himself up about that, you know? He thinks he should have known. You should have seen him when he knew Katherine had you. You should have seen his face. I've never seen a man so scared.' He laughed harshly, pushed back his red hair. 'Hell, I've never *been* so scared. But one thing was pretty clear. He cares about you, Emily. He cares a lot.'

'I know.' She could still see Cord's eyes, that deep, passionate blue, leveled right on her as he'd told her he loved her. She wished he were telling her that right now.

'He racked his brains to figure out a way to get you away safely. The drive to the school was pretty tense – we knew how far away the sheriff was and we knew we were your only hope. It was hard for him, knowing Katherine had you.'

'Yes,' she said softly. She knew how much Cord loved Katherine, could only imagine what he felt now.

'He drove like a maniac.'

'I bet.'

'He didn't want me to come, and I got mad.'

'Not you,' she said dryly.

'Until I realized he didn't want to put me in danger too. That was weird – realizing he liked me.'

Josh looked at her and she smiled. 'He's a good man, Josh.'

He nodded. 'At the school he tried to make me wait in the truck, but I couldn't. That got him mad. But when we didn't see you, he forgot about me not listening.'

'We've been on our own too long,' Emily managed with a small laugh. 'Neither of us respects authority all that well.'

Josh didn't smile. 'Not knowing where you were was . . . the worst.'

'I'm sorry, Josh.'

He sighed and took her hand. 'I'm not trying to make you feel bad. I'm trying to tell you the guy's not as bad as I thought.'

'Oh.' She smiled suddenly. 'And . . .?'

'And maybe . . . you could . . . you know, have something with him.'

'*Have something*?'

'Like a relationship,' he mumbled, his face turning

red. 'There, I said it. Now leave me alone about it.'

'Josh – '

'I just wanted you to know it would be all right with me is all. The guy's okay.'

She squeezed his hand. 'He is, isn't he?' Despite the horrendous headache, she felt enlightened. Hopeful. And, for the first time in far too long, sure of her future. She wanted Cord in her life, she wanted his love, she wanted it all.

She didn't know what she had been waiting for or why she had hesitated. And, as is often the case with newfound knowledge, she couldn't wait to share it. With Cord.

She couldn't wait to tell him she loved him.

But he never came.

She was released and, true to Cord's word, Sheriff Stone drove them home. Her truck had already been delivered. It seemed like ages since she'd seen her own apartment – so much had happened, but it hurt to think about it. Her head hurt.

Before she could dwell on the fact that Cord still hadn't come to see her – or even called – Josh helped her settle in her own bed.

Sleep claimed her immediately.

Emily slept for two straight days, waking only to stumble to the bathroom and then to swallow down some soup made by Josh. When she finally managed to shower and dress, she felt like a new person.

Except for her broken heart.

Cord hadn't so much as sent a card. Not a good

sign, she decided. But she kept herself busy by painting the other wall of her patio.

Her heart ached unbearably.

Seth came to visit, arms loaded with flowers and gifts. He expressed his horror at what she'd gone through, his deep sorrow for Katherine, his huge relief that his own ordeal was over. But he said not one word about Cord and she was far too proud to ask.

He insisted she still paint murals on their office walls and demanded a commitment from her. Between that and the county's job she'd been awarded, she'd be busy all summer. And though it seemed as if her dream about painting murals could finally become a reality, it didn't mean as much as she'd once thought it would.

She did have one major disagreement with Seth as he left.

He handed her a check, trying to pay her in full for the paint job at Cord's house. The check was for three times the amount owed her – and signed by Cord himself.

It was simple. Cord didn't want her to finish the work.

After Seth had gone, Emily tore the check to shreds. When she looked up, practically blinded by tears, she saw Josh's face.

'We don't need it,' she said defensively, tossing the pieces of paper aside.

'No,' Josh agreed quietly. 'We'll make more.'

'We won't go hungry,' she said quickly, hoping he

wouldn't worry. She'd never actually thrown money away before – never *had* it to throw away. 'I promise you.'

'I know.'

She looked at him and saw that he wasn't shocked, as she'd thought, but full of sympathy. She didn't want sympathy. 'Stop it,' she said. 'Stop feeling sorry for me.'

'I'm not.'

'I was fired, Josh. *Fired*. I've never had that happen before.'

'He doesn't mean it,' Josh said lamely, lifting his shoulders. 'He's not himself.'

All she could do was sniff and nod. And hope.

She wasn't insensitive enough not to understand. The woman Cord thought of as his mother had murdered. Repeatedly. He had a lot of things to work out. She imagined him sick with worry over Katherine, throwing himself into work to forget it.

As busy as he was, he wouldn't stop loving Emily. Or would he?

The truth was, Cord wasn't a man to throw himself into anything to avoid problems. He tended to face them head-on. So why didn't he face her, damn him?

If she thought about it too much, she'd go insane. So, on the first day she felt able, she got into her truck and drove to Cord's office.

He wasn't in.

'He's at home,' Seth said, watching her from the reception doorway. 'Why don't you go up there and beat some sense into him?'

'Does he need some? Sense?'

Seth smiled gently. 'He needs *you*, Emily. He just doesn't want to think so. Go there?'

She nodded and turned toward the door. 'Emily?' Seth called. 'Do me a favor? Just don't tell him *I* sent you.'

Without hesitation, she headed for Cord's house, not knowing what she was going to say. Okay, so he'd avoided her. It didn't mean his love for her had faded away. He'd suffered a huge loss. There were things in his life other than her.

They didn't have a commitment – which, by the way, she had no one but herself to thank for. He'd wanted one and she'd panicked.

She pulled up his driveway, slowing in spite of her resolve. Maybe he wouldn't be happy to see her. Maybe he wasn't *ready* to see her.

It didn't matter. She needed to tell him how she felt.

What if he didn't want her love? a small voice asked, deep inside her. *What if she was too late?*

Never, she assured herself. You can never be too late for love.

She hoped.

Cord cut another piece of tile, squinting against the spray of water coming off the tile-cutter. When he'd finished, he straightened and sighed. His back killed him. Hell, fifteen straight hours of physical exertion would kill anyone.

If he couldn't sleep himself into oblivion, he could certainly work himself into it.

Hell. Who was he fooling? Even work couldn't take his mind off things. Like how Katherine had looked when he'd let the sheriff take her away. Or how much blood had been flowing over Emily when he'd first seen her. He knew he'd never forget the sight of her huddled, terrified, on the window ledge, holding on for dear life.

He couldn't believe his own stupidity had nearly gotten her killed. He didn't think he'd ever be able to forgive himself for that.

Just thinking about her hurt. His heart ached with it, but he had to force his mind off it because he'd die otherwise. He leaned over the loud machine and forced himself to cut more tile, ignoring his screaming muscles.

He had to face facts. In saving her life he had made sure Emily McKay was lost to him forever. How could she ever forgive him? And, even if she managed to do that, how could she ever forget that it had been his fault that she'd nearly been killed? *His* fault, damn it, and there was nothing he could do about it now.

Except nurse his broken heart and finish the house. He loved this house. But he just couldn't imagine being happy in it without Emily. He wanted her and he wanted her children. Their children. And so, since he could settle for no less, he had to sell the house the minute it was finished.

He wondered how Emily felt. If she was painting right this minute. Picturing her long red braid, her paint-spattered overalls, her frown of concentration, he nearly smiled.

And broke a piece of tile. Cursing, he flipped off the loud tile-cutter. He couldn't work. And sleep was completely out of the question. Maybe a dip in the hot tub would help.

The silence, after the loud roar of the tile-cutter, was complete. In the kitchen he stopped to strip off his shirt. Unbuttoning his jeans, he walked out.

Halfway to the patio he heard the bubbling of the jets. Frowning, for he was sure he hadn't left the thing on, he glanced out the foyer windows as he passed.

His heart stopped.

In his driveway was Emily's old, beat-up truck.

CHAPTER 19

'What the *hell* are you doing?' Cord demanded, hands on his hips. He looked down, rocked to the core. Emily sat in his hot tub, wearing nothing but a soft smile.

'What does it look like? I'm soaking.' She closed her eyes and leaned back in the picture-perfect pose of relaxation. But he wasn't fooled. He'd seen the brief flash of fear and nerves in her eyes.

And what the hell should *she* be afraid of? he wondered. It was *his* heart that was crumpled, *his* life that was destroyed. Okay, so he felt a little melodramatic, but God, he was dead tired. And the shock of seeing her again, of realizing she was everything he remembered, was difficult.

Maybe if she loved him . . . but she didn't. And now she never would.

He stepped closer. 'You drove all the way up here to soak?'

'Mmm-hmm.'

She didn't bother to open her eyes, but even through the steamy mist he could see the frantic pulse beating at the base of her neck. Even now she wasn't completely immune to him.

He couldn't handle it. Seeing her again was torture. And the white patch of bandage on her forehead was a cruel reminder of what she'd suffered. *Because of him.*

'Does it hurt?' he asked tensely, his voice hoarse.

Her beautiful green eyes opened and settled on him. 'What?'

He swallowed. 'Your head.'

She looked at him for a long minute. 'If I said yes,' she asked him finally, her voice very soft, 'would you come kiss it?'

Oh, God.

She straightened slowly, exposing wet, gleaming shoulders and the tips of her beautiful breasts.

'Would you?'

He stared at her, willing his body to follow along with his mind. 'I can't,' he said simply. If he did, he'd never let her go and the guilt would kill him.

She pushed off the seat of the hot tub and stood, dripping wet, in the center of the tub, clearly visible to her waist.

His mouth fell open – from shock or arousal, he had no idea. 'Em, please,' he begged, lifting his hands as if to ward her off. 'Don't do this to me.'

She tilted her head, her mouth still softly curved in a smile that was meant for him. How many times had he wanted to see her smile that way at him? Too many to count, and yet here she was. His for the taking.

And he couldn't.

'What am I doing to you?' she asked, dangling her fingertips in the water. She took another step in the water, bringing her even closer.

He grabbed a towel off a nearby chair and came to the edge of the tub. Squatting close, he held it out to her. She didn't take it. 'Answer me, Cord.'

'You're killing me. Now get out of there.'

She watched him another minute, then shook her head. She sank back down into the tub, mercifully hiding her glorious curves from him. He sighed in relief.

'You didn't come to see me,' she said, her eyes shadowed.

A vivid picture of Katherine, with her wild, insane eyes, swinging at her, had him sucking in his breath. 'I couldn't.'

'Why?'

The pain in her voice made him answer truthfully. He owed her that much. 'How could I after what Katherine put you through? For over a month she stalked you, and nearly managed to kill you, thanks to me.'

'So you . . . feel guilty?'

The question, mixed in with her disbelieving, incredulous tone, was too much. 'Hell, yes. What did you think I would feel?'

He'd got her there, he could tell. Her mouth worked, but no words came out. Of its own will, his gaze dropped to her wet limbs. 'Please, get out of there, Em.' Her hair clung to her neck and her eyes glowed. A faint blush tinged her cheeks. She'd never looked better.

'I never thought of that,' she said, looking thoughtful. 'You feel guilty.'

He sighed and dropped his head between his shoulders.

'Guilt is a wasted emotion, Cord.'

What was she saying? That she never bothered with it, or that he shouldn't feel it? 'Tell that to my heart.'

'It wasn't your fault. None of it. You've got to know that.'

If only he could believe it. But hindsight was twenty-twenty, and he couldn't understand how he hadn't seen Katherine's illness sooner. People had *died* because he hadn't.

'Nobody blames you, least of all me,' she said softly.

All right, he *could* believe that. She was the most forgiving person he knew. And, strangely enough, just explaining his feelings to her had helped ease them somewhat. He imagined he'd carry around some pain for the rest of his life, yet already he was beginning to believe he could live with it. But he could hear the sympathy in her voice, and he didn't want her pity. He wanted her love. He could settle for nothing less.

'I thought we were friends.' Her eyes seemed shadowed by regret.

Friends. Lord. 'We are.'

'You fired me, Cord.'

How could he possibly explain? He had thought –
no, he'd been *sure* – she wouldn't want to work for
him again. He'd thought she wouldn't want to see
him ever again. 'It was for the best.'

'Best for who?'

He couldn't stand the reproach in her voice and he
tried to make her understand. 'My mother tried to
kill you,' he said dryly. 'Remember?'

'Yeah,' she said, touching her head. 'I remember.
But that has nothing to do with us.'

He wished. 'Please, Em.' He held out his hand to
help her up.

'Come get me out.'

He stared at her. 'What?'

Unbelievably, she closed her eyes, leaned back. 'If
you want me out, come and get me out. Better yet,
join me. It feels great.'

'You're naked.'

She smiled then, and he knew why. They'd once
had this very conversation, in reverse, that night
they'd made unforgettable love.

'So I'm naked,' she said agreeably, though her
voice shook slightly with what he would have sworn
were nerves. 'And you don't have a bathing suit. So?
Tell you what – I'll keep my eyes closed and promise
not to peek.'

'Emily.' This was not funny. 'Come on, get out of
there.'

'Nope. Join me.' He narrowed his eyes when she
laughed softly. She was *teasing* him.

And he was just ornery enough, and desperate

enough, to do it. He kicked off his shoes, yanked off his socks and stepped out of his jeans. He tossed his shirt across the deck and didn't stop to fold it.

She gasped and her eyes flew open when he joined her with a noisy splash. He caught her arms and drew her close, forcing her head back. 'You play dirty,' he said. 'But this changes nothing – '

'I love you,' she whispered.

' – because I need more than you can . . . *what*?' He shook her, his eyes intense and confused. '*What did you just say?*' A small glimmer of hope shimmied through him as he finally saw the truth before him. Everything she was, everything she felt, showed in her eyes.

'I love you,' she said again. 'I've always loved you, but I was just so afraid.' She touched his face. 'I'm not afraid now, Cord. And more than anything in this world I want to be Mrs Cord Harrison.'

His heart leaped, and for a minute he simply couldn't speak.

'I'm sorry it took me so long to figure that out. Please say that I'm not too late. That you still love me too.'

He dropped his forehead to hers and laughed, the vise on his heart loosening for the first time in days. 'Oh, Em. How could you even ask?'

'Better yet,' she whispered, pulling close and pressing her wet body tight against his. 'Show me.'

**THE EXCITING NEW NAME
IN WOMEN'S FICTION!**

PLEASE HELP ME TO HELP YOU!

Dear *Scarlet* Reader,

As promised, I have some excellent news for you this month –
we are beginning a super Prize Draw, which means that **you
could win 6 months' worth of free Scarlets!** Just return
your completed questionnaire to us (see addresses at end of
questionnaire) before 31 July 1997 and you will automatically
be entered in the draw that takes place on that day. If you are
lucky enough to be one of the first two names out of the hat we
will send you four new Scarlet romances every month for six
months, and for each of twenty runners up there will be a sassy
Scarlet T-shirt.

So don't delay – return your form straight away!*

Sally Cooper

Editor-in-Chief, *Scarlet*

QUESTIONNAIRE

Please tick the appropriate boxes to indicate your answers

1 Where did you get this Scarlet title?
Bought in supermarket ☐
Bought at my local bookstore ☐ Bought at chain bookstore ☐
Bought at book exchange or used bookstore ☐
Borrowed from a friend ☐
Other (please indicate) _____

2 Did you enjoy reading it?
A lot ☐   A little ☐   Not at all ☐

3 What did you particularly like about this book?
Believable characters ☐   Easy to read ☐
Good value for money ☐   Enjoyable locations ☐
Interesting story ☐   Modern setting ☐
Other _____

4 What did you particularly dislike about this book?
_____

5 Would you buy another Scarlet book?
Yes ☐   No ☐

6 What other kinds of book do you enjoy reading?
Horror ☐   Puzzle books ☐   Historical fiction ☐
General fiction ☐   Crime/Detective ☐   Cookery ☐
Other (please indicate) _____

7 Which magazines do you enjoy reading?
1. _____
2. _____
3. _____

And now a little about you –
8 How old are you?
Under 25 ☐   25–34 ☐   35–44 ☐
45–54 ☐   55–64 ☐   over 65 ☐

cont.

9 What is your marital status?

Single ☐   Married/living with partner ☐

Widowed ☐   Separated/divorced ☐

10 What is your current occupation?

Employed full-time ☐   Employed part-time ☐

Student ☐   Housewife full-time ☐

Unemployed ☐   Retired ☐

11 Do you have children? If so, how many and how old are they?

_____

_____

12 What is your annual household income?

under $15,000	☐	or	£10,000	☐
$15–25,000	☐	or	£10–20,000	☐
$25–35,000	☐	or	£20–30,000	☐
$35–50,000	☐	or	£30–40,000	☐
over $50,000	☐	or	£40,000	☐

Miss/Mrs/Ms _____

Address _____

_____

_____

Thank you for completing this questionnaire. Now tear it out – put it in an envelope and send it to:

Sally Cooper, Editor-in-Chief

USA/Can. address
SCARLET c/o London Bridge
85 River Rock Drive
Suite 202
Buffalo
NY 14207
USA

UK address/No stamp required
SCARLET
FREEPOST LON 3335
LONDON W8 4BR
Please use block capitals for address

TITRU/3/97

Scarlet titles coming next month:

MASTER OF THE HOUSE Margaret Callaghan
Ella has just started a new life as housekeeper to the wealthy, newly engaged Fliss. But when Fliss's fiancé comes home, Ella's troubles really begin! For Jack Keegan is Ella's ex-husband – the only man she's ever loved . . .

SATIN AND LACE Danielle Shaw
The last proposal Sally Palmer expects to hear from her boss, Hugh Barrington, is 'Will you be my mistress?' Surprising even herself, Sally embarks on the affair with consequences which affect everyone around her!

NO GENTLEMAN Andrea Young
When Nick comes back into Daisy's life, she's convinced she's immune to his charm. She's going to marry safe, handsome and loving Simon. So let Nick do his darnedest to persuade Daisy that it's excitement *not* security she desires. She's already made her choice, and nothing will change her mind . . . or will it?

NOBODY'S BABY Elizabeth Smith
Neither Joe Devlin nor Stevie Parker tell the truth when they meet. He thinks *she's* a writer, she thinks *he's* in PR. After a wonderful night together, Joe leaves with no explanation. So Stevie takes her revenge . . . then Joe plots his!